"*Amazon Moon* is the sort of novel that grabs you by the throat on the first page and doesn't let go until the last. It is an exciting story and, at the same time, something more. It is a fable about one man's redemption, his rediscovery of innocence."

Nicholas Guild—New York Times Best Selling Author
The Assyrian, The Berlin Warning, The President's Man

"With *Amazon Moon*, Starkey has done it again—lured me in, set me up and wrung me out! Splendid."

Jeff Mudgett—Author of *Bloodstains*

Also by Glenn Starkey

SOLOMON'S MEN

THE COBRA AND SCARAB

YEAR OF THE RAM

Amazon Moon

Glenn Starkey

Copyright © 2013 Glenn Starkey.

Artwork by Ryan A. Bibby of Novel Branding.

All rights reserved. No part of this book may be used or reproduced by any means, graphic, electronic, or mechanical, including photocopying, recording, taping or by any information storage retrieval system without the written permission of the publisher except in the case of brief quotations embodied in critical articles and reviews.

This is a work of fiction. All characters, places, organizations and events portrayed in this novel are either products of the author's imagination or are used fictitiously.

Abbott Press books may be ordered through booksellers or by contacting:

Abbott Press
1663 Liberty Drive
Bloomington, IN 47403
www.abbottpress.com
Phone: 1-866-697-5310

Because of the dynamic nature of the Internet, any web addresses or links contained in this book may have changed since publication and may no longer be valid. The views expressed in this work are solely those of the author and do not necessarily reflect the views of the publisher, and the publisher hereby disclaims any responsibility for them.

Any people depicted in stock imagery provided by Thinkstock are models, and such images are being used for illustrative purposes only.

Certain stock imagery © Thinkstock.

ISBN: 978-1-4582-1102-6 (sc)
ISBN: 978-1-4582-1101-9 (hc)
ISBN: 978-1-4582-1100-2 (e)

Library of Congress Control Number: 2013914602

Printed in the United States of America.

Abbott Press rev. date: 08/20/2013

For my family, Donna, Jake, Caleb, and Cindy, who inspire me each day to be better than I was before. You are the beats of my heart.

And to Nick, mentor and friend, thank you for the encouragement you unknowingly provide.

Glenn

"I may not have gone where I intended to go, but I think I have ended up where I needed to be."

Douglas Adams,
The Long Dark Tea-Time of the Soul

Chapter One

November 1995,
Ucayali River, Peru
East of the Pacaya Samiria National Reserve

"Remember to keep watch, Ignacio," said the elder. He brushed a circling fly from before his face and then lowered the hand to rest once again on the grip of a belted machete as time worn as its owner. "If a caiman has you for his morning meal, I will have no one to carry the jugs for me."

A hint of a grin broke the stoic expression his mixed Spanish and Indian ancestry usually held. Gaze sweeping the shoreline, he maintained his vigil as his grandson walked into the river.

Slender and bronzed from a merciless sun, the boy stopped and bent to fill the jugs when the water reached his shins. At the reminder of the fierce brother to the alligator, Ignacio cast a wary glance in the direction of every splash he heard about him. He frowned and shook his head.

"Papito," he sighed with exasperation, calling his *abuelo* by the family nickname. "Every day we come to the river and every day you tell me the same thing. I am a man now! When will you stop warning me of the caiman as if I were a child?"

The leathery-skinned man benevolently nodded agreement. Unfortunately, his grandson had become a man, forced to grow beyond his years in a land that allowed little time for children to enjoy their youth. Jungle predators, the harsh climate, disease, poverty, drug runners, armed bands of leftist guerillas, these and more cared nothing for the innocence of a child. They demanded the strong survive, and the weak perish cruelly.

"Only when the dirt is tossed on my grave will you no longer hear me speak of the caimans! They are like this river, the *cabrones*—treacherous and unforgiving. Someday you too will be standing here warning your children of them."

The jungle weathered elder drew sullen. When he spoke again, his tone held regret. "Our lives are hard enough, Ignacio, without our seeing a loved one torn apart before our eyes."

The willowy boy rose from the water, his thin arms straining against the weight of the jugs. Whipping his head to move thick locks of black hair from his face, Ignacio turned to face his beloved *abuelo* standing on the shore. His eyebrows drew downward as he tried to understand the change in his grandfather. Such was the manner of old men who kept dark secrets well-guarded, allowing fragments to escape against their will.

Fear clutched the boy's throat when Papito's eyes flared.

"Jump, Ignacio! *Jump away!*"

Adrenaline flooded the young man's body. He released his hold on the jugs and tried to leap to the bank, but his feet held fast to the river bed. The heavy weight of the water-filled jugs had sunk him deeper than he realized into the mushy mud. He lost balance and fell forward into the shallow water. Jerking his legs frantically to free himself, he clawed and crawled his way toward shore, spraying a wall of mud-swirled water and river debris about him.

The machete cut an arc through the air as it cleared its sheath. Arm waving over his head, Papito raced past his grandson toward the river, ready to make a stand against the black caiman drifting slowly in their direction.

"You will not take this one!" Years of anguish, anger, and fear permeated his voice. Papito shook the razor-sharp weapon with a deadly grip, yet the long, blackish figure in the river only floated closer, undisturbed by the old man's readiness for mortal combat.

Ignacio stood blinking and wiping mud from his face. He stared at the caiman a moment, squinted to better focus, and then ran to his grandfather, laying a hand on his taut arm. "Wait, Papito. Do you see? It is a man holding onto a log!"

The boy crept toward the water's edge as the elder gradually lowered his machete to chest level. They stood cautiously studying the log and figure drifting toward them. Leaves, blades of grass and streaks of mud painted the wide back of a man, camouflaging his skin. His head was turned to the log with mouth open, hard-pressed against the bark, barely above the waterline. An arm of knotted muscle draped the log.

Ignoring any dangers, Ignacio raced into the river until he was almost waist-deep. He pulled the log toward shore, all the while trying to keep the stranger's face upright to prevent drowning. When the log lodged into the riverbank, the boy tried to lift the unconscious man. The limp weight was too great for him and the arm about the log held it in a death grip.

A feeble groan came from the lips of the mud-streaked, naked giant. One eye opened briefly, rolled and showed white then closed.

"Help me, Papito. Hurry, he's alive!"

The elder jabbed his machete into the ground and grabbed a wrist. Papito and his grandson pried the arm from the log and together tugged until the body slid through the mud and lay fully ashore.

Ignacio knelt by the nearly lifeless man's head and gently rubbed the river's filth from his face. Another low groan flowed from the man's lips, only this time carrying with it the mental suffering of a wounded soul. The boy leaned close, his ear almost touching the river giant's mouth.

"*Que dice?* What does he say?" Papito asked anxiously, examining the half-dead stranger as he sat beside him across from his grandson.

No reply. Ignacio remained bent over the man, eyes half-closed, straining to hear the slightest word.

Sympathetically shaking his head, Papito slowly sat upright, his eyes flushed with pity. He made the sign of the cross.

"*Madre de Dios,* this poor creature looks as if he has been tortured or beaten. Do you see the bruises and scars on his body?"

The grandfather gently brushed mud and strings of river weeds from the battered man's chest, carefully eyeing the red splotches left by dozens of ant and insect bites.

"Here . . . look . . . these are from a whip or a knife." Papito traced several of the wounds with a fingertip and shook his head. He leaned closer to study them. "No, they were made by the claws of an animal."

Still stunned by their discovery of the stranger, the boy eased back onto his heels, glanced at the wounds, and stared at the warrior-like features of the man who now lay upon death's doorway. Compared to the people of his village, here was a giant among men that easily stood a head taller than any of them. Ignacio had never seen anyone so muscled and strong in appearance.

Long black hair imbedded with twigs, mud, and grass hung matted from his head, and a wild, mud-smeared beard veiled his cheeks and throat. His deeply tanned skin told of relentless days under the jungle sun, but about his groin where a tattered loin cloth of some form had once been, a paler tint portrayed his true color.

"Tell me, Ignacio. Did he say who did this to him?" The grandfather's brown eyes were stretched wide on his wrinkled face, his gaze blending curiosity and dismay.

At first the boy shrugged then turned to him with an innocent expression. "He keeps saying *Moloc*."

Horror swathed the old man's face. Mouth agape, he recoiled from the wounded giant as if he were a viper about to strike. The elder rose, grabbing his grandson's arm with such force the boy fell back into the dirt.

"Come away from him. *Pronto!* Do as I say."

Shocked by Papito's sudden change, the boy slid back from the motionless body. "But he's hurt! We cannot leave him here to die."

Papito stepped back and motioned his grandson to him as he stared at the stranger. When Ignacio drew near, the old man wrapped his arms tightly about the boy, kissed the top of his head, and fervently made the sign of the cross when he looked at the tortured man again. Watching the stranger as if anticipating he would rise and attack them, the elder retrieved his machete. He lightly pushed his grandson back until they were ten paces away.

Sweat trickled down Papito's temples. The jungle air felt thicker to him, more humid than only moments before. Rising to its zenith, the sun cooked the land and all within its reach. The old man knelt and jabbed the machete into the ground, letting his hand rest on its handle. Conflict showed in his eyes as he struggled with his thoughts.

"We must take him to our—"

"*No, Ignacio!* It is better he dies."

For the first time in his life Ignacio saw dread mounting in his *abuelo's* eyes, and the sight of it frightened him. Yet something about the hurt giant silently cried out for help and Ignacio could not leave him to the fate of the jungle.

Papito's eyes slowly closed, his face somberly masked with the resolution of a determined action. Pulling the machete from the ground as he rose, he exhaled deeply, never removing his gaze from the stranger. His grip tightened on the machete's handle until his knuckles grew white.

"You cannot kill him!" the boy shouted, arms held out to block his grandfather's path. "He has done nothing to us." Ignacio stood his ground but across his face was uncertainty about what he should do next.

"*Silencio,* Ignacio!" Papito's voice rang hard. "Now leave me. Return to the village. You must not see this." The grandfather started around the boy, staring all the while at the unconscious man.

Fingers feebly moved on the stranger's right hand. A pain-drenched groan carried louder than before into the air.

"Why, Papito? Why must you kill him?" the boy asked, shifting his position to remain in front of his grandfather.

As the dread gripping the old man broke its hold, his gaze softened. He looked at his grandson with a desire to speak all he had been holding so long within his heart. He pointed with the machete to the battered man.

"He has been touched by the devil, Ignacio. Evil follows him and we must protect our *familia* from the dangers."

"Protect our family from *what* dangers? How do you know such things about him?"

Lowering his gaze to meet Ignacio's, Papito turned and gestured eastward to where the Ucayali River became the Amazon and then swung his hand toward the south.

"Out there, *nieto,* is a place where evil lives—and all who venture near it are cursed for life."

Immediately he made the sign of the cross and nervously looked at the stranger, almost expecting him to rise in demon form.

Ignacio readied himself to argue more, but a strained voice from behind startled him. In a single leap he was beside his grandfather, staring as wide-eyed as Papito at the grimacing man in the dirt.

"Let him kill me, boy. What I know must die with me."

The wounded stranger gazed glossy-eyed in the direction of the voices he had heard. He tried to speak again. A wrenching agony shot throughout him, sending him back into oblivion. His head fell hard back into the mud.

"*Por favor,* Papito. Please. He is not evil. I know it, I know it. *Por favor.* Let me go to the village and bring the others to carry him. Look at his body. Someone has done these things to him. He needs our help," the boy pleaded. He held fast to his grandfather's arm.

An eerie silence settled over the jungle as if the ruthless land awaited the old man's declaration of a death sentence. But it never came. Glancing from Ignacio to the unconscious man, Papito nodded begrudgingly.

"Very well," he said, wiping his machete clean on a nearby broad-leafed plant. "Go for your *hermanos,* your brothers. Tell them to bring the men of the village. This *hombre* is heavy and it will take many to carry him."

Ignacio smiled and raced into the jungle. The grandfather watched him leave then turned toward the wounded man and sighed wearily. He sheathed the machete and stood staring at the stranger.

"May God forgive me, *hombre,* for what I was about to do." He paused, drew a deep breath, and looked eastward across the river into the dense jungle. "But I remember the last man who came as you did. He went mad, staring at the sun and moon, screaming *'Moloc'* until the pain within his mind was too great to bear."

★ ★ ★ ★

Ignacio sat patiently near the stranger's mat, leaving only to do his chores, and always returning quickly in hopes of being present when the sleeping man awoke. Two weeks passed before the stranger's health allowed him to sit upright and remain awake for any length of time. When given soups filled with crushed coca beans and healing herbs, he slurped the bowls empty like a starved animal and watched the villagers outside the thatched-roof hut as if they were brutal captors. By the third week of the stranger's resurrection from the dead, Ignacio had not heard the man speak other than to cry out from the nightmares that seemed to regularly travel the dark canyons of his mind. But on the first day of the fourth week, the ruggedly built man surprised him.

"Are you the boy from the river?" asked a gentle voice.

Stirring from his afternoon nap, Ignacio rubbed sleep from his eyes and looked about in confusion. He was startled when he realized the stranger had spoken. He nodded hesitantly as he stared at the man sitting on a mat across the hut from him.

"*Si, señor*, I am Ignacio. *Mi abuelo* and I pulled you from the river. We have cared for you since that day."

The deep blue eyes of the stranger gradually closed as fatigue overcame him. A second later they opened with the glare of a troubled man. He glanced at his fresh loin cloth, and then to the multitude of scars and wounds lacing his chest. Raising a hand, he touched his shaven face and felt of his hair. It was clean and clipped short. Wearily he shifted his gaze to the young boy studying him.

"*Mi abuela,* my grandmother, washed your wounds, bathed you and prepared the medicines to make you sleep and heal."

The stranger nodded approval and watched the dark-skinned boy's smile widen.

Papito paused as if choosing his words carefully. "I thought you would die, but she says a *hombre* like you never dies easily."

No reply or hint of thought came from the stranger as he looked at the boy.

"So, the mud-giant has come to life," Papito said, his voice carrying a cheerful tone as he walked up the hut's rickety steps. He halted at the foot of the stranger's mat and stood with a hand resting casually on the handle of his machete. Not wanting to appear as if he were staring, he let his gaze carry a moment about the open-sided hut then returned his eyes to the silent man.

At a glance it was evident immense strength lay beneath the tautly stretched skin. Iron-like muscles flexed with the stranger's slightest movement, and yet he seemingly retained the agility of a jungle cat. Without his matted mane and mud-caked beard, he was surprisingly handsome, with high cheekbones, chiseled chin, and an aquiline nose. His superb physical conditioning hid his age well, but about the coldly staring eyes that watched the world with the alertness of a wild animal, were faint wrinkles which told of matured years. Although the man now sat on a mat, Papito remembered how tall he was when the villagers first lifted him from the riverbank to carry him here.

"*Mi familia* calls me Papito, and this is my *nieto*, grandson, Ignacio. You are welcome to stay with us until your health returns. *Mi esposa,* my wife, has cooked a monkey for us to eat. If you wish, I will have some brought to you."

Struggling against the agony raking his body, the stranger extended an open hand to the old man. "My name is Alvarez. John Alvarez. Thank you for all you have done."

They shook hands and Papito observed a fleeting glimpse of amity appear in Alvarez's eyes. The old man's apprehensions about the stranger lessened, yet he remained cautious.

"Ignacio, go tell Willita to bring the food she has cooked. Tell her we have a man here who is hungry for something more in his belly than soup!"

Anxious to report the stranger's condition to his grandmother, Ignacio dashed from the hut, clearing the steps to the ground in a single leap. Papito warmly smiled as he watched the boy race away. Turning, his smile faded when he found Alvarez staring at him, face devoid of emotion. Unnerved at first, Papito took a cross-legged seat on the hut floor, casually adjusting his machete into an easily grasped position.

Alvarez closed his eyes and rolled his head on his shoulders then slowly raised his arms above his head and stretched like a cat after a long nap. His face mirrored the pain coursing his aching body from the movement as his open hands clenched into knotted fists at the agony, yet he continued to flex as if needing to test his agility.

The village elder sat fascinated by Alvarez. In all of his seventy years, as best he could recall, he had never seen such a man. The skin appeared ready to rip from the constant strain of being stretched over hardened muscles. Along Alvarez's chest, legs, and arms lay a visible network of veins, thick as twine. But of all that captivated Papito, the faraway stare of the blue eyes disturbed him most—a stare saturated with suffering, hate, brutality, and compassion, all wrapped within the same gaze, leaving one to wonder what Alvarez's next action might be.

"You are not of this land, *señor*. You speak like a *Norte Americano*. Is this true?"

Alvarez nodded and glanced at the growing crowd of villagers gathering outside his hut. The elder waited, hoping Alvarez would provide more information about himself, but only silence filled the void between them.

"Excuse my people for staring. They do not know if they should be afraid or happy you live." Papito grinned and lifted his arms, gesturing to his biceps before pointing to Alvarez. "We have never had someone like you in this village and my people embrace every jungle superstition."

The old man's smile dwindled. His tone grew somber; eyes intently watching for a reaction. "Many believe the tribal tales of *demonios,* demons, in the jungle."

Papito's words struck a violent chord. Alvarez's deep blue eyes narrowed and burned wildly with animalistic madness. The tension sweeping through him was obvious. His nostrils flared and his chest rapidly rose and fell as his breathing became labored.

"Calm yourself, *Señor* Alvarez. You are among *amigos,* friends, here. No one means you harm. I apologize for disturbing you as I have." Papito realized his initial fears of the man were warranted.

Yes, my big friend, you have been to the land of evil, he thought, keeping watch on Alvarez. *For a man such as you to fear the mere mention of demonios means they have held your heart in their hands and squeezed the life from it.*

Nothing more was spoken between them while they waited for the food to be brought. Minutes passed before Alvarez calmed enough to sit vacantly staring at the children who giggled, smiled and pointed to him. He wrung his hands slowly, at times squeezing so tightly the knuckles grew white, then whatever fire burning his soul settled and he drew still.

Papito took note of the immense sadness dwelling in the stranger's eyes as he watched the children of the village. Such was the look of a man who had witnessed far more than a hundred lifetimes could bear. But as quickly as it came, the wretched mood left Alvarez, replaced by a cruel gaze which held him spellbound.

Ignacio elbowed his way through the villagers on the steps and proudly carried a bowl to Alvarez. The savory aroma of roasted monkey meat, cooked yams, and fresh bananas immediately permeated the hut.

Ignoring the crowd of curious onlookers, Alvarez glanced at the bowl then to Papito. *"Gracias, señor."* His thanks in Spanish fluently rolled off his tongue. Stomach growling from hunger, he began to devour the food.

"Bueno, bueno. Such is good," Papito remarked, smiling at Alvarez having spoken Spanish. "With a name as you have, I wondered if you spoke *español."*

Alvarez nodded and continued to eat.

"Here, in my village, we have learned to speak *inglés* from the *sacerdote,* the priest, who comes and stays at our village. He says we should learn this because it is *importante* to know if we are to trade with those doing business in the Amazon. This is why my *nieto* speaks your language. I wish to make his life better than mine." Papito lovingly hugged Ignacio and ruffled his thick mane of black hair.

A frown of embarrassment spread over the young man's face as he squirmed beside his grandfather.

Setting the empty bowl in front of Ignacio, Alvarez nodded appreciatively and wiped his mouth with the back of a hand. He looked at Papito as if all the man had spoken went unheard.

"Thank you for the food," he said softly, fatigue masking his face. Without further word Alvarez rolled back onto his mat and closed his eyes.

Ignacio watched Alvarez's chest rise and fall in slow, measured movements. He glanced questioningly at his *abuelo* with raised eyebrows.

The grandfather gestured for him to be quiet and together they left Alvarez sleeping in the hut.

"Did you see, Papito? He is not an evil man. He will not hurt us," Ignacio said, walking beside his grandfather.

"Yes, I believe he is not evil. Neither are the jaguars of the jungle, but they will hurt you when they are afraid," the old man replied, resting a hand on his grandson's shoulder.

"*Medroso?* Afraid? What does a man as big as *Señor* Alvarez have to be afraid of?"

Papito let his hand slide from the boy's shoulder and looked to the orange glow of the setting sun. "Of the *demonios* that dwell in his dreams, Ignacio . . . of the *demonios* who have touched his soul," said the elder, voice barely above a whisper.

* * * *

Weeks passed before Alvarez was able to walk about the small village without the assistance of a staff to steady his balance. Although the adults no longer watched his every move, swarms of children excitedly trailed him at a respectful distance and remained his constant shadow. The flesh wounds crisscrossing Alvarez's chest and back healed, leaving a patchwork of scars that unknowing to all except Papito, ran deeper than the skin. As his health improved, so did his appetite and strength. Once able to work, Alvarez repaid the kindness of Papito's family by chopping wood and carrying their heavy bundles.

Standing out of sight, Papito would watch in amazement as Alvarez relentlessly swung a heavy axe for hours, often driving its steel blade through a log with sheer brute force. Naked except for a loin cloth, sweat dripping from his body, the quiet giant pushed himself to extremes each day, seemingly punishing himself as if the pain he created was penance for past horrible deeds. At day's end, exhausted from the grueling labors, Alvarez bathed in the river and sat alone for hours on the bank to watch the river flow lazily past.

Against his better judgment Papito grew to like Alvarez, yet always there remained an element of fear within him—fear that one day the *Americano* would explode in a violent rage and vent the troubles plaguing his soul. After weeks of observing Alvarez's mounting restlessness, Papito realized he must find the right moment to talk with him.

A full moon rose over the jungle into the Amazon night, its perfect white orb illuminating the village and surrounding land in a tender blanket of light. Across the sky, stars glittered and sparkled like precious gems in an overflowing treasure chest. The noise of the village settled into peaceful silence as children fell fast asleep for the night and the creatures of the jungle silently prowled until dawn. An occasional cry of fright momentarily cut the air when an infant awoke but soon serenity returned once more to the rows of huts.

The elder drew a deep breath, knowing the time to talk had arrived.

"Here, take this, *señor*." Papito handed Alvarez a dented metal cup of steaming coffee then took a seat beside him on the hut steps. He lifted his own cup and sniffed its strong aroma. A gentle smile formed.

"On a night such as this it is good to sit with *amigos,* drink *café,* and watch the stars. Life is good, no?"

Alvarez barely turned his head enough to look at the village elder then let his gaze return to the cup held tenderly in his hands.

"Thank you for the coffee," he said in a voice slightly above a whisper.

Disappointment passed through Papito. He truly believed Alvarez would use the opportunity to say more than he had. But the night was young, and there was still time to probe the stranger's heart.

They drank their coffee in silence, gazing at the stars and staring at the shadows of the night cast by large pit fires set about the village to ward off jungle predators. An hour passed with Alvarez doing little more than occasionally swatting a mosquito and sighing remorsefully at times when he looked heavenward.

Glancing at Alvarez, Papito felt a sense of guilt at having once thought of killing him. A sudden, driving compulsion to apologize forced words to the tip of Papito's tongue, yet he lacked the courage to speak. But, as if Alvarez had read the old man's mind, he turned his face to look at him.

"Why didn't you kill me when you found me at the river?"

The elder was about to sip his coffee but stopped, lowered the cup and exhaled hard.

"In truth, John, it was Ignacio who stopped me. He saw good in you. But I must be honest, when he told me the name you kept saying, I knew you had been touched by *el diablo*, the devil." The elder paused as if garnering courage to continue. "I am not a murderer, *señor*. No, yet I would do so to guard my family and village against the evil."

The coldness in Alvarez's blue eyes faded and was replaced with regret. A wet sheen on them reflected the firelight. "No, you are not a murderer—but if you had killed me, you would have only been putting an animal out of its misery."

"Animal?" Papito sensed the deeply rooted pain emanating from Alvarez. It sent a maelstrom of emotions swirling through his mind. When he spoke again it was with the voice of a father who suffers each day with the longing to talk to his son once more, yet knowing he never will.

"John, why do you say this? You are not an animal. Yes, I was afraid of you—of where you had been and what could happen to *mí familia*. That is why I thought it better you die at the river." He hung his head in shame and gazed dejectedly at his bare feet. "You must understand, when I saw you and heard you call the name—" Papito paused and made the sign of the cross. "I remembered my son, Ignacio's father. May God forgive me for my sins." The voice trailed off. The elder could no longer talk.

Alvarez sat back on the steps and leaned against a broad hut post. Questions were poised on his lips, and his expression became one of wonderment, yet he held himself in restraint. "Your son went *there* and lived to come back?"

The old man nodded as if the movement tore at his heart.

"Marco was headstrong and stubborn like his mother. After Ignacio was born, my son said he was going to a place in Amazonia where he could get enough money to care for all of us. We were hungry in those days and having money for food is always a dream of the poor. But Marco had heard the tales of a place where gold sits like a mountain, and is there for the brave to take."

Eyes brimmed with tears, Papito's gaze rose to meet Alvarez's cold stare. "I begged him not to go because my father, and his father before him, had always said it was the devil's gold. They warned everyone to stay far away from that land because no one ever returned from the devil as they had left."

"But your son *did* return?"

"Yes, five years later. One day I found him like you on the riverbank, tortured and half-dead. He would only say *that* name. Even now I am afraid to speak it."

"What came of him? Did he live to tell you about—"

"He lived, if that is what it may be called. His mind was lost from him. *Como se dice—loco?*"

Alvarez exhaled hard, understanding all too well what Papito was trying to say. "He went mad . . . insane."

Sorrow pierced the old man's soul at the memory.

"Yes, my Marco went insane. He began to stare at the sky as if the sunlight would cleanse him—but when the moon rose full in the night . . ." Papito paused and pointed to the white orb over the jungle canopy, ". . . it was on those nights Marco trembled as a frightened child does, and he spoke *that name.* Each day grew worse, *señor.* I became more afraid for *mi familia.*"

Beads of sweat dotted Papito's brow. He wrung his hands nervously. "One morning Marco and I stood at the river. He cried in my arms and begged me to end his suffering. I refused and he tried to take my machete. We fought and he knocked me to the ground . . . Never had he done such a thing! But I could see in his face the pain had become too great for him to bear. He raced to the river, screaming things I did not understand. I tried to stop him but Marco was young and strong—not as strong as you, *hombre,* but strong enough to fight me and win. He ran into the water and swam far out into the river."

Eyes glistening in the firelight, Papito inhaled deeply to stem the hurt rising fast in his throat. When his gaze carried to Alvarez once more, the suffering made it difficult for him to speak.

"It was then the black caiman took him. All I could do was stand and listen to his screams until there were no more. To this day I have never told my family what happened to him. In their minds Marco is still alive. I told them he left to live in some other land."

Alvarez sat staring at the old man, torn between his grief and the understanding of the torment Marco had endured.

Tears trailed Papito's cheeks as he looked at Alvarez. When anguish at last overpowered him, he lowered his face and sobbed without shame. The floodgates of his heart opened. Years of concealing his pain flowed freely from him.

Laying a consoling hand on Papito's shoulder, Alvarez waited patiently until he regained his composure.

Minutes passed before the elder raised his head to look at Alvarez. "The day we found you, I thought of my son and was afraid. I have lived all these years with the memory of his death, but always there are the questions with no answers. What evil is in that land? What did my Marco see to drive him mad? You have been there. Tell me so I can understand why a good man as my son would return with such terror in his mind."

Alvarez drew rigid, breathing labored. He felt his chest constrict and heart pound as if it were struggling to break the confines of his body. The blood coursing his veins raced like a raging river, becoming scalding and seemingly burning his flesh. His arms shook in spasm while his hands flexed into knotted balls. He shut his eyes, forcing himself to calm before savage memories took hold and began to rake his mind.

"*Madre de Dios,* I did not mean to give you such pain!"

Papito's apology went unheard. Alvarez's mind finally obeyed him and blanked in self-protection. The moon had shifted positions across the sky before he looked at the village elder again, yet when he did, a blend of cruelty and bitterness lay below the fragile surface of his calm gaze.

"If your son was a good man before he left, remember him that way—forget how he was in the end. He did not deserve to die, but if the madness wouldn't leave him, he knew he was dangerous to his family."

"And you, John? Can you fight the madness? I have seen you chop wood, punishing your body because your mind cannot forget.

You speak as if you believe you too truly deserve to die." Papito paused and drew a weary breath. "Tell me, *hombre*. Were you good before you went to the evil land?"

Alvarez never blinked as he stared into the questioning eyes of the old man. He shook his head tediously slow. "No. I was a convicted killer living my life out in prison . . . and most of the time in solitary confinement."

"You?" A mask of confusion shot over Papito's face. "But I have seen you with Ignacio! Your heart is good. When the village children climbed on you and played their games as if you were a tree, you were gentle and kind to them. I cannot believe such things you say."

Glancing at the full moon, Alvarez repositioned himself against the hut post and let his gaze travel across the gleaming stars. He exhaled a hard blast and looked at Papito regretfully. "I will leave tomorrow. I have unfinished business with two men."

"We cannot keep you here if you must go, but you are welcome to stay in my village for as long as you wish. Ignacio has grown fond of you and will be hurt when you leave."

A pleading look filled the elder's eyes. "If you must go, I ask only one favor."

"What? I already owe you more than I can ever repay."

"I ask only that you tell me what made you go to the evil land. My son went because we were poor and he wanted to bring us gold. Tell me of your *familia*. Were they poor people like us and that is why you went? But no, John, I cannot rest until I know what drove my son mad. I must know what is in the evil land. *Por favor,* please. Do this for a father who has lost his son and has no answers to the questions in his heart."

"The truth may hurt your more than you realize. Are you prepared to live with more pain?" Alvarez's tone grew unsympathetic. His own mental suffering dwelled within him like a volcano on the verge of eruption, and unknowingly he wanted to release the mounting pressure.

"We have all night to talk, John. The *sacerdote* says confession is good for our souls and cleanses us. Already I have told you more than my own *familia,* even the *sacerdote,* knows about my son. I have kept the black secret in my heart all these years, but telling you has let me breathe once again. I will carry Marco's death to my grave, and what you say to me this night will go with it. On this I swear before God." Papito made the sign of the cross.

Alvarez scowled. "Confession may be good for the soul, but first you have to believe God exists—that there's a heaven and a hell."

The village elder abruptly straightened on the hut's hard steps and gazed confusedly at the muscled man beside him. He shook his head. "I do not understand. I *do* believe in God."

Alvarez nodded. "Good, because I know there is a hell. I've been there." In the pervading moonlight his features took on the stoic appearance of cold granite.

Whether it came from the fire burning in his soul or was an illusion of the night, the old man observed an inferno of madness ignite in Alvarez's blue eyes.

"Very well, Papito. I'll tell you. I owe you that much. But you must hold onto your beliefs as never before because when I finish, you will not know what to believe."

And having spoken, Alvarez solemnly took a deep breath, looked at the Amazon moon, and began his macabre tale . . . .

Chapter Two

If I had known what awaited me in the Amazon, I would have killed the three men the day they arrived at the prison to ask me to undergo the journey. In doing so, I could have lived out my life behind concrete and steel and continued to believe in mankind as I knew it. I realize how strange that sounds, choosing imprisonment over freedom. But if I had remained there, I might still have *something* to believe in—something to anchor my sanity to.

Now, I am no longer sure what is fact or the fabrication of a deviant mind. My life has become a ship lost at sea, sailing without direction on storm-driven waves. I'll survive though. I always have. I learned early in life to live with pain.

★ ★ ★ ★

There were four in my family; my father Santiago, my mother Quintana, my older sister Melinda, and me. We lived in a small Texas town and were neither rich nor poor, existing in that middle-class of society where men struggle for a better life and rarely succeed. Yet, my father was a proud man, burning with determination to accomplish great things for his family. He refused to accept anything less, and with my mother by his side, they stalwartly set about their plans to elevate our well-being.

At the age of ten and still immature, all of that meant little to me. While my father labored without complaint from dawn to dusk in the oilfields then rushed to attend his night college classes, I only grew angrier over his absence from me. How was I to understand the sacrifices he made were intended to provide a better future for us? My youth refused to accept mature reasoning and I grew rebellious, unconsciously determined to attract my father's attention.

My days were dedicated to making my sister's life miserable and becoming the best fighter in school. I cannot recall the number of times I was expelled for drawing blood on other boys. With each fight I proudly accepted my punishment from the teachers as if a badge of honor was being bestowed. My strength and size were rapidly increasing and I relished the power they gave me. Having achieved a reputation for myself in school as one not to cross, I turned on Melinda with equal fervor.

Melinda was eight years older than me and a budding rose in my parents' eyes. I, on the other hand, had grown to be the thorn in their sides. Although I never realized it then, she was beautiful, gracious, and intelligent. Standing beside my mother, they were mirror images. Their long, raven black hair was so rich and thick that when the sun caught it, blue streaks danced its entire length. Golden honey painted their eyes and their skin was soft and wonderfully tinted. Yes, my mother and sister were beautiful and turned many a man's head in admiration. But Melinda was a young flower, and like all flowers do in spring, she attracted every male bee for miles.

There is no doubt that I was jealous of my parents' constant doting over her. They praised her appearance, her maturity, her academic skills, and on, and on. She was truly deserving of the tributes, and again, I can only blame the stupidity of my youth for feeling neglected by them.

I tired quickly of committing the usual brotherly acts of vandalism against her. There is no need to list them. Let your imagination run rampant then know I acted with malice. Her angry shouts were music to my ears and sweet revenge for the attention she received from my parents. In time, her cries grew to be a monotonous song. I chose a different strategy and selected a new battlefield for my war against the favored child. As the bees came in swarms hoping to pollinate the flower, I would be there to swat them.

On the first day I managed to sing a rock through the windshield of her suitor's car. By the end of the second day, I succeeded in sending her next friend home with a headache from my well-thrown baseball. After a week passed and my parents' rage settled, I waited patiently until another love-struck young man came to court her. The poor fellow sat so still in a chair that I almost took pity on him and thought not to follow through with my plan. But my father's determination also ran bone-deep within me—and carrying the name of Alvarez meant I could never turn away from a challenge.

"Here, Melinda. I brought you something to drink," I said innocently, walking into the living room, balancing a large pitcher of lemonade on the tray in my hands.

Naturally, she panicked. Her golden brown eyes instantly narrowed into a fiery, hate-filled glare. Melinda wasn't easily fooled and realized there had to be some devilment in my courtesy. Yet I remained a perfect gentleman and after setting the tray carefully on a short table before her, I poured her a cool, refreshing glass without incident.

Melinda watched me like a hawk, talons ready to soar in for the kill. I knew I would have to act swiftly or all would be lost.

"Thank you, John. I'll pour my friend's glass," she remarked, eyeing me as if she wished I would turn into a pillar of salt and crumble to the ground. But her hands had not reached out fast enough, and mine had.

"I can do it," I replied eagerly. It was then I turned to the grinning fellow in the chair as I lifted the tray.

Oh, my theatrics were superb. Even now, reflecting upon that moment with my sweet sister, it warms my heart. The tray rose into the air; the pitcher full with the exception of one lone glass. I expertly tripped over my feet, cried out as if I were afraid to fall then joyfully watched as the tray and pitcher crashed into the young man's lap. He bellowed like a wounded bull and sprang from the chair, groin drenched in well-iced lemonade.

"You brat!" she shouted and swung a rolled newspaper to strike me.

Agile for my size and ready for action, I dropped low to avoid the blow. Unfortunately, my sister's admirer was blind to her move, and bent forward to swipe his trousers clean.

SMACK! Melinda struck him in the head with the vengeance of a woman smashing an annoying insect. And from that day forward there was one less bee flying around our home.

But I was not ready for retirement yet and bade my time until the opportunity for mischief presented itself once more.

Out of respect and love for the memory of my sister, I will not relate the details as I wish, but the hour was late and my parents were asleep for the night. I heard Melinda returning home after spending an evening with the man she had grown more than fond of.

The clanks and clatters of his car were distinctive. Over the past months I had come to know them well. From my bedroom window I watched the sleek, red polished car slow to a halt and park in the blackest shadows outside our house. I thought it peculiar the windows were up on such a warm night. After sneaking out into the yard, within minutes I heard thumps and muffled moans carrying from the car.

In a stroke of juvenile genius, I remembered my father's recent purchase of a motorized camera, and how blinding its flash was when he took our photographs for the family album. My mother and he had decided they needed photos of us so they could sit in the autumn of their life and look back with warm memories. For weeks Melinda and I had been plagued at every turn with the whir of a rapidly clicking camera and its brilliant flashes.

"Yes," I whispered with a proud, wry grin, "My parents will thank me for giving them these memories."

Rushing into the house I found the camera loaded and ready like a hunter's gun waiting to be taken up for the hunt. As I returned to the car, the strained moans from within had grown louder and were carrying into the still night. The car began to rock slightly and I became confused by its motion. But that did not prevent me from approaching.

My father believed in explaining the mechanics of everything to me. It came from his love of engineering, and too, he hoped to interest me in a vocation other than fighting. Armed with his teachings I was well versed in the proper use of the camera, its buttons, its flash attachment, and more especially, its action grabbing, high speed motor.

The car windows were fogged, blocking my chances for a clear shot through the window. I scouted for a better view then realized my only alternative was to open the driver's door.

A small, blinking light atop the camera told me the flash was fully charged. By then my heart was pounding against my chest. The excitement of the moment was becoming too much for my young mind to bear. With one hand on the door handle, the other holding the camera, finger poised over the button, I flung open the door and yelled, "Smile!"

I was not prepared for Melinda's bloodcurdling scream or the spectacle before me on the car seat. Stunned, my finger depressed the button and refused to release its pressure. The camera's motor whirred loudly. *Clicks* reverberated in my ears and the strobing flashes of radiant light blinded my half-naked sister and her friend. My mission was accomplished. I had caught on film, and for my parent's photo album, the flower being pollinated by the bee.

With heels wildly spurring the air and legs spread as far as the cramped confines of the car would permit, Melinda laid buried beneath a young man with trousers down about his ankles and whose buttocks presented me with odd winks. I could only stand in shock while my sister yelled and beat her fists against her lover to gain his attention. Caught up in the throes of passion, it took him several seconds to regain his wits before scrambling from Melinda's flower garden.

His hands rose to protect his eyes from the vibrant flashes of light and his head struck the car's roof with a harsh *thump*. He feverishly tugged at his trousers while attempting to kick back at me as a mule defensively does, but his foot caught in the steering wheel and the car's horn blared through our quiet neighborhood. Madness erupted in the car's front seat as the two lovers fought for space to dress themselves.

Meanwhile, the camera in my hands relentlessly hummed and flashed, capturing all upon film. In the mayhem I observed parts of Melinda's anatomy I had seen before when I walked unannounced into her room. As I said earlier, out of respect for her memory I will not go into detail except to say her body was in full bloom. Her companion unwillingly displayed himself too and I averted my gaze.

It was then an iron-like grip settled over my shoulder and my father's deep, hardened voice shook me to the very foundation of my soul.

"Into the house, John," he said, and took the camera from me. As I hurried away, I looked back to see him standing with hands on hips, staring at my sister and the terrified young man in the car. I knew my father well and the more quiet he was, the greater his fury. At that moment there was the purest silence I had ever known.

My dear mother, frightened and confused by all that was occurring, ushered me to a chair and then returned to her vigil by the front door. She clutched her robe closed at the throat and waited anxiously for my father's return. I believe she realized what had transpired, but a mother always hopes for the best when her children are involved.

Melinda entered the house first, head hung low in embarrassment, clothes disheveled. She glanced at me and the embarrassment changed to fiery anger. Closely following her into the house, no longer the impassioned lover and pollinator of flowers, came her companion. His clothes were equally unkempt with shirt buttons mismatched to their holes and shoe laces untied. My father stepped into view and gave the camera to my distraught mother. His face was a confusing mask of rage and hurt, and his hands closed into knotted balls as hard as sledgehammers.

"Go to your room, John. Your mother and I must talk to your sister."

I did as told, and quickly too, for I had heard such a steel-ring in his voice once before and knew his Hispanic blood now reached its boiling point.

All night the front door of our home opened and closed with force. A steady stream of people entered and there were arguments, cries, and pleas for understanding. While I recognized some voices as those of my family, I assumed the others came from my sister's lover and his parents. An authoritarian voice moderated the discussions, yet I failed to comprehend who it belonged to. The night seemed to drag on forever as I sat on the edge of my bed listening to the storm raging in the other room. For the first time, I was truly bothered by my mischievous antics and the misery I had caused my family.

At dawn my father entered my room. I was awake and had slept very little during the night. The creak of the door made my body draw taut and I nervously watched him take a seat beside me on the bed.

Never had I seen him so weary looking, almost broken-hearted. His proud features, the thick dark hair, the penetrating black eyes, wide-shoulders, and arms that appeared to me as big as trunks of a tree, all now looked worn and aged. Years of hard labor in the oil fields had given him the strength of a bull. Yet this single dilemma with my sister took its toll on him.

He laid a tough-skinned hand on my shoulder and affectionately smiled, but there was no humor to be seen in the black pearls staring at me. I expected the worst and assumed my punishment would match my deed. At such a young age I felt death was imminent, and I was unprepared for his wounded emotions.

"John, I never meant for us to grow apart," he said, the words carrying an apologetic tone. "In trying to make a better life for our family, I assumed you knew how much I loved you. Now, I realize I should have spent more time to tell you."

His words stabbed my heart and I grew weak, ashamed of all I had thought about him over the years.

"Every time I look into your blue eyes, I think of my father. He too had eyes the color of the ocean. When your grandfather came from Mexico, he worked in the fields like an animal because he could not get a job better than manual labor. Yet, he took care of his family and we always had food on our table. We laughed, sang, and danced in our home, never realizing we were poor. We were happy with each other and not for the material things that could be bought. But my father was a proud man and wanted us to succeed in America. He wanted his family to be equal to everyone, and over that he constantly worried about our future."

I listened intently. My father rarely talked of his impoverished upbringing to anyone other than my mother.

"Your grandfather spoke very little English, but he eventually became an American citizen. He worked hard all his life and died with only one wish—that his children would never have to endure the same hardships. On his deathbed, he made me promise to go to school and not work in the fields all of my life. I'm telling you this so you may understand why I have been gone from home so much. I left for work in the mornings before you were awake and often didn't return home until long after you were asleep. When my back ached and my muscles were sore, when the sun burned me in summer and the cold winds cut me in winter, I had to remind myself of one thing—that I was doing it to help us—to better your life, Melinda's, and your mother's."

The mention of his absence infuriated me. He saw the anger in my eyes because he rubbed my shoulder and smiled as a father does when he realizes a child cannot understand the complexities of providing for a family.

"But I'm through with college and I have a better job now. I have a degree as my father wanted and I've moved from the fields to an office. You and I will start doing more together, becoming friends, becoming a father and son again. There is much we can learn from each other. For us to be a true family though, you must promise you will stop pestering your sister and fighting in school. Promise me you'll always try to be good in your life, and will always remember we love you."

I could only nod in answer. Joy choked my throat and refused to allow me to speak sensibly. I was confused by feeling so happy, and within the same moment, wanting to cry. These were words I had longed to hear, and now, I was unable to make the slightest reply.

"Next week I must go to Brazil for several weeks and inspect an area of the Amazon near the Peruvian border. My company wants to explore for oil and because I speak Spanish, they've asked me to look at several sites. It could mean a promotion for me in the future."

Excitement gorged me. I envisioned us together and began to dream of that unknown land—the Amazon. Before I could talk, he patted my shoulder.

"It will be a short trip. Your mother is going with me to look at the towns and houses." My father glanced at the door, his face growing somber. "And it seems your sister will be going with us so we can keep an eye on her."

"What of me?" I asked. "Why can't I go too?" Rejection set in and I felt alone in the world as before. I protested but he remained steadfast in his decision.

"Your mother wants you to stay with her parents while we are gone. There's still another month of school left before summer comes. You must finish it. Melinda isn't in school anymore and will go to help your mother. Who knows what the future holds? We may all be moving to Brazil."

I found no consolation in his reasons why I should remain while they go. Although he said it was only to be a short trip, my stomach tightened without reason. Words escaped me. I felt frightened by something I was unable to understand at such an age. It was my first experience with true fear of the unknown. Even now I grow disturbed as I think of our talk that night.

My father kindly smiled, wrapped his powerful arms about me, and squeezed until I believed I would surely burst. After a few minutes, he relaxed his hold and we sat talking as men do about the dreams they have for their futures. But the dread which churned my stomach refused to leave for days and I could only find comfort when he held me close.

The following week on a fog-shrouded morning with my heart in my throat, I stood on my grandparents' doorstep and waved goodbye as my family departed for the airport. From the backseat, Melinda's futile attempt to smile matched the sorrow in her eyes as she returned my wave. Yet it was my mother's expression which disturbed me most, piercing my soul with her angelic presence. She pressed her fingertips against the window as if to feel my face and I longed for her touch. All I saw of my father was his waving hand and the side of his head as they drove away. Within seconds the car became a mere outline in the fog and next they were gone from my sight, enveloped by the gray blanket. A great weight set upon me. The sickening fear that had swirled within me the week before suddenly returned with a vengeance.

Four days passed without word from my father as he had promised me. I grew nervous watching my grandfather, Alejandro, slowly pace the kitchen, pausing only to light his pipe and glance at the telephone. A constant pillar of smoke rose from the scarred pipe's bowl, trailing him about the room. The furrows upon his brow seemingly deepened by the hour, and his gaze often grew distant as he stared at the floor.

In mid-afternoon of the fifth day a police car slowly passed my grandparents' house then returned. The car entered the driveway and parked. Sitting beneath an oak tree in the yard, I watched the somber-faced officer step from it and look toward my grandfather who stood equally solemn on the porch.

"Is this the Madeira residence?"

At first I believed my grandfather was not going to answer, and then he nodded. The front door eased opened and my grandmother stepped out, ashen faced and wide-eyed.

"Mr. Madeira, I'm sorry to—" The officer caught sight of me and immediately drew silent. He walked to the porch and from the distance I was unable to hear his whispers to them.

My grandmother burst into tears and rushed into the house with a hand over her mouth as if she were sick. I sensed the uniformed man's ill news related to me, yet did not know how. After the officer left, my grandfather stared at me with intense pain in his eyes and summoned me to the porch.

He slowly sat on the steps, easing himself down as if the weight of the world pressed heavily upon his back. As I stood before him I was almost unable to breathe from the panic choking me. Tears rimmed his harvest brown eyes and made them glisten in the afternoon sunlight. His bottom lip quivered as he struggled to speak.

"You must be strong, John," he said, laying his pipe beside him on the steps. His hands gripped my shoulders and squeezed so tightly that I winced. "Be strong because what I must say will make you hurt."

I cannot recall all he spoke that day. My mind numbed as anguish flooded my heart. His words gradually faded from my ears but I do remember, "The airplane crashed in the Amazon and can't be found. They believe everyone is dead."

At ten years of age, I lost my family.

★ ★ ★ ★

To this day, the greatest regret I carry is having wasted so many years doubting my father's love for me. Such is the advantage of hindsight. A man's vision is always crystal clear when viewing his past and thinking of all he should have done correctly. I could always say, "If my family had not died, my life would have turned out differently." But is that merely wishful thinking? I will never know.

The first time the police had ever come to my grandparents' house was the day they brought news of the plane crash. Unfortunately, that was not to be their last visit. In the following years many a police car came and went, bringing me home in handcuffs to the humiliation of my grandparents. I believe the officers pitied them for having to raise a worthless kid like me. There were so many times when I should have been thrown in jail and was not.

Bitterness became the nourishment of my heart. I let anger become addictive to me. My grandparents were not to blame. They provided for my every need as best they could, and their love never faltered regardless of the petty crimes I committed. It was I who turned away from the gentle world they offered. I had been cheated in life, cheated of having a family. Never again was I to hear my mother's words of love or feel her soft kisses upon my brow. No one could replace the strong arms of my father who wrapped them about me and squeezed with the strength of a bear. There would never be another Melinda to chase me away in fury then later wearily grin at my brotherly antics. Yes, I had been cheated from ever knowing those things again, and my rage burned with the force of an inferno.

In my seventeenth year, and not entirely of my own choice, I embarked upon a new path in life. One that would expertly temper the metal of my soul, pound it until the red-hot glow became a double-edged sword, then polish and sharpen it to a keen, razor's edge.

"Robert John Alvarez," the gray-haired county judge said coldly, peering at me over the rim of his black, plastic framed glasses. "You are charged with public intoxication, resisting arrest, and three counts of assault on police officers. Damn your hide, son! I thought you promised me the last time you were arrested that you were going to get your life straight?"

I stood handcuffed before his wide desk, calmly awaiting my fate. Three policemen stood nearby, each wearing bruises and moving sorely from our struggle the night before. My grandparents sat off to one side of the room and as usual, my grandfather could only despairingly shake his head at the trouble I had brought upon myself. Beside him sat a granite-faced Marine Sergeant who eyed me from head to foot and appeared to nod approvingly at the charges against me.

I briefly looked his way and was awestruck by his Spartan demeanor and the rows of campaign awards decorating his chest. The creases of his tailored uniform appeared as if they would slice a finger if touched, and the shine of his black shoes mirrored the light in the room. When our gazes met, he stared at me with a dispassionate expression. The hint of a droll grin formed on his lips and left me confused.

"John," the esteemed judge said, hammering the top of his desk with a balled fist. "I've known your family for a long time. They are good people, too good for you to ruin their reputation—and lives."

This was not what I expected. Judge Whitmore always gave me a lecture of damnation before sending me off to serve my sentence performing a variety of grueling public services. Now though, the tone of his voice held an odd ring and I paid closer attention to his every word.

Leaning back in his chair, Judge Whitmore gestured toward my grandfather. "We've been discussing your future and have come to an agreement."

The judge sternly looked at me as he motioned for the Marine Sergeant to approach. "John, I want you to listen, and listen good because you have two choices; either you go to prison or join the Marine Corps. I—"

My grandmother's sobs interrupted Judge Whitmore's talk. He sympathetically looked at her and gestured for my grandfather to calm her.

"Now, now, Josefina. You know as well as I do this is the best thing for the boy," the judge said, adding a confirming nod to his words. When she quieted, he turned to me and slid several sheets of paper across his desk. "I'm giving you a chance to finally make something of your life. At the rate you are going, well—there are the enlistment papers, all you have to do is sign them. If you don't, I'll put you in prison for sure."

What choice did I have? At that age, prison sounded as if it would be the end of my life. There was such finality in it. But my other option carried the promise of still doing as I pleased, and I thought nothing of what it truly entailed. I looked about the room and observed the anxiety in everyone's face as they awaited my decision. Everyone except the tall Marine Sergeant who drolly grinned. He knew what my life would be if I signed the papers, yet he was not about to speak the truth.

Judge Whitmore drummed his fingers on the desktop and pursed his lips. His stare never wavered from me and I realized he would gladly send me away.

As I leaned forward and took up a pen, my handcuffs *clinked* and the sound made me pause. Without reason it shattered my fragile world of thought and suddenly I felt ashamed for having caused my grandparents so much grief in their elder years. They had suffered enough with the loss of my mother and I compounded their sorrow with my wildness.

I stood to full height, squared my shoulders, and looked at the old judge. "Sir, I'll sign them but only with these off," and I held out my wrists to the policeman standing closest to me.

Judge Whitmore smiled and motioned to the officers. I observed a glint of respect in the Marine's dark eyes for my words. His nod came almost imperceptibly, but I had caught it.

Rubbing my wrists, I breathed deeply and looked to my grandparents. "Next month I'm supposed to receive the insurance money from my father's death. There should be two-hundred-thousand dollars in that trust fund. Before I leave, I'll ask Judge Whitmore to write a paper for me to sign, giving it all to you," I said slowly, suddenly feeling better about my life. "It cannot repay all you have done for me these past years, and it cannot undo the worries I gave you. But it will make your lives easier, and I want you to know I love you both dearly."

Josefina sorrowfully shook her head and covered her face with a handkerchief. My grandfather rose and came to me, his face painted with sadness. He started to speak, but I would not allow it for I knew he wanted to refuse my gift.

"Will you do that for me, your honor?" I asked the judge. He nodded softly and remained silent, evidently too moved by the spark of humanity still left in my wasted soul. "Then I'm ready," and without hesitation, I signed my name to each page the Marine Sergeant laid before me.

"Alejandro, we'll need your signature too since John is only seventeen and you are his legal guardian," Judge Whitmore said, handing the pen to my grandfather.

The last time I remembered seeing my grandfather cry was the day the police told him of the airplane crash. Now, he swiped tears from his eyes as he lifted the pen. I slid the papers to him and affectionately smiled. He signed and gently laid the pen on the desk.

"Welcome to the Corps, Mr. Alvarez," the sharply dressed Sergeant said, shaking my hand as he wryly grinned.

We stood eye to eye and the strength in his grip surprised me. Whereas I had always used my height and size to bluff my way through life, here calmly stood a courageous man who had been tried and tested in combat.

Sergeant Steven Mulvain kept his gaze on me as he spoke to my grandmother. "Don't you worry about a thing, Mrs. Madeira. The Marine Corps will take good care of John. We'll teach him skills he has never known and he will travel to lands he's only read about. Yes, ma'am. Don't worry about John. He'll be a different man the next time you see him."

The devilish gleam in Sergeant Mulvain's eyes should have triggered a warning within me. But it did not and I wrongly presumed his droll grin was only of joy over my enlistment.

I cannot deny he spoke the truth that day. I would learn new skills and travel to foreign lands. Unfortunately, as I later discovered, the Marine Corps' idea of skills and travel greatly differed from that of the civilian world.

Chapter Three

There are two Marine Corps Recruit Depots, Parris Island on the east coast and San Diego on the west. A recruit can go to either location depending upon how full each is on any given day, but geography primarily dictates which is to be your first military home. The Mississippi River serves as the divisional line, and being from Texas, my formal introduction to the Corps began in San Diego, California. So in November of 1967, and only four months into my seventeenth year, I said goodbye to my grandparents as Sergeant Mulvain placidly watched in the airport terminal.

It was an emotional parting, one the veteran Marine had witnessed many times in his recruiting career. Josefina wept and agonizingly shook her head as if her world had collapsed. Although Alejandro did not cry, he stood in silence, staring at me with such a grief-stricken gaze that I believed he would do so later in the solitude of his home. When we embraced he trembled in my arms, but I was too consumed with the excitement of my unknown future to comprehend their sorrows.

For the young and adventurous there is always an indefinable exhilaration which precedes a harrowing journey. My heart was pounding and though a part of me wanted to remain with them, another part was anxious to leave and venture out into the world. I was eager to spread my wings and soar into a new life, anxious to meet the challenges Sergeant Mulvain had spoken of for the last week. I wanted to board the plane and fly away from my past. No goodbyes, no nothing, just leave and never look back.

In all fairness to Sergeant Mulvain, I must say he spoke only the truth in every conversation we held. There are stories of recruiters who lied to their enlistees and only related the tales of Marine heroics, courage, and glory, but Mulvain had not. His calm descriptions of the hardships I was to endure in the Corps only fueled the fires of my warrior nature.

I believe he sensed from the first day we met in Judge Whitmore's office that I was better suited for the rigors of war than life among civilians. In me, he found the clay for the Marine Corps to sculpt into a conscienceless killer.

As I sat in silence on the plane the night we departed, oblivious to the long hours of flight to San Diego, I thought very little about my grieving grandparents and deceased family. My memories of them faded quickly and Sergeant Mulvain's grim forewarning rose above all other thoughts like a black-mane lion defiantly challenging anyone to enter his domain.

"When you believe you have reached your mental breaking point, the Corps will push you beyond it. You won't like it. No one does, but you will learn to keep going under the cruelest of conditions while others accept failure and stop to cry. The weak quit when confronted with extreme adversity. That's what makes the Corps different from other branches of military service. We train you to walk through the fires of Hell and come out on the other side, ready to fight—and win."

For hours Mulvain's words echoed in my head, drowning out the monotonous drone of the airplane's engines. I enjoyed the ring of each word, yet did not have the slightest notion of what I was to undergo in the coming nine weeks of boot camp—nor what I would become in the following years.

★ ★ ★ ★

I paid no attention to the number of men accompanying me on the flight. After we landed and were assembled into a vague semblance of order, I roughly estimated our count to be one-hundred or more. We were ushered into specially constructed trailers that appeared to have previously hauled cattle. Their metal walls were high, with small windows set near its roof so only glimpses of street lights were seen as we made our way to the depot.

We sat in the dark on hard bench seats with terror gnawing at our throats. Although we were under orders to remain silent, I doubt if anyone could have spoken. My parched mouth could barely find the saliva to swallow.

No breeze flowed in the cattle-car. The air was stale and suffocating with its noxious odor of sweating men. I believe the driver took pleasure in striking every bump in the road. When he did, it jostled us about and heightened the unexplainable fear that had taken its grip on our souls.

Finally, the cattle-car slowed to a halt and the engine died. Faint light shone through the high placed windows and illuminated the trailer's interior, enough for me to make out the faces of the men surrounding me. They were young, old, smooth-skinned, ruddy, pockmarked, black, brown, and white—yet all bore an ashen look of fear as I assumed I wore.

The cattle-car's front door swung open and crashed against the side of the trailer, startling everyone within from its resounding *boom*. My muscles wrenched tighter and when silence returned, I heard men's labored breathing about me. Next came the dull thuds of heavy booted footsteps as someone boarded the trailer.

"Sweet Jesus in the morning! Those fucking recruiters are scraping the bottom of the puke barrel. We need Marines for Nam and all they send me is dog-shit in civvies," the wide-shouldered, coal-black, drill instructor said in disgust, shaking his head as his icy gaze swept over us. His *Smokey Bear*, the flat-brimmed, World War I style campaign hat, sat low over his eyes and rode high on the rear of his head. He stood like a granite statue outlined by the night's shadows. His drab green battle dress uniform was heavily starched and his black boots were polished to a mirror shine. Gradually he scowled and leaned to the nearest terrified recruit until their faces were mere inches apart. "What'd you say, maggot?"

No one had spoken except for the drill instructor.

From midway back in the trailer I watched as the powerful drill instructor drove his black-gloved fist deep into the recruit's face. The unknown man's head whipped violently then he went limp and fell from the bench seat.

"Shut up, ladies! You're about to piss me off," the drill instructor shouted. His eyes narrowed into mere slits as the veins along the side of his neck became hard chords. "When I give the order, I want every swinging dick to unass this trailer and be standing tall on the yellow footprints outside."

Tension rose in my body and I sensed it in the men about me. I wondered if I had mistakenly arrived at an insane asylum rather than a military base. The only sounds in the trailer were all made by the drill instructor, yet he accused us of talking and had vented his anger on an innocent man. This became the first of many lessons I would learn. Physical abuse was a major cornerstone to the training in Marine boot camp.

The drill instructor glared at us a final time and turned to leave. Someone coughed and the uniformed black warrior abruptly spun toward us. "You bunch of pecker-heads don't listen, do you? You want to play silly fucking games and not obey orders to be quiet. Well, slime-balls, we'll play silly fucking games." He backed several steps until near the door, his face masked with sadistic glee. "You've got five seconds to unass this trailer and four of them are already gone! *MOVE! MOVE! MOVE!*"

The stampede for the door began. As men neared the DI, he pelted them with his rock-hard fists and cursed the day of their birth. I do not know how I made it past him without being struck, but my luck ran out when I leaped from the trailer door. There were five more drill instructors standing outside the cattle-car waiting for us to unload. And they were as angry as the one inside.

Curses, shouts, and pile-driving blows to our stomachs bombarded us as we raced to the rows of well worn, yellow-painted footprints in the parking lot. A drill instructor stepped in front of me, barring my way, standing so close the hard brim of his *Smokey Bear* bumped my brow as he yelled. The tirade of degradation he bellowed so swiftly was difficult to understand, but there is no need to recount his exact words. I will only say from that night on, I was called by names I never knew existed, and my vocabulary increased tenfold with words which can never be spoken in refined circles.

The drill instructors strode through our ranks, bashing men to the ground and berating everyone they passed. One by one we were ordered to run into a building where the hair was sheared from our heads as if we were sheep. We were herded into another building and issued military clothing which did not fit except for the combat boots. Every step we took, a maniac in a brown *Smokey Bear* followed; cursing, yelling, and punching, never allowing the chaos to settle. Cardboard boxes were thrown at us to carry and few men caught them because our arms were already heavily laden with clothes. From there we ran to a different building and piled everything we had been issued onto tables.

"Strip, maggots!" a wiry built, hatchet-faced Marine ordered. He stood with feet splayed, fists resting on his hips as he stared at us from beneath the brim of his *Smokey Bear*. Staff Sergeant Waldrip appeared ready to rip the head off the first recruit who dared to disobey him.

"Strip and throw those civvies in the box, then write your home address on it. Remove all photographs from your wallets and throw them in the box. I don't need you lying in the rack, pounding your pud and looking at pictures of Suzy Rottencrotch. If you're married, forget your wife! If you have a girlfriend, forget her too! Don't worry, ladies. In another week, they won't remember your names. Some Marine on leave will be pulling shore duty on their asses," he shouted with a sarcastic grin.

Listening to him, I realized little was sacred in the Corps. We were systematically being stripped of more than our clothes. We were referred to as "maggots, slime-balls, dog-pukes," and more, but never anything faintly resembling a member of the human race. Every shred of dignity, humanity, and ties to the outside world were being torn from us, only to be replaced by the ingredients the Corps chose to provide.

Placing my clothes in the box, I wondered what Josefina would think when it arrived and she discovered so much of my clipped hair inside. Naturally, she would fear the worst for me. But I had neither the time nor liberty to do other than what I was told.

"You've got five seconds to shower, ladies. Don't waste it skinning your dicks. When you exit, you will shave whether you need to or not!" came a booming voice over the barrage of insults being cast by the half-dozen drill instructors about us.

The black drill instructor from the cattle-car walked among us taking enjoyment in our debasement. He nodded approval to the wiry Sergeant Waldrip. They shook their heads in amusement before turning on us again with vengeance. *"Move! Move! Move!"*

For three days we went with virtually no sleep. Around the clock we were stuck with vaccination needles, physically examined, prodded and probed. Although bone-tired and often falling asleep while standing in formation, we took countless written tests which determined our future military occupations. The bombardment of obscenities, brutal blows to the body, and extreme levels of stress were relentlessly maintained, yet I never realized the drill instructors had changed at various times. I did not know they worked in shifts for it was only a job to them. They were the keepers of the asylum.

* * * *

With each passing day I began to understand Sergeant Mulvain's warnings more. I believed I was walking through the fires of Hell, yet my breaking point had not been reached as other recruits had. Possibly because I was too frightened of being maimed by one of my three maniacal drill instructors or my tolerance for pain was far higher than I realized. I have no explanation, but of those men that did break, there were some who never returned to sanity again.

At night, lying in bed, I often listened to the older men weep as if they were children, crying out to their god to save them. One man, a stout-built cowboy from Nevada, told us the stress had grown to be too much to bear and on a moonless night he tried to slip away. We later heard of his arrest by the military police as he tried to climb the fence about the base. We never learned his fate, but punishment for being AWOL, absent without leave, is imprisonment.

The close proximity of the San Diego Airport to the Marine Corps Recruit Depot did little to help our wavering mental strength. We could hear the 'freedom birds' as their engines roared on departures, and this alone wore heavily on many a man's nerves. Where was there to run to? Prison awaited me as much at home as it did if I 'went over the hill' to attempt escape from boot camp. But rather than allow my fears to run rampant within me as others had, I harnessed my terror and used it as a driving force to accomplish every order I was given. Without realizing what I was doing, I put into action one of the main principles the Corps wanted to instill in us—*use the force of fear to keep functioning.*

We lived in half-moon shaped aluminum buildings with concrete floors called quonset huts. Rickety steel bunks were our beds and a diesel-fired, pot belly stove took the chill from the night. Each recruit had a wooden footlocker for his clothes and toiletries. These were to be the most creature comforts we would have for nine weeks.

If we were not running, the DI's were herding us from one location to another. I say *herd* because that is exactly how it was. We were bunched together so tightly we stumbled over one another as we walked. The DI's made it a form of punishment. Since we could not learn to march like marines, we were nothing more than a herd of cattle. The embarrassment drove the message home. We grew nimble on our feet and precise in our movements.

I believe in the first forty-eight hours I received less than an hour's sleep before a DI entered my hut and threw a metal trash can across the floor. He shouted a barrage of obscenities as he jerked mattresses off the racks with us still upon them. His lunacy made me believe the hour of the apocalypse had arrived. It confirmed my belief that Marine boot camp is nothing more than a training site for insanity.

Regardless of whether it was midnight or noon, our drill instructors were always immaculately dressed and moved with exactness. In contrast, we were a comical looking lot; shaved-heads, wide-eyed from constant shock, wearing ill-fitted uniforms as we tripped over each other in our rush to obey incessant commands.

An hour never passed without our platoon being cursed. Psychologically, we were deprived of pride and personal beliefs, then like empty jars, our minds were refilled with volatile thoughts.

"I've got nine weeks to make you into marines even if I have to kill you doing it," Gunnery Sergeant Buckner told us repeatedly.

I believed him and for the remainder of boot camp, he, along with two additional drill instructors, became our constant shadows around the clock.

"I'm your mother, your father, your sister and brother for the next nine weeks. I'm the only family you're going to have until this living

Hell is complete," the hatchet-faced Staff Sergeant Waldrip declared on our third night in boot camp as we stood in platoon formation before him. Short and wiry, the ferocity of his glare could back a tiger into a cage and make it cringe.

"I don't give a damn what color you jerk-offs were when you arrived because now you are *green*—Marine Corps green!"

Waldrip had an endearing way with words. That was the closest he would ever come to saying he liked us and was racially unbiased.

Like Buckner and our third DI, Staff Sergeant Cummins, Waldrip was a blooded veteran of Vietnam. They had lived through some of the fiercest fighting to date in a land which was only a name to me at the time. Whenever they spoke of war, their voices changed to an emotionless tone, something I would not fully comprehend until I later drew blood in battle myself. They were bitter, angry, and yet sad within the same breath. In their eyes I often observed a maelstrom of hate, and the madness which overcomes men who have experienced far more than any mortal should. But Waldrip, in his granite manner, often warmed and spoke with mixed emotions as he scanned our lost soul expressions.

"Listen, ladies. You're here to learn how to kill the enemy and stay alive in the process. Nothing else. We are the best killers in the world . . . and proud of it." The grisly-faced DI loved to walk the length of our platoon and pause at times to glare at a recruit. "Nam needs warm bodies and we're supplying them. If you want sympathy, look in the dictionary between shit and syphilis because after I get through with you, you dog-turds won't back down from the devil himself."

My brawny size and tall height always made me an immediate target for his lectures. At first I considered myself only a poor victim picked out of the masses. Later came the understanding he saw in me what Mulvain had—a true fighting machine.

"What's your name, maggot?" Waldrip growled, looking up at me. He eased close until I believed the brim of his *Smokey Bear* would bump my face.

"Sir, the private's name is Alvarez, sir!" I learned quickly to speak only in the required third person whenever addressing a drill instructor. To speak otherwise brought on a minimum of an hour's physical torture through exercises designed to enhance your bodily pain.

"What're you here to learn, dick-drip?"

"Sir, to kill, sir!" Never removing my gaze from straight ahead, my words were shouted as if he were a football field away.

Waldrip backed a step and looked me over from head to foot, pleased with my answer. He pointed to my hands and bellowed, "Hold those dick-skinners out."

I did, palm up, and felt tension take hold of my body.

The wiry sergeant glanced at my hands, motioned me to lower them and stepped closer, squinting as he stared into my eyes.

"Look at me, Alvarez," he whispered in a voice which sliced through me and cut to the bone.

His order caught me off guard. Direct eye contact with a drill instructor was forbidden and never did they call us by name. But I looked at him, afraid at any moment his steely gaze might turn me to stone.

He studied my face as an artist carefully inspects the first brush strokes upon a canvas. His voice reached into my mind and carved his words into my brain. "In combat, we shoot our rifles until they're empty then we use them as clubs until they break. After that we draw our Kabar and gut the enemy—and when the blades break, we use our hands to rip the enemy's throat out. We never stop fighting until we are graveyard dead!"

Waldrip's voice lowered until only my ears alone could hear. He faintly gestured to the men surrounding us as we stared at one another. "These bastards might stop, Alvarez, but you won't. Quitting isn't in you. I can tell."

His piercing gaze was chilling and remorseless. Within the depths of his dark brown eyes I saw my own reflection. A taut line formed across his lips as he stared at my face and nodded.

"I've seen that look before, and the men that had them were the best killers I've ever known. No, bastards like you don't stop butchering until someone puts a bullet through their gourd."

He raised a finger and lightly tapped the side of my head. As he lowered his hand, he backed away and smiled smugly, "But while you are here, if you ever lay one of those dick-skinners on me, I'll take a toe hold on your belt buckle and skull fuck you!"

I knew at that moment the same love of combat flowed through us, coursing through our veins like a flood-gorged river. Combat was the temptress who willingly shared her bed with each of us. We suckled upon the same breasts, caressed the same thighs, and relished the addiction and agony it evoked within our souls. Combat was our penance for the miserable lives we lived, the miserable souls we were. In time, I would be baptized in battle by the blood of my enemies, and this grisly-faced Marine and I would forever be brothers in the fraternal order of war.

Chapter Four

In boot camp the recruits come from every nook and corner across the United States, often places I never knew existed. Some of the men were as young as me while others were in their late twenties and early thirties. Short, tall, slim, obese; we represented every race, creed, and color America embraced.

The overweight men were shipped off to the 'Fat-Farm' for weight reduction. Our platoon began training with a hundred men, and each day the numbers dwindled until we reached seventy. Some were released from the Corps on a Section Eight medical discharge as mentally unfit. I now wonder if they truly were. Possibly I was the crazy one for managing to remain.

There were men who stated they were homosexual in hopes of being discharged. Those who did were often subjected to degradation by having to stand before the platoon and shout about what they sexually enjoyed. Staff Sergeant Cummins retained an exceptionally cruel streak and took personal pleasure in taunting them.

The Corps did not waste time weeding out the weak. As Sergeant Waldrip always said, the Corps needed marines in Nam and was pushing troops through as fast as possible. Later I learned boot camp is actually twelve weeks long, but due to the war, it had been reduced to nine.

★ ★ ★ ★

Running was our sole mode of transportation. We ran to our classes, then ran back to our Quonset huts and changed into different uniforms so we could run to our physical training area. We ran, and ran, and ran. We never stopped running and always to the cadence chant of "Kill, kill, kill."

Each evening after our meals in the mess hall we returned to our huts, polished boots, wrote letters if we had the desire to write, and awaited orders from our DI's. One of the three drill instructors might enter the hut unexpectedly and you were to stand at attention until he directed otherwise. He might simply say "Lights out, maggots," and we went to sleep until the next morning. But never did our eyes close before we prayed for God to safeguard Chesty Puller, a legendary marine in the Corps.

Yes, the DI's tucked us in at night and woke us in the mornings. We learned to be ready for action on a split-second's notice. The DI's loved to throw trash cans and enter a hut, shouting and pulling everyone from the racks as fast as mattresses could be grabbed. I crashed into the unforgiving concrete floor several times before learning to sleep as light as a cat.

"You better listen good, shit-birds! One day your life may depend on how light you sleep and how fast you can react," Gunny Buckner yelled one brisk morning after dumping recruits from their racks. Survival and killing were the essence of every drill instructor's talk with us.

As our training progressed and we marched in formations rather than herds, cadence was called out to us by the DI's in a language vaguely resembling English, yet was fully understood by Marines. No other branches of military service use such jargon as they call cadence for their troops.

Inch by inch, the Corps rebuilt us into what it wanted. New terminologies were learned, words of which can start fights within the blink of an eye. In only a few short weeks your body undergoes a metamorphosis no one could possibly understand except another individual who has gone through the same torture. You wonder how with such little sleep and constant physical exertion and stress, could a human manage to put on weight, strengthen, and become as hard as tempered steel. You have strained and tasked yourself to the very limits and beyond, and at times, your body hurt in places you never believed muscles existed.

The Corps pushes a man until he often feels death would be welcomed many times over, yet I always lived through the physical torment. Mentally, we were shredded and cemented whole once more with an ideology completely different from when we arrived.

Our minds were solely oriented to combat and teamwork, for there was no more fence-riding attitudes within us. It was either Yes or No. All remnants of soft emotions were discarded and replaced with the creeds of violence and destruction. Within a split second you could become a savage beast ready to fight, and the next, you were a fully controlled machine, finely tuned.

With each hour I became a different person and felt more at ease with my new being. Whether for good or bad I cannot be the judge of that, but the mindset I was achieving would fair me well in my years to come. I was being trained to fight like a "Devil Dog," a title marines had bloodily earned long ago on the battlefield of a foreign land.

We changed physically and mentally without realizing change had come about. The days of carefree thoughts were now all behind me. My life centered upon my rifle and how it fully functioned. Our rifles were kept immaculately clean, and we practiced their assembly and disassembly in daylight and dark.

I rarely thought of my past. My roots had become entrenched in the Corps.

As the weeks sped by, our mental and physical strengths only increased. No more were there dreams with boyhood fantasies. Our thoughts were solely honed to effectively destroy as a military unit. The training was purely Spartan.

Once, while preparing for a high level inspection with our rifles, I watched Gunnery Sergeant Buckner take a rifle from a recruit and butt-stroke him into unconsciousness simply because there was a speck of dirt in the chamber. But in our minds we weighed the action as justified. A speck of dirt might jam the weapon and get him or another marine killed in combat.

The Corps believed in fighting; with your hands; with weapons, it did not matter. We practiced on each other, choking and attempting to kill under controlled training conditions. With bayonets fixed on the ends of our rifles, we were taught how to split and slice a human open, then swiftly smash their skulls into fragments of bone. Often we stood about circles drawn in the dirt, and like gladiators in an arena, tried to beat each other to death with 'pugil sticks,' heavy staffs padded on both ends to simulate empty rifles. In those circles, we fought until only the victors stood and the vanquished lay bleeding on the ground.

We were honed to a fine razor's edge and slowly converted to what the Corps wanted us to be—heartless warriors of a modern age. Brainwashing or training, I do not know which it may best be called, but the Marine Corps' program of organized chaos worked. I never knew when the transition came within me, but my priorities changed in life.

My mind was consumed with thoughts of war and methods of destroying a human being. No longer did I resemble those friends I had left behind at home. *Home.* The word represented nothing more to me than a vague memory of a previous lifetime before I was reborn and given true life by the Corps.

Now my dreams were occupied with the armies of nations to confront and conquer. While my friends back home thought only of chasing teenage girls and jobs in pizza parlors, I grew anxious to explore the world and stake my claim to it.

★ ★ ★ ★

The days swept past within the blink of an eye and instead of being a *herd* or a *mob*, we now spoke and moved as a formal military unit. At first we had only worried about surviving boot camp and never realized when our thoughts shifted to graduation.

Day by day our lives grew easier because we were accustomed to the hardships. My rifle became an extension of my arm, and we departed for range training at Camp Pendleton in the desolate mountains of California.

The weather grew harsh and icy cold with a drab gray painting the clouds. Out upon those open expanses of land the wind blew relentlessly, piercing what little soul remained within us. Lying on the cold ground, trying to concentrate on firing a rifle was difficult, yet we survived as always. My mind focused on making a kill with one shot rather than the reality that I was using it to take a life.

I had never held a rifle before entering the Marines, much less fired one. For some of the recruits, weapons were nothing special. Those men came from the mountains of Tennessee, the majestic terrain of Wyoming, and the western plains of Texas. Shooting a rifle was as natural to them as eating breakfast in the morning.

After the brief escape from boot camp, we left the range and returned to the comforts of 'Hell.' Our DI's said we had grown soft while at the range and renewed our physical training until we continuously ached again from head to toe.

★ ★ ★ ★

Each day drew us closer to graduation. We were fitted with uniforms that conformed to our new physiques. Less than a week remained, but the DI's still took pleasure in finding something wrong with our actions in order to punish us. Their favorite practice was to have us stand with arms outstretched, palms down, with our rifles lying atop our fingertips. The first time Gunny Buckner introduced us to this torture, rifles fell from weary arms within minutes. By the end of boot camp though we could stand for long periods of time before the first rifle fell and thought nothing of the tirade of verbal abuse which always followed.

For better or worse I was now different. The world before me was only to be conquered. My mind relished the demanding life of the Corps with all its discussions of war, the enemy, battles fought and those yet to be won. In some strange manner, the Corps had become my home and I thought only of my grandparents' house as a place to visit for a brief period of time.

I took pleasure in my new self, never realizing how crucial my training would become in the years ahead. Such are the problems of youth, ignoring the future and focusing only on what is immediately at hand. It's unfortunate though that at such an early age, I bore more internal scars than I wish to recall.

A stone wall had risen about my heart and I vowed to never allow anyone to enter. This was my means of self-preservation and the wall felt good. Within its confines lay protection and peace, and each day its mortar was fortified until I was assured no weaknesses existed. But time steadily chips away at every man. Years later, my protective walls would be breached against my will for no man can withstand the onslaught of love.

★ ★ ★ ★

The Corps provided stability and gave purpose to my existence. For the first time, my life had direction. I washed away my past and began anew. My internal clock awakened me each morning long before the shouting DI's barged into our hut. I slept lighter, aware of every sound in the night, ready for whatever might approach. We ran miles upon miles and my body was no longer tormented as compared to my arrival at boot camp. My knowledge of military history, habits, protocol, and weaponry expanded. Tactics with which to slay the enemy held great importance. My own life, or a fellow Marine's, might one day depend upon the knowledge.

Humans are a curious lot. Under normal conditions we do not believe mental or physical change may come about so swiftly. But placed in the proper environment, the transformation will come. My own experiences testify to this.

You can take a peaceful individual and turn him into a murderous machine which borders on self-destruction yet remains in check. Separate a man from everything he has known; strip him of his clothes; shave his head; degrade him, deny him any connection with the person he once thought of as himself, and fill him with only the understanding you want him to hear. Do this and any human will evolve into a different personality—or go insane.

A fine blend of fear and adrenaline sustained me, providing the necessary strength to rise each morning and complete the day. I never cried nor wailed into the night as other men often did. No, I simply withdrew behind my protective wall and found tranquility if but only for a few minutes. We were pushed to extremes, taken to the very edge of mental breakdown then as a team, crossed over an invisible, internal line. We crossed it physically and mentally, and discovered we were still alive.

The worst battlefield scenarios were always presented to us. They became challenges to mentally conquer. To me the worst was being captured and tortured in war for its potential to become reality was the greatest. We often joked among ourselves that being a prisoner of war would be an easier life than boot camp. Yet we knew that was not true and accepted such talk only as a means to ease our apprehensions.

Surprisingly though, we were never bothered by the idea of being killed. Our drill instructors kept us busy thinking of killing the enemy and soon believed ourselves to be invincible. *The enemy was going to die, not us.* Within such thoughts, however, lay a greater contradiction. We were constantly told of the high numbers of marines being killed in Vietnam each day.

In the heart of all the madness there were moments which did not fit; moments so out of character I often wondered if I was truly in an insane asylum or living a nightmarish dream.

"Lights out, ladies," Gunny Buckner yelled as he walked the sidewalk parallel to our huts.

On that night I was anxious to climb into my top bunk and sleep. We had undergone a miserably rough day and as I stretched my arms, I felt the sore muscles of my shoulders draw into knots. Lying on my back grew uncomfortable so I turned onto my stomach and bunched the pillow beneath my head. Restlessness gnawed at me, but as my eyelids grew heavy, I listened to Buckner and Waldrip talk. It was lighthearted conversation, something definitely unusual to hear coming from the two warriors.

My hut window was open and from my bed, I could see them standing on the sidewalk. Buckner left and the grisly-faced Waldrip assumed the duty. He scanned the area as if searching the terrain for infiltrators, and walked into his hut.

It is odd how a man can feel peace within himself at the strangest of times. As I lay in bed, staring out my lone window to the world, a sense of serenity overcame me. The pain of my body vanished and soon my thoughts began to drift. The mournful, heart-wrenching tune of *Taps* came across the depot loudspeaker, its sorrowful tone inundating my mind. I thought of my father standing with coffee cup in hand on our back porch, quietly admiring the sunrise. My mother touched my head and ruffled my hair. My sister angrily chased me from her room. Then I envisioned them holding tight to one another as their plane crashed and burst into flames.

No longer was there any concept of time as I lay staring out the window at the shadows of the night. The breeze caressed my face and gently kissed my brow. An hour, possibly two, passed without my notice. My mind had blanked. I gazed at the beam of light shining from the DI's hut as if it were hypnotic, and then music flowed through the night air.

At first I believed it all to be surreal. To hear operatic arias in this militant, barbaric depot was unimaginable, as out of place as the Pope holding mass in a whore house. In those years I knew nothing of arias, tenors, and the classics of great composers. Yet the music I heard captivated my heart and never released its hold for the remainder of my life. Disturbing emotions stirred within me that contrasted greatly with the ruthless bastard I would later become.

I grew lost in a sea of tranquility, tossed about on the crashing waves of the orchestra's instruments. My heart became light; my thoughts were no longer black and dreary. The singer's tenor voice cried out in a universal language surpassing all barriers and shook the very pillars of a man's shrouded emotions. It was the first time I had heard Placido Domingo sing Leoncavallo's magnificent aria *"Vesti La Giubba"* from the opera *Pagliacci*. The great tenor sang with such depth and passion I was moved beyond words and felt my heart being torn by the anguish in his voice. I hurt without reason and wept in silence.

The next moment, Luciano Pavarotti's tenor voice rose with clarity as he sang *"Nessun Dorma!"* from Puccini's third act in *Turandot*. Although he spoke in Italian, my mind translated each word because of their similarity to the Spanish my family spoke:

> *"None must sleep! None must sleep*
> *But my mystery is locked within me,*
> *No one shall know my name!*
> *Vanish, o night!*
> *Fade, stars!*
> *At dawn, I shall win!"*

As I listened to the entrancing music, my gaze focused on the shadows outside. A lone uniformed figure stood by the drill instructors' hut, away from the window's soft beamed light. The man's slender build and the distinct shape of a *Smokey Bear* told me it was Waldrip. But in my mind, the man and the music were mismatched. I was stunned to see him staring at the stars and listening to the arias with such repose.

Sergeant Waldrip leisurely smoked his cigarette, but although he stood in safety, assured of no harm befalling him, he cupped his cigarette in combat fashion with one hand to hide its red glow in the night. The smoke rose in a wispy trail and was caught up by a faint breeze. When the music ceased, I observed a change come over him as if he were saddened by his trance being broken. Silence fell over the depot again. He exhaled almost regretfully; field stripped the remains of his cigarette, scanned the area a last time, and slowly walked into his hut.

This served as a valuable lesson to me for the future. Regardless of the vileness we may perceive in others and believe exists in ourselves, there are always tender sides hidden deep within the souls of the worst men—tender sides which rise at the most unexpected moments.

★ ★ ★ ★

As all things eventually draw to an end, so did our nine weeks of training. We graduated in a ceremony filled with pomp and veneration, listened to speeches of traditions we upheld and the honor it would take for us to do so. Our hour of glory passed quickly and with it came the official end.

My platoon departed in silence the next day for Camp Pendleton. It was not until after graduation that I heard our drill instructors call us "Marines" for the first time. Gunny Buckner and Staff Sergeant Cummins laughed as they watched us leave.

I heard them jokingly yell, "Goodbye, maggots," and we accepted it with the warmest of feelings. But as the bus pulled away, I looked out the window. A strange sensation traveled up my spine and made the hairs at the base of my skull rise.

Glancing across the wide parking lot I saw Staff Sergeant Waldrip. He solemnly stared at me as if he knew what lay ahead in my future, yet I could not tell if his expression was of pity or envy. Our gazes held fast to one another and time seemed to stand still. At last he nodded almost imperceptibly and slowly walked away. I remained silent during the entire duration of our bus ride to Pendleton, curious why I felt so disturbed.

We endured several more months of infantry training in the California mountains. The smell of war was in the air and I found myself breathing deeply of it each day.

It is only now I understand Waldrip knew at least half of us would never return from Vietnam. He realized he was watching "the walking dead." Unfortunately his foresight proved correct.

At the end of our training we received new unit orders and prepared to ship out. Half of my platoon was ordered to the infantry, to be *grunts*, while the remainder of the men went on to communications school. Later I learned the majority of those grunts were killed in combat.

I was one of the few who survived.

Chapter Five

I do not speak of my family's death or my first months in the Corps to evoke your sympathy. No, my only wish is for there to be an understanding of the circumstances which stoked the inferno within me and left my heart charred. Those events were the beginning of a long journey upon a treacherous path.

At seventeen, by Marine Corps regulations, I was too young to be sent to a combat zone. But I was old enough to undergo "Force Recon" trainings in preparation for it. In the following year as I waited to come of age, I rappelled down mountain cliffs, parachuted into black voids and landed ready for night assaults. I swam miles to shore through frigid ocean waters and planted explosives on beach targets before moving miles inland to continue destruction. My mind and body were fine tuned and equal to the alert senses of a jungle animal, yet still I was forced to bide my time for actual war.

Once, between trainings, I managed to obtain leave to visit my grandparents. The money I had given them provided material comforts they would never have been able to afford otherwise. Knowing they had received some bit of happiness warmed my heart, although it did not make up for the misery I gave them through the years.

They were happy I was home again, especially Josephina. She took delight in my sharp-fitting uniform and military bearing, but I paced their house like a caged tiger until the day arrived for my departure.

"Why are you so restless, John?" Josefina asked as we sat drinking coffee in the kitchen. The morning sky was cloudless and the sun warmed the kitchen with its brilliant, thick beams shining through the windows. Alejandro lit his pipe and watched the smoke swirl and float through the angled rays of sunshine like ghosts of an ancient tale.

I rose, walked to the window and stared out across the yard, thinking how best to reply. The vanilla fragrance of Alejandro's blended tobacco drifted through the room and stirred my emotions. I should have been filled with peace, but my heart longed to be far away where battles now raged day and night.

When I turned and leaned against the kitchen sink counter, Josefina's eyes pierced my heart and read my thoughts. "You will be leaving soon enough. For now, let us spend this last time together enjoying each other's company." Her voice was gentle and tears rimmed her eyes.

"Last time?" I asked, unable to conceal my confusion at her words. "I'll only be in Vietnam a year."

Josefina shook her head and lovingly reached across the table to take my grandfather's hand in hers. She sighed wearily and spoke in almost a whisper. "I'm afraid we will never see each other again, John."

Walking to her chair, I knelt and took her soft, wrinkled hand in mine. I laughed at her worry over me. "I'll come back."

She withdrew her hand and reached out, pulling my head to her. Kissing me on the forehead, she spoke but the words came so low I could not understand what had been said.

Two months later I received orders and immediately shipped out to a Force Reconnaissance unit based out of Da Nang, South Vietnam. It was during my first tour in that ravaged land I received the letter informing me of their deaths. Josefina, at the age of seventy-six, passed quietly away in her sleep, and Alejandro died within a week of her funeral. Although the letter said his heart simply ceased to beat, I believe he grieved himself to death and no longer found reason to live.

The night was moonless and the letter was read by flashlight as I waited with my team to board the Huey helicopter carrying us into a "hot LZ," a landing zone where fighting could be expected upon arrival. We had a simple mission; locate and destroy a VC, Viet Cong, unit responsible for mortaring a Marine outpost near our base.

After reading the letter I carefully folded and stowed it in my pack. I turned off my flashlight, thankful for the dark. It hid the wet sheen of my eyes.

By dawn we were in ambush position one *klick*, kilometer, east of the Laotian border, laying alongside a route to the Ho Chi Minh trail. The morning mist appeared thicker than usual, limiting our visibility to less than twenty feet. Although I knew my team members were near, I felt alone in the silent sea of gray fog. My thoughts strayed to Josefina and Alejandro. Anguish swirled within me like a tornado. The pain of their deaths, the muddled anger I felt toward myself for the grief I had given them, all constantly built pressure in my mind until I believed I would surely explode. But release came when the first VC eased into view.

This was my twentieth mission into the jungle yet I grew as anxious as if it were my first when I saw the black pajama-dressed man creep out of the mist. We laid in waiting, watching the small VC unit move quietly past our camouflaged positions, allowing them to draw deeper into our invisible net of death. When I heard the first of our Claymore mines explode, years of internal anger flowed from me like a dam bursting under the strain of a flood gorged river. I will not relate all that followed. The details of such butchery serve no purpose.

Minutes later, my team and I were hacking our way through the jungle, rushing to the extraction point, leaving eight crimson-drenched black pajamas strewn along the trail. As I raced behind my team leader, I felt the small pouch on my hip bouncing wildly and pressed my hand over its flap to ensure it was secured. I did not want to lose my prizes.

★ ★ ★

By fall of 1969, I had almost completed two tours in Vietnam and was fortunate to have survived more recon missions than anyone in-country could recall. I had been promoted to Sergeant and led my own four-man team. Not having family to return to in "the world," America as we referred to it, I intended to remain for a third tour. The number of dead Americans climbed into the thousands and men with my talents were desperately needed.

My recon team, Iron Raven, was based out of Da Nang and was well known for its daring exploits into North Vietnam. Bounties were placed on each of our heads, with an exceptionally high value upon mine. I paid no heed to the reports other than taking pleasure in the fact I was so well known and feared by my enemies. Our intelligence officer told me the VC referred to me as "Big Raven" because of my height and muscularity. Knowing the VC's ability to gather information, I assumed they had probably questioned the Vietnamese workers who cleaned our bunkers and cooked our meals in camp. Only through those means could they have known as much about me as they did, for I left no VC alive I made contact with on a mission.

There were four of us in the nine months I ran Iron Raven. Nakai, a full-blooded Sioux who did honor to his ancestors by his ability to read trail signs and slip silently past the enemy; Stern, a mountain-bred cowboy who never tired and was always so calm under fire; Franklin, a black man raised as an alligator poacher in the swamps of Louisiana, and myself from Texas. Even now their names are on my lips as if I had only seen them yesterday. There were no differences of color, race or religion among us. We were brothers of war, comrades in arms, and the only family of importance any more to each other.

Being on my second tour and having undergone such a high number of missions, I was often called "a lucky bastard" by my warrior peers. In camp, I retained few comforts in my bunker because I wanted to remain accustomed to the harshness life in the jungle provided me. But I did allow myself one pleasure I used greatly after every mission; a tape player to listen to my assorted recordings of operatic arias.

Upon completion of every mission, my men never disturbed me for at least three hours while I unwound by drinking Jack Daniels Black and lay listening to the voices of great tenors. I realize how odd that may be, a butcher calmed by whiskey and classical music. Yet I discovered it worked well in helping me make the transition from combat to the relative safety of our base. And from the cold-blooded reputation I had earned in the field, there was no one in camp who dared to laugh at my eccentricities.

My team tempted fate each time we underwent a mission, but it was our uncanny skill to read each other's minds and know how we would react which helped us survive. We destroyed VC safe havens, North Vietnamese Army hospital sites and logistical bases, called in artillery and air strikes on NVA battalions, captured dozens of prisoners for interrogation, and underwent many a running firefight before being extracted by helicopter in a hail of bullets.

Our kill record was far higher than other recon team and we had sustained only minor wounds. But our good fortune vanished the day the commanding officer entered my bunker with two CIA agents.

★ ★ ★ ★

"Keep your seat, Sergeant," Captain Lockhart said, motioning for me to remain on my cot. The familiar stub of an unlit cigar protruded from his mouth as he glanced about my bare-walled bunker. He grinned. "This is probably the only bunker in camp that doesn't have foldouts of tits and ass hanging all over it."

The two men accompanying him made no effort to conceal their curiosity about my quarters. By their wandering gazes I realized they were searching for something specific, something to provide them with insight into my thinking.

"No, sir," I answered, sitting on the edge of my bed, watching the strangers. "I don't spend enough time here to worry about dressing the place up." My shirt was off and I observed the taller of the two agents looking at my body like a man inspecting a horse before buying it.

Captain Lockhart removed the soggy cigar stub from his mouth and spit a tobacco string toward the door. He looked at the agents as if awaiting their approval. When one nodded, Lockhart spoke.

"Alvarez, these men have a mission they want to discuss with you. It's strictly a volunteer thing, but they asked specifically for your team."

I remained silent, wondering what fantasy assignment the Central Intelligence Agency had dreamed up for us. The only thing the CIA had managed to do in Vietnam was get good men killed with hair-brained ideas which never proved fruitful.

The agents had a deceitful look about them and my gut-feeling was to distrust them. Both were dressed in combat boots, BDU battle dress uniform trousers, and loose fitting, plain styled, civilian shirts with the sleeves rolled up into bunched knots. They carried semi-automatic pistols in shoulder holsters and wore sweat stained, major league baseball caps. The taller man removed his cap and scratched his crew-cut head as he walked to one of my two footlockers. He paused to examine them carefully then took a seat upon one.

"My name is Leonard, and his is Rogers. We're with SOG here in Da Nang."

Rogers made a curt nod then glanced outside to see if anyone was within earshot. I saw him touch the butt of his gun as he leaned toward the door. Satisfied no one was near he remained by the door and gradually brought his gaze back to me.

At a glance I could tell he was an arrogant son-of-a-bitch, willing to do whatever he deemed necessary to accomplish a mission. Leonard looked more like a weasel, his slender face and gaunt features giving him a more sinister appearance in the bunker's dim light. But these men lived in a dark world all to itself, and he probably felt at home.

"We're working on a little project up north and would like you to be a part of it. Are you game?"

SOG, the CIA's Naval Advisory Detachment of the Studies and Observation Group, was better known as the Special Operations Group. They held the authority and decision making power for conducting cross-border operations into every country surrounding Vietnam. Kidnaping; assassinations; psychological operations; training and dispatching agents into North Vietnam; their activities were endless and all were conducted under the umbrella of utter secrecy. While rumors floated about what SOG did, only those with a need to know were ever allowed true knowledge of their dirty tricks. But, as I was to discover, even when deeply involved in one of their missions, this group often failed to fully advise its operatives of the intelligence it had gathered.

I chose to remain silent and only nodded in reply to Leonard's question. Rogers stared at me, his face as devoid of human emotion as a weathered statue in a city park. Captain Lockhart evidently sensed my dislike for them. His stubby cigar fervently rose and fell as he chewed on it and looked from man to man in the bunker.

Leonard casually eased his New York Yankee baseball cap further back on his head and glanced at the footlocker he was sitting on. He touched its lock and drolly grinned. "Is this where 'Big Raven' keeps his *necklaces?*"

Again I nodded, my dislike for them growing rapidly. They had done their homework better than the VC and wanted to use their newfound information as leverage on me. But I chose to play their game by my own rules, not theirs.

"Every time we go out, I leave a necklace of VC ears hanging off a branch as my calling card," I said.

"Jesus Christ, Alvarez!" Lockhart spouted. His cigar stub almost fell from his mouth. "Have you gone Section Eight on me? Get rid of those goddamned things—and don't let me hear about you leaving any more *calling cards.*"

Captain Lockhart shook his head in disgust and grabbed the nearby bottle of Jack Daniels from my cot. His first swig was small then he took another that was long and deep. He hissed a loud blast of air at the potency of the whiskey and wiped his mouth as he gave me the bottle. I stared at Rogers as I upended the bottle and drank as if it were water. When I lowered it, Leonard and Rogers exchanged smirking glances. They approved of either my ability to drink or my not being afraid to speak of the ears in front of Lockhart.

"No, Captain. Sergeant Alvarez hasn't gone crazy. He's simply learned how to deal with the Viet Cong on their own terms. They respect him. Or should I say *fear* him?" Leonard remarked, gazing at me.

I shrugged, not caring what the agents thought of my tactics.

Rogers smiled in sadistic enjoyment. "From the reports we've received, you've left a necklace at twenty different sites for the VC to find—and on each necklace is at least a half-dozen ears. That's a lot of kills for one man."

Lockhart grabbed the bottle and took another deep gulp to settle his nerves from the revelation. "How many more necklaces do you have, Alvarez?"

"There's only one left, Captain. I got tired of collecting them. Now I just cut them off and leave them on their chests."

A chuckle broke the air.

Leonard nodded. "We've been following your mission reports fairly close and like the way you operate. One pilot told us you threw a bound prisoner out of the chopper on the way back to base because he didn't answer your questions fast enough."

"That's not true."

"Oh? Then what was the reason?"

"We had three prisoners and only needed two. I threw the third one out because he had souvenirs from dead Marines in his pockets."

Leonard laughed. "Well, I'm sure he was *trying* to escape."

I held my blank expression and never removed my gaze from him. "Cut the crap and tell me what the mission is or get the fuck out of my hooch."

Rogers braced. It was evident he was used to having people hold him in some sort of reverence because he was with the CIA's special ops group.

My bluntness never fazed Leonard. He smiled and looked me over with his horse buyer's eye. "Good, good. We can get down to business and dispense with the small talk." He glanced at Rogers and watched as the shorter man readjusted his Mets baseball cap and looked out the door. When Rogers signaled the all clear, Leonard's smile melted into a somber facade.

"In two weeks we want to drop your team into Xam Nua, Laos and have you collect information on a high-level meeting that will take place. You'll do a high altitude parachute drop at night and move in close enough to radio reports of everyone you see coming and going from a certain villa. After the meeting is concluded, your team will hike to Bung Kan, Thailand and be extracted by chopper. That's all." Leonard sat back on the footlocker and lit a cigarette as if he had just discussed an afternoon family outing.

Captain Lockhart's shocked expression told me this was the first time he had heard what the mission entailed. I stared at Leonard's gaunt features, curious if he had undergone any similar missions.

"Xam Nua is 600 klicks north of here. That's only 100 klicks southwest of Hanoi. They must be throwing a pretty good party up there if the CIA is passing out invitations to attend," I said, wary of what all was truly involved. "Then you want us to walk across Laos before we can get a chopper out of there?"

"Yep," Rogers stated without a hint of concern for the danger. "We'll supply you with radios that utilize satellite linkups to transmit, and field glasses that will let you see the pimples on an elephant's ass at five hundred yards. All you have to do is radio information of who comes and goes from the villa then leave. Regardless of what goes on there, you are under orders to only gather intelligence."

Leonard spoke before I could ask more questions.

"Actually, it's 650 kilometers to Xam Nua and you'll be 200 kilometers southwest of Hanoi. Don't worry. If you run into trouble while leaving the villa, we can get a special ops team to extract you if it gets too hot in the frying pan."

"Who lives at this villa? They must be important."

The CIA agents adamantly shook their heads in perfect synchronization. "We've already explained more than we should. If your team accepts the mission, we'll fully brief you—but first you say Yes or No," Leonard demanded calmly.

I knew he was lying. Bastards like them never spoke more than they should.

"I'll talk to my team and give you our answer tomorrow."

Captain Lockhart nodded and anxiously walked to the door, apparently glad to leave. Leonard and Rogers appeared surprised I had not jumped upon the opportunity to work for the CIA. They exchanged stunned glances and started away.

Leonard stopped abruptly. "Here," the tall man said, reaching into a deep trouser pocket. He threw a thick wad of money onto my bed. "Take your Iron Raven team out and get them laid courtesy of SOG." His evil smile matched his dark profession. He was a man who thought nothing of dealing in human flesh.

Later that day I met with Nakai, Stern, and Franklin. There was actually nothing to discuss. I explained what I knew and they pretended to be insulted I had asked if they wanted to go with me. After the jokes settled about my doubts in them, we went to the nearest whorehouse and spent Leonard's money in the finest of Marine Corps traditions. For the expensive price we would pay on the SOG mission, Leonard had bought our lives dirt cheap.

Chapter Six

Two days later Iron Raven went into isolation to prepare ourselves for the mission. Although Leonard and Rogers stated SOG would provide all equipment needed, Stern and Nakai *procured* extras from the CIA compound while Franklin and I kept the two agents' attention diverted. We counted on no one but ourselves to know what we would and would not need in the bush.

"Mikhail Borjanovich, a Russian Colonel, lives here and directs Soviet advisors in tactical and interrogation techniques," Leonard explained, pointing to a reconnaissance plane photograph thumb-tacked to a briefing room wall. "He's the big duck in the pond we're mainly interested in, but you'll see other Russians at the villa. Count heads and radio every detail that you can about them individually. We don't care if they scratch their balls. Tell us what hand they're using and describe their rank and appearance. There will be some NVA brass arriving too, so keep us informed on what they're doing."

"Why don't some of your spies get this information for you?" Franklin asked innocently.

I thought the question to be quite normal under the circumstances.

Rogers, whose haughty attitude had become more irritating to us by the day, rose from his chair and leaned across a table, resting the full weight of his body on his splayed hands.

"You dumb fucking nigger!" he snapped. "If we *had* someone to report this meeting, don't you think we would *use* them?"

I was proud of Franklin that evening. He immediately obeyed my silent hand signal without hesitation and remained as still in his chair as he would have out on ambush. But he was seething, and I knew the rage within him was at boiling point.

Standing across the table from Rogers, I watched him sarcastically grin and shake his head. I waited until he was about to speak. With practiced ease, I withdrew my razor-sharp Kabar and accurately stabbed the heavy blade deep into the wood between his open fingers, barely missing the thin web of skin stretched tautly between them. Rogers' mouth shot agape and his eyes flared as his ashen face rose to me.

"The next time you call Corporal Franklin a nigger, I won't miss. Is that clear?" My voice was low, guttural, yet controlled. My emotionless stare never wavered from his eyes for I wanted him to fully understand my sincerity.

Rogers' face flushed beet red. I could see his body trembling with pent-up anger, but he was smart enough to nod and slowly step away from the table in silence. After that evening we rarely saw Rogers. But when we did, his arrogance toward us had diminished considerably.

★ ★ ★ ★

In the following week we made practice jumps using free fall techniques at the highest altitudes possible without having to use oxygen. We carried the same equivalent weight as we would have on the night of the mission and attempted to find every problem we might encounter. By day we test fired the weapons we would carry, and by night we sat in our private quarters in the SOG compound and reviewed our own plans and maps. We packed, unpacked, and packed again until assured nothing vital to the mission and our safety was overlooked. The last day as we lay on our bunks resting, I heard Stern talking to Nakai.

"What do you think, Chief? Are we coming back from this one?" the cowboy asked hesitantly.

"No," Nakai replied softly. He turned over on his bunk as if to go to sleep.

I wanted to bolster their spirits and make light of their apprehensions, but my stomach had drawn tight. I realized I felt the same as them.

★ ★ ★ ★

No other light than a red bulb illuminated the cargo bay. We sat staring at our boots and dozing as best we could, unable to talk without shouting to be heard over the drone of the airplane's engines. There was no further need to check our gear. We had pulled, tugged, and tightened every strap possible at least ten times and were forced to sit idle until time to jump.

A crewman appeared and gestured "five minutes" to me, then lowered the rear ramp we would leap from. It was the longest five minutes I have ever lived.

Stern and Nakai sat across from Franklin and me. Nakai leaned forward and extended his hand. I gripped it tightly and held fast while Stern laid his hand over mine, and Franklin wrapped his paw-like hand over them all. We looked at each other, nodded, then broke the grip and moved to the ramp.

Each of us wore black coveralls over our tiger-striped uniforms to better blend with the moonless night as we descended. Even our parachutes were pitch-black to mask us in the sky. This was the worst part of the mission. The slightest error could create the greatest havoc for us. The plane might overshoot the drop zone and we could easily land well into North Vietnam. We had to stay close to avoid getting separated and lost, yet be careful to avoid a midair collision that might leave one of us unconscious as we plummeted to the ground. We might all land in gnarly trees. So much could go wrong so quickly.

The red light changed to green. The crew member gestured with a 'thumb up' before pointing toward the dark void awaiting us. One moment we stood together on the bay ramp with the deafening roar of rushing wind and engines bombarding us, the next, we were free-falling toward the massive black pit below.

Since Stern had the most jump experience, he was responsible for releasing the chute on our reinforced equipment bag. The remainder of the team had only to be concerned with waiting until the last possible moment to open our chutes and avoid becoming entangled in lines. But we landed safely with only minor brush cuts and miraculously managed to find each other within minutes. Again, we had cheated death.

We stripped from our coveralls and emptied the duffle bag's equipment. Shoving coveralls and chutes into it, we buried the bag in a hastily dug hole in the thickest jungle undergrowth that could be found and then set off at a swift pace to distance ourselves from the drop zone.

Adrenaline fueled our bodies and carried us nonstop for hours. We paused only to radio our safe landing and stare through Starlight scopes into the black surroundings. Nakai took point and when he stopped to listen to the sounds of the night, so did we. Only when he was satisfied did we relentlessly push on through the jungle.

★ ★ ★ ★

The remainder of the night and next day we crossed streams, fields, rivers, and traveled through the worst jungle brush we had ever encountered as a team. We skirted villages and once had a Laotian patrol pass within mere feet of our position. But by dusk we arrived at the sloping mountainside we would call home for the next three days and set about camouflaging ourselves to blend with the terrain.

Faces smeared with green, black, and gray grease paints in erratic lines to break the contour of our heads, we tied leaves and branches about our bodies until we were undetectable at close range. Stern and I setup the powerful field glasses to begin monitoring and relaying the events inside the villa to Franklin, who would in turn radio each detail to Da Nang. But it was Nakai's superb senses and warrior abilities we relied upon most. He kept watch about the area and protected us as we concentrated on our duties.

The colonial two-story French villa was lavish by Laotian standards. A high stone wall shrouded it from sight at ground level, but we were fortunate to be well elevated and could clearly see into the villa's interior through its large open doors and windows. Terraces were adjacent to bedrooms and massive areas we took to be meeting rooms and offices. Guards on the wall and about the villa were minimal in number, though we believed that came from the Russians' false sense of security at being so near Hanoi.

On the first day we observed little activity and slept in shifts to avoid overly tiring ourselves. Our meals were cold and no fires were ever lit to warm water for coffee. We buried our trash and were careful to avoid disturbing the vegetation. We never left signs of our presence in case we had to reposition to safer ground. As it turned out, Nakai spotted a five-man patrol of young Laotian soldiers moving toward us, making a final sweep of the mountain in preparation for the coming meeting. We were forced to move, but luck had not deserted us yet and our new observation post provided a better vantage point than before.

I watched Nakai as he listened to the passing patrol. Like all inexperienced soldiers of the world, the patrol moved along the trail as noisy as a herd of water buffalos in a mating frenzy. After they passed and we were no longer in harm's way, Nakai looked at me and gave hand signals I had come to understand. *We could have killed them with no problem.*

★ ★ ★ ★

At dusk Franklin touched my arm and I instantly awoke, alert to my surroundings. He pointed to the villa and nodded. I rolled onto my stomach and focused my field glasses. Franklin was settled between Stern and myself to better hear the information we whispered. The powerful CIA radio was pressed close to his lips and he lay ready for us to begin. There was little need to look for Nakai. He was somewhere nearby, watching over us as he was supposed to.

It was not difficult to spot Colonel Mikhail Borjanovich. He had a swarthy walk and appeared to be as arrogant to everyone as Rogers in Da Nang had been. By the way aides jumped and ran to obey the shaven-headed, mustached man's commands, no doubt he was our main person to observe throughout the meeting.

Highly polished black sedans bearing Russian and North Vietnamese flags began to arrive promptly at 1800 hours. As they did, we radioed the number of occupants and brief descriptions of each. I must admit, the field glasses were excellent because I felt as if I could reach out and touch the uniforms of the officers exiting each car.

"Lots of stars and bars on those bastards," Stern whispered.

"Yeah, and look at all the booze being hauled in for them. Think the CIA is picking up the tab?" I remarked, wishing I could have a drink and relax.

Franklin chuckled. "You want me to radio that to Da Nang?"

I nudged him with my elbow and felt him chuckle.

"*Party time,*" Stern whispered gleefully, adjusting the focus on his binoculars.

Immediately I spotted what he had observed. Three large vans had come to a halt. A steady stream of beautiful, well-dressed women, surely ladies of pleasure, stepped from the vehicles and entered the villa. I counted at least thirty women before stopping.

"What? Who is it? *What, dammit?*" Franklin asked anxiously.

I never removed my eyes from the field glasses and spoke in a low voice. "Nothing, nothing. The main course for dinner is being delivered." It was difficult to hold my laughter. "Sure looks good. Doesn't it, Stern?"

The mountain-bred cowboy sighed longingly as if he were a child standing before the window of a candy store. "Yep, probably the best beef you can buy around here."

Franklin shook his head and nestled back into position. "Wish y'all quit talking about food. You're making me hungry."

★ ★ ★ ★

As night blanketed the land and lamps lit the villa rooms, our ability to clearly see inside increased. Apart from Borjanovich and his three aides, six Russians had arrived with fifteen North Vietnamese Army high-grade officers. Their ranks were stair-stepped and possibly some of the NVA were aides, but all carried a heavy weight in North Vietnam.

The earlier entourage of hostesses entered a main room and spread throughout the crowd. There was no difficulty in spotting the NVA generals. They were the ones with raven-haired temptresses hanging off of each arm. Six well-endowed women appeared that we had not seen before; three blondes and three redheads. They appeared European but were probably Russian, and by the manner of their dress and way in which they flitted with ease from man to man, I was sure they were professionals of an age old trade. They gradually replaced the Vietnamese women clutching the NVA generals' arms, and for the remainder of the night never left their sides.

Throughout the evening we watched as tables of food were devoured and cases of expensive liquor were emptied. There may have been people starving in North Vietnam, but these NVA officers appeared never to have known hunger. The women teased and hand-fed their new 'friends,' holding slivers of meat over the officers' mouths as if they were dogs anxious for a morsel. At times bits of fruit were placed in the cleavage of a particular blonde and an NVA general would root the tidbits out, burrowing his mouth between the melon-breasts to the applause and delight of the crowd.

We watched drinks being spilt and sloshed by the NVA guests, and observed Borjanovich smirk as he made his way about the room. Evidently all was going as he wanted. This night would break any resistance the NVA had toward him or his wishes.

There seemed to be no serious talks taking place, only the prelude to what would later come. I grew tired at times and saw nothing of importance to relay to SOG. After all, what would we have reported, "Two Stars just grabbed a handful of Red's ass and she tugged his mule."

I observed Borjanovich make a last round through the crowd, patting his NVA guests on the back as if wishing them well with the ladies. He made his way to the door and disappeared. Scanning the length of the building, minutes later I saw him enter a room I took to be his private quarters. He unbuttoned his shirt, poured himself a drink and eased into an oversized chair to read a newspaper. Within thirty minutes he turned his lamp off and retired for the evening.

By midnight every upstairs' room in the villa had at least two women in bed with each man, but the senior NVA general had the three blondes to care for his needs while the three redheads catered to a junior grade general. It was a night of debauchery, an orgy with no sexual feat having been overlooked. Stern and I lay in the jungle watching the room windows as if each were its own pornographic movie.

In the first room, women performed acts on each other to the cheers of a drunken soldier who played with himself; in the second, Vietnamese officers double-teamed a woman while another long-haired beauty slithered over the trio in feigned rapture. Naked women seductively swayed before lecherous men in the third room, and in the fourth, bodies writhed in one huge pile on the bed. Every room held a different spectacle, but one particular window provided a unique sight.

Through it we watched as an NVA officer bent and was whipped with wide leather belts by two eager ladies of the night.

At first I found it all amusing, then grew bored. I heard Stern's heavy breathing and laughed inwardly each time he mumbled, "Oh, baby!"

Eventually, Franklin comprehended what we were watching and kept asking me to describe it. Nothing was happening that I wanted to report so I let him take a brief look through the binoculars.

"You two are lower than whale shit!" he whispered to Stern and me. "They were delivering the *main course*, huh? Y'all are no damn good." He shook his head yet never removed his eyes from the field glasses. "This is some mission. I hope my mother doesn't ask me what I did in Nam 'cause this'll be awfully hard to explain."

Stern stifled his laughter.

"Yes, but remember. Those bastards in that villa are responsible for a lot of dead Americans."

It was the first time all evening I had heard Nakai speak. His voice rang with such clarity of truth that it brutally stabbed my soul. My amusement and boredom gradually transformed into a cold anger.

"They leave day after tomorrow?" Stern asked softly.

"Yes."

"Damn, they'll be doing this tomorrow night too."

"Yeah, too bad we aren't here to kill 'em," I said, taking the field glasses from Franklin to return to my vigil.

★ ★ ★ ★

By three in the morning, the men in every room were asleep or passed out from too much liquor. We observed very few of the women drink and now they lay sprawled naked across the men or partially dressed in the officers' uniform coats. The six women we believed to be Russian operatives had switched partners and lay in each other's arms, fast asleep alongside of their assigned NVA general. When no further activity could be seen, I ordered my men to get some rest. I'm glad I did because it was to be the last we would receive for days.

★ ★ ★ ★

Waking long before dawn, I scanned the villa grounds. Half of the Laotian guards were asleep while the others appeared busy discussing what they had witnessed from their posts atop the high stone wall. Sweeping each of the windows I observed everyone still sprawled on the beds except for one of the blondes who slid from her general's arms.

I recognized her as Venus, or at least I should say that was the nickname we gave the blonde love goddess. She was the best built of all the women in the villa. Her magnificent breasts, with an equally fine body, could make a sane man go crazy. And from what I had seen of her talents during the night, she was what every Marine prayed for at least once in his lifetime. But there was something peculiar in her mannerisms as she edged from the bed and I watched her closely.

Venus slipped into a robe and never bothered to close it as she hurriedly left. I lost sight of her and scanned the villa windows. Borjanovich was awake in his room, fully dressed in his Soviet military uniform. He sat at his desk, reviewing papers in a folder as he drank coffee and smoked a large cigar. I had a feeling Venus would be arriving soon and my hunch played true. She entered, robe flying behind her as she walked, still appearing unconcerned with it being open.

The swarthy Russian officer sipped his coffee, unmoved by the fabulous body standing before him. She appeared to be briefing Borjanovich on the two-star general's pillow talk, and at times I saw the Russian curtly nod and swing his hands in questioning gestures. Venus must have plied a great deal of information from her victim because her briefing took several minutes. When at last she finished, I thought she would leave immediately to return to the NVA general, but she did not.

Borjanovich poured her coffee and I was surprised to see her take his cigar and smoke it with pleasure. By their actions, I could tell they were long time friends and must have worked similar assignments in the past. She moved about the room in a relaxed fashion, robe open, sipping her coffee and smoking his cigar. The Russian officer returned to his desk and rustled through a stack of papers until he found a specific one. After a few seconds of reading, he nodded and smiled to her. Whatever information she was assigned to retrieve, she must have done it well for Borjanovich rose and joyfully walked to her.

I kept watching through the field glasses, expecting her to leave. But I was wrong again. When Borjanovich approached her, she opened her robe wide for his pleasure. They kissed and she lifted one of her long legs and slid it up his side. His hands were beneath the robe, hidden from my sight, but I could tell there was no place not being explored by his traveling fingers.

The Russian had more internal strength than me or possibly he knew something about her which helped his restraint. When Venus backed to his bed and spread herself out for his taking, Borjanovich only shook his head and returned to the desk.

He must have had an iron constitution because she teased him so erotically with her body that I felt my own will power breaking. I wanted to run down the mountain and jump on her myself.

★ ★ ★ ★

By the time the sun rose over the horizon, bathing the mountain skyline in golden light, everyone was awake in the villa. The women were no longer to be seen and a formal air returned to the high-level gathering. The guests sat about a long table on a terrace, the medals on their uniforms gleaming from the brilliant sunlight. They enjoyed a leisurely breakfast as if passing time until their meeting hour arrived.

Nakai's restlessness made my nerves tingle. I had come to know him well. He never grew agitated unless something ill-fated was about to occur. Unfortunately, his senses proved accurate as usual and within an hour, a heavily guarded truck squealed to a halt in front of the villa.

"What do you think?" Stern asked, unable to see what the truck carried because of its tarp shrouded bed.

I anxiously searched for any hint of what laid hidden beneath the tarp. The ten-man detachment guarding it was strictly professional and looked similar to some of the NVA that had relentlessly chased us in the past through the jungle. My team respected the formal NVA units. They were well disciplined and as intent on winning the war as we were.

The squad immediately established a protective perimeter about the truck. There was no comparison between them and the lackadaisical Laotians guarding the villa.

"Franklin, get ready to call Da Nang. I think we're about to find out what's in—" But I froze, mentally unprepared to see a handcuffed, weary looking American prisoner of war step from the rear of the truck.

My worst fears for the man rose into my throat like a knotted fist. I felt sick of my stomach and briefly closed my eyes. Suddenly, I remembered Leonard saying, "Borjanovich directs Soviet advisors in interrogational techniques," and I believed I knew why the prisoner had been brought. When I found my voice again, I could only say, "Mother of God, please, no."

Stern echoed my words as he turned away from his field glasses.

Chapter Seven

"What do we have, John?" Franklin slowly lowered his radio microphone and stared at me, waiting for an answer. The tension in his voice was thick as the lump in my throat.

I glanced at Stern, but he had returned to his vigil of the terrace. "They have an American," I stated, looking at Franklin. "He could be a downed pilot, a grunt grabbed off a patrol—I don't know. One thing is for sure. He's a POW."

Franklin grimaced. He turned his face in the direction of the villa. "It's gonna be a *long* day. A real long day."

And it was.

★ ★ ★ ★

The NVA detachment escorted their prisoner into the villa and directly to the terrace where everyone still sat around the table. Borjanovich motioned for a chair to be placed next to him and an aide hurriedly obeyed.

Head down, shoulders slumped, the slender POW was ordered to sit as if he were a trained dog. When I observed a guard shove the poor man with a rifle butt for moving too slow, I felt my heartbeat race as the purest rage I had ever known gorged my veins.

Borjanovich casually rose from his chair and arrogantly strode the length of the table. His face tightened, brows dramatically drawn into a long, thin line with each glance at the captive. He pointed at him and then laughed when the prisoner's chin lowered.

"I don't like it. The son-of-a-bitch is enjoying the fear he's creating in the prisoner. He keeps telling him something," Stern whispered.

I could see it for myself through the field glasses. Borjanovich had spoken to the American and received the reactions he wanted. My thoughts came aloud, not really wanting confirmation. "I bet the Colonel invited the NVA to bring their toughest prisoner. He's going to give them a demonstration on how to break him."

"Damn, I hope you're wrong," Stern softly replied. He adjusted the focus ring on his binoculars. "But it looks like you're right."

Borjanovich swung his hands like a symphony conductor and walked around the prisoner, talking to his guests. The two-star NVA general appeared pleased and nodded. He disdainfully gazed at the prisoner then lifted his cup to a nearby servant. The cup was refilled and the general sipped it with relish as he watched the prisoner.

The Russian ordered his aides to strip the POW of his shirt and bind the man tightly to the chair. He gestured for a briefcase to be placed on the table then opened it with reverence. Through the powerful binoculars I could see his mirthful expression as he looked upon its contents. Nausea crept up my throat and into my mouth, leaving a vile, bitter taste. I gestured for Franklin to give me the radio.

"Crow's Nest, this is Iron Raven. Do you copy?" The wait for a reply seemed like an eternity.

"Roger, go, Iron Raven."

I recognized Leonard's voice instantly. "Crow's Nest, they brought a POW to the party. Caucasian; approximately five foot nine; dark hair; slender build; appears to have been a POW for a while. Ivan's going to work on him. Request permission to intervene. Do you copy?" Again, a long silence fell.

"Negative, Iron Raven. Maintain your orders. He might be there for another reason. Do not attempt extraction."

"Oh, Jesus!" Stern muttered.

I had been staring at him as I talked to Crow's Nest and saw his eyes shut. Immediately I dropped back to my binoculars, realizing the torture had begun.

Borjanovich slowly broke every finger on the prisoner's right hand with an odd tool resembling a pair of pliers. Each time I saw the prisoner wince, cry out, and fight his restraints, I could almost hear the *snap* and *crack* of his bones in my head. The Russian colonel glanced at his guests and grinned. He drove long silver pins into the captive's neck, arms, and chest, leaving them to enhance the suffering. With the use of odd shaped instruments, Borjanovich probed and prodded pressure points with the slightest of strength, then paused to lecture on the pain he evoked. The Russian officers that had arrived with the NVA appeared ready to applaud their superior's actions.

In the crisp morning light I watched the glistening blood trails from the pins grow wider and longer. I saw the prisoner's head whip left and right as his suffering intensified. He slowly shook his head in answer to Borjanovich's questions, but the Russian only smiled and renewed his brutal interrogation. The bound man's lips curled inward and he clenched his teeth against the pain when Borjanovich tapped the ends of the pins and drove them deeper. A violent tremble swept over the prisoner. Tears trailed his cheeks when the Russian stopped applying pressure.

As the prisoner cried, my heart wept with him. I had to force myself to continue my observation. My mouth was parched, throat constricted into a taut chord, and I ran my tongue over my lips to wet them before I could speak.

"Crow's Nest, this is Iron Raven. Be advised, the poor bastard's being tortured."

★ ★ ★ ★

Borjanovich was relentless, determined to obtain answers from the prisoner so as to please his guests and prove his prowess. I thought of a pompous college professor egotistically parading before his students. He invitingly motioned for the men about the table to approach and take their turn at inflicting pain. All I could do was lay in the dirt, teeth clenched, hands knotted into white knuckled fists, and watch helplessly as NVA and Russian officers questioned and tortured the American under Borjanovich's close supervision.

My gaze carried the length of the terrace, studying the assembly. A one-star Vietnamese casually picked through the assortment of fruit on a tray; another yawned as if bored with the prisoner's agony. Two men talked and gestured during their conversation as if debating the best methods to use back in Hanoi, while one man sat intently observing the sadism with an expression of sexual gratification. When I scanned the three servants standing by a wide terrace door, they were flinching and covering their mouths in horror.

I swung my field glasses back to the bound man. His mouth shot agape and his eyes scrunched shut, cheeks drenched in his tears. A smirking NVA officer stepped away and released his hold on the prisoner's right forearm. It crashed onto the armrest of the chair, wrist swinging without control. A Russian aide cruelly retied the arm to the chair.

Borjanovich was a master at his work. He knew how to gauge the physical and mental limits of his victim, and always stopped as the POW wavered at the edge of the black abyss of unconsciousness. Each torture he performed or supervised took only minutes. Yet to me, ordered to watch this poor soul be put through such agony, it felt as if hours passed before the Russian halted.

By the time the sun was directly overhead the gathering appeared weary of experimenting on the prisoner and sat about the table discussing the morning's events. Servants carried dishes of food and drinks to each man, always careful to avoid walking near the beaten prisoner. As the officers ate, the scantily clad prostitutes appeared and stood by them, hand-feeding them, teasing them, providing entertainment. In that moment I wanted nothing more in life than to be on the terrace and slaughter everyone present.

Venus walked out onto the terrace with the air of a queen gracing her subjects with her presence. In the sunlight her thick blonde hair gave her a dazzling appearance in contrast to her black-haired Vietnamese counterparts. The other blondes and redheads followed, but it was easy to tell they had been instructed to let Venus be the star of the show. She wore a long silken red robe which taunted a man's imagination and was secured by a single button at the navel. On her fingers were shining objects I believed were sharp metal fingernails. Her wicked smile to the two-star NVA general made my blood run hot. She walked to the prisoner and with each step my hatred for her intensified.

The general lustfully smiled as she teased him by erotically rubbing her womanhood on the American's shoulder. She feigned an orgasm to the delight of the crowd then pressed on the pins and pursed her lips when the prisoner winced and screamed. Swinging her leg over the armrests, she straddled him and rocked to and fro as if he was a pitching horse. I lost sight of the prisoner yet knew he must have been enduring extreme suffering because of her weight on his broken body. Borjanovich laughed heartily. The gathering of NVA pointed to the tortured man, chuckled and lifted their drinks in toast to Venus. When she rose from the prisoner, his face was contorted from pain and his eyes held a distant, glazed look. It was then I saw the fresh wounds on his chest where she had sunk her talons deeply into him.

Calling Crow's Nest, I bluntly requested permission to extract the POW, but was again denied approval. Leonard said to forget him and continue my mission as ordered. Yet, how could I displace the man's torture from my mind when I was being forced to watch it occur? How could I lay there and calmly report the NVA and Russians were having a grand time at the brutal expense of my countryman? My team was shattered by all we witnessed, and each of us wanted to destroy the villa with a vengeance.

★ ★ ★ ★

After the noon meal, Borjanovich returned to his teachings and skillfully broke more bones and wounded the American with an assortment of instruments. By now the prisoner had begun to pass out with regularity and the Russian colonel was forced to halt for the day. The NVA patrol carried the near lifeless POW from the terrace. We watched them return him to the truck, but they didn't leave. Instead, they camped about it, cooked meals, and spread blankets on the dirt as if to stay until the next day.

"We still leaving after midnight?" a voice asked from the brush to my immediate left. I nodded, already knowing what Nakai was about to say. "I'd sure like to take him with us."

"Me too," Stern whispered, glancing at Franklin who was already nodding to me.

I looked through the field glasses and watched the gathering of enemy officers leave the table to follow Borjanovich into the villa. Their schooling was over for the day.

Easing away from my field glasses, I sat up and gazed at my team. There was no need to discuss the hardships we would encounter by trying to flee across Laos with a half-dead man, much less the problems we faced in simply getting to him.

We had cast our lots and knew none of us could return and ever hold our heads up with pride if we left the POW behind—especially after having seen all he had endured. I slowly nodded, proud we were a team. Proud I knew such unselfish, courageous men.

"We've got a lot of planning to do before dark," I said, glancing at the villa with renewed interest. "Nakai, find the Laotian guards' armory. We'll need a few supplies." Without waiting for a reply I motioned to the villa as I glanced at Stern. "Can you make it a parking lot?"

His grin made me smile.

★ ★ ★ ★

Daylight faded and dusk draped the land in faint light, creating splotches of black shadows which seeped toward one another until becoming a solid blanket of darkness. The evening meal for Borjanovich's guests was a feast of imported delicacies and fine liquor. I assumed he wanted the NVA to leave the villa in a favorable frame of mind for he never stopped circulating through the crowd. He encouraged them to drink and kept their glasses full; obscenely gestured to the women's bodies and motioned to the rooms upstairs, then wryly grinned as he walked away. Although he carried a drink, I rarely saw Borjanovich take a sip. When standing by his guests he feigned intoxication and easily could have shamed the best actors of a Broadway play.

The crowd thinned as men and women filtered toward the bedrooms. Within the hour the orgies had begun with the same vigor as the night before. Soon, only Borjanovich stood alone in the banquet room. He set his full glass on the table and strode smartly toward the door.

Our greatest concern was how we would manage to assault the NVA detachment and grab the prisoner before the entire villa was awakened. Stern and I studied each bedroom window, pleased to see naked, sweaty bodies in the passionate throes of lovemaking. This night we wanted everyone eagerly engaged with no idle minds to care about the noises outside their rooms. But Borjanovich unknowingly assisted us and had the prisoner brought to his private room. By the manner he brusquely ordered the guards away, I believe the colonel intended to drain the captive of information he did not want the NVA to know existed.

Stern kept watch on the orgies while I observed Borjanovich calmly sit in a chair before the prisoner. The swarthy Russian had chosen a different approach to his interrogation and only talked to the sunken-eyed captive. Listless, suffering from shock and pain, the American slumped in his chair, shirt splotched with dried blood from his wounds.

I waited until midnight when the debauchery was at its height in the villa before putting my field glasses away. The brush moved beside me and Nakai silently appeared from within its black shadows. Franklin secured his radio while Stern inspected his weapons. Gradually we drew to a halt, glanced at each other, and knew the hour had come to repay Borjanovich for his hospitality to the prisoner.

In the past we had never wasted time discussing the validity of the war or the manner in which it was fought. No, Stern, Franklin, Nakai, and I realized our job in Nam was to follow orders, kill when and where the Corps chose, and do so without reservation. Now though we were purposely violating orders, choosing to make our own private war, choosing who *we* wanted to kill. And it felt good to be predators again.

Chapter Eight

Simplicity is often a warrior's best ally. Lengthy details; intricate plans and tactics; elaborate codes and signals; all can be the undermining of a hazardous mission. The old saying of, *"expect the unexpected,"* is the one constant which can be relied upon to occur. Something will always go wrong during a mission and changes must be made. Bearing this in mind, we intended to use the simplest methods of attack and evasion.

While the Laotian guards atop the high wall were engrossed in watching the bedroom performances, Nakai and Franklin slithered to each and stealthily terminated them. Receiving the 'all clear' signal, Stern and I climbed the wall and lowered ourselves onto the villa grounds. Franklin followed, leaving Nakai to provide cover fire for us from his lofty position. Borjanovich's false sense of security about the villa worked to our advantage because we encountered few guards about the residence and dispatched those we found without problems.

The exterior walls of the villa were wide brick set in a careful pattern which provided us excellent handholds. We decided the best avenue of attack was from the second-floor terrace running the length of the villa along the rooms. Every bed was in plain view of the windows, and the greatest kill ratio could be achieved in the swiftest, safest manner.

Stern moved to the far end to better see the NVA patrol sleeping beside the truck below. Easing next to the first window, Franklin pressed his back to the wall to wait while I crept toward Borjanovich's glass-pane terrace door. We were spread thin and could barely see each other in the half-moon's light, but my team was waiting for me to kill Borjanovich—and the massacre would begin.

At Borjanovich's door, I looked in and saw his back to me as he sat before the American. Sweat stung my eyes and the heat of the night was suffocating, yet my blood ran as cold as an Arctic stream. I needed a clear shot, one which did not risk passing through the Russian and striking the prisoner. I eased to the window wall and held my bush gun at the ready. Glancing toward Franklin, then Stern, I raised my hand into the air. I knew Nakai was watching. When my hand dropped back onto my weapon, I spun, aiming into the room.

Borjanovich turned in my direction, eyes flared, the whites of them spread like wind caught sails on a schooner. In that split second as he looked at me I realized he held a pistol and saw it rise toward the beaten captive. I squeezed off a short burst and watched the Russian's arm and shoulder explode, showering the air with a fine pinkish mist. He toppled sideways and crashed to the floor in his chair. Franklin started toward me, tossing grenades into each window he raced past. From his high perch, Nakai opened fire into the windows ahead of Franklin, shooting entangled lovers before they could rise and flee. This allowed my Louisiana poacher time to pull pins and throw his fragmentation grenades inside the rooms.

Stern was doing his part well. I heard several grenades explode and glanced in his direction. He must have been fortunate to strike ammunition crates in the truck because a mushrooming, red-orange cloud spiraled into the night sky.

Leaping through the window I rushed to the prisoner. He was half-conscious. As I approached he peered at me in expectation of more torture. I must have been a frightening sight to him; my face streaked in wide diagonal black and gray grease paint lines; ammunition, grenades, knives, pieces of leaves and grass protruding from my tiger-striped jungle uniform. Pushing my floppy wide-brimmed recon cover off my head in hopes he would better recognize me as friendly, I withdrew my Kabar and sliced his ropes. He almost fell from the chair, barely able to hold himself upright. I grimaced at the agony swathing his face but never slowed.

"We're Marine Recon. You're going home. Can you stand?"

He weakly shook his head and slowly raised his gaze. I knelt before him so he could better see me, all the while aiming at the door, ready for guards to enter. The villa shook from the continuous grenade explosions and between the blasts I heard my team's automatic rifles singing their sweet songs of mayhem.

"I can't make it," he groaned. "Listen to me—" He coughed and the specks of blood appearing on his lips told me of his internal wounds. "My arms and hands are broke. My leg and ribs too. They tore me up inside with pins and—"

My heart twisted into knots as I looked upon the poor creature who once had been a handsome, strong man.

"We know what they did. I'll carry you, but we're taking you home," I said, reaching out to lift him onto my shoulders. I'll never forget his howl of anguish when I took hold of his shirt and pulled slightly. It made me freeze, then release my grip.

My God, I thought, *how can I ever get this man across Laos? To safety through miles of the worst jungle?*

Under the best of conditions, without being hunted by NVA and Laotian troops, I had no chance of saving his life after the tortures he had endured. When he next spoke, his voice scalded my soul and tore at my heart.

"Kill me. Don't leave me to them. Kill me. I'm dying anyway. You would put a wounded animal out of its misery. Do it for me. I'm begging you. Do it . . . I'm begging you." Then he wept like a battered child.

I stood, knowing he was right. If he remained, they would kill him. If he went with us, he would surely die from the travel. My mind and heart were being ripped apart by his request. I tried to swallow the knot in my throat but could not.

"What's your name?" I asked softly.

He must have realized by the tone of my voice I was at war with myself. Fighting his torment he proudly lifted his head to stare at me with brown eyes consumed with suffering. "Promise me you'll tell my family I loved them to the end."

I nodded. "You have my word of honor."

A look of peace swept his face. "Major John Packard, United States Air Force. My wife's name is Stella. She's in Lufkin, Texas. Find her. Find my children and—" Pain shot through him and he winced horribly. He coughed and more blood appeared on his lips.

"I gave you my word and I never go back on it."

Major Packard weakly nodded and smiled for the first time. He drew in a deep breath and stared directly into my eyes.

"Now, do it—and God bless you."

I gently rubbed his head as if he were my own hurt brother then gradually slid my fingers over his eyes to close them. I cannot describe what I felt at that moment, but the pain within me surely equaled his. Lowering my hand I looked at the serenity painting his face. His eyes remained shut and I'm glad. I did not want him to see my rifle rise to his forehead.

"No, Major John Packard," I whispered, "May God bless you." Then I squeezed the trigger.

★ ★ ★ ★

"John! *Dammit*, let's move out!"

Franklin's voice sounded a thousand miles away. I did not know if he had witnessed what I had done, but I was beyond caring. My fury erupted and I screamed to release the torturous pressure in my soul. Turning from Packard, I looked down at Borjanovich. The world became a brilliant red before my eyes. I emptied a full magazine into him until he was no more than a shredded pulp of meat and bones.

The crazed beast within me thirsted for blood. Instead of leaving by the window, I strode toward the door leading out into the hall. Franklin shouted at me, but I paid him no heed. There was butchers' work to be done and I knew best how to do it.

With a razor-sharp Kabar in one hand and my bush gun in the other, I started down the hall searching for survivors. I went berserk.

I found wounded and stunned NVA officers attempting to flee. Bleeding, half-dressed women screamed and tried to dash past me. Russian officers, limping and tripping over each other, raced away from me. Yet, none survived my murderous spree. Those I did not shoot, I savagely slashed with my blade. And when my rifle was empty, I clubbed them to death. I never stopped. If Staff Sergeant Waldrip had been present, he would have surely been proud of me.

The white hall walls were splattered with ghastly streaks of vermilion as if a madman had swung a paint drenched brush while entranced in a wild dervish. Smeared, bloody hand prints trailed toward the floor where the dying had grasped for a final hold. The floor was slick with the entrails of my enemies. Apart from Borjanovich and his followers, there was one more person whose death I direly wanted before leaving. Venus.

I was inspecting my handiwork when I saw the naked bitch stumble into the hall. She glanced at me, dazed from her wounds, and tried to run. Her senses had not fully recovered and she tripped over an NVA officer's body and tumbled to the floor.

Slowly I walked to her, relishing the terror in her eyes as she watched my approach. She was bigger in person than I realized. Possibly it was the distance I had been observing her from which made me think she was of average height. My thoughts raced as I stood over her with rage pulsating in my brain. Adrenaline pumped my body and fueled my muscles. I wrapped a hand about her throat and brutally pulled her to her feet. Fear paralyzed her.

Slamming her hard against the wall, I squeezed as I lifted her above me. Unable to breathe, she began to fight. Her legs flailed the air and struck my chest. Her fists swung at my face but missed. Her breasts bounced wildly against my arm.

"This is for Packard," I said gutturally and extended my arm to full length, holding her high off the ground. My mind blanked as I choked her, and again I fell into the depths of madness. Visions flashed before my eyes. I saw her having an orgasm on Packard's shoulder while he cried in pain at the slightest touch. I saw her astride him, her ass squirming on his lap as her gleaming talons dug into his chest, adding to his misery, all at the delight of her NVA audience. But worse, I heard him begging for me to end his suffering—to end his life.

"John! John!" shouted Franklin. "She's dead! Jesus, man, let's get the fuck out of here!"

Sanity returned and I let Venus drop into a lifeless pile on the floor. Stern ran toward us, stopping long enough to grab my rifle and Kabar. He gave them to me and shook his head as he glanced at the carnage along the hall.

"Where's the American?" he asked, trying to control his panting breaths.

"He's dead." I stared at him solemnly for a second before turning to leave, sheathing my Kabar and reloading as I began to run.

Chapter Nine

Franklin and I joined Nakai at the villa's arched gateway. Together we fled into the jungle to await Stern. Within minutes, he came wildly running out of the villa, motioning for us to leave. Nakai took point, heading out on a route already mapped in his mind to Bung Kan, Thailand. I never questioned the full-blooded Sioux. He had always been our point-man and could move across the thickest of jungles and worst terrain as swiftly as a wolf racing through a forest.

We maintained our distance of several arm's length apart and slipped through the black jungle like animals born to it. At times we paused to listen and ensure we were not rushing headlong into a trap. Once Nakai was satisfied all was clear, we were on the move again.

Nakai led us across a small valley and halted on a hillside to scout the area and get his bearings. He glanced at the sky and briefly studied the stars. In the pale moonlight came his odd grin I'd grown so accustomed to and knew we were traveling in the right direction.

A warning *grunt* sound came from Stern. We froze in place and waited until he signaled again. Looking back to the villa I observed a steady stream of headlights moving toward it. Stern edged forward to me and motioned to his watch. He depressed its side and stared at the emerald illuminated face. When the light went out, he nodded and glanced back in the direction of the villa. I turned too for I knew what was about to occur would be more spectacular than a Fourth of July fireworks display.

The first explosion sent a massive, swirling fireball soaring into the air, and then the second and third came so closely together I almost believed they were one. Fire shot skyward, belching debris and twisting orange-red streaks into the night. Secondary explosions erupted from the Laotian guards' armory and engulfed the villa in flames. From across the valley we felt the ground tremble and smiled at Stern's parting gift to the truckloads of soldiers responding to reports of an attack on Borjanovich's estate. That cowboy may have been raised on a ranch, but he surely held a natural talent with C-4.

A final explosion erupted, spewing spirals of smoke, immense mangled fireballs, and more flaming debris higher into the air than the previous blasts. We listened to the rumble of the villa as it crumbled to the ground.

"Take us home, Nakai," I said softly, and the full-blooded Sioux melted into the night.

★ ★ ★ ★

We crawled past sleeping villages, crossed raging rivers, and sloshed through rice paddies. Vines tore at our clothes and raked our hands and faces. Sweat stung our eyes and set fire to the bleeding wounds made by needle-like thorns and sharp blades of elephant grass. There were open valleys, gentle sloping hills then we faced jungle so thick our flight came to a halt. The towering tree canopy blocked all traces of moonlight and transformed the jungle into a black abyss. Branches and limbs from the jungle undergrowth seemingly gripped us like arms and held fast until we blindly hacked ourselves free. But we trusted Nakai and knew this route was necessary. Our pursuers would expect us to take the easiest flight to safety, and we were accustomed to doing the unexpected.

By dawn we sat two mountains away from the villa, staring back at the land we had traveled at a grueling pace. Our strength was direly taxed, yet we never slowed until Nakai believed it safe. The sun rose brilliant and crisp over the horizon, creating spectacular hues of green and brown across the countryside. It was truly a wonderful sight to behold, yet there was no time to admire nature's beauty. I knew Laotian and NVA troops were in hot pursuit of us in that palette of colors. They would be joined by more in the hunt, each wanting to claim us as their prize catch.

On the evening of the third day I ordered Nakai to halt. We were bone-weary, needed rest, and food. I had begun to think we might make it because of our stealth and swift speed. But I was wrong and that night would prove it so.

I had maintained radio silence, wanting to be as far away from the villa as possible. Our radio was powerful and we were supposedly linked to some CIA satellite with scrambled voice abilities for the security of our operation. Yet, I did not want to risk a signal being tracked by the NVA. When I realized we were near Phou Bia Mountain, I decided to radio Leonard and confirm our extraction zone or any alterations in the plan.

"Crow's Nest, this is Iron Raven. Do you copy?" The wait grew long and I was about to transmit again when Roger's voice came loud and clear.

"You had to be a hero, didn't you?" His cold, sarcastic tone told me the CIA already knew of our assault on the villa. But I did not care. I wanted my team out of Laos alive and would worry about the repercussions of my killing spree later in the safety of a Da Nang compound.

"Crow's Nest, this is Iron Raven. Request confirmation of LZ. Are there changes?" The last thing I wanted was an argument with him over the radio. We needed food, water, and the sun was rapidly setting. Valuable time was being wasted.

"Fuck your extraction, Alvarez! You went free-agent and now my partner and I are neck-deep in shit trying to cover your tracks. But I've got a little surprise for you. We're going to cut our losses—real quick!"

His words stunned me. Sitting back on the ground, staring at the radio, I realized we were going to be abandoned. When my senses returned, I squeezed the microphone as if I were still choking Venus. "Listen good, Rogers. Get a chopper in here now!" Anger mounted within me. I wanted to scream but knew better than to do so and announce our position to every Laotian in the valley.

I listened to Rogers laugh. It drove me insane.

"Hey, Alvarez. Your team is going to be one of those big unanswered questions when the war is over. But I don't give a fuck!

You're expendable! And you've got a surprise coming. You're walking into a crack NVA battalion. You better tell your nigger to run fast 'cause they might be the Klan!" His laughter shot chills up my spine.

"If you don't send a chopper, I'll kill you. You've got my word on that." The rage within me made my hands tremble, but my voice surprised me at how smooth and controlled it sounded.

No reply came. I called him again and still he refused to answer. Rogers had turned his radio off.

In the faint dusk light I could see the solemn, camouflage painted faces of my men staring at me. Closing his eyes, Franklin lowered his head. Stern wet his lips and looked skyward, sweat trickling down his temple. But Nakai never broke his gaze.

I slowly put the radio away and looked at them. "We've been burnt. I think that son-of-a-bitch let the NVA know which way we're heading."

There comes a time in every man's life when all seems lost, yet it is his sheer willpower and anger which keeps him going. At that moment, we each knew there was little chance of us making it through the tight net of a well-trained battalion. But we were not about to give up. Our determination to survive was fueled by our hatred for Rogers and Leonard leaving us to die.

Shaking his head, Stern was about to speak but Nakai's senses had alerted him to something. The Indian raised a hand and vanished into the jungle.

"*John!*" Nakai whispered excitedly. There was no need to wonder what had created such an alarm in him. I heard the sharp squeal of truck wheels grinding to an abrupt halt.

Nakai was a master at blending into the environment and it took several seconds to find him in the undergrowth. Crawling to his side, I edged up to look out into the valley. Several hundred yards ahead sat a seemingly never-ending row of transport trucks with uniformed soldiers. Scanning left and right I observed platoons of men fanning out, maintaining precise formation as they moved. Suddenly, in the distance to our rear, more trucks stopped on the highway we had crossed only minutes before. Every platoon was directed by fiercely shouting officers. They were quickly closing their net about us. Either

Rogers had covertly notified them of our position or they had tracked our radio transmission signal. It did not matter anymore. They had found us and were anxious for the kill.

"How long do you think we have?" I asked Nakai.

He glanced across the valley and looked at me. "Thirty minutes before the first group is on us. Maybe an hour if they drag their feet," he replied somberly.

"You know what to do," I said, sliding the pack off my back. And each man immediately went into action.

Nakai looked at the terrain and selected our best defensive position. Stern followed him, opening the large pack of goodies stolen from the villa's armory. From my pack, I threw Franklin the small radio we had *borrowed* from Leonard and Rogers' office. Within seconds he had it transmitting a "downed pilot distress signal" to the Air Force base in Udorn, Thailand.

I moved to Stern and we feverishly established a last stand defense in a large, wagon wheel formation about us. Nakai and Franklin raced behind us, bringing Laotian grenades, ammunition, and explosives as we needed to set the traps.

We moved and worked as one man, each knowing what the other required and were about to do. Not a word passed among us. Within minutes we were settling into the thick jungle-growth of the valley to await our pursuers.

It's odd how I never felt fear at that moment. By all rights, I should have been terrified. But I wasn't. As I lay soaked in sweat beneath the branches of wide-leafed plants and gnarled shrubs, I could only think of how I would kill Rogers and Leonard when we returned to Da Nang.

Darkness engulfed us like a black ocean. The angry voices of NVA officers leading their men across the valley grew louder, more distinct by the second. Trucks clanked and clattered as they rolled over the broken ground, attempting to make an impenetrable wall behind the anxiously searching troops. The first of Stern's traps exploded thirty yards to our north and the fight was on.

Anguished screams blended with the thundering explosion of the Claymore mine. *POP!* A flare shot into the air and illuminated night into day with an orange-yellowish tint. Another flare popped and spiraled skyward. Small-arms fire erupted, followed by automatic weapons raking the brush to my far left as the NVA unleashed a wild, aimless volley of bullets. A second and third Claymore was detonated by running men, and in the eerie light of the flares, I watched two bodies sail lifelessly through the air. A truck exploded, then another, and another from their close proximity to each other.

The NVA knew we were near, but had not been able to spot our position. We maintained fire discipline and waited for them to draw further into our traps. Then, as a Claymore detonated behind us, I realized we were almost fully encircled by the NVA.

I silently mouthed the words, "Now, Stern," and as if he was listening, he set off the first wide circle of charges about us. The blasts were deafening and although I hugged the ground as tightly as possible, the concussions rocked me. A fiery wall of flames, dirt, jungle limbs, and shredded plants rose about us. Blood and pieces of bodies rained down while debris pounded us. A broken rifle crashed into the ground by my head and the ground shook like a wild horse trying to buck an unwanted rider.

Two more trucks exploded, their cargoes of ammunition and fuel cans aiding our defense. Vietnamese voices shouted angrily, cried out for help, and screamed in pain. I heard Nakai's savage battle-cry as his bush gun began to howl relentlessly. More flares popped and shot into the air. Rising to my knees, I unleashed my rifle on the men running toward me.

Stern madly hurled grenades in all directions and Franklin mowed down a sea of men rushing him. Gradually I was building a wall of dead about me as the NVA learned too late where I lay hidden. I glanced to my right and saw wind-fanned flames leap skyward in a solid wall. Our stolen explosives had helped to spread the trucks' burning fuels and set the valley and jungle afire. Smoke twisted and churned into the illuminated night in macabre fashion. But there was more to come, for Stern still held one final surprise in reserve.

The NVA came at us from all directions and I believe they accounted for more of their own dead than we did. They were caught in crossfires yet were helpless to regroup and redefine their attack. In the excitement of being so close to capturing us, their officers had pressed them into the assault without giving thought to the consequences of directly facing their comrades. Possibly their communication had faltered or the taste of victory was too addictive to allow clear thinking; whatever the reasons may have been, they shot each other like opposing armies.

Nakai's position was overrun. The wall of fire behind him carved a perfect silhouette of his body and I could see him in hand-to-hand combat with a swarming mountain of soldiers. I lost sight of him then heard his bloodcurdling screams muffle and fade.

A wide-eyed soldier, half my height, jumped in front of me and stood stunned by the sight of my size and features. With my face painted in long diagonal lines of black and gray and the whites of my eyes so distinct, I must have appeared like some demon of the underworld to him. He stood petrified with mouth agape. But I was not and rammed the barrel of my bush gun into his mouth and pulled the trigger. His head exploded, spraying me with brain, bone, and blood. Franklin yelled to my left and I wheeled to see four soldiers trying to wrestle him to the ground. The Louisiana poacher stood with men clambering over his shoulders, arms, and chest. I started toward him, but in the madness of his battle, he looked my way and cried out, "Stay back!" It was then I saw the grenades in his hands and observed their spoons take flight.

Diving to the ground I rolled clear of him. The blasts struck me and knocked the wind from my lungs. At his death I felt my heart being savagely torn from me. My mind reeled. I rose from the dirt and saw the flares floating downward with smoke and a fog-like haze slowly trailing them. The grassfire swept the land, pushing and holding back additional platoons of soldiers anxious to join the fierce battle.

"John!"

I heard Stern's anguished scream and spun to find him staggering blindly toward the towering wall of fire. Shouting soldiers ran between us and blocked him from my sight. They raised their rifles and the steady staccato of their automatic weapons bore into my mind. As they moved apart, I watched Stern spasmodically dance until his legs gave way and he fell. But I dove to the ground again because I had seen him about to squeeze the small box in his hands.

The DET cord stretched like a lariat about us erupted in a brilliant flash with lightning speed, detonating the Laotian explosives Stern had so deftly secured to it in several places. *WHOOM*! My ears rang and the world became a twisted, jumbled, abortion of war. The screams of the dying rose in a horrible wail which flooded my mind. Bodiless arms and legs struck my back. Jagged chunks of metal from the trucks rained from the sky. A helmet with a head still strapped within it landed on my neck and countless soldiers fell about me. Stern, in his last heroic act, had probably killed fifty to a hundred men who raced madly into his circle of death.

Kicking my way free I rose like some fool in a movie, throwing grenades and firing into the rushing waves of soldiers flowing toward me. With flares steadily being shot into the air and the smoke rising from the burning grass, it all mixed to form a surreal illuminated fog that swooped down and blanketed me from the NVA's sight.

They were as lost as me in it once the smoke swirled and spread across the land. I heard their officers shouting to cease fire because now the realization had struck they were only shooting each other. But I never stopped until my magazines were empty.

Without thought I started walking through the flare-lit fogbank of smoke. Whenever someone neared me, I stabbed and slit them open with my Kabar before stumbling onward to find another victim. The smoke was to my advantage, yet I was beyond caring. I was searching for more NVA to taste my blade.

Unnerving quiet settled over the land, broken only by the moans of the wounded and dying. There were no more explosions, rifles firing, or flares popping into the air.

I tripped over bodies and staggered blindly through the almost translucent smoke. The flares began to gradually burn out and the grassfires were diminishing. Darkness seeped over the land again and I could scarcely see my hands as I held them up before me. Gripping my Kabar tightly, I began to walk across the battlefield, protected by the blanket of smoke shrouding me. I felt numb, mentally dead, but I never stopped walking.

★ ★ ★ ★

A brilliant glare directly overhead blinded me. I squinted against the harsh light and heard a constant ringing in my ears. My thoughts spun like a maelstrom as I woke. The acrid smells of medicines filled my nostrils. A voice, soft and crystal clear as if it came from an angel, called out to me. At first I believed I was hallucinating or dead. But I was neither. The only angels I knew of did not wear nurses' uniforms and the bright light over me was a lamp. I was in a hospital ward. The nurses were American. And I was alive.

Our distress signal had done its job. Search and Rescue Teams had flown daily missions into Laos until spotting me sprawled on the ground twenty *klicks* from the Thailand border. From the bits of information my nurse related, the Rescue Team estimated I walked for three days after the firefight and miraculously eluded the NVA. Since my arrival, she said I had slept four days without waking. I listened but against my will fell into a deep sleep once again. I awoke only to be fed and bathed by the comely brunette who seemed to always be at my side when my eyes opened.

In her own right, she was truly an angel. Her voice soothed my soul and the touch of her hand upon my arm felt wonderful. Looking into my eyes she knew pain flowed deep within me, and she found something worthwhile in my worthless life.

After three weeks in the hospital my health was sufficiently regained from the severe dehydration, exhaustion, and starvation I had suffered. Taking control of my mind and body again, my sole purpose for living returned to avenging the deaths of my fallen brothers.

I always keep my word.

Chapter Ten

When my strength returned, I left the hospital. There was little difficulty in doing so. Hospitals are always a madhouse of activity day or night. Neither was securing passage to Da Nang a problem. In every war, simply understanding how the military machine works is sufficient to bypass the tons of rules and regulations that give my government its very existence.

Through careful questioning of Karen, my nurse, I learned the intricacies of the base and who best could aid my flight. She suspected my intentions because she came to my ward bed constantly and feigned some brief examination. Once, I caught her sadly gazing at me and was moved to a sense of guilt at having deceived her so in our conversations.

On the night I chose to leave, Karen came in the early morning hours and asked to join me in my walk. To avoid suspicion I made it a nightly habit to stroll the halls in pre-dawn hours, and had successfully argued with the nurses to wear clothes rather than hospital gowns. But upon this day, rather than me leading the way along my normal winding route, she led me by the hand to a secluded linen closet in an obscure wing of the hospital. There, on a makeshift bed of clean sheets and towels, my angel in a nurse's uniform gave me a parting gift of love that to this day brings special warmth when I recall her memory.

When we left the closet, I walked one direction and she another, never looking back because we knew my time had come to leave.

Outside the hospital I retrieved the few personal effects I had carefully hidden away then made good my escape. At the landing field I found the transport planes exactly where Karen had said. With a bottle of bourbon and a sad tale of having missed my plane, I bribed a flight control sergeant into letting me catch a hop back to Da Nang.

Military hops are a normal occurrence at air bases. Servicemen can take their leave in another country by simply boarding any plane yielding available space. So it was in the quiet morning hours, I climbed into a cargo plane destined for Vietnam.

There I sat among crates of supplies and empty coffins, planning my next course of action.

★ ★ ★ ★

There is no reason to relate the specifics of how I hid and waited until the time was right to catch Rogers and Leonard by themselves. For three days I followed them from the SOG compound and shadowed them to the bars and whorehouses they regularly frequented. Men such as they, who work in dark professions and secretive worlds, would normally have taken precautions in their travels. But they did not and I have no doubts their arrogance and sense of invincibility made them careless.

Executing Leonard came almost too easy, nearly spoiling my pleasure of revenge. On the fourth night I waited in the dismal shadows of a back street alley and caught him as he drunkenly walked from a bar. Ten steps into the dimly lit alley he paused and stood weaving, chin lowered to chest, urinating as if writing his name upon the wall. I chose not to let him finish and approached from the rear, pressing the tip of my Kabar into the base of his skull.

"Stern, Franklin, and Nakai," was all I whispered.

In the quiet of the alley I heard the forceful blast of his urine increase and smiled at the fact he recognized me. That was all I wanted—him to know his executioner—and have a second to think about the reason for his coming death.

Skewering his brain, I took glee as the blade twisted. He rose onto his toes, body shaking violently before his legs folded beneath him. His falling weight freed my knife and with it came slivers of brain matter. He did not die instantly, although I knew he would die soon. But until his final moment came, he would live as a vegetable, heart pumping life to a brain dead man.

Rogers' death came as swiftly as his partner's. The SOG man shared a house with a bar-girl and I slipped through the yard to await his arrival. The past two nights he had walked through the house then stepped out onto the small veranda to gaze at the city like a gloating king. That night his actions were no different. I stood in the shadows of the veranda and struck with the speed of a panther.

A brutal blow to the stomach dropped him to his knees. He gasped for air; his eyes flared and mouth agape. I gripped his head, my hands closing tighter, fingers digging into his skin. My arms trembled from the blinding rage racing throughout me.

"I told you I'd come back," and having waited long enough, I snapped his neck as if it were straw. At first I could not open my hands and held him aloft. The adrenaline pumping my heart made him weightless. Grief for my fallen friends consumed me to the brink of explosion and his death was not enough to satisfy me.

Blanking into a thrashing sea of mental pain I took one last pleasure before leaving for my bare-walled bunker at the Recon base.

★ ★ ★ ★

"Sergeant Alvarez?"

I recognized Captain Lockhart's voice. Although I tried to open my eyes, mental exhaustion had taken its toll and I could only lie in my bunk and softly answer, "Yes, sir."

"Wake up, John. We have to talk."

Drawing upon what little strength remained within me I pulled myself upright on the edge of the bed and glanced at the four granite-faced Marines standing with automatic weapons trained on my chest.

Captain Lockhart rolled his soggy, stub of a cigar from one side of his mouth to the other as he stared at me. I looked at my bare chest and saw streaks of dried blood, but it was not mine. They came from the lone pair of ears hanging off the necklace about my neck.

"My God, are those Rogers'?" he asked wearily, slowly raising a hand and removing his cigar.

There was no need to lie. I was beyond caring what happened to me. I nodded solemnly and stood, awaiting his orders.

"Where's your team?"

"Dead, sir."

Lockhart closed his eyes like a father receiving fatal news of his sons.

"Rogers and Leonard burned us to the NVA."

"I'm sorry . . . I'm sorry." His words seemed to choke him. Turning to the door he called back in a gentle voice, "Go with these men, John. Don't give them any trouble. I promise I'll do all I can for you," and he walked out into the sunlight with the steps of a man who had aged years in mere seconds.

Captain Lockhart was true to his word and attempted every possible defense to save me from the gallows. He called in every favor owed him by Pentagon generals, and secured the best military defense lawyers that were available at the time. His testimony of my team's kinship, and the voluminous report of our heroic missions while under his command, stirred the hearts of my tribunal and incited wrath against the CIA. Yet in the end, the truth of SOG's betrayal was whitewashed better than a picket fence. I was portrayed as a bloodthirsty monster, a killer of innocent people, and a pathological liar about the existence of a POW. Washington bureaucrats avoided involvement, not wanting their hands dirtied by the entire affair because the angry tide of public opinion was continuously rising over the senseless deaths of Americans in the war. The scandal of a government agency willingly leaving a POW and a Recon team to die would wreck havoc on their careers and destroy many a political kingdom.

After seeing the bleak direction my trial was taking, I saw no further reason to testify and sat in silence, listening to the accusations made against me by CIA encouraged prosecutors. It was to be swift justice against me because I had become an embarrassment to SOG's efforts in Vietnam regardless of how they labeled me.

The outcome of the trial came as expected, but I held no regrets over slaying Leonard and Rogers. I was beyond caring about myself. My family was dead. I had witnessed the cruel deaths of men who were like brothers to me. I learned what the Corps taught me, and was only guilty of having learned those lessons all too well. My country had ordered me to war and I went without reservation, doing all that was required at whatever the costs. But my life in the Corps drew to an end and I was turned away in disgrace from my only remaining family.

At the age of twenty-one and dishonorably discharged from the Marine Corps, I was sentenced to life without parole in a federal prison for the murders of two CIA agents.

★ ★ ★ ★

With legs and arms heavily shackled like a wild animal, authorities shipped me from one penitentiary to the next over the span of a year. The transfers were not from reasons of my making. No, at each prison I believed the inmate attempts to kill me were CIA sponsored. Someone wanted to insure permanent silence about the mission. Those foolish enough to try their hand received injuries to last them the remainder of their lives. In one assault, I was forced to kill two of my attackers. They left me no alternative and I slit them open with the very instruments intended to be used on me. After the second prisoner's death I was placed in solitary confinement in a maximum security cellblock, far from the inmate population.

Prison life seemed quite pleasurable compared to living in the jungles of Vietnam. My days were spent lifting weights, exercising, reading, or lying in my bunk listening to the few operatic arias the warden permitted me to have. Calendars and clocks meant nothing to me and I refused to have them in my cell. I was sentenced to life imprisonment and had no use for the time or date to serve as a reminder.

The weeks became months, and the months, years. Guards came and went, their faces always displaying the same expression of curiosity as they peered through the bars at me as if I were a hideous creature, docile only while in captivity.

There were those who were cordial though, almost sympathetic at times when we sat and talked, me on the floor in my cell and them in the hall on a chair. 'Benny' Bentley, a bulky guard who was two years from retirement, was one of them. He had lost a son to the war and bitterly blamed every politician for the death. To Benny, Vietnam had only been a governmental playground where good men died and rich kids were kept safely exempt with their college status.

"What're you reading today, John?" he asked, stroking his silver mustache as he eased into his chair by my cell. I enjoyed his company and set the book aside. Our talks lasted hours, broken only by him taking time to make his rounds about the cellblock. Often he would speak Spanish to me, saying it helped him retain what little fluency of the language he had. But I believe he did so to comfort me and ease my pain whenever I began to talk with a lonely tone.

"Assyrian history. It was quite a civilization," I replied, stretching my legs out before me on the floor. "If you want, I'll give it to you after I'm through."

He laughed and his belly bounced. "Hell's bells, man. I don't need to educate my mind. What I need is a good skin magazine to stir my coals and help me get lucky with Martha. Damn, that woman's cantankerous. But she gives me a roll in the sack once a year like clockwork," he stated, and glanced about him as if his wife might hear. He craned his neck to look into my cell. "By the way, what's today's date? I don't want to be working and her start without me?"

His laughter poured out from deep within him as he scratched the yellowing silver hair I had seen change through the years.

"Don't know, Benny. I don't keep track of the days," I said, leaning my head against the cement wall.

The old man straightened in his chair, embarrassment edging across his face. "Sorry, I forgot. I didn't mean anything by it. Just kidding around," he remarked softly. "Coffee?" he asked, unscrewing the cap of his Thermos.

I gestured no and watched steam rise from the cup he poured. The aroma flowed into my cell and the moment was as peaceful as any a man may have in prison.

"Hey, John. I heard some scuttlebutt this evening when I was coming on duty. Maybe I shouldn't tell you but I think you ought to know," he whispered in a conspiratorial tone.

Again I watched as he glanced about him, only this time as if searching for eavesdroppers. I did not speak but raised my brows in question, believing he had some jailhouse gossip. His voice lowered and I strained to hear him.

"The word is that some men were in the warden's office today asking about you and looking at your file."

The news was unexpected. I grew puzzled by who might be asking and why. I had been left to myself for years and had not created problems. A thousand questions without answers flooded my mind. I eased closer to the bars of my cell and leaned forward.

"What do you think? Parole officials?"

Benny's face comically scrunched as he shrugged.

"Beats the hell out of me. From what I hear, they weren't saying too much about themselves. Kind of quiet guys who answer questions with a question and you never know where you stand with them."

Confusion rose within me. The disturbing sensation that began to churn my stomach sent a sense of alarm up the back of my neck. I settled against the wall and gazed across my cell. "Government agents, Benny?"

The old guard sipped his coffee and glanced down the hall. "I think so, John," he replied. "I guess the government wasn't satisfied with killing my son and almost killing you. Maybe they're gonna try and finish the job."

"No, it's been too many years for them to try and make a hit on me. They must be looking at my prison records to make sure I'm still here," I said, speaking to my aged friend with a lack of confidence in my voice. "Oh well, I should be easy to find."

I realized how odd my words sounded and half-heartedly laughed. But Benny never smiled.

"I would appreciate you keeping an ear open and letting me know what's going on."

"Damn straight, I will. I'll snoop around tomorrow and check the registry logs where they signed in today. That should tell me real quick who the bastards are," Benny said defiantly.

Nodding my thanks, I relaxed, never in my imagination envisioning the perils which lay ahead in meeting those men. Oh, how I can look back now and see my mistakes. If I had only foreseen the slightest glimpse of the madness and suffering I would endure at the whims of Moloc, I surely would have killed the three men the moment they proposed the mission.

Chapter Eleven

Throughout the night I thought about Benny's news and slept restlessly. Long forgotten memories resurfaced and laid heavy on my mind. Dawn found me awake, staring at my cell's ceiling, and I was glad to take my hour on the rooftop courtyard.

It is amazing how we can derive such pleasure from simple things when our freedom is taken away. I watched patches of clouds drift carefree across a crystal blue sky and listened to the birds along the high walls about me. The sun had not fully risen and its rays covered half the courtyard, pleasantly warming it. Moving into the light I let it bathe me, delighted by the cleansing feel upon my face.

Although I had only an hour to enjoy my freedom in the courtyard, I spent several minutes with eyes softly closed in silent gratitude of the moment. There was peace in my heart, my mind, my soul, and for that brief second I no longer felt bound by steel, concrete, and barbed wire. When I opened my eyes again, I saw the stern-faced tower guard, rifle cradled in his arms, watching me. I thought he was about to wave and started to raise my hand in friendship. He turned his back to me and I was reminded of being an outcast, to not be afforded the least common decency. The sun still warmed me and the birds continued to sing, but I felt another brick being added to the wall about my heart.

Yes, it was a foolish moment on my part; a brief time of feeling I was a member of the world again. But reality has a cruel way of enforcing our station in life and the sight of the guard's back quickly turned me cold.

Having spent so many years in solitude, I knew how to void myself of all thoughts and function only as a machine. I glanced at the guard as I began to jog. Within seconds he was washed from my mind and I concentrated solely on my daily run along the courtyard walls. Two-hundred steps in length, then turn and travel one-hundred more before turning again.

I could run it with my eyes closed and, to break monotony, had on several occasions. Twenty laps one day, maybe twenty-five the next, running so near the wall my shoulder often scraped it, and each day promising myself to measure the total distance. I never did, though. In prison everything has limits, parameters as to what can and cannot be done, with walls serving as boundaries that never allow you to go past them. Possibly I wanted to believe in the freedom of my run and did not want to ruin it by knowing the exact distance. Whatever the reason, I never measured the jog.

Heart pounding, I dropped to the weight bench in the center of the yard and attempted to punish myself more. My body fought me, and was a good adversary, but that never stopped me from constantly increasing the weight on the barbells. After the rigorous workout I walked about the courtyard to cool off, yet on this particular morning my free time was cut short. Two prison guards came with wrist and leg irons then shackled me and led me away.

Initially I was confused and grew frustrated when they refused to explain why I was being treated so. They led me to an elevator and down to the warden's office in silence. The trip was slow because my chains only allowed short steps. Yet as we drew near the office, I grew eager to arrive, assuming the unknown men Benny had spoken of were involved in this.

"Inside," ordered the tallest of my escorts. He tugged my arm toward the closed door. It was then I observed his apprehensive look and wondered who truly awaited me. "And remember, we'll be out here in case you make trouble," he remarked.

My grin angered him for he knew I was not intimidated by his presence, whether shackled or not. As I opened the door and started in, I glanced his way and whispered, "If I get scared, will you come save me?" And I left him standing red-faced.

★ ★ ★ ★

"Prisoner 30914," declared a well-tanned, athletic looking man in a gray sports coat as I entered. He sat in the warden's high-backed leather chair, adjusted his tie, and gestured to the chair before the wide executive desk. "Come in. Have a seat. We need to discuss a little business." His smile was as fake as a two-dollar whore's moan.

I glanced about the office before moving. The warden was gone and a neatly groomed, brown-haired young man in a tan coat stood by the window, staring with fascination at the prison yard. On the couch against the wall, a salt-and-pepper, frazzle-haired man sat in a wrinkled suit, studying me as if I were a perplexing problem to solve. By his disheveled appearance I wondered if he was scatterbrained, but his eyes were alert and attentive and I took him to be no man's fool.

My senses tingled and curiosity pushed me on. I shuffled to the chair, chains clinking. The man at the window glanced my way and wryly grinned at my captivity before returning his attention to the window.

The man at Warden Kennedy's desk lit a cigarette and held the pack out to me. I shook my head and he shrugged as he slid them into his shirt pocket. He leaned forward, scratched his brow with his thumb and opened a folder. "Whoa, what a record!"

I was not in good humor and did not appreciate being played the fool. There was an air about them which cast a vile mood over the room, one I remembered well from the SOG men in Vietnam. The man on the couch earnestly watched me. He turned his head to look at the man sitting at the warden's desk, his eyes displaying a dislike for him.

Settling back in the chair with my file folder in his lap, the man blew a cloud of smoke into the air as he leveled his gaze onto me.

"People pay good money to go to the movies and see stories like these," he remarked, lazily gesturing to my file. "Unfortunately, all that bravery is going to waste in a place like this. What's it been—eighteen or twenty years now? That's a long time to be in prison, especially when you're kept in solitude most of the time because you keep killing people," he said, a wry grin edging across his mouth.

There was no reason to reply. He was laying out the game he wanted to play and I had no choice but to listen.

When he realized he could not evoke a response, he smoked his cigarette in silence, all the while staring at me as if searching for some type of opening. At last he snuffed the cigarette out. "You never have visitors; you don't write to anyone; you don't make problems for the guards, all you do is read, listen to music, and exercise in the courtyard. In all these years, you've only made one phone call, and that was to someone in Lufkin, Texas. You're a strange character, Alvarez. On one hand you're a stone-cold killer, and on the other, you're like a monk in a monastery," he stated, attempting to hook my emotions and lure me into his web. "One thing's for sure, your sex life is like a monk's."

The brown-haired man at the window appeared frustrated with his companion's tactics and began to walk about the office studying Warden Kennedy's plaques on the walls. He paused to inspect his suitcoat then brushed something from his chest.

"Why did you kill two federal agents?" he asked, brow rising as he turned toward me slowly. His tone was as smooth and tranquil as a gently flowing stream. He shrugged. "I read the court transcripts, but I want to hear it from you."

"If you read the transcripts, you know all there is to know," I stated, distrusting his act of sincerity.

The warden's chair creaked as the athletic-looking man leaned forward onto the desk. He stared at me a moment then glanced at the wrinkle-suited man on the couch.

"Mr. Alvarez, my name is Standish. Ezekiel Standish." The frazzle-haired man rose from the couch and walked to the desk to lean against it. "This is Mr. Henderson and Mr. Clements," he remarked, motioning first toward the warden's chair and then to the brown-haired man moving about the room. "If you will be so kind as to answer a few questions, they may have a proposition worthy of your attention."

Standish had taken the role of peacemaker to alleviate mounting tensions. He was a likable fellow, not forceful, yet determined. His slovenly manner of dress spoke of a man more interested in academic pursuits than trivial cat and mouse word games and antics.

Henderson shot an irritated look at Standish and Clements. I suppose he wanted to drag the game out longer, lull me into some belief they had come out of the benevolence of their hearts to make me an offer. But Standish paid him no heed and Clements only brushed his sleeve clean then turned a hand to inspect his nails.

When Standish left the desk to return to the couch, Clements pulled a key from his coat pocket and pointed to my shackles. "If you say yes to what I'm going to ask, I'll remove the shackles and you can leave this prison with us."

There is no denying a part of me was excited over the thought of freedom, but another part screamed to be cautious. I forced myself to remain calm. This entire meeting was not what I expected to hear, yet, in the back of my mind, it was. Clements and Henderson reeked of covert operations, of black secrets which cost good men their lives and no one caring about the price paid.

"But what about later . . . after I've done what you want? Do I come back here to be locked away so no one will ever know the mission?" I asked, looking at each man's face. Henderson grinned cagily and I knew my assumptions about their professions were correct. "Tell me," I said, not waiting for them to reply, "Are you CIA?"

At Clements' chuckle, I followed him with my gaze, curious as to what he found so humorous about my question. He walked to the warden's desk, poured a glass of water from the decanter and offered it to me. I shook my head and watched as he drank. He scowled and quickly set the glass down. I held my laughter in check. It had taken me months to become accustomed to the strong, chemically treated prison water. But after twenty years of imprisonment, I rarely thought of it anymore.

Wiping his mouth with a napkin as if it would help rid him of the foul taste, Clements turned to me. *"CIA?* No, they're child's play compared to us."

My look of confusion drew a devilish grin from him.

"Mr. Alvarez, while you have wasted your life in here," he haughtily remarked, gesturing to the outside prison walls, "the world has changed. New governments, countries, the formulation of world orders, have all come about. Technology has leaped far beyond what you knew it to be when you were free." He shook his head sympathetically. "I could spend hours simply telling you about the latest changes in warfare and battlefield equipment—but we're not here to set up school."

His expression reminded me of a rich kid looking down his nose at the illiterate, poverty-stricken masses. Clements was at least fifteen years younger than me and from the way he constantly cleaned himself like a cat, I felt sure he had never undergone a quarter of the dangers I had.

"But the people of the world haven't changed," I said, looking him directly in the eyes. "And whatever it is you want from me, you can't achieve it with your toys—and that's why you're here. You need me, *but I don't need you.*"

A frown formed on Henderson's face as he glanced at his partner. "I told you we shouldn't waste our time with him."

Clements coyly smiled in answer and turned his attention to me again.

"You're partially correct. My organization does need you for an assignment, but it could be accomplished through other means. You have a unique talent for survival in the jungle and we need you to escort someone into and out of a hostile tropical environment. Our proposal is simple. You do the escort, and upon its *successful* completion, you'll be paroled with sufficient funds to disappear and live like a king anywhere you wish. Now, choose between prison and freedom." Clements glanced at his watch. "I don't mean to pressure you, but you have five minutes to decide."

Clements picked lint from his suit and patted his head of thick brown hair to ensure his neat appearance. Occasionally, he checked the passing time, undisturbed by my silence. At last he sighed and walked to Standish. "He's not going. We can make other arrangements."

"May I talk to him?" Standish asked, already walking toward me. He wrung his hands and wiped them dry on his wrinkled suit.

"Yes, but you can't tell him anything unless he agrees to accept the assignment," Clements stated in an exasperated voice.

Standish nodded and kept his gaze on me as he sat on the edge of the desk. "Mr. Alvarez, I won't plead with you to say yes, but I can't tell you about Melinda unless you do."

"*Melinda?*" I braced and the chains about my wrists clinked. I was struck hard by my sister's name, unable to comprehend what she and these men would have in common. My mouth opened, yet I could not force words to come. Shock swept over me then rage consumed me at the thought of this being a cruel joke.

Walking to Standish, Clements looked at me and grinned. "I believe you have his fullest attention, Ezekial. Go ahead, tell him more."

Standish nodded, masked in sincerity. "Agree to what these men want and you have a chance of finding her—and living out your life in freedom, wherever you want," he said earnestly. Upon his brow were small beads of sweat and he wrung his hands again.

I regained my senses enough to cautiously choose my words. "If you're not the CIA, who are you?"

The warden's chair creaked and Henderson rose into sight from behind Standish and Clements. He walked around the desk to stand beside them. "Sorry, Prisoner 30914. You know enough to make a decision. If you make the right one, we'll answer your questions. You make the wrong one—well, let's just say you will definitely be here until you die—and always wondering about your sister."

There was little surprise in what he said. It was what I expected from men of his caliber. They dealt in blackmail with comfort and ease, never knowing remorse for the grief they caused in others. To use my sister's name to achieve their goals meant nothing to them. But in Standish's eyes I observed a hint of humanity, something which set him apart from his companions. I glanced at Clements and Henderson, thinking how similar they were to Rogers and Leonard, even though they said they were not with the CIA.

"All right, I agree."

Standish sighed in relief as he gazed at me. Henderson and Clements smugly grinned at each other.

"Who are you and what does my dead sister have to do with this?" I asked, feeling tension mount in me. The chain between my wrists was stretched taut as I held fast to the arms of my chair while waiting for an explanation.

"*Armageddon*, Mr. Alvarez. We are with an elite organization known as Armageddon. The name's a bit theatrical, but definitive. Only a handful of people know of our existence and we prefer it that way," Clements said calmly. "Fifteen years ago the President realized the government and its intelligence community were on the verge of complete failure due to corruption, leaks, moles, double-agents, and petty jealousies between agencies. Armageddon was born from those troubles and given ultimate authorization to do *whatever* is necessary to eliminate America's problems." A smile formed on his lips, yet there was no warmth in his eyes. "We battle evil, Mr. Alvarez. Wherever we find it and by whatever means is necessary."

This revelation made me want to laugh. They were murderers the same as me although they were allowed to walk the streets while I was not. I had killed during a war, under the authority of the same government Clements served. But he viewed himself as engaged in the final conflict, the great battle of good against evil. I suppose a look of skepticism crossed my face because he nodded understandingly.

"Hard to believe? Accept it as the truth and don't waste your time trying to think it out. We don't interfere or become involved in government matters unless we perceive a threat to national security."

The finality in his voice disturbed me. I realized that rather than improving itself, America had only become more infected by the twisted mindsets of men like Clements, Henderson, Rogers, and Leonard. But what did Melinda have to do with them? And why did Standish appear so nervous? My silence only made Clements believe I agreed with him.

"Zeek, tell him about his sister," Henderson ordered, staring at me, keeping close watch on my every reaction.

Ezekial Standish wet his lips and wiped his hands dry on his wrinkled trousers. He glanced at Clements who nodded reassuringly then he turned to me.

"Three years ago, while in a village in the Amazonia region, I happened upon an American woman who was called Melinda by the people. Although she rarely spoke, I learned she survived an airplane crash as a young girl and had been living in the village ever since she was found."

Again, I could find no words to speak. Pain scourged my soul and evoked sorrowful memories of my parents' deaths. But at the thought of Melinda still being alive, an undefinable joy sprang from my well of anguish.

"Where is she?" I asked anxiously. "You didn't leave her there?"

Standish shook his head and momentarily lowered his gaze, making me sense more lay within his story than he had volunteered. "I had to leave quickly, and wasn't traveling by a route which accommodated a woman's presence." Several seconds passed before Standish could raise his gaze to look me in the eye.

Something was wrong. I felt it in my gut and sensed it as vividly as an animal suddenly finds hunters at every turn. But I glanced at Clements and pressed on with my questions.

"What's my assignment? If all you need is a guide on a jungle expedition, then why me?"

No answer came immediately. Clements only pointed to Standish and the older man nodded consentingly.

"I need someone capable of taking me into the jungle and bringing me back safely—someone who can serve as my bodyguard as well as my guide," Standish explained. "We will travel through the village where I last saw your sister. After I gather the necessary information, you can bring her back to America and go your own way."

Each man's expression was a mixture of contrasting emotions. Standish appeared nervous, as if his conscience bothered him. I knew Clements and Henderson did not have such a problem. They probably had no conscience. They appeared only concerned with the cover-up of my exodus from prison.

Still, I trusted none of them and was willing to risk all to search for my sister. Standing, I looked at Standish, mentally gauging him for the journey. He was far shorter than me and probably in no better physical condition than his wrinkled suit. There was no doubt as to his intelligence, his eyes displayed the gleam of a man who constantly must know what makes things tick or would find rapture in a new discovery. Looking at the gray in his hair I guessed him to be at least ten years older than me. His nose was long and thin, set between a wide forehead and a rugged chin. I gazed at him a few seconds and realized there was something in his manner which set him apart from his companions. What it was, I do not know. Yet I felt that he was not comfortable with deceiving people as Clements and Henderson did.

I extended my hands to Clements and remained silent while he removed the chains from my wrists and legs. The sensation of freedom from them reminded me of when I had stood before the judge as a young man with no alternative but to leave or go to prison. My life had come full circle for now I was forced to choose between prison and leaving.

Henderson appeared nervous at the fact I was unshackled. Before, when my movements were limited, he had viewed me as one who could easily be defeated. Now, after stretching my arms wide and towering above him, his lips were drawn into a thin line and he edged away as if to avoid my reach.

Opening my file on the desk, Clements signed a sheet lying loose in its folder. He withdrew an envelope from inside his coat and set it on the desk. "That's it, Alvarez. You're my property now and free to go with us."

"What about my clothes?" I asked, for even I knew once outside the prison I could be mistaken for an escaped convict and risked being shot on sight.

"We have a car waiting to take us straight to a jet. You can change after we board. Don't worry. We have clothes for you. In three or four hours, you'll be in a secure area where we can begin the briefing," Clements responded, already starting for the door.

Henderson held back and indicated he wanted me in front of him.

"Before we walk out that door, is there anything you've *forgotten* to tell me," I asked, glancing from Clements to Standish. Immediately, Henderson backed a step and slid a hand beneath his coat. I knew what he was touching, but felt no alarm. If he had pulled a gun, I could have easily reached him before he had a chance to fire the first shot.

"What?" Clements asked as he turned to face me. His brows crept downward and pulled together tightly. He shook his head. "You'll be briefed on mission specifics later, but that's nothing more than logistical information."

"I don't want surprises. If I'm going into a civil war or we're going to assassinate someone, I want to know up front." I observed Standish's eyes widen as he spun toward Clements. There *was* more to the mission and Standish had confirmed it.

Clements laughed and walked closer to me. He motioned Henderson to relax. "You are to escort Zeek into a secluded region of the Amazon, let him gather information and do his thing, then bring him out—*alive*. Protect him, do whatever is necessary, but that's your assignment—and all you're going to be told until the briefing at our safe house. Any more questions?" he asked, staring directly into my eyes.

I shook my head. "No. I just want the truth."

Standish breathed a sigh of relief and hurried to the door, but Clements remained standing in front of me, his gaze roaming over my face. "Hey, I tell you what. If you get down there and find out I've lied, come back and kill me like you did those other federal agents." His stone face gradually broke into a grin then a wide smile.

"Oh, you've got my word I will," I replied, returning a similar smile. Without saying more, I walked around him to follow Standish.

"Now that's something I can count on. A convict's word of honor," Clements said as casually as if we had been discussing the weather.

I paused at the door, glanced at him and softly spoke. "I always keep my word."

We stared at each other a moment then I left the prison that had been my home for twenty years. Never once looking back, never once envisioning what lay ahead.

Chapter Twelve

It is difficult to imagine what it is like to be locked away from the world for so many years and then one day, walk freely among people and see so many wondrous sights. Everything was new and fascinated me as if I were a child in a toy store. I had read countless books and magazines to keep myself abreast of the changes in society. Yet seeing the marvels of new cars, building's architectural designs, and hordes of people rushing madly about me were astounding.

There was another unsettling aspect of my new found freedom which made me realize how much I missed in my life—*women*. In prison I learned to subdue and bury my sexual urges beneath the mountain of readings I did each day. I displaced the thought of a woman's touch upon my body and taught myself, with great difficulty at first, how to live in a state of celibacy. But now, seeing women walking about in tight, form fitting clothes teased my senses and aroused uncontrollable fires within my loins.

Unfortunately, my discomfort must have been obvious. Henderson continually pointed out every beautiful woman we passed, and Clements laughed and intentionally slowed the car for a better look. Sitting in the front seat with Clements, Standish chuckled although he attempted to keep himself in restraint. At first I felt like a fool, embarrassed by the urges rushing throughout me as I gazed at every goddess. But within a half-hour of Henderson's jokes and lewd comments, I found myself laughing with them at my love-starved stares.

"Don't worry, Alvarez. I'll make sure you have the chance to clean the rust out of your pipes. First, we have to get you lined out for the mission," Clements said, smiling at me as he looked in the rear view mirror.

I nodded to him but wasted no time in returning my attention to the wonderful women of the city.

★ ★ ★ ★

At the airport, Clements flashed an identification wallet and official looking papers at a naive appearing young man. I watched Clements' every move and listened intently as he declared, "FBI. We're taking this prisoner back with us."

The guard immediately straightened and drew somber, hurrying away to his gate office. He waved to us as the draw-arm across the entrance rose and we drove past.

Henderson smiled, gave an abbreviated salute to the guard then glanced at Clements. "I thought we were going to be Secret Service today?"

"Hell, I just reached in my pocket and grabbed the first ID my fingers touched. FBI, Secret Service, ATF, it doesn't matter. Any of them will work," Clements said, leaning forward to look along the flight line. He groaned wearily and looked at Standish. "Do you see it?"

Standish shrouded his eyes against the glare of the sun and gazed at the rows of jets. "There," he stated, pointing to the far end of an unused runway.

I followed his aim and observed a sleek black Lear jet parked off to one side by itself. Clements wasted no time in driving to it, and as we drew near, a slender man in a dark sport's coat called to someone in the jet. An attractive woman appeared in the doorway, her long golden brown hair cascading about her face as she leaned out to look about the area. At the sight of our approach she walked down the ramp, adjusting her gray business suit and stood beside the man I took to be the pilot.

Parking clear of the aircraft's wing Clements stepped from the car and slipped a semiautomatic into his waistband. It was then I realized he had kept a weapon lying beside him since we left the prison. He smiled mischievously as I watched him adjust his coat over the pistol.

"A little insurance in case you decided to change your mind and take off," he remarked, walking past me.

I nodded complacently, unbothered by his caution, and followed him and Standish to the jet. Again, Henderson waited for me to take the lead before he moved.

The aircraft was magnificent and naturally in my eyes, like none I had ever seen. Midnight black, highly polished, and ominous in appearance, it fit well into Clements' organization and I am sure no cost had been spared in its purchase. I was too engaged in my inspection of the jet to see who Clements had spoken to, but heard him ask, "Captain, can we leave?"

"Yes, sir. Fueled and ready for departure," came a soft voice which further fanned the fire in my loins.

When I turned abruptly, Standish smiled at my shocked expression. He nodded toward the ramp and I looked up in time to see the blonde entering the craft.

"Times have changed, Mr. Alvarez. She's the pilot—" Standish motioned to the slender man taking Clements and Henderson's briefcases. "—and he's the attendant."

★ ★ ★ ★

The pilot's flight expertise impressed me as much as the jet. Within seconds after taxing into position, we smoothly shot down the runway and catapulted into the sky. The ground instantly fell away and cars became mere specks dotting the landscape. Angling onto its side, the craft gradually leveled as our course was established.

The jet was spacious and plush in its furnishing. There was easily room for twenty passengers, with areas designed for small conferences. At a glance I could tell the jet was a comfort my traveling companions were accustomed to for they seemed quite at home.

Standish moved to the seat beside me and loosened his tie as he glanced at Clements and Henderson sitting at the front of the cabin. Looking behind us, he gestured to the flight attendant. "Two Black Jacks on the rocks, Henry," he said when the man drew near.

Watching the attendant leave, he turned to me. "Hope you don't mind me ordering for us," he said, relaxing back into the well-cushioned seat. "If memory serves me correct, I read in your dossier that you used to enjoy Jack Daniels' Black."

I nodded slowly, a bit disturbed by the depth of information these men knew about me. The drinks came and initially I could only stare at my glass as I held it. There had been so many firsts on this day. Cars, buildings, people—and now, I held my first drink in years.

Like a connoisseur of fine wines, I lifted the crystal glass and sniffed its fragrance. My grin made Standish chuckle, but when I sipped the whiskey and coughed at its potency, he laughed aloud. I sipped it again, only this time the drink smoothly flowed down my throat.

"After you're finished, go with Henry. He has a change of clothes for you," Standish said, studying me as he gently shook his glass to make the ice swirl.

I started to speak but, having seen the expression on my face, Standish raised his free hand to stop me. He glanced toward Clements and Henderson then leaned his head toward me. "I know you're filled with questions, but be patient and wait until we land and can speak freely. You and I will be together for quite some time to come, so I hope you'll trust me."

"Very well, Mr. Standish," I whispered. "I do have questions, and a lot of them. I'll wait until you believe it's safe."

A genuine smile warmed Standish's face. "Call me Zeek," he said, nodding as he extended his hand. We shook and something in his eyes set my mind at ease. I finished my drink and summoned Henry, ready to wear my first civilian clothes in many years.

★ ★ ★ ★

Our flight took us southward for three hours and by the roar of the engines, I knew we were swiftly putting miles behind us. I kept watch on the position of the sun, wondering when we would veer to a different direction. Yet, we never did and I estimated we were somewhere over Texas.

I looked out my window to gaze at the ground below. A thick blanket of clouds blocked it from my sight, but my thoughts were wandering and it did not matter. As I stared at the rolling, silvery texture of the sun drenched clouds, I wondered if we had passed over Lufkin.

Did you ever accept my lies, Mrs. Packard? Telephoning you tore at my heart but I gave my word to your husband.

On that day, so long ago, I had tried to steel myself against the sorrow I knew would come in her voice. Not all I said to her was a lie. Packard's last words were that he loved her and their children, and he had died a hero in my eyes. I've never known a braver man. But it was when she asked how I came to know these things that I spoke words practiced so often before making the call.

"All I am at liberty to say, Mrs. Packard, is he died from injuries sustained in his airplane's crash and I was with him when he drew his last breath."

To this day, I can still close my eyes and hear her weep. It was a long, mournful cry, one born from the depths of her soul.

Sitting in the jet, watching the clouds below, I let the fingertips of my right hand softly rest upon the window's glass as if I were touching a tear upon her cheek.

Her quivering voice is embedded in my mind and haunts my sleep. But then there are nights when in the dark, I see Major John Packard sitting before me, waiting for his suffering to end.

It is on those nights I realize I am damned for all eternity.

Chapter Thirteen

Something shook me awake and briefly my world spun in confusion. I looked about the interior of the jet and at the different clothes I wore. Standish sat watching me, amused.

"Air turbulence," he commented and leaned across me to look out the cabin window. He studied the clouds and brief glimpses of land below. "You were daydreaming and fell asleep."

His brow rose as he glanced at my face. Standish's eyes were consumed with questions and I thought he was going to ask what I had been dreaming, but he settled back into his seat. "It might take a while for you to get used to drinking again."

I nodded and turned my attention to the window, glad he had not pursued his curiosity. The roar of the jet's engines decreased and I heard the drone of the landing gears as they lowered. My ears popped from our swift drop in altitude and I felt the jet angle slightly to my left. As we cleared the bank of clouds, I tried to place the rough hewn, desolate terrain that came into sight. Our descent was as quick as the takeoff and within minutes we were gliding along a runway with no signs of civilization anywhere about.

When the jet came to a halt and the cabin door opened, Henderson and Clements rose from their seats. I registered that something was different about them then I realized while I slept each of my traveling companions had changed into the same type of casual shirts, jeans, and boots as I had been given to wear.

Standish called out to me as he pulled a suitcase from an overhead compartment, "You can go on if you like. We'll meet outside."

Having no personal effects to carry, I walked to the door, looked out at the land then back to him, hesitant to move. Unfortunately, years of prison life still bound me with its invisible chains. But at Standish's gentle nod and warm smile, I stepped through the door and slowly walked down the ramp.

The day was lightly overcast yet held a glare that made me squint. Once my eyes adjusted to the afternoon light, I scanned the surrounding hills and rocky land. Although the runway was well-kept and bordered by lights for night landings, there were no buildings within sight and only a single dirt road led to and from it. The humidity in the air struck me odd because years had passed since I last felt my clothes stick to my body.

"Welcome to Mexico, Alvarez," Clements said, setting his leather flight bag beside him on the ground. He glanced at his watch and let his gaze sweep the land. "Not exactly the most picturesque spot of the world, but I'm sure anything looks better to you than prison."

I nodded, too caught up in the exhilaration of my freedom to speak. There were no walls, no armed tower guards at every turn. The vast expanse of open land, the virgin scent and freshness of the air, even the feel of my clothes with their tailored fit, all sent contrasting emotions throughout me. Having been imprisoned, I had forced so much of life's simplicities from my mind, and suddenly, I found myself troubled by all I had missed—and how my life had evolved.

Standish and Henderson dropped their luggage beside Clements', and Henderson immediately lit a cigarette. His expression of relief told me he was glad to finally be on the ground, but Standish walked about us in a wide circle, stretching his arms as he anxiously glanced at the road. I looked at him and wanted to laugh because his appearance was as slovenly in jeans as it had been in the suit. But I do not think he gave his appearance much thought.

"They're on the way, Mr. Clements."

The wonderful suppleness within the voice stirred my primal senses and I turned in time to see the golden-haired pilot start down the ramp. She was beautiful or at least I thought so at the time. But it was the closest I had been to a woman in twenty years, and any woman whose heart still beat and blood ran warm would have been a goddess in my eyes.

The flight attendant followed her out the door and laid his clothing bag atop her suitcase. He looked at me, pleasantly smiled, and gave a soft nod. I thought nothing of it and returned his nod, but Standish chuckled and lowered his gaze to the ground. My curiosity got the best of me and I casually moved to him.

"What's wrong?" I whispered so none about us could hear.

"I believe Henry likes you," Standish replied equally low.

My throat tightened. I stepped back from Standish and looked at Henry. Years of prison life with its constant threat of gang rapes, unexpectedly rose in my thoughts.

Standish found the change in my demeanor amusing.

"Don't read more into it than that. Henry is a good man." Standish nodded and smiled. "He's a pilot and quite a capable one too. He's our back-up in case something happens to her," Standish said, glancing at the attractive captain. "Things have changed while you were locked away."

I turned to face him. "Okay . . . but a pilot working as an attendant? That doesn't seem right?"

Standish shrugged. "If you were paid as good as him, you wouldn't care what your job title is. Matter-of-fact, if you're going to be working for this merry group, don't be surprised by anyone you come in contact with. Armageddon pays top dollar, far beyond your imagination, but it employs the most multi-talented people you'll ever meet."

"What about them?" I asked, nonchalantly gesturing to Henderson and Clements. I could only guess at what unknown expertise they might hold.

"Clements and Henderson have skills I'd prefer not to know about," Standish said, scratching his graying hair as he looked at the men. He scowled and sighed in disgust. "I'd hide my pet gerbils from Henderson if I had any. Watch out. He's no good and I wouldn't put anything past him."

Against my will I laughed aloud. Standish had given me valuable insight to men I already distrusted.

★ ★ ★ ★

Two cars arrived in a thick cloud of dust, both driven by men who made no efforts to conceal their automatic weapons. They loaded the luggage in silence and as best I can remember, never spoke more than three words. Our journey took less than thirty minutes, but it seemed never ending the way the drivers struck every bump and hole in the treacherous road.

The rugged landscape transformed from rocky hills to a flat, wide valley surrounded by majestic mountains in the distance. In the middle of the valley sat a regal hacienda with thick, high walls about it for ultimate privacy. My thoughts returned to the federal prison I had left, but the more I gazed at the lavish ranch, I realized how similar the structure was to the Laotian villa of long ago. Why someone felt the need for high walls in such a desolate location of Mexico I do not know, because I felt confident the nearest civilization was far away.

We passed through a wide gate archway and instantly entered an oasis. Where outside the walls everything was tan, brown, and tinted with grays, here were brilliant festive colors which drew a smile to one's face. Grinning servants stood on the porches and lined the steps, waiting to obey the slightest request and assist whenever possible. There were exquisite gardens, fountains, wrought-iron lined verandas with marbled floors, and cool, tree shaded, cobble-stoned paths around the villa. The hacienda's interior was as pleasing as its grounds and I can only guess at the expense of the hidden paradise.

By the abruptness with which Henderson and Clements departed for their rooms I was sure they no longer worried about my escaping. Standish took the time to tell me to relax and make myself at home then he too left, trailed by servants bearing towels and his luggage. I was still amazed by my surroundings and stood taking pleasure in its decor. My senses had not dulled though and I turned to locate the reason for my faint alert. As I glanced at the winding stairs leading up to the second floor, I caught sight of the pilot watching me as she followed Henry. She maintained eye contact for several steps and smiled as she disappeared into a hall.

I wandered about the first floor, exploring it like a child in a maze, constantly surprised at the hacienda's immense size and richly furnished rooms. Without being asked, a chubby, comely faced woman, half my height, approached and introduced herself as Elisa, then handed me a drink. I thanked her and sipped it gingerly, wondering what it was. She gave a motherly smile when my brows rose in surprise. It was Jack Daniels Black, and perfectly iced. I could only wonder how much everyone already knew about me.

Elisa and I instantly became friends and for the remainder of my stay there, she grew to be my constant shadow. When she was not trying to serve me food and drinks, she scurried about the lavish house ensuring I had fresh clothes, linen, and toiletries. From her I learned the lengthy history of the La Rosa Rancho during past Mexican revolutions, and how Armageddon had years ago purchased vast sections of the land for its private use. Although she had been born in Mexico to poor parents of Yaqui and Aztec descent, she spoke fluent English and was well educated. Whenever she talked, I listened intently because there was always something to learn from her. Yet, I always remembered Standish telling me to never be surprised at the people Armageddon employed.

My spacious room was fascinating and I had difficulty believing it was mine alone. I slept on a monstrously wide bed with silk sheets and overly thick pillows. Ceiling fans churned a constant, gentle breeze and kept the polished, stone floors cool to the touch. In the closets were a variety of clothes all tailored to my size. There were leather chairs, a mahogany desk, and outside the double-wide doors was a private veranda to lounge upon if I so desired. My transition from a prison cell with no freedoms to the luxuries of La Rosa stunned my mind, but I quickly adapted to it and took enjoyment when I could.

On the first evening we dined in a banquet room large enough to seat fifty or more people. That night Standish, who insisted I call him Zeek, observed how the golden-haired pilot kept glancing in my direction. He leaned to me and whispered she had formerly been with the CIA and readily changed agencies due to a mission which soured out of no fault of her own.

Sam, actually Samantha, was a story in her own right. Thirtyish, strong-willed, independent, her self-assuredness was so perfectly maintained that it magnified her beauty. It was not until evening that I got my first good look at her, and then it was from one end of the table to the other for she kept her distance from me. But I was captivated by her emerald green eyes and the long blonde hair sensuously outlining her smooth facial features. She moved with an athlete's agility and by the contours of her lithe body in the dress she wore, I imagined she rarely missed the opportunity to exercise. Knowing my concentration was broken by her presence, I tried to avoid her gaze throughout the evening. But I did so with extreme difficulty.

After a meal that bordered on being called a feast, Sam and Henry retired to a separate part of the hacienda while Standish, Henderson and Clements walked with me to a rustic den with a massive stone fireplace. There was a chill in the night air and I stood by the hearth, enjoying the warmth of the crackling fire. I do not know how long I was entranced by the dancing flames, but when I turned everyone was watching me as if awaiting my reply.

Henderson gestured to an open wooden box on the glass table before him and leaned back in an oversized chair to sip cognac and smoke the log protruding from his mouth. I glanced at the Cuban cigars in the finely carved box and shook my head. He shrugged and looked to Zeek who was lighting a Meerschaum pipe that had burned many a bowl of tobacco. Clements upended his whiskey glass and held it aloft for a servant to refill. When it was taken, he dabbed his fingers with a napkin and examined his chest for any drippings from the glass. I smiled inwardly at his constant preening, wondering what he would be like on a long-range mission behind enemy lines when you were often forced to urinate in your trousers because you had to remain hidden.

Elisa brought me the cup of coffee I had asked for earlier at dinner. I needed a clear head and knew until I was accustomed to hard liquor again, coffee would be to my advantage.

"All right, Alvarez," Henderson stated, peering at me over his cognac. "You're bound to have a thousand questions, so ask away. We can talk freely here."

I drank my coffee as leisurely as he sipped his drink, using the time to organize my thoughts. *Talk freely?* That was the last thing I knew would occur between us, but I was quickly reviving my old Recon training that had gone unused for so long.

"Who all is going on this jaunt?"

"You and Zeek."

"How are we traveling?"

"Sam and Henry will fly you to the airport in Iquitos, Peru. From there you cross the Amazon River by ferry and walk inland to an area Zeek will show you on a map tomorrow."

"Weapons?"

"Anything you want."

"What about extraction after Zeek obtains his information?"

"Return to the airport. Sam will be there. She'll bring Zeek here and fly you to where ever you want—and she'll have a deposit slip for funds placed in a bank in your name."

I studied Henderson's face, curious as to what he had left unsaid. Zeek puffed away on his pipe and by the way pillars of smoke rose into the air, I realized he was slightly nervous. Clements, on the other hand, sat back in his chair, eyes closed, appearing as calm as a man on strong dosages of Valium. But at the rate he had been putting away his drinks, I was not surprised.

"If I'm to be Zeek's bodyguard as well as tour-guide, who am I protecting him from?"

Clements chuckled and opened his eyes. He gazed at me with a glassy, fogged look which made me grin at his inebriation. "You're our two-for-one special of the day. You can guide him and make sure he doesn't trip over his feet and get hurt."

Motioning with his empty glass toward Zeek, Clements drunkenly nodded and grinned sarcastically. "Hell, he's so absent-minded at times he'd probably walk into a headhunters' village and be their main course." Clements chuckled and handed his glass to a servant. "You'll be more of a nursemaid than a bodyguard, and as old as you both are, I'm sure you have something in common."

The liquor had definitely taken its hold on the arrogant bastard and loosened his thick tongue. But from experience I knew youth and whiskey were a poor combination, often turning mice into lions. Or in Clements case into a jackass.

I glanced at Zeek but he lightly shook his head and looked at me with an expression of, *"Don't worry. We'll talk later."*

"It's been a long day and I'm going to bed," Henderson moaned, easing out of his chair. He walked to the fireplace and tossed his cigar into it. "All right," he said, pulling on Clements' arm. "You've had enough for the night. Come on. I'll help you to your room."

Clements stood and weaved in place. His world was spinning and I drew pleasure from the thought of how hung-over he might be the next morning.

"We'll start the briefing in the morning," Henderson told me as he escorted Clements to the door.

I motioned for Elisa to bring more coffee and smiled at the sight of America's elite protectors stumbling from the room. Zeek took a cup and we sat for another hour by the fire, mostly in silence, generally making light conversation to know each other better. I liked him although I felt sure he was not telling me all he knew about the mission. Yet I believed as we drew closer to leaving he would feel confident enough to explain more.

"What scares you, John?" he asked, eyes narrowed with the passion of thought which comes from the black recesses of a troubled soul. "No, let me clarify that. What's your worst fear? Or do you have any? I've read Armageddon's dossier on you and can't imagine what it would be."

Every man holds some form of fear deep within himself. I have known men who were frightened of spiders; men who feared growing old, the dark of night, or failure in their lives. But Zeek's question took me by surprise. Many a day I had sat in my prison cell, staring at the walls, contemplating the rights and wrongs of my life. His was a question I had given little consideration to for I had long ago learned to control fear to my advantage. If I could control it then, under the worst of conditions in combat, what should I fear?

I know such thinking can be debated for hours by scholars of philosophy and psychology, but I could only answer his question with a shrug and sit in silence.

Zeek lowered his gaze to the floor and sat quietly. His ashen face was confusing and I wondered what battle he waged with himself. On that night though, I knew nothing of substance about him to associate his inner turmoil with the journey we were to undergo.

"Don't let Clements' remarks annoy you. He's always been an obnoxious drunk as long as I've known him," Zeek said calmly, regaining his composure. "He doesn't have the balls to go to the Amazon with me. That's why he searched so hard to find you."

I watched him slowly rise from his chair and walk away, heavily burdened by his thoughts.

"Zeek?"

"Yes?" He halted by the door to pack his pipe with fresh tobacco.

"What do *you* fear?"

He stared for several seconds, hands frozen upon the pipe with one finger still in its bowl. The ashen look returned and I saw heartfelt terror in his eyes.

"Meeting the devil, John," he whispered then walked from the room like a man heading to the gallows.

Chapter Fourteen

The next morning I rose before dawn and showered in cold water to awaken my senses. Although I kept in good physical condition while in prison, I knew how taxing the jungle could be. The high humidity and constant sweating drains a man's strength, and the least exertion swiftly produces a fatigue which clouds his decisions. There were other factors to consider, but from experience, I knew I needed to push myself harder each day in preparation for the mission.

I found paramilitary clothes in my closet and after changing into a comfortable pair of boots and trousers, I left shirtless for a grueling run. Initially, the guard refused to open the gate and allow me to leave, but Zeek waved approval from his balcony and I passed through.

The rocky valley and surrounding majestic mountains were beautiful in their own right, but the orange-streaked sunrise painting the skyline captured my attention. I ran along the dirt road, keeping my gaze on the horizon. When I felt my heart pounding against my chest, fighting to be free, I left the road and headed straight for the nearest mountain, pitting myself against the rugged terrain. Another half hour passed and I turned toward the hacienda.

At La Rosa's archway I walked in wide circles, gasping for air like a fish out of water. Sweat trailed down my face, chest, and back as if I stood beneath an open water tap. My trousers were wet and darkly splotched from the waist to below the pockets, and I knew the next day must be worse if I was to be in adequate shape for the Amazon.

My liberation from prison had heightened my senses, awakened my mind. I caught the faint fragrance of perfume and paused to let it tease my nose. The breeze swirled the flowery essence about me then faded. I started up the stairs of the hacienda, but stopped at the sight of Samantha standing partially hidden by the dining room door. Her vixen gaze set me afire and I turned away, desperately needing a cold shower for more reasons than cleanliness. Two days passed before I saw her again.

On the first day of briefing I studied topographical maps, scanned satellite reconnaissance photographs that appeared to be intentionally blurred in spots, discussed alternate routes in the event of problems, and talked to Zeek about our supply needs. Henderson was always nearby, monitoring our conversations and interrupting when it seemed my questions drew too near the truth. After my morning run on the second day, I was taken by jeep to a remote area established for tactical training. What had once been a modest village of adobe buildings now stood abandoned and riddled with bullet holes. At a glance I could see the destructive effect grenades and explosive charges have, and wondered how often this village had been used for practice.

Henderson opened a footlocker and loftily swept his hand over an array of arms like none I had ever seen. He smirked at my hesitation to select a weapon, then lifted several automatics from the chest and laid them on the hood of the jeep.

"I've got UZIs, MACs, LAAWs... What do you want? German, British, Israeli? There's polymers, high impact plastic—"

I hated to interrupt his boastful speech, but most of what he had were useless to me. My Recon training had all been with much simpler weapons. This was all just expensive junk.

A weapon in the corner of the chest drew my interest and I lifted it for him to see. Naturally, he frowned at my choice, having wanted me to select one of his more exotic prizes. But the semiautomatic's weight and balance were superb and I relished the feel in my hand. I cannot explain the bond between a warrior and his weapons, yet it is like a perfect marriage when soul mates unite.

"Beretta, 40S&W. Ten-shot magazine, decocking lever—"

Oblivious to his description, I began a closer inspection. Anxious to test my skill, I loaded several spare magazines and shoved them into my belt line as I walked toward the nearest building.

Henderson followed me and said, "Targets are in the windows and doors. Pick something and shoot before you drown in your drool." He shook his head languidly and tossed me a pair of ear muffs.

I was twenty yards from the building. My first shot splintered the door frame to the right of a life-sized photograph of a masked terrorist holding a woman hostage. The second cut a hole to the left of the gunman's ear. I knew I was only becoming acquainted with the weapon's trigger pull and recoil, but I heard Henderson's laughter between the blasts and grew irritated.

"Maybe Zeek should be your bodyguard!" he yelled.

I turned my back to the target as if searching for something else to shoot. Henderson chuckled and from his sarcastic expression, I could tell he had already formed an opinion of my marksmanship. But I waited, listening, growing angrier by the second. Finally, I decided to change his mind.

Wheeling toward the target, I fired until the pistol was empty, dropped the empty magazine and before it hit the dirt, had reloaded. I know it was showing off and should not have done so, but I had taken enough guff from him and chose to end it. Again, I rapidly fired until the slide locked back upon an empty magazine. I stared at the target and grinned. Light shined through the erratic hole I had cut in the terrorist's forehead.

I heard no more laughter from Henderson. And for the remainder of the day, I played with his chest of toys, expending ammunition until my hands hurt.

"Okay, which one do you want?" he politely asked, gesturing to the pile of space-age looking weapons.

"This one," I stated, holding the Beretta aloft. "And I want a sawed-off, 12 gauge pump shotgun, a CAR-15, and a Kabar."

Henderson scowled and shook his head, annoyed by my requests for outdated weapons. "How about a musket too?"

★ ★ ★ ★

Retiring to my room early on the third evening, I wanted to relax and mentally prepare myself for the mission. Of all I had been told and the maps I had seen, a number of unanswered questions still remained.

Zeek's reply when asked what he feared fueled my curiosity too. *Meeting the devil.* There had been a suggestion of terror in him at that moment, and the voice within told me he believed he would truly meet the devil on our mission. But I scoffed at the idiocy of my thoughts and searched for some plausible meaning.

The night air was crisp and felt good upon my naked body as I walked out onto the veranda. Stars glittered in the cloudless sky like jewels in a king's treasure chest, and the land was bathed in the light of a moon so full the outlines upon its face were vividly distinct. I breathed deeply and filled my lungs with air so clean its purity was intoxicating. As had been my habit each night in prison when the lights were ordered off, I flowed through the ancient Chinese exercises of Tai Chi, bringing peace and harmony to my body, mind, and soul. Yet, before I could complete my movements, I drew still, alerted to someone's presence.

I eased upright and returned inside. Fortunately, only one lamp lit my quarters and I casually turned it off to bait my attacker. *If it is Henderson or Clements testing me,* I thought, *I will give them more than they wanted in answer.*

Moonlight illuminated my room and I crept to a better vantage point. The curtains of the windows and veranda door swayed from the gentle breeze and with the backdrop of moonlight, anyone who approached would cast a perfect silhouette upon them.

I waited, watching the veranda, wondering if I had misjudged my senses because nothing came into view and there was only silence. Then a flowery essence drifted to me on the night air and my body unexpectedly drew hard as tempered steel.

The silhouette flowed toward the veranda door with an athletic grace I had observed before in the hacienda. But there were distinct portions of its outline I had not seen in years. *Breasts.* My pulse quickened, beating with the ferocity of tribal drums in my head. The dark figure paused at the door. I moved to one side and observed long fingers part the curtains. My mystery guest entered and at the sight of the first long, lithe leg that came through, the drumming in my head ran rampant.

Samantha stepped fully into view and glanced about the room. When she saw me standing off to one side, she did not startle. She was as naked as I, and there was no hint of shame in her face for the manner in which she had arrived. I let my gaze roam over her wonderful body, feasting upon it like a starved man coming out of the wilderness. A temptress' smile eased across her lips as she glided toward me. I was about to speak when she pressed her finger gently upon my lips to silence me.

There was no need for words between us. I did not care why she had come as she did and she never volunteered a reason. Her insatiable appetite that night matched mine and when she left my bed before dawn, I wished the sun had never risen.

In the week I was at the hacienda that was the only morning I did not go for my daily run. I remained in bed, nourishing the fragrance of her perfume as if it were delicious nectar.

In the following days she passed by me as before, in silence and with only a brief hint of a smile. It was not until my last night at La Rosa Rancho that she came to me again, appearing magically upon the moonlit veranda to share my bed without a word having passed between us.

Chapter Fifteen

I stood on the runway and watched Henry carry our gear aboard the midnight black jet. In the sunlight streaming over the jagged ridges of the mountain, the jet resembled a magnificent raptor, anxious to be airborne, aloft in the clouds where it belonged.

Clipboard in hand, Sam walked about the aircraft intently conducting her pre-flight inspection. Although I was near, her attention rested solely upon the jet and she moved past me as if I was invisible. In honesty I must say my ego was a bit bruised by her indifference, for we had spent two nights together which sorely taxed our physical endurance. But she was a professional and her conduct reminded me we had not been love-struck teenagers caught up in the exploration of sexual frontiers. It was not until she completed her inspection and started up the ramp did she glance my way. As she entered the craft, she stopped to brush golden strands of hair from her face and winked at me.

Henderson waited by his car, smoking cigarettes and gazing at the rugged landscape while Clements gave Zeek last minute instructions. I could have heard more of their conversation but the whine of the jet's engines being warmed for take-off cut short my eavesdropping. But I heard enough and chose to wait until Zeek and I were alone before pursuing any questions.

A dull red flooded Zeek's face and without warning, he jabbed a bony finger deeply into Clements' chest. Clements eyes flared and as I would expect, he glanced at his shirt and immediately smoothed the cloth. He angrily called out to Zeek, but his words were ignored.

"Let's go before I get one of your guns and shoot that son-of-a-bitch," Zeek yelled through the whine of the engines.

I smiled and followed him aboard, anxious to leave, for I had begun to think of my sister. A chance existed I would find Melinda alive after years of believing she had died in the Amazon so long ago. Hope is a strange emotion, and much can be said about how it renews our lives. Yes, my mind was clouded by the prospect of our joyous reunion, and I never gave thought to the truths I would learn about her. But for that brief time, I was the happiest I had been in many a year.

★ ★ ★ ★

We settled into our flight path and the Lear jet's engines became a muffled rumble to my ears. Henry, attentive to his duties, appeared by my side bearing a selection of coffee, juice, and whiskey. It was too early for liquor and I wanted nothing to impair my thinking. I chose coffee and grinned when Zeek reached out from across the aisle to take the whiskey intended for me.

"No need letting it go to waste," he said smugly, a glass in each hand. He gulped them like a man wanting to drown his misery and when ice clinked in the glasses, he called for more.

I waited until his third drink was emptied and moved to the seat beside him, stretching my legs out into a comfortable position.

"Clements said Armageddon only gets involved with matters of national security. If that's true, why are we *really* going to the Amazon?"

He stared at the seat in front of him and hastily gulped a fourth drink to garner courage. "Have you ever chased a dream only to find a nightmare instead?"

Answering my question with a question was not what I expected from him. Face scrunched into a mask of deep worry, he lethargically shook his head and lowered his gaze to the melting ice in his glass.

"I'm an archeologist, John. Not a killer like Henderson and Clements. All I ever wanted was to explore historical ruins and unfold the secrets of the past."

I sat quiet, allowing him to speak his troubled heart. The liquor's effect was evident in his eyes and greatly assisted in loosening his tongue. Whatever the reasons were for his outcry of pain, I was an avid audience.

"If what I found three years ago is true, then it *must* be destroyed." Zeek's voice trailed off into a haunting whisper. His gaze rose to my face and in his eyes I observed a fine blend of fear, remorse, and fatalistic truth. "*Moloc*," he stated, talking more to himself than to me.

It was the singular word I had distinctly overheard Clements say on the runway before Zeek's anger overcame him and forced him to walk away. But to say, *"It must be destroyed,"* cast my thoughts to secret missile silo complexes endangering America; a drug lord's hideaway from which the world was being poisoned by the fruits of his labors; an insane dictator who threatened to unleash a deadly virus for his own benefit. I mistakenly took Moloc to be the code name of the location we were heading toward, never suspecting it would be the sole threat to the sanity of the world.

"Then why are you going, Zeek? I could have taken a team in to *eliminate* the problem." I spoke with such confidence and innocence Zeek peered at me with the understanding gaze of a father whose son believes he is worldly and would not accept the truth if it were placed in his hands.

"It's not that simple. We must know how deeply we've been infected before we—" My frazzle-haired friend wearily rubbed his face and massaged his temples. He lowered his hands and sadly looked at them. Darkness enshrouded him as it does with all men who must undergo a task which flows against their peaceful nature. His gaze rose to meet mine.

"I searched for good and found only evil, John. Now it's up to me to find some way to destroy it." He leaned close and clutched my hand, squeezing with a strength born from the purest fear. "In that jungle lays a kingdom as none you've ever read or heard about. I saw it only once, at a distance in the faint light of dusk, and my mind still refuses to believe what my eyes saw. We were forced to flee for our lives before I could learn more, and yet, even the chase gave proof to the superstitious tales I had heard from the Indian tribes."

"We? What proof?" I asked, adrift on a sea of questions. My mind was boggled by his rush of disjointed information. "Zeek, were you on an expedition for Armageddon?"

He nodded and released my hand to ease back into his seat. "I had been working for them all along and didn't know it. They controlled the government purse strings funding my trip." Zeek shook his head in exasperation. "I should have suspected something wasn't right when Clements first came to me with the money. He held too keen an interest in my research. With every question he asked, I felt he already knew the answer."

"What research? How would he have known?"

"Through the years I deciphered passages in a dozen ancient texts which referred to a ruler who controlled the world as no other had. Based on my research, I narrowed the location of his kingdom down to an area along the border of Peru and Brazil. Somehow Clements intercepted my request for a government grant and read the summary of what I hoped to discover."

The explanation made sense. Possibly Clements had read Zeek's summary. I believed there was more and decided to push our conversation further.

"An agency like Armageddon doesn't get involved unless national security is at stake—and so far, I haven't heard anything significant enough to draw their attention to an archeological expedition. A passage you found in a book in some primitive country? That's not . . . ."

Zeek's odd expression made me draw silent. He leaned toward me and remarked, "I said *passages* in ancient *texts*, and I never said it was only *one* country. They all referred to the same ruler!" Having spoken, he proudly straightened and drank the ice water in his glass, allowing me time to digest his words.

"John, I discovered the same references to this ruler in Egyptian temples, Chinese monasteries, Hindu manuscripts, European castles, Bolivian texts and Aztec carvings." He swung a hand through the air before him. "Don't you see? This ruler, whoever he is or was, harnessed some type of power for his benefit. Not only did he have power, but he had control over countries spanning the globe. My God, John! Think about it. How could one person govern so much without us having learned of him before? That isn't all though. Each of the passages I deciphered came from a *different* time period. To the best of my calculations, this ruler would have been born long before Christ and lived for four thousand years or more!"

At that point I thought the whiskey had loosened Zeek's mind as well as his tongue. "And what did this guy look like?"

Zeek scratched his scalp and laughed. "No, the question is what *does* he look like?" He gazed at me with whiskey glazed eyes. "Either one man has lived thousands of years or his descendants have carried on using his disguise."

I shook my head sympathetically. Zeek's years of researching dusty manuscripts had addled his brain. "Okay, what *does* he look like?" I asked, already assuming our trek through the jungle would result in finding nothing more than a vine covered rubble of chiseled rocks.

"Bah," he scoffed, waving a hand at me. "This part's nothing more than exaggerated superstitions." Zeek sighed and raised his glass for Henry to see. He waited until the flight attendant brought a fresh drink and walked away before speaking again.

"Bear in mind these texts were written when people still believed dragons were over every hill and you would fall off the end of the earth if you sailed too far. But the descriptions of this ruler all hold a similarity; tall and stronger than ten men; half-man, half-monster; crueler than any beast that ever walked upon the face of earth. He retains an army of mutants called Drolids and—"

I could not contain myself any longer and laughed aloud at Zeek's sincerity. *"Drolids?"*

"To hell with you—and Clements and Henderson. To hell with the whole lot of you!" he stammered and took a large swig of his drink. "You wouldn't be laughing if it had been you chased through the jungle by a bunch of grunting freaks of nature!"

I stopped laughing when I observed dread in his eyes. This was the proof he had mentioned earlier only I had become too enthralled by his tale to ask.

"You personally saw them? No one told you about them?"

"Dammit to hell, John! Remember when we first met and I told you I couldn't bring your sister back with me?"

I nodded anxiously.

"My expedition began with twenty-five men and ended with one—me. We passed through Melinda's village on the way to the forbidden region, and it was when we found the ruler's kingdom that his army *found* us. They chased us relentlessly. As my porters fell in exhaustion, pleading for mercy, those mutant bastards tore the limbs from them."

Zeek lowered his head until his chin touched his chest. He remained motionless for so long I thought he had fallen asleep. When I started to rise and return to my seat across the aisle, he raised his face to me.

"I've never seen anything like them . . . and I don't want to again."

What could I say? I couldn't deny he had seen *something* which struck panic in his heart. From experience I knew the horror of being chased through a jungle with an unknown number of men in hot pursuit, all anxious to inflict pain if they captured me. But he had only witnessed the deaths of porters, hired men he did not truly know. I had seen my team, men who had shared months of their lives with me, be brutally killed before my eyes. Yes, I understood far more of what he was feeling than I was willing to tell him.

I stood and took the drink from his trembling hand. His eyes closed as I spread a blanket over him and reclined his seat.

"Don't worry, Zeek. I'll take care of you in the jungle. You'll see," I said softly, not realizing how difficult my promise would be to keep.

★ ★ ★ ★

Zeek slept, if it can be called that. From across the aisle I watched him startle and vacantly gaze about the cabin, then when reassured of his safety, close his eyes again. At times he mumbled and fretfully tossed about in his seat, and once he jumped as if an electric shock had raced through his body. I do not know what demons chased him in his dreams, but I can recall nights when I awoke drenched in sweat or tears.

I grew bored with sitting in my seat and strolled about the cabin to stretch and prowl the craft. There was little a person could want that was not available to help pass the hours. Books, magazines, taped movies, a wide range of recorded music. Each time I looked in a cabinet or lifted a book, Henry appeared, asking if he could be of assistance.

I found him to be quite a good conversationalist. Our topics flowed from political affairs to everyday life and he made no attempt to deceive me or lead our talks in any specific direction. My curiosity rose about my midnight hacienda visitor and when I inquired about Samantha's past, he diplomatically smiled and said, "Sir, what she wishes you to know of her, must come from her. But I will assure you of one thing that may set your mind at ease. If she extends her *friendship* to you, then you should feel honored. She is quite selective." His lips parted, forming a devilish smile which displayed a full set of pearly teeth.

I grinned, believing he knew very well the exact nights she had come to my room. Whether he observed her walking by his window and assumed it or they had sat and discussed her rendezvous as old friends often exchange confidences, I do not know which. But he knew of our liaisons and I respected his discretion.

We landed twice for refueling and each time were on the ground no longer than it took to ready ourselves for the next stage of our flight. At the second landing I found the airport to be as desolate as the La Rosa Rancho runway—with one exception. The surrounding landscape was a plush green, thick with jungle and air so oppressive and humid that my shirt immediately stuck to my chest. My skin grew clammy and was strange to my senses because it had been Vietnam since I last felt such a miserable sensation.

Standing on the jet's boarding ramp and basking in the tropical sun, the reality of our mission stuck me hard. I recalled Zeek's tale. A ruler who controlled the world for centuries? Mutants called Drolids? Questions buzzed in my head like a swarm of angry bees, all pestering me.

We, as common-sense thinking beings, must have stability and logical explanations to balance our every thought and action. When confronted with questions, we search ourselves for concrete answers by which we can form sound opinions to allow us to continue in some structured fashion. But to think of an ancient ruler being immortal, and worse, having a mutant army that still exists in this modern age? No, posing such a question to your mind is like looking up at the stars and wondering how such a great void can continue endlessly. There is no answer, and we quickly turn from the question to search for something we can explain.

★ ★ ★ ★

I wished we had landed at Iquitos, Peru in daylight because I would have enjoyed an aerial inspection of the immense river. But the spectacular night view was equally fascinating with the Amazon moon reflecting off the great watery snake's back.

For someone such as me, who had traveled upon many a large river in my military days, there were no comparisons to the Amazon. We were over two-thousand miles inland from its mouth and the river was still massive enough to sustain the traffic of ocean-going vessels, barges, and ferries without a sign of congestion. As we circled the airport I studied the grayish black mass of rain forest lying dismally to the south, awaiting us. The eerie moonlight painted erratic shadows across its rolling canopy and glistened on the bordering river. The entire sight was one few people seldom see.

Iquitos was a city alive and illuminated by thousands of glittering lights cast off buildings and its ships at anchor. Cars, with their headlights streaming on the roads before them, awkwardly resembled ants trudging in single file to their mounds after a long day's work. For a man who has spent years in prison, it was all a wonderful view regardless of how poverty-stricken and filthy it truly was in the sunlight.

We landed and taxied to a remote section of the airport. There we were taken by tight-lipped, armed men in a caravan of trucks and cars to another remote area where high chain-link fences and razor-sharp barbed-wire surrounded a guarded compound of plain buildings. There were no windows on any of the structures and lighting about the grounds was positioned so on-lookers from far away were blinded. The entire location virtually screamed covert operations, but in this land, where foreigners freely plied their trades in exchange for enormous sums of under-the-table money, I was not surprised.

Pack slung over a shoulder, I lifted my weapons bag so no one would carry it away. A pot-bellied man reeking of foul body odor directed us to individual buildings then vanished into the night. Although I had several questions, I was glad to see him leave. I do not know how much longer I could have held my breath in his presence.

My home for the night was simple and clean. After having stayed in such a lavish hacienda, I found myself unintentionally comparing the two. The bed looked comfortable enough, and after testing the shower, I believed I had all the comforts a man could want. But when the door creaked open and my golden-haired pilot entered with an inviting smile, I realized immediately I now had all a man could want.

Chapter Sixteen

The next morning I rose and dressed in silence, fighting the urge to slide back into bed and make love to Samantha a last time. She was beautiful, laying there with her hair tousled about her soft shoulders and angelic face, her nipples peeking at me from beneath a gently folded arm. Through the night we had thrashed like wild mating animals then settled into the passionate throes of lovers soon to be parted forever. I chose to leave with those memories etched into my mind. As I left her sleeping, I smiled and eased the door closed behind me.

Zeek stood on his porch, solemnly staring at the dawn breaking over the horizon. How he had ever managed to survive archeological expeditions is beyond my understanding. The mere sight of him on the porch; slovenly dressed in mismatched clothes; his backpack perilously hanging off one shoulder; frazzled hair sticking out from beneath a wide-brimmed hat set back on his head; all made me wonder if he had ever truly been afield.

Seeing me approach, he laid his pack on the porch and returned inside his building. I waited on the steps, scanning the compound's high fence and razor-sharp wire. It was definitely a secretive stopover for people who did not want their business known. I did not care though. We were leaving, and, for a place where visitors were supposed to remain anonymous, it was itself pretty conspicuous.

"Here," Zeek murmured, handing me a steaming cup. "This may be the last decent coffee we get in quite a while. I'm not the best cook in the world, so don't bitch when we're in the jungle."

I chuckled and adjusted the sling of my shotgun so it was free of my pack's strap. Zeek looked at its sawed-off barrel then glanced at my Kabar and multitude of magazine pouches I wore for my semiautomatic.

"You planning on starting a war?" he asked, motioning to the bandoliers of shotgun ammunition crisscrossing my chest. He sipped his coffee and worriedly shook his head.

"No, they're for snakes. I hate snakes," I replied, forcing myself not to laugh at his apparent nervousness of returning to the jungle.

We drank our coffee and made small talk, the type that eases the tensions of men facing the unknown on a dangerous mission. I pulled at my shirt to fan a breeze over my sweating chest. It was only dawn and already I felt drenched in perspiration. That sticky, suffocating feeling remained with me for days, yet, after a couple of weeks I would grow acclimated to the thick humidity.

I set my cup on the porch and looked to Zeek, wondering how long he would tarry. He sighed and placed his cup beside mine. Without a word he nodded and started for the compound's gate, struggling to put his pack on as he walked. I glanced back at the door of my own building, inwardly hoping to see Samantha standing there, waving goodbye. But she was not and I felt hurt at not having someone to love in my life, at not having someone to await my return.

★ ★ ★ ★

Zeek knew the best route to the river and all I had to do was follow. We crossed open fields and cut through the city's outskirts. Gaunt-faced men leaned against walls and bumped one another's elbows as they gestured to my weapons. I believe they would have tried to take them from me, but by their gestures I could also see they thought best not to try me. My shirt sleeves were rolled up high onto my biceps and whenever we passed a sleazy-eyed group, I intentionally flexed the muscles in my arm and squeezed my fist to make them grow hard as iron. Yet I was not foolish enough to forget that a large number of men gives a group false courage, and always I kept a watchful eye behind me.

Poverty wears the same face in every country around the world. Where unpolluted water is as valuable as gold, the clothes of the poor are always dirty and threadbare and a stench of excrement always permeates the air. And in every child's eyes one sees the hollow stare of hunger.

Life holds little hope for people when their futures revolve solely around a day by day existence. Thievery, prostitution and murder, born from that struggle, become so commonplace that they are accepted with the same indifference as the sun's setting.

Having spent so many years in prison, I had forgotten these sights and smells. But it did not take long for the memories of war-ravaged lands to resurface and I was glad when we arrived at the Amazon River.

Zeek scratched his head and scanned the dilapidated river boats along the docks. He smiled as if he had spotted an old friend and pushed his way through the travelers toward a two-story river boat.

"That's her," he said proudly, gazing at the floating deathtrap. "She may not look like much but she's as worthy a craft on the river as you'll ever get."

I didn't bother responding. The remaining fleet along the shoreline looked equally as pathetic as Zeek's rotting river queen. Every gangplank seemed to overflow with brown-skinned people carrying caged animals, cardboard boxes, and crates on their shoulders. I followed Zeek aboard. Not wanting to lose my weapons to quick-fingered artists, I slung the shotgun across my chest and laid a hand over my pistol's grip.

We stood on the deck, bunched tightly in the mass of humanity, barely able to move our arms, and still more passengers flowed aboard until I believed we would surely sink. Zeek forced his way to the railing and I was glad because I was beginning to feel claustrophobic. I listened to chickens, ducks, and pigs as they loudly protested their confinement. Children sat on the railings, engaged in contests of spitting into the water, all the while laughing, never thinking about drowning if they fell into the river. The pungent odor of strong tobacco flowed through the air as old men rolled cigarettes and smoked them with an almost regal air of leisure. Then the morning breeze shifted and the musty fragrances of unwashed, sweaty bodies swept past me.

The majority of the *caboclos*, the peasants, were barefooted and clothed in ragged attire or old multi-color faded shirts with American advertising logos across them. I scanned their faces and observed the influence of mixed European and Indian blood. There were passengers of purer Indian blood, and those stood with reflective gazes and faces painted or tattooed in ancient designs, patiently awaiting their return to the jungle.

These were new sights and I stared at the facial art in sincere interest until Zeek tugged at my arm and whispered, "If you look too long and anger them, our heads could wind up on a tree limb in their backyard. It's not uncommon for people to go into the jungle and never be heard from again." I heeded his advice and returned my attention to the river.

I found the Amazon to be a river of life, teeming with contrasts. Yet I was only witnessing a mere fragment of its activity as we lazily sailed across to the far bank. Zeek told me of the senseless murders of Indians lumbermen committed when angered at having to cease their butchery of the rain forest, and how all along the great river's length were serene villages broken by violence, rape, and disease.

"Upriver," Zeek said, gesturing to the west, "You'll find leftist guerillas and drug runners in flak jackets, wielding the best weapons money can buy." His arm swung eastward then lowered to support his weight on the railing. "Down there you have corrupt politicians, ruthless lumbermen, and cocaine traffic. But between them you'll find villages with people who want nothing more than to be left alone."

Zeek shook his head in disgust and spit into the river as if to rid himself of a foul taste. "*Civilization*—a must for all primitive societies," he stated with a hint of anger. "The Europeans came here the same as they did to America, killing what they couldn't enslave and stealing what they wanted. Did you know in the 1500's there were three million Indians in South America?"

Shaking my head, I remained silent because I could see how disturbed he was becoming.

"Now there are only fifty-thousand," he said flatly. "Murder and rape wasn't enough to satisfy the *civilized* nations staking their claim to this land. No, they wrought more misery on the Indians by introducing them to influenza, smallpox, measles, tuberculosis, and venereal diseases."

Zeek was entering a dark mood. I had seen it slowly mounting over the last few days. It was as if the closer we drew to our destination, the more morbid he became. I leaned over the rail to gaze at the ripples created in the water by our overburdened river queen, thinking about all he said.

Minutes passed before we spoke again. Water, whether it is a gentle brook or a massive river, has a calming effect on troubled souls. As I stared at the Amazon and listened to the din of animal cries, people's voices, and the boat's straining engine, I recalled the books I had read in prison and how they related similar tragic stories. Unfortunately, the savagery Zeek had spoken of was how our world had evolved, and few nations were not stained by the horrors of conquest.

Who was I to stand and make judgments on the villainy of society? I had witnessed and taken part in enough cruelties to last a lifetime. I was a convict; a murderer; an orphaned man who had silently grown to hate God for the loneliness in life I had endured. I only cried out his name when I was drunk and spending my seed between the legs of a whore. No, I had no right to judge anyone.

★ ★ ★ ★

We disembarked on a rickety dock which shook under the stampede of anxious travelers. I was glad to be ashore and move freely without striking someone at every turn. Zeek's black mood had infected my senses and only the presence of the ominous jungle ahead seemed to displace it.

Surrounding the dock was a nameless town with as much squalor and poverty as we had just left across the river. Zeek slowly walked along its dirt street, eyeing the ramshackle huts and buildings as if he would never see their likes again and wanted to etch their memory into his mind. It was only eight in the morning and we were already drenched in sweat and carried the same odor as the river boat's voyagers. I halted beside the paint-bare walls of a general store and stood examining my maps and compass.

"Two or three days south then turn southeast and travel three more," Zeek commented, having moved beside me to peer at the map.

"After that, we should be at the village where I last saw your sister. From there we're only a few days . . ."

Zeek's abrupt silence made me glance at his face.

"From Moloc?" I asked, still associating the name with some type of covert military site.

He somberly nodded in reply and started toward the jungle.

Chapter Seventeen

Our journey to the border of Moloc's land took ten days instead of the five as Zeek had thought. His health could not sustain a grueling pace, and although in far better condition than he, at each day's end I found myself drained of strength.

We waded through waist-deep streams, crossed treacherous caiman infested rivers, and hacked our way through walls of tangled vines in the Amazon forest. Anacondas were always a major concern, but the Bushie pit vipers kept me most alert. Luckily we saw very few and they were always at a safe distance. There were times when I felt as if we were being followed, yet I never saw anyone.

"It's the local tribes," Zeek remarked calmly, seeing me stop to scan the forest about us. "They're curious about the white men crossing through their lands."

Nodding to him, I disliked the sensation their invisible presence created within me.

"I must compliment your senses, John. Most men would never realize the Indians' were near," Zeek said, mopping his brow with a soiled handkerchief. "I doubt they mean us harm. We would already be dead if they wanted our heads."

Thinking about his words, I knew he was right. We were trailed for days and they had had sufficient opportunities during that time to attack. Yet, I did not like being followed by unseen men. Especially after Zeek told me some of the tribes were known to be headhunters.

Zeek's uneasiness increased the deeper we traveled into the Amazon. He spoke little and whenever I asked him a question, I often had to repeat it to capture his attention. Several times I caught glimpses of fear in his eyes that later changed to vacant stares.

On the afternoon of the ninth day Zeek asked to make camp early rather than wait until near dusk as had been our habit. We arrived at a clearing on the bank of a small river and Zeek wanted a moment to rest. At a glance I could see how weary he was, so I left him sitting on a log while I scouted the area.

My former Recon habits were swiftly returning. Moving in a wide circle about the camp, looking, searching, preparing our night's safety, I then followed the river's shoreline back to the clearing. Zeek had a fire made and was kneeling beside it, feeding twigs into the meager flames.

"Satisfied?" he asked at my approach.

"For now," I replied, undecided whether to speak of all I had discovered.

We ate a light meal and sat in silence. By the time we finished eating, night had fallen and the campfire's light made shadows dance on the trees about us. A full moon rose and Zeek sat almost terrified as he looked at the white orb.

"John?"

Rubbing oil over my shotgun, I stopped and laid it across my lap to listen. Through the days of our journey we had grown to be friends, and I could tell he was disturbed by some secret locked within his soul.

At that moment he appeared to have aged ten years. Possibly it was the campfire playing tricks with my mind. But the wrinkles upon his face had grown deeper, more defined than mere minutes before. I did not answer him and sat in silence. Finally, he removed his gaze from the stars and looked directly into my eyes.

"The moon, John. We're very near Moloc's land and you must promise me you will use extreme caution whenever there is an Amazon moon in the sky."

"The moon?" I asked, leaning forward to better see his eyes. The horror in them was none as I had ever seen there before. "How could a full moon bother you?"

"It's not only me. Every village within Moloc's grasp fears it. The raids generally come on those nights, and by dawn, few people have escaped tragedy."

"Who raids the villages? I thought Moloc was a missile site or some type of secret project?"

Ezekiel Standish briefly closed his eyes. When he opened them again, tears rimmed his eyes and glistened from the campfire's light.

"Moloc's the ruler of this land. His Drolids raid the villages for him in search of fresh meat." Zeek's voice tapered off into silence.

I waited for my friend to continue but he only sat staring into the dying campfire, lost within his mind. When I realized he was not going to speak more, I pressed him for answers to the thousand questions I had been holding back.

"Who is this Moloc you are so frightened of? If his army is only stealing cattle, why don't the villagers take him meat every month?" I paused. Finally, I asked him straightforward. "What are we *really* doing here?"

My questions fell on deaf ears. We sat in silence; Zeek staring at the campfire, me waiting for him to speak.

"He's an animal—or at least part one, I believe. The fresh meat his men search for are people. *People, John!* Men, women, and children. What the Drolids don't rape and slaughter, they carry back as captives to Moloc so he may do as he pleases with them." Zeek drew a deep breath and looked at my face. "You and I are here to learn how he can be killed."

"Is that all? Some South American son-of-a-bitch set himself up as boss and our government wants him killed? You could have told me all this in the beginning."

"You don't understand, John. He's an animal that has controlled—"

"Don't feed me anymore crap! Most of these third-world leaders are animals. They have their own little kingdoms out here in the boonies. Hell, flesh is bought and sold all the time. So Moloc's a pervert who has his own private whorehouse of men and women, and his army keeps it well stocked. There's more you're not telling me. We'll be in Moloc's land tomorrow, but before we step one foot across his border, I want the truth!"

Zeek stared at me and solemnly said, "Remember when I told you about your sister? Melinda was captured by Moloc's army. If she's still alive, she's in that whorehouse you spoke of." He looked at his hands lying in his lap and gently rubbed them. "I hate to say such a thing, John, but it would be better for her if she died before arriving there."

Rage swept over me in tidal waves. I understood perfectly what he meant. The thought of my sister being violated by some bastard ruler, or his soldiers, drove me to the brink of insanity. But in the midst of my fury, I sensed danger approaching.

Water splashed in the river as it does against a leg moving too swiftly through it. Behind us, a vine shook beneath the weight of a heavy foot. A muffled cry came from the direction where I had stretched wire and placed several sharpened stakes to both sides of a well-trodden path.

Thankfully, our campfire had burned itself down to glowing embers. Caught up in our talk, we failed to stoke it, but worse, I had failed to remain aware of our surroundings.

Zeek heard the noises and in the moonlight I saw his face grow ashen. He started to speak but I was already beside him and clamped my hand over his mouth.

"Be quiet and follow me," I whispered into his ear. He nodded, looked about him then crawled behind me into the dark forest.

Before returning to camp after my scouting mission, I had established a small hideaway within the middle of several fallen trees. In hindsight, I am glad I did. The jungle brush blocked us from view and the thick tree trunks provided ample protection against bullets. I had stowed part of our supplies there, along with much of my ammunition and CAR bush gun. In the event we were overrun during the night, I did not want to lose everything in our flight to escape.

We crawled through a small opening formed by one tree leaning atop another. Zeek failed to keep his head low enough and I heard a dull thud. His fear kept him silent though and for that I was grateful.

Sweat trailed down my face as I slowly raised my head over a tree trunk to watch our unwelcome guests of the night. At first I could not see them in the black shadows of the forest, but as they stepped out into the moonlit clearing I counted at least eight well-armed soldiers.

Two had come from the river while the others crept through the jungle.

They whispered in their native tongue and I could not understand their conversations. A man I presumed to be their leader pointed to our campfire and swept a hand across the jungle as he talked. There was no difficulty in understanding the sign language. He was ordering a search.

Rather than wait, I chose to take the battle to them on my own terms.

"No matter what you hear, don't come out until I call you by name," I whispered. The night camouflaged Zeek's face, but I felt his confirming taps on my arm.

Moonlight illuminated the forest where trees had fallen and created gaps in the canopy. I stayed clear of the light and deftly moved within the black shadows. Rising to full height, I stood with my back pressed against a tree.

A soldier walked within my reach and I snapped his neck as if it were a twig. The next man stopped at the sound of his nearby comrade falling into the brush. His pause was enough to allow me to draw close and wrap an arm about his throat.

The first two died swiftly, victims of their own stupidity and inadequate training. But the remaining six were fanned out through the forest, forcing me to stalk them.

Life and death are simple matters in combat. You must live and the enemy must die. In hand-to-hand fighting there is no time for mercy, conscience, or second-thoughts. A pilot may impassively watch from the sky as his bombs detonate and the earth erupts. He knows people have died, but the deaths are unreal and there are no faces for him to remember. An artilleryman fires a round and has no realization of the true havoc it wrecks miles away. But to kill with a knife or bare hands is to hear your enemy's cry and feel his heart pounding its last beat. Then in those final seconds of his life, looking into his eyes, you see into the depths of his soul.

There are men who would be disturbed by such things, and there are those who are cold-blooded and without remorse. I was the latter and moved through the jungle after my prey, a predator on the hunt. I dispatched the third and fourth soldiers with my Kabar. One felt my blade through his ribs, lung, and into his heart. The other never knew what struck him when the razor-sharp steel drove through his throat and upward into his brain.

The next two tasted the butt of my shotgun and were silenced forever with swift knife strokes. Not a shot had been fired and only the muffled sounds of bodies falling into the foliage had broken the quiet of the night. But I relaxed too soon and suddenly heard bullets cutting the air about me.

It was indiscriminate firing, the type which comes from desperate men raking the terrain out of fear. The silhouettes of the last two soldiers came into view. I grew motionless and watched as they spun and fired at the jungle behind them. It was then I realized they had no knowledge of my position and their deaths came easily. When they had spent their last round and were feverishly trying to reload, I merely raised my shotgun and fired. My first shot took both men to the ground, but the second and third ended the night's battle.

I cannot say what emotions moved through me because I truly do not remember having had any. Eight men were dead and I had functioned solely as a well-oiled machine—a killing machine. All I do recall is that I immediately melted into the black shadows to wait for anyone I might have overlooked.

"Zeek," I whispered minutes later, confident the area was at last safe. "Zeek, you can come out."

Branches rustled and leaves scraped cloth. Zeek slowly appeared, eyes stretched wide, mouth agape as he passed through patches of moonlit forest.

"Pack up. We're moving on," I ordered.

"Who are they?"

"I don't know." Reloading my shotgun, I glanced about the area without interest. They could have been drug runners or a patrol of leftist guerillas. The Shining Path were known to be in the region. There was not enough light to fully inspect them and there was no need to do so. Surrounding our camp and trying to sneak in had signed their death warrants as far as I was concerned. From that point on, it became a matter of their lives or ours.

"You knew they were coming, didn't you?"

"No," I replied. "Earlier I found enough boot prints to tell me this was a well traveled area." I pointed to the river's southern shoreline. "And the scrape marks in the mud weren't made by Indian canoes either. They're from flat bottomed, metal boats. I just wanted to be ready if anyone did come."

Zeek nodded and stared at me.

In the moonlight painting his face, I saw a blend of fear, disgust, and curiosity about the kind of man I was.

If he had asked I could not have answered, nor would I if I knew. I did not want to know the truth about myself.

* * * *

We traveled two miles then slept the remainder of the night well hidden within the cover of dense brush. By dawn we were back on the trail and did not halt for an hour.

An uneasy feeling settled over me. I kept scanning the forest as we walked. Each time I looked back, Zeek would be staring at me.

"It must be the Indians again," I remarked.

"No. Listen to the jungle for a moment."

Drawing to a halt I listened and let my gaze rise to the tops of the trees. Nothing. No birds calling and flying about. No monkeys or wildlife were in sight. Only silence filled my ears. It was then I lowered my eyes to Zeek and slowly shrugged my shoulders.

"We're in Moloc's land," Zeek said softly, glancing at the surrounding landscape. "Even the animals fear this place."

Remaining silent, I looked at the Amazon forest. My friend was right. A somber air hung over the area and even the birds could find nothing to sing about.

Without further word between us, we continued our trek for another hour and walked into the cleared outskirts of a village.

* * * *

At first glance the village appeared no different than any other in jungle lands. The thatched roof huts had open sides for ventilation, and all were elevated two or more feet off the ground to protect the people from seasonal floods and crawling insects. Cooking fires were lit at every turn and the scents of meat roasting on spits, stews boiling, and wood burning, drifted upon the breeze. But the longer I stood looking at the village the more I came to realize its oddities.

No dogs ran about the huts chasing children. In every village I knew of, whether the jungles of Vietnam or the rainforests of the Amazon, local wildlife is often kept as pets. Monkeys might be seen climbing on the shoulders of children; parrots would sit squawking on perches, and snakes always slithered on the arms of older boys. Yet, none of these were present that I could see.

Silence greeted us, and this in itself seemed odd. Gradually villagers appeared from behind the huts and trees. First the men and then came the women and children. They were as curious about us as we were of them. Yet as I gazed at their faces I realized the magnitude of sadness their eyes held, and how beaten their spirits were.

Zeek stepped forward and waved them near. A wrinkled man, burnt dark under decades of a hot tropical sun, raised his hand in a gesture of peace. I remained silent and listened to the elder and Zeek speak in a dialect which held no meaning to me.

"They are impressed by your size and wonder if you are a great warrior in your land," Zeek said, glancing at me. A hint of a smile crossed his lips as he returned to his conversation with the village leader. There was much hand-swinging, nodding, grunts, and head shaking. Within a few minutes, the elder turned to his people, pointed to me, spoke several words in his native tongue, and the villagers began to walk away.

I was surprised by how quickly they dispersed and went about their daily lives. One moment they appeared frightened of us, and the next, it was as if we had been accepted by them and were no longer a novelty. Several children remained by my side, staring upward with necks craned back.

"They've never seen a man with blue eyes," Zeek chuckled, scratching the head of a dirty-faced boy. His hand slid away and he stared at me. "But the chief wants to know if you have come to free them?"

"Free them?"

"The chief says tribal legends tell of a man who will come to free them from their sorrows. A great warrior who will suffer much before he conquers evil."

Shaking my head, I looked at Zeek. "They have me confused with someone who gives a damn."

"Maybe," Zeek softly replied.

★ ★ ★ ★

We spent the day walking about the village. Whenever Zeek stopped to talk with the people, I would stand quietly back and watch their terrified reactions. I needed no translator to know he was asking about Moloc or to understand their answers. Several men turned away and often times the women grabbed children up into their arms and rushed into the huts. But Zeek was persistent and found men brave enough to whisper answers to his inquiries.

I estimated the village's population to be far less than a hundred, yet of their total, few young women had been seen. The ages seemingly jumped from mere children to old, and I thought this odd until I remembered Zeek talking about the moonlight raids.

"Beauty and youth are curses to our women," a crippled man remarked as we sat beside him on the steps of his half-fallen hut. "Years ago we hid the women in the jungle, but eventually they were found. This was the reward I received for helping my people hide their wives and daughters." And having spoken, the time-worn man slowly pointed to his mangled legs.

By late afternoon I had heard enough stories about Moloc's atrocities to last me three lifetimes. They were difficult to believe, each being filled with descriptions of beast-like men who formed the Drolid army and savagely preyed upon innocent villagers.

★ ★ ★ ★

By dusk Zeek had grown extremely agitated and kept glancing at the sky. He feared the rising of the moon, but there was nothing I could do to alleviate his anxieties. I had begun to think of my family again, my sister's fate, and had my own concerns.

"Is this the village Melinda was in?"

Zeek nodded slowly and gazed at the ground. He stood in silence for a minute then looked at me. "These people found her in the jungle after your family's airplane crashed. She lived here until Moloc's army captured her." Zeek drew a deep breath before continuing. "The old man we talked with today—the crippled one on the steps—one of the women he was hiding from Moloc was Melinda. He knew what they would do to her if she was found."

Each word he spoke burned me like red hot pokers freshly drawn from a fire. So many questions laid heavy on my mind, yet I dreaded the answers I might receive. My anguish became anger then fueled itself into a height of rage as I had never known. I wanted retribution for my sister's life, my family's death, and all I believed had been stolen from me through the years. I wanted Moloc's death.

There were no thoughts of ever seeing Melinda alive again. After hearing the tales of cruelties the captives underwent at Moloc's hands, I adamantly crushed such a wish. My only hope was when the end arrived for her, death came swift.

"When do we leave to find Moloc?" I asked. My cold tone made Zeek turn and look at me.

His answer came in a voice barely above a whisper, and I observed dread in his eyes.

"Tomorrow."

★ ★ ★ ★

If I had not been in such a dark mood, I would have enjoyed the delicious meal prepared for us by a kind village woman. We ate in silence and, having lost most of my appetite, I finished quickly and set about cleaning my weapons. As I rubbed them with oil and reloaded each, I could only think of the pleasure I would take in killing Moloc.

Such thoughts may be grisly and abhorred by the civilized world, but to a man in the jungle, a man whose miserable past only gave sight to a bleak future, revenge becomes the flame that warms his soul.

A hint of a breeze moved through the jungle and mosquitos came and went in swarms. My body was adjusting to the thick humidity and my mind was swiftly regaining its former Recon state. As I sat with the shotgun across my lap, staring down the road leading into the village, I recalled every piece of information about Moloc and the Drolids that Zeek had gathered.

Moloc was just another man who had become barbaric and ruled with a heavy hand. His feared army had made a reputation for themselves across the land. I saw everything as being explainable. To Zeek, this was no more than a fact finding mission; one to gather the information on how the cruel South American leader could be killed. Yet, to me, this was to be Moloc's end. I would not leave until he laid dead at my feet or me at his.

The villagers had said the Drolids were long overdue. There had been no raids in six months. Although the moon was again rising full into the sky, they hoped this month would pass as the last; long nights filled only with fear until the dawn came.

As the moon grew brighter, I observed the villagers melt into the surrounding jungle shadows to hide. Soon I found myself alone with only the crackle of cooking fires to keep me company. Even Zeek took refuge from the night.

Hours passed before an unsettling noise broke the jungle's silence. The clamor grew and I rose to my feet, scanning the empty village for signs of the source. Then the bedlam made itself known to me.

Initially, I stood doubting my senses yet there they were, marching steadily toward me on the road leading into the village.

How was I to know this was only to be the first of many such experiences in which I denied what my eyes observed? I had been told of these *soldiers* and scoffed at their description. Now I realize how foolish and naive it was for me to believe the villagers had fabricated their tales.

At a distance they were no more than a wide, dark blotch, clumsily bobbing on the road as it moved toward me to the cadence of unseen drums. As they drew closer, the shapes of men, if that is what they may be called, became more defined. I stood stunned at the sight of them.

Though they were not as precise as the worst army of the world, the soldiers maintained a semblance of military formation as they marched. They were short in height with bodies formed of large lumps of muscle. Their bald heads appeared to be shoved down between their shoulders, eliminating the need for necks. Upon their chests were crude leather breastplates and pieces of chain-mail, and about their forearms were gauntlets comprised of animal skins. While some wore sandals with thongs bound about the legs, others looked to be bare-footed. Wide belts and straps encircled their waists, and from each hip swung a sword, battle-axe, or mace-like club that appeared well used. On both sides of their formation strode angry, grunting creatures that were equally as horrid. They savagely cracked whips to enforce discipline with the brutal, cutting sting of leather.

The air was thick with tension, the dull boom of drums, and the guttural grunts which I later learned were their only means of speech. I thought of Cro-Magnon men lost in time, draped in the attire of barbarian armies. Yet, as I stared at the oncoming horde, I thought of apes having bred with humans and giving birth to mutant offspring. Such was the confusion I faced, unable to comprehend what I saw, yet forced to accept the reality of their approach.

The cracks of the whips became as deafening as pistol shots, and the arms swinging the black leather whips appeared as thick as oak limbs. The flesh covering the grunting creatures' bodies bled each time a lash struck them, but they appeared impervious to pain and never broke their loping stride.

Within seconds the main force entered the village and spread ranks to begin an assault. Human screams rose into the night. I realized the Drolids had encircled the village to flush the people from the jungle.

Madness fell as men, women, and children fled past me in all directions. Then the main Drolid force was unleashed by their commanders and the village was engulfed in a tidal wave of savagery.

Racing back into the village I searched for Zeek. People crashed into me at every turn. Hoping to force a break in the Drolids' rapidly closing net, I set fire to every hut I passed. Flying embers set adjacent huts afire. Soon a massive wall of flames rose through the middle of the village.

A soldier ran past me, arms outstretched to grab a fleeing boy. I pumped two shotgun rounds into the burly creature and watched him writhe on the ground. His beast-like features staggered my senses. More soldiers came, grunting as they loped behind fleeing villagers. The madness intensified about me. A Drolid ripped an arm from an elderly village woman, danced about, and swung the limb over his head in victory. Another soldier waded into a cowering mass of people, smashing a swathe of death with his club. A girl's shrill scream rose from behind me and I spun with the shotgun leveled to fire. A grunting, monstrous pile of muscle knelt on a child, pinning the girl to the ground with his knee.

My mind snapped. Insanity had taken hold of me. The shotgun bucked in my hands and fire spewed from the muzzle. I coldly watched the Drolid crumple to the ground beside the girl.

Zeek fled to the jungle when the fighting began, but I quickly forgot about him as I walked through the roaring fires of the village huts on my killing spree. Shooting the Drolids did not necessarily mean their deaths. I discovered only at close range, with a shot directly to their heads, was I able to swiftly take their lives.

At first I used only the shotgun, fearing my CAR bush gun on full automatic would catch the villagers in my line of fire. But once into the melee of butchery, I realized avoiding them was an impossible feat. The Drolids displayed no mercy toward the people, and I took none on them. When my shotgun ammunition was exhausted, I used the weapon as a club until it broke. I switched to the bush gun and fired until it emptied then used it to bash the soldier's faces.

"John!" a voice cried out. "John!"

I spun at the sound of my name and saw Zeek frantically looking about the area as he ran among a throng of villagers.

"Here, Zeek!" I yelled, waving an arm to capture his attention. He saw me and turned in my direction. I started toward him, colliding with screaming villagers at each step. All I could hope for in this madness was to reach Zeek and make good an escape. Fighting was useless. There were too many Drolids for me to make a stand.

Hulking masses ran after him, reached out and caught his shirt. Zeek's feet flew upward as he was violently yanked to a halt. A Drolid soldier stepped in front of Zeek and blocked my view. My friend's terrified cries filled the air as Drolids fell upon him.

Running to Zeek I pulled a half-buried, battle-axe from the ground and threw it with all my strength. It spun end over end, becoming a blur before sinking deep into the back of the Drolid standing before Zeek.

"No! No!" Zeek's screams tore at my heart.

The wounded Drolid clumsily spun on his feet then crashed to the ground like a falling oak tree. Zeek came into view once more and I saw his arms and legs thrashing wildly in an attempt to break free of his captors. My focus was solely upon him when a massive arm swung and struck me hard in the chest with the force of a battering ram.

The wind shot out of my lungs in a forceful blast and I reeled sideways, thrown off balance by the blow. My face dug deep into mud. Rolling onto my back, I gasped for air and caught sight of Drolids carrying my struggling friend away.

A Drolid, whip in hand, stood over me. When a fleeing Indian crashed into the creature it provided enough distraction for me to crawl clear of the Drolid's reach.

I rose to my feet and looked about the area. Zeek was gone.

Blood ran in streams across the ground, gleaming from the reflections of firelight. Smoke swirled from the rooftops of the huts and spread in thick clouds across the night sky. The screams of the villagers bombarded my ears as Drolids fell upon them. I have witnessed many violent deaths in my life, but never to the extent as I did that night beneath the Amazon moon.

I do not know how long my fight lasted, nor can I recall the number of Drolids I killed before they overpowered me. With my pistol in one hand and the Kabar in the other, I fought until the ammunition was spent and the blade of my knife broke on chain-mail. After that, the last I remember was being tackled by three Drolid soldiers who swung their fists with the force of iron clubs. A sea of black enveloped me and washed consciousness from my mind.

Chapter Eighteen

My captors held each arm in a steel grip and although I was taller, I could not break free. An iron collar encircled my neck and from behind me, a guard harshly jerked its heavy chain each time I struggled. The grunting beasts pulled me along stone paved halls until we arrived at a massive pair of rugged wood doors. The brief glances I managed as we walked only served to confuse me more because my surroundings were like a medieval castle, and equally as dark and dank. Torches protruded from the wall sconces, fluttering and crackling as they made eerie shadows dance along the walls and floor.

With the collar cutting into my throat at the slightest resistance, I could not see my naked body but my arms were held aloft and in plain sight. I was smeared in mud and excrement from wherever I had been kept while unconscious. My skin appeared as dark as any Indian's in the Amazon, but my size and height made me stand out above all others. Later I learned it was my blue eyes which held these dumb creatures' interest, and even in my horrid state, I was a rare sight. I was their prize from the ruthless raid on the village and I was to be presented to their leader in chains.

Torchlight silhouetted us against the ancient doors, and in the wavering shadows the Drolids' bodies appeared to be nothing more than a mountain of lumps. The doors swung open on rusted hinges, groaning as begrudgingly as an aged man rising from bed in the morning. My guards impatiently shifted their weight from foot to foot, heads lowered as if afraid to face what awaited them inside. Their grunting conversation dwindled to silence as the doors drew open and gave sight to within.

A brutish Drolid shoved his way through the mass of soldiers about me to take the lead. He stood with his back to me; chin down, awaiting permission to enter. I took him to be their commander, or at least a ranking officer, for I had briefly seen him in the village directing the assault, savagely whipping his troops whenever they failed to obey him swiftly enough. His manner of dress was better than the rest, with each belt, strap, and leather protective plate he wore being oiled to a deep luster and less marred.

He turned to glare at me and I observed his left eye was a scarred, burned out crevice. The contemptuous look on his pockmarked face left me with no doubts he would have preferred to impale me upon his sword. Possibly I had been saved from such an agony because I was to be brought before his ruler. Of this I'm unsure, but his stare was sufficient to raise the idea in my mind.

Extending a paw-like hand, he took my chain leash from a soldier. I readied myself to be violently jerked to the floor. When he lifted the chain and tightened his grip, I knew my neck was about to be broken. Yet, he did not and only glared for a second longer before turning back to wait.

A blaring, hard voice carried from within the enormous chamber. The leader briskly started forward. Although I had voluntarily begun to follow, not wanting to feel the iron dig into my neck again, I was almost dragged.

The cavernous room magnified the claps of my guards' sandals on the stone floor, creating a dull thunder which rolled through the air like an approaching storm. Their primitive weapons clanked and bumped against their sides, and, although there were only a few soldiers, I could have closed my eyes and easily believed an army was on the march. My nostrils were immediately assaulted by the rancorous odor of burning incense, yet the incense was a fragrant perfume compared to the foul smell of my guards and the retched stench rising from my own body.

We entered the room at such a quick step my head was thrust back by the harsh pull of my leash. My gaze swept the high, arched ceiling and its thick beams as we marched at least twenty steps before sharply turning to travel another twenty. The cyclops captain abruptly stopped and with a vicious yank on the chain brought me sprawling to the floor. Only by sheer luck did I manage to buffer my head with my hands before crashing into the unforgiving stone. The fall stunned me, yet as the tense silence of the room filled my mind, I wondered if this was to be the moment of my death.

No longer were my ears bombarded by the thunder and clatter raised by the soldiers. Now, the only sound pulsating in my head came from the throbbing beat of my heart. I have fought fear many times in my life and tasted its vile bitterness upon my tongue, but there, laying naked and expecting to be driven through with a spear, fear enveloped me. I felt helpless to combat it. Sweat stung my eyes and blurred my vision. I squinted to clear them and felt my skin crack where mud and excrement had caked upon my face.

The commander's weight was on the chain, his filthy foot so close to my nose that with each breath I inhaled his stench. In casting me to the floor, he had knelt, head bowed, gaze fixed on me as he awaited his orders. I could see hatred for me fiercely burning within him.

The muffled clinks of chains came and I heard what I believed to be the purring of huge cats. With my head pressed hard against the cool stone floor, I could see nothing around me except the captain's dirty foot and his glaring, one-eyed face. Then a cold, echoing voice spoke, burning itself so deeply into my mind that it will take five lifetimes to forget.

"Guelf, you loyal, imbecilic oaf. Must I constantly remind you not to bring me gifts until you have washed them?"

The calm tone was deceiving because I sensed the ire in the speaker.

Heavy steps approached and I felt their reverberations through the stone floor. I observed the one-eyed captain draw taut. A whip lashed his bent back, once, twice, three times so swiftly their *cracks* blended into one. I flinched and tried to move, yet could not from being pinned so strongly to the floor. The ferocity of the lashes would have made a normal man scream in agony, but the Drolid leader remained motionless, never so much as blinking his one good eye with each strike.

"There now, Guelf. Will that help you to remember?"

The soldier grunted his reply in an odd mixture of low gasps drawn from deep within his chest.

"Good, good," said the calloused voice. "I know you are not trying to upset me, and I'm glad. You know how I dislike becoming angry."

Guelf urgently mumbled in his primal tongue as he slid his foot off my leash. His paw-like hand wrapped itself about the chain and I braced for another brutal jerk. But my one-eyed captor remained kneeling with head bowed, awaiting permission to rise.

"What? I see nothing special before me."

Again, the Drolid leader anxiously grunted.

"You forget your place, Guelf, speaking to me in such a tone. Fortunately, I'm in a generous mood and will see what you have brought *before* I have you skinned. Very well, show me and be quick."

There was no hesitation in the soldier's actions. He jumped to his feet and pulled me upward with him. Pain flashed throughout my body as the iron collar dug once more into my throat. I closed my eyes and squeezed my hands into hard knotted balls to combat the suffering, but when I stood at full height and opened my eyes, my suffering became shock.

A marble dais stretched the width of the room and behind it stood twelve polished granite pillars, each at least fifteen feet apart and so huge in girth four men with hands clasped together could barely encircle one. Steps led upward to the dais, and upon them, four chained, black leopards lay intently watching me as if I were to be their next meal. They were large, magnificently muscled animals, and their coats shimmered in the light cast from hundreds of white candles and the fires in braziers to both sides of the dais.

Behind the great cats were six women stretched felinely along the top step, nude except for the glittering jewelry they wore. Their smooth, unblemished skins were the fine hues of sunlight streaming through honey, and the raven black hair that sensually draped their faces and cascaded onto their shoulders, shimmered with tints of blue. Prone, they held their erotic poses, staring at me through cat-like eyes with the same hunger as the leopards lying before them. Even in my pathetic state of captivity I could not help but be awestruck by their bodies. Never had I seen such women except in the fantasy artworks of Frank Frazetta who painted warrior-like temptresses clinging to the legs and arms of barbarians—women who appeared as natural with a sword in their hand as they did writhing with backs arched upon silken sheets.

Two men, one black as a moonless night and head shaven, the other with a thick mane of hair and skin as dark as freshly tanned leather, both stood splayed-footed to each side of their ruler's mammoth throne on the dais. Their hands rested on the hilts of long, wide-bladed swords slung from their hips, and they peered at me through narrowed eyes. Gold bands wrapped their necks, biceps, and wrists, while loincloths barely concealed their genitals. They were as tall and muscled as me, and differed greatly from the mutant Drolids.

I had lifted weights for years to mold my body, but their rippling muscles appeared to have been chiseled from grueling years of slavery. From their sadistic expressions I felt sure they had been born under the lash of a ruthless taskmaster's whip. These were men who looked as if they had never known mercy and would give none in return.

At the black's sandaled feet laid a curled whip, freshly wet with blood. I recalled Guelf's lashing and wondered if this mastodon had administered the punishment. If he had, then the one-eyed leader surely received a beating that would have immediately killed a normal man.

My mind became a storm driven sea of madness. I told myself none of this could be true. I told myself it was all a nightmare in which I had been hurled back into ancient times and would soon awaken back in my prison cell. But how could I deny the living proofs before me! The men, the women, the animals were there before me. No, I had not gone mad yet.

But, I reached the brink of insanity when my gaze fell on the cloaked ruler seated upon the massive throne.

At first glance I thought of a monstrous, demonic genie that had escaped from its lamp. The longer I gazed at him the more I wondered what man-like reptilian abhorrence he truly was.

He sat upright and motionless with long fingers curled about the armrests of his throne as if posed for an artist to paint him. A fine crimson cloak with swaths of red and silver from the room's light draped his torso so only his ghastly head, powerful hands, and thick muscled legs were visible.

I could only stare in astonishment. A faint shade of emerald green blended with the grayish tone of his skin to present a creature as none I had ever seen. When at last he moved his head, his color changed like a chameleon. His ears were large and rose in points to extend outward like the horns of a bull. Across his forehead were deep furrowed lines which joined and curved downward to a wide flattened nose with nostrils flaring in time to his breath. The skin atop his slick head was stretched so tight I could see every indentation of the skull. At the rear of his head swung a tail of black hair, bound with golden rings. The rings formed a long stem, and at its end, a wild tuft fanned outward. His lips, thick and swollen, slowly parted to show sharp teeth no different from the leopards' upon the steps.

My gaze raced over his alien features and abruptly halted as I looked into his marbled eyes. They held a merciless stare and silently spoke of the purest evil I will ever know. Their outlines drew toward his temples in exaggerated Oriental fashion and it was not until then I realized he had no eyebrows. Possibly this enhanced his evil countenance, but I could feel his malignant gaze reach into me and clutch my soul in its black talons.

Dumbfounded, I stupidly stepped forward as if a closer look would clear the hallucinations from my mind. Guelf harshly jerked my leash and yanked me back. I grabbed for the collar and the great cats instantly sprang to the ends of their chains, claws slicing the air to reach me, their screams filling my ears. A rippling effect flowed the length of the dais as the naked vixens rose onto hands and knees, lips curled, hissing like angered house cats. In their flared eyes shined the same hunger for my flesh.

The ruler stood, gaze sweeping the women and animals. He never spoke nor raised a finger, yet the leopards cowered at his stare and the enchantresses submissively slunk back onto the step. As silence enveloped the great hall, he raised his mighty arms and let the crimson cloak slide from his massive body.

Surely, I thought, *nothing is left to stun my mind*. But I was wrong.

As the cloak cascaded to his feet, I stared at a naked, man-like anatomy towering at least seven feet in height. He was muscled with what appeared to be the strength of ten Spanish fighting bulls, and the veins beneath his taut skin were like steel chords. The definition of his body was so profound that each muscle moved against the next like colliding blocks of granite. From between his legs swung a battering ram that when rigid I believed could split a woman in two with a single thrust. But as the last shreds of reason and sanity escaped me, a tail longer and equal to the girth of my arm, slowly whipped into view from behind the creature.

"Blue eyes, Guelf? Where did you find such a specimen?" he asked, as intrigued with my eyes as I was by his leviathan appearance. Without waiting for the Drolid to reply, he nodded in a scholarly manner and gleefully said, "You've done well for one who has the intelligence of a rock."

The one-eyed commander grunted excitedly. He bowed then rose to his feet, every crooked black-streaked tooth in his mouth bared to the world in joy.

"As your reward, I shall allow you to retain your sully skin another day," the creature said, stepping to the edge of the dais. Although he spoke to the Drolid, his attention fully rested upon me. His tail incessantly flailed the air in reptilian fashion.

"Wash him," he stated in an aloof voice, returning to the throne.

Guelf viciously jerked my chain and dropped me to my knees. I held fast to the collar, clenching my teeth against the bolts of pain shooting through my legs. The captain stood with the chain wrapped about his hand, holding it taut to keep me unbalanced. Soldiers splashed me with buckets of water until I thought I would drown. At least a dozen naked Indian women, some mere children, others wrinkled, aged, and frail, rushed forward to scrub my body and wash my hair. They kept their eyes downcast and wore the defeated expressions of people who had come to accept cruelty as a way of life. But when I caught the fleeting gaze of one of the children, I observed a dead, hollow stare in her eyes.

Although I suffered from my collar and the harsh impact of when first thrown to the stone floor, the Indians' zombie-like motions made me curious as to the tortures they had endured at the hands of the fiendish ruler. They scrubbed until I believed my skin would surely be scraped from me. Without giving the women a chance to move aside, the soldiers threw more buckets of water onto me.

I choked and gasped, coughed and spit, yet the deluge never slowed until Guelf yanked me to my feet and gutturally grunted. By the time my eyes cleared and I could freely breathe again, the women were gone. My skin held a pinkish tint from their rough cloths and brushes, and I smelled strongly of orchids. Only Guelf remained by me and we stood awaiting the ruler's pleasure.

The creature sat leaning on the armrest of his immense throne, peering at me through mere slits as he slowly stroked his chin. His eyes suddenly widened as if he were struck with a novel idea, and his lips curled until his pearl white teeth were clearly visible. One of the vixens at his feet raised herself onto an arm, resting her weight on a hand. She slid to him and twisted until her breasts brushed his leg. As her fingers glided over his skin, she wantonly gazed at me, her face and magnificent body enticing my mind. The ruler reached out and stroked her head as a huntsman pets his beloved hound.

"It has been many a year since I last looked upon a blue-eyed earthling," the creature said, appearing to be calmed by the woman's touch. "Have you come to kill me as the others have tried?"

Earthling? My mind raced and thoughts stumbled over each other. *My God,* I thought, *what is this creature that rules as if he were a king? And who are the others he speaks of?*

The vixen's hand slid over his thigh like an anaconda slithering toward its prey. She hungrily smiled at finding the object of her search. No sooner had her fingers begun to stroke his member than he snarled like a furious jungle cat and a vile hiss escaped him. Her face whipped upward as he clamped onto her raven black hair and pulled until her back arched and breasts rose into the air. I expected to hear her bones crack at any second, but with a wave of his hand he sent her careening across the dais. When at last she came to a halt, she crawled away uninjured, as if such an act were commonplace.

"Your species never ceases to amaze me with your love for primitive religious cultures," he said, wrath subsiding as he focused his attention on me again.

"Why do you always cry out to God whenever you are frightened?" He chuckled rebukingly and rose from his throne, taking a defiant stance as he swung his arms open wide. "Well, look, earthling. Look upon a true creator. It was I, Moloc, who gave your species all of those storybook tales."

His laughter boomed across the cavernous room as he shook his head slowly.

"The Bible, the Koran, the Tora! Bah! A concoction of ramblings I found amusing—but you pathetic creatures exist best when you have good and evil on which to blame your failures." He laughed again, only this time its sinister tone held no hint of humor. "Your superstitious natures are so primitive."

My mind was engaged in a monumental struggle to combat the madness besieging me. He had read my mind as if it were an open book then boasted of authoring the Bible for his own perverse whims. But he had called himself Moloc, and suddenly I realized this *thing* in a time-locked barbarous realm was what Zeek and I had come to destroy.

Moloc eased back onto his throne, never removing his eerie gaze from me. His eyes narrowed, studying me—or reading my mind.

"Have you lost your tongue, earthling? Yes, I know your thoughts when it suits me, but I prefer the spoken word. Look about you. You see I have few to talk to." Disgusted, he gestured to Guelf and the feline-like vixens sprawled along the floor. "Dumb brutes and nymphs that only breed more of the same."

"Where is my friend, the man captured with me?" I asked, coming to grips with the insanity I was embroiled in.

The ruler curiously looked to Guelf, and the Drolid leader grunted in a low, almost apologetic manner. Moloc wearily shook his head.

"I'm afraid your friend—Zeek, I believe you called him—was not as fortunate to survive as you. It seems Guelf remembered him from a previous hunt and was still quite upset at having lost him after an extensive chase."

Motioning to the lump-muscled Drolid, Moloc leaned forward in his throne as he looked at me. "Prisoners who exhibit high degrees of intelligence are to be brought to me. My commander took it upon himself to torture Zeek without my permission."

There was such finality in the reptilian-king's voice I could only hope Zeek's life had ended swiftly. But again, I was disturbed. Moloc had read my mind, drawing Zeek's name from me without a hint of effort.

Guelf shifted his stance and released his hold on my chain. The weight of the falling leash tugged slightly on my neck and I looked at the soldier. His mouth was agape, slobbery tongue slowly painting his lips. I observed fear spread across his grotesque face. His eye rapidly blinked and he stumbled back several steps, never removing his gaze from the dais. When I turned to Moloc, he had risen and stood glaring at the commander. It was then I recalled how coldly he had said Guelf tortured Zeek without permission.

The four great cats focused solely on Guelf, their ears flattening against the backs of their skulls. They were aroused by Moloc's nearness as if it signaled some coming threat.

The barbarians beside the throne strode past Moloc and unleashed the leopards. I slid a hand about the chain hanging by my leg, ready to wield it to defend myself. Each great cat was superbly muscled and their claws appeared as big and sharp as sickles. Their yellow eyes narrowed as folds of black fur drew back to display gleaming white fangs. I had often wondered through the years how my life would end. Yet, being ripped and shredded had never entered my mind until now.

Atop the dais, the vixens grew as inflamed as the leopards, anxious for a kill, eager to partake in the blood-letting. They squirmed on the steps, flooded with anticipation.

Guelf's pleading grunts fell upon deaf ears for there was no one present who cared about his fate. He nervously glanced about the cavernous room then spun toward the door.

Savage, ear-piercing screams erupted from the leopards as they catapulted from the steps. I took a death grip on my leash and fought the petrifying fear rising from within my stomach. My knuckles drew white as wind-driven snow and my feet were rooted like oak trees to the stone floor. I was determined not to die without a fight. But the leopards were faster than I thought. They leaped so closely past me that I felt their hot breaths upon my face and their fur brushed my arms. I was stunned by their speed and appalled at how helpless I would have been against their onslaught.

Guelf's muscle lumped body held his flight to a clumsy, waddling run, and the great cats caught him in three powerful leaps. His agonizing screams drowned out their feral cries, and in a wildly thrashing pile of legs, arms, and slashing paws, the Drolid and the leopards crashed to the floor.

I have caused many a man's death and witnessed the murders of more than I care to recall, but never have I seen so horrible a spectacle as Guelf's death. Crimson streaks shot like fountain streams into the air. Wide, pinkish sprays rose and fell over the fighting mass. Claws raked the Drolid's body, slicing him open with each stroke. Black fur turned to a glistening ruby, and white fangs became dripping red. The great cats tore chunks of flesh from the bellowing commander and in their feeding frenzy fought among themselves for the meat. At last, Guelf's anguished voice was silenced and his struggle ended as a fierce leopard severed the one-eyed head from its lumpy shoulder.

Moloc watched impassively as his pets devoured the Drolid. I gazed at him, curious what my own fate was to be, all the while listening to the snarls and slurps of the leopards. He gestured to the blood-smeared cats and the black warrior chained and led them from the room. The hollow-eyed women and girls who had bathed me entered to remove Guelf's ravaged remains. Once the stone floor was scrubbed, they left on silent feet, their gazes downcast as if afraid to draw attention to themselves.

Moloc walked down the steps, scrutinizing my body with renewed interest. Halting before me, he stared into my blue eyes, towering over me by at least a foot. Compared to his massive build, I felt tiny and weak. Reaching out, he took the leash from my hand and pulled it taut, yet never with enough strength to take me off balance.

"You will serve me well," he said, letting his gaze roam over my shoulders and arms. "With you I can breed the traits I have long desired to have in my stock." His fingers unfolded and let the heavy chain fall onto me.

I braced against its impact and struggled to remain still. What he was proposing, using me as a stallion to his mares, numbed my mind. The thought of being treated like an animal suddenly infuriated me.

"And if I don't *serve* you?" I asked, finding strength in my anger.

The reptilian-king's sedate expression never changed as he reached out and took a firm hold on both sides of my collar. Muscles rippled in his arms. I heard a metallic *crack*, and without feeling it break, realized he had torn the iron collar apart.

Moloc held the broken halves for me to see then cast them into the air with a flick of his wrists. Their *clank* and *clatter* as they bounced along the floor reverberated through the room.

"Only the dead do not do as I want," he answered bluntly.

He returned to his throne, pausing on the steps to scan the women at his feet. His tail curled and slowly swung as if he were in deep thought, then he continued his walk.

"You show great promise—" The creature abruptly drew silent and turned to face me as he lowered himself onto the throne. "What is your name? You must have one."

"Alvarez."

Moloc rubbed his chin and briefly glanced at the high ceiling. "I may change it later, but for now, it suits me," he stated, relaxing in the chair. He let his strong hands dangle over the ends of the armrest and lifted a finger. Responding to his gesture, one of the alluring women along the steps rose onto hands and knees and moved to him with feline grace. Her breasts, jeweled belt, and necklaces all swung freely beneath her in a gentle rocking motion. She settled into an erotic pose by his leg and caressed his green tinted skin, looking at me with a seductress' gaze. He laid his hand upon her head and absent mindedly stroked her hair as if enjoying its soft texture.

"Do not think of defying me. Pharaohs, emperors, and monarchs through the ages brazenly tried after I allowed them to rule. They grew pompous and disobedient, and I was forced to teach each of them harsh lessons," Moloc said, truth carrying cruelly in his voice. He canted his head and stared. "You puzzle me. You ask no questions and although fear invades you, I sense an aggressive nature equal to my leopards. Should I kill you now, Alvarez? Save myself the trouble of doing so later?"

He shook his head and studied me as a sculptor gazes at a granite block and sees its vast potential. "No, I think not."

Through the ages? My God, how old is he? No, what is he? I asked myself. My thoughts were so jumbled, lost in a fog of confusion that I spoke with the innocence of a child. "Are you the devil?"

The creature tossed his hideous head back, heartily laughing at my candor. His deep laughter boomed through the air, magnified by the cavernous room. I was about to cover my ears against the deafening bombardment when the sound of his voice trailed to silence and he leaned forward in his throne. Moloc shoved the temptress away and his gaze grew as cold as an Arctic blast.

"When my race exiled me to this planet, your species were still cowering in caves and hurling rocks. This was to be my prison, but I made it a kingdom." He smashed his iron-like chest with a knotted fist, marbled eyes glowing with fury. "I bred them in experiments until they could walk erect and speak. I gave them knowledge and guided their progress as I desired. I needed amusements and your species provided them."

Easing deeper into his throne, Moloc glanced at the floor, his gaze filled with loathing. "But your species multiplied faster than intended and developed minds of their own. I discovered your innate love for brutality and honed it to perfection." He raised his head to stare at me. "I set my creations to war, nation against nation, race against race, filling their rulers' heads with the desire to attack and conquer, to decimate and vanquish their foes without mercy. Over the centuries, your race has committed their bloodiest acts of genocide for me when they carried religious prejudices as their edicts of righteousness."

He mockingly laughed and shook his head with a cruel glee. "You disappoint me, Alvarez. Must it be spelled out for you to comprehend? If I assisted so many mindless fools in the creation of your religions, and made your world as ruthless as it is today, haven't you come to the realization of who I truly am?"

I stood baffled by his boasting, too mentally spent to make sense of his conceited riddle. But as a morning mist slowly rises to give sight to the land it shrouds, the reptilian-king's name began to replay itself, growing louder until it rumbled in my head like the coming of a volcano's eruption.

Molech—Moloch—Moloc! An ancient name for the demon believed to be the Prince of Hell. I recalled it from something I had read once.

My eyes flared and mouth shot agape. I felt like a fool. His arrogance should have alerted me to his egotistical conceptions. All along, I had been standing before the very devil himself, the single model for evil through the ages, and was too blind to see. I was too captivated by his appearance and savagery to Guelf to hear what he had said.

A maelstrom of conflicting thoughts swirled within me and I reeled from my internal battle to set everything into balance. All I had been taught as a child and learned through adulthood was a twisted mind's fabrications. This *thing* before me had played mankind as if it were a puppet on a string. *He alone had set the world, set civilizations, upon the path they followed through centuries, providing only the knowledge needed to progress to the next level he wished man to achieve.*

Moloc nodded slightly and his mouth formed a heartless grin.

"Excellent, Alvarez. You haven't disappointed me. You must be well read. I was afraid you would turn out to be another such muscled idiot as those who surround me." He leaned forward on the throne, gazing at me with renewed life in his marbled eyes. His voice lowered and held a malevolent tone. "No, you have a mind and weigh your thoughts. That's good—good. I want that! You may well be what I have searched for so long."

In my delusion I forgot the creature-king could read my mind. Thoughts of escape would have to be masked, hidden behind a facade of submission. Flight now would serve no purpose. I did not have enough knowledge of Moloc's palace to evade the Drolids. I realized at that moment only through keeping my wits would I ever see the outside world again.

Chapter Nineteen

Moloc settled back in his throne and stared at me in silence for several minutes. At last he stood and walked down the steps toward me. His bodyguards followed, yet remained back several paces.

The women on the dais rose onto their hands and knees, their gazes focused on me with animalistic hunger. Their beauty was deceiving and I considered them to be as dangerous in their own right as the leopards.

"Choose one if you wish," Moloc said, nonchalantly waving an arm toward the cat-like women. "If none suit you, there are more. They are mute though, so it will do you no good to befriend one in hopes of gaining information."

The creature-king grinned in a manner which sent a chill racing up my spine.

Did he already know my plan? Was it futile now to pretend to submit to him? The questions rose within me. The closer Moloc drew the more tense my body became. Yet all he did was slowly walk around me as if inspecting me for flaws.

"Matu," Moloc said softly from behind me.

The word had barely left his mouth when the dark-skinned, Indian bodyguard lunged at me with sword drawn.

Instinctive reflex made me turn sufficiently to allow the gleaming blade to miss my chest. I glanced at the man's eyes and in that instant knew he wanted my death. As his weight carried him forward, I stepped into him, caught his sword-hand and deftly twisted as I dropped to my knees. The movement sent him airborne over me. When he crashed into the stone floor, I harshly twisted his hand and locked his arm into such a position as to keep him pinned face-down. I glanced about me for his sword but did not see it, then remembered the second bodyguard.

"Release him." It was Moloc's cold voice. He stood staring at me.

I turned my head and saw his black bodyguard holding the Indian's sword at the ready, awaiting the command to attack.

My grip loosened on the Indian's hand and his arm fell to the floor.

"Watch and learn," the creature-king said. His tone held a ring of warning to me.

The Amazon Indian was rising to his feet when Moloc moved a long finger in his direction. Without hesitation, the black bodyguard drove the sword to the hilt through his former companion. There were a few seconds of gasping and struggling, but the blade pierced vital organs and the Indian's end came quickly.

"Do you see, Alvarez? I do not accept failure. Matu failed me when I ordered him to run you through. Such an offense carries swift punishment in my realm." Moloc casually glanced at the dead bodyguard and walked to his throne, talking without ever glancing back at me. His voice echoed in the cavernous room.

"I needed to know if you held any combative skills. A cut or two would have done you no harm and I intended to halt the attack before he killed you."

Moloc walked up the steps and sat on his throne. The black bodyguard moved to his side and became motionless, staring at me with a face as stolid as his ruler.

The barbarous contest was for Moloc's pleasure, and the guard's execution, my lesson that life and death were of little importance in this land.

"It's true," the creature said, nodding to me before he drank from a golden chalice. The drink, whatever it was, dribbled down both sides of his chin as he raised the cup on end. He tossed the chalice to the floor and wiped his mouth clean with his cloak. "Life and death are trivial matters. It is only the butchery which lies between them that intrigues me."

Anger swept through me when I realized he had again read my mind. *How would I make my way to freedom if he knows my every thought?*

"The Roman era, when I allowed conceited fools to rule and proclaim themselves gods, held great interest for me. I simply planted the seeds of atrocity and perversion and the emperors nourished them." Moloc closed his eyes as if relishing joyous memories in his life.

Confusion must have shown on my face because when he looked at me, he continued his boasting.

"Surely you've read about the great circuses? The gladiatorial games? To honor me for allowing him to rule as emperor, Trajan staged a spectacular circus lasting one-hundred twenty-three days." Moloc's eyes widened with excitement as savage images flowed through his head. "Over five thousand humans and eleven thousand animals were slaughtered in contests against each other. It was a glorious sight to behold and I shall never forget it! Yes, your species is a murderous lot. Even though the ground had become a mud pit from the blood of the dying and dead, the forty-five thousand spectators wanted more. They actually cried out and pleaded with Trajan for it not to end."

Nausea consumed me. I fought back the bile taste rising into my mouth.

"Now," Moloc said, his voice growing calm. "You will not fail me." The creature swung a hand toward the vixens along the dais. "Select what you want to breed. Eventually you will mount them all, as well as some of my slaves from the surrounding tribes. If you sire the right bloodline, in time I may grow generous and provide some manner of reward. But if no worthy offspring are born from your loins—well, you know how I feel about failure." He sighed deeply and looked at me with indifference.

I stood quietly, veiling my true thoughts with rambling mental images. The creature-king's head tilted to one side, then the other, and his eyes narrowed. As I watched his curiosity grow, I realized he had difficulty reading my jumbled thoughts.

"May I have a few days to replenish my strength? The past weeks have taken their toll on me and I need food and rest." I glanced at the sex-starved glow in the women's eyes then forced a grin as I looked at Moloc. "If I am to satisfy them, I may need all my strength."

Amazon Moon

There was no need to lie. My body had undergone much abuse from the Drolids. I wanted time alone to think, and too, I was about to learn if my veiled truths could conceal my inner thoughts.

Moloc grinned and as he did, an odd mixture of hiss and growl poured from him. Across the dais, the nymphs smiled and slowly rocked on their hands and knees. At first I wondered if the creature was angry, then I realized he was pleased and the nymphs were merely reacting to his delight.

There were a thousand unanswered questions in my mind. *How old was Moloc? Why didn't he age? Had he truly changed history to be as he wanted? Where was my sister Melinda? How could Moloc be killed?*

"Food will be brought and you may have a day of rest. Obey me and your years here will be as other men have only dreamed of."

Moloc slowly leaned forward, face growing somber as he stared at me. "Always remember though, better men than you have tried to play me a fool. Displease me and your life ends."

The creature-king waved his hand and Drolids moved to my sides and behind me. A heavily scarred soldier grunted lightly and pulled at my arm to lead me away.

Moloc turned his attention from me and gently laid a paw-like hand atop the raven hair of a nearby vixen. She seemingly purred at his touch and rubbed herself against him as if she were a house cat.

As the creature-king sat relaxed and silent on his throne, he truly appeared to be evil personified. It was then, with torches and braziers casting elusive shadows over him, I realized I had seen him before—in demonic portrayals of the artworks of ancient civilizations. His every feature had been drawn through the ages in texts to warn of his malevolence. The Sumerian writings, the Mayan carvings, Hindu manuscripts telling of the serpent from the gods; all had described him, and yet modern man scoffed at the pointed ears and curled tail in the books and paintings, calling them the exaggerations of superstitious, uneducated people. Yes, piece by piece, all Moloc said was fitting together.

The scar-faced soldier pulled my arm and grunted, breaking my stupor. Surrounded by lump-muscled, foul smelling Drolids, I started toward the massive wooden doors leading out of the great hall.

As I was about to walk through them, Moloc's heartless voice echoed through the air.

"Alvarez."

I stopped and turned with a sense of dread.

"Your sister is dead."

It took all my strength to stand still and not react to the pain which stabbed my heart.

"I did not kill her," Moloc stated complacently. "She died by her own hands."

The agony within me intensified. I squeezed my hands into knotted balls and felt my arms shake.

Moloc's lips parted in a piecemeal smile and his white fangs appeared. He shrugged his shoulders and glanced at the nymph by his leg. "I suppose she could not live with her shame after a night of sport with my soldiers. You humans are strange about such things."

Rage flooded me. The need for revenge blinded me. I had intended to bide my time and find the right moment to kill him, but his taunting changed that. Now, I wanted to hold his head high into the air and watch his blood flow across the stone floor.

Breaking from my escort of soldiers, I raced toward him. A dozen Drolids fell upon me and beat me with their hammer-like fists until a black abyss of unconsciousness began to sweep over me.

All I remember as the Drolids dragged me away was the sound of the horrid creature's laughter booming throughout the great hall.

★ ★ ★ ★

I do not know how long I was unconscious or the number of beatings I received from the soldiers. They left me heavily bruised and my eyes were almost swollen closed. The slightest movement shot streaks of pain throughout my body, but no bones were broken. My good fortune must have come from Moloc not wanting his prized stallion permanently injured, and thus ordering the Drolids merely to show me the cost of disobedience.

When the swelling passed and my vision cleared, I found myself locked in a dismal stone cell with iron bars along the hall's wall. Chains shackled my wrists and legs, but with short steps I could walk about my new home. A barred window allowed me to look out over open fields and huts I believed were the houses for Moloc's Indian slaves. For the first few weeks of captivity I could do nothing more than nurse my injuries, but as my health improved, thoughts of escape returned.

Daylight coming through the window lit my cell, but at night, every inch was blanketed in darkness. Three rats scurried past me at all hours, unafraid of my presence. Often they would sit upright and watch as I exercised. As much as I dislike the repulsive creatures, I grew to accept their company and talked to them to avoid growing mad in my imprisonment.

Little breeze passed through the window, and what did merely made my cell more humid and stifling. The walls constantly held a fine sheen of moisture, and in some areas, blackish mildew had formed. A stench permeated the cell, yet I soon found myself becoming accustomed to it.

Good food and clean water were always brought and such luxuries silently spoke of my value to Moloc. If I were to break and submit to his will, he wanted me in fair health rather than a state of starvation.

For the first month of my imprisonment the only person with whom I had contact with was a scar-faced Drolid who acted as my jailer. He brought food each day at noon and waited by the cell door, grunting until I looked at the plate on the floor. After being assured I knew the food was there, he left.

Such an act infuriated me and one day I refused to glance at my meal, feigning ignorance of his grunts. Within a week, the lump-muscled beast became so frustrated with my act of stupidity he passed my plate through the bars to me directly, rather than slide it into my cell on the floor. If I was in fair humor at mealtime, I would test my jailer to see how much he understood and to what extent I could plan my flight.

"Thank you, Scar Face," I said, nodding to him as I slowly took the plate in hand. "Tell me, are your mother and father as butt ugly as you?"

The brute canted his head and grunted. His brown eyes intently watched me, yet I could tell he had no concept of what had been said.

He childishly swung his arms, sniffed the air, and looked about my cell.

Smiling, I concentrated on a single thought, curious whether he could read my mind as Moloc did. But Scar Face never glanced at my plate of food on which I had focused my thoughts.

"That's very good," I remarked with a coy grin. "You are as dumb as a tree stump." My gaze lowered to his hip and the three-foot-long sword hanging from his belt. A wide, warm smile spread across my lips as I spoke. "If I ever get my hands on it—"

An angry, guttural growl cut short my entertainment. Scar Face dropped to his knees, bald head bowed, and his entire body trembling.

"If your hands ever touch a sword, be prepared to lose them," Moloc stated, walking into view. He released another guttural sound and Scar Face fled down the hall.

A squad of Drolids and several of the women I had seen on the dais stood behind Moloc, staring at me. From their faces I could only imagine how a zoo animal feels as he waits to see what the crowd will do to him. My waiting did not last long. Moloc stepped close to the iron bars and grinned in his vile fashion. He motioned to the cell door and a Drolid rushed forward to unlock it. The hinges creaked sharply as the door swung open, yet no one moved to enter my cell.

The chains of my shackles rattled as I stepped back and braced myself, expecting some act of cruelty. I waited, but the creature-king merely gazed at me.

Moloc motioned to the women and their eyes sparkled with anticipation. "The Scaths beg me to give them time alone with you while my soldiers, on the other hand, ask for your death. Which should I choose, Alvarez?" He paused and gestured to the slimy stone walls. "Surely you do not wish to spend the remaining days of your life in here? You have the opportunity to live like a king. There is nothing you can ask for that would not be given! Agree to sire the new race I want and generations from now your name will be spoken with reverence."

Moloc's eyes flared and in them I observed the madness that absolute power brings. Looking at him, I wanted his death and the destruction of his kingdom—revenge for Melinda's death, and too late I remembered he knew my thoughts.

"I like your spirit, Alvarez, but too much can be detrimental to your health," he remarked and raised a bony finger.

In the hall, the Scath women frowned as the Drolids marched past them. The soldiers entered my cell, beat me more brutally than before, and each day for a week at some unexpected hour, they returned to dispense more havoc upon my body.

★ ★ ★ ★

Three months passed uneventfully. From my window I watched the naked Indian slaves work the fields, whether under a burning sun or in a torrential downpour. Most were women and children. Those men I did see walked with shoulders slumped, down-trodden, never raising their faces.

One afternoon as I napped on the cool stone floor, I awoke to children's terrified cries and women's screams. Climbing to the window I helplessly watched as a Drolid patrol brutally separated mothers from their offspring.

Mercy is unknown to Drolids. When a mother fought to save her child, she was cruelly struck down and left in the dirt to recover, if she ever did. Every soldier except for the patrol's leader had a child tucked under an arm. He stood alone, studying the captives as if to insure no child had been overlooked.

My blood ran hot, scalding me each time I saw a soldier bash a woman's face or furiously shake a child to quell its cries. The captives were innocent beings, undeserving of such ruthless treatment. Gripping the window's bars, I squeezed until my knuckles were white, wishing all the while I could break free to defend the Indians.

A young woman rushed from a gathering of slaves and ran to the leader. I could hear her pleas but did not understand her tribal language. Yet her weeping was a universal language, and I felt her agony at the soldiers stealing her child.

The Drolid leader dispassionately stared at her then with the back of his hand sent her careening into the dirt. She landed on her hands and knees, dazed, with blood dripping from her mouth.

"Hey! Hey!" I shouted, hoping to distract him as he slowly walked to her. I waved my hand, shook my chains, and yelled again. "Come here, you bastard! Try that on me!"

The heavily lumped leader halted at her and scanned the field, squinting against the bright sunlight. At last he saw my waving hand and paused to listen to my shouts. I believe he realized I was attempting to draw his attention away from her or possibly he wanted to show me how powerless I truly was in Moloc's land. Whatever was his reason, his next action made me sick to my stomach.

Stepping up behind the woman, he reached beneath his loin cloth. The bastard looked at me, bent his legs, and drove his hips into her. I closed my eyes and ground my teeth, unable to watch. But nothing could prevent her chilling scream from consuming my mind.

When courage finally returned, I looked out to the field once more. The woman lay motionless in the dirt, and the patrol walked away with frightened children clutched in their arms.

In the months which followed I witnessed many a cruel act in that field. It was a place where tears watered the crops more than the monsoon rains.

* * * *

On my prison wall each day I scratched a mark with my chains to track the length of my imprisonment. One day the realization came that almost a year had passed since I had first entered the Amazon jungle.

Through the months, the Drolids came and beat me with sticks or their balled fists. There was no pattern to the abuse and I can only suppose Moloc ordered them to do so merely to remind me of his rule.

Moloc himself came to my cell every few months to ask if I had changed my mind. I could anticipate his visits days in advance by the better treatment I received. But afterwards, if I still refused to be a stallion to his mares, I could also anticipate a visit from his soldiers.

Three times Moloc had me brought to his throne room, where I was forced to kneel before him for hours while we talked. On those occasions, whether from boredom or to coax me into a receptive state, he spoke at length about his time on our planet. He allowed me to ask questions and answered as if we were old friends sharing secrets.

"In past centuries I freely traveled by foot or ship as it pleased me, making myself known only to those I permitted to rule. If a peasant or farmer saw me, there was little to fear. They always ran babbling to others about the devil seen in the forest or near their home. Superstitious as everyone was, the tales only grew and no one dared to trail me," the creature-king boasted one particular afternoon.

"This century has become increasingly difficult for me to move about. Your species surprised me and advanced faster than I realized. Now, with the advent of better communications, if I were observed, such news would be spread world-wide within minutes—and I would have hordes of explorers in search of me. No, I have remained here in my kingdom for quite some time, venturing out into the world only when the need is great . . . or some pathetic ruler needs to be reminded of who is truly his superior."

"But, of all places, why remain here in the Amazon?"

Moloc shook his ugly head and glanced about the cavernous room. "The climate is close to my native planet and serves my health well. My aging process has virtually come to a halt because of your sun's effects upon my body. Why should I live elsewhere when my life is best sustained by this thick humidity?"

There were times when the thousand questions I had about him jumbled in my head and he laughed at my confusion. Yet it served to remind me he could read my thoughts unless I veiled them among unrelated images. The easiest way I discovered was to recall photographs from the many books I had read in prison. His ability to read my mind could then be defeated.

"I have always allowed only specific individuals, those with true controlling powers within every world government, to be aware of my presence. At times I supplied certain rulers with information and technology which gave them victory in battle with their neighbors." Moloc paused and stood to walk the length of the dais.

"I have played nation against nation as if they were all pawns in a chess game. Yet, your land continually seeks my end. Your country fears I will destroy it—and I may yet do so . . . ." He paused and gently laid a hand upon the head of a Scath woman pressed hard against his muscled leg.

From these talks I learned much about this creature king of the jungle, yet never enough to plan to destroy him and his precious lot of Drolids. When in a good mood Moloc waved his tail to and fro, but when he grew angry, it drew still. Somewhere within his stone palace supposedly were vaults of gold, tribute paid to him by countries about the globe. While we regarded gold as wealth, on his planet gold was used for more than I understood and was the reason for the alien exploration and mining of earth. He intended to buy his freedom and victoriously return home if his race ever returned again.

On one occasion he remarked how the vaults of Fort Knox in America were actually empty because of the tributes paid to him. Hearing this reminded me of a conspiracy theory I once read which detailed how no one was permitted to ever inspect the vaults because the gold had long ago been secretly removed.

In one talk though, only with fleeting reference to his Drolids' ransacking patrols, Moloc mentioned a cache of weapons his mutants had collected and stored near the gold. My ears perked up at the news, yet I knew to be cautious and not reveal my interest. The Drolids had at times come in contact with well-armed drug runners and guerilla factions crossing through Moloc's territory. Leaving no one alive and proud of their victories, the mutants carried the weapons and equipment to Moloc as prizes in hopes of gaining their ruler's favor.

There was a braggart's streak within him for he always wanted me to know how primitive earthlings were in comparison with his advanced race. Having been a mercenary in his own world and convicted for treasonous acts of some form, he had been brought to our planet to work until death in the mining of our resources. When the operations abruptly ceased due to the outbreak of interplanetary wars, he was abandoned along with other prisoners who soon died. From his manner of talk, I felt confident he had played a major role in their demise.

The ruins at Puma Punku in Bolivia and the 'Band of Holes' in the mountains of Peru were stated to be proof of their former mining operations on earth, yet we as humans were unable in our ignorance to comprehend the evidence left there. In Egypt, the pyramids were aligned with the Orion and Sirius constellations to assist his people in the entry of time portals for their travels across the universe. He spoke of thirteen crystal skulls hidden around the world. They had served as beacons during the time of mining operations, yet when placed together in a circle, they created a power far beyond our human comprehension and ability to harness.

The creature's stories went on until my mind reeled. I recalled having read accounts of archaeological expeditions at the locations he spoke of, and his stories paralleled many of the scientific conclusions explorers had drawn. But how could I accept his words as truth? If I did, it would mean that all I knew as real was merely a fabrication of a twisted mind. Yet how could I deny the reality of his presence, a creature from another world physically sitting before me?

Only upon one occasion, for whatever reason, he spoke of his early life. I was brought before him one afternoon and forced to kneel as usual. From his throne he solemnly stared at me, remaining silent for what seemed to be an hour, and only the slightest movement of his fingers on the armrest told me he was alive.

"I come from a warrior culture," he said in a whispering voice. "One which strongly retains a caste system. With the right bloodline there are few limitations in your life, yet with the wrong blood you were the lowest dregs of our society . . ."

I remained still, not wanting to interrupt him for fear he might stop. Everything I could learn about him might later prove valuable in my escape.

Moloc wearily let his gaze flow across the great hall then focused on me again. His mood was far different than I had ever seen before. Arrogance no longer carried in his voice.

"My youth has no memories worth recalling unless cruelties are of value. I have no knowledge as to who bore me because I was left in a street to die . . ." The creature slowly raised his hand and barely waved it through the air. ". . . And all because who either bore me or sired me was of the wrong blood."

A morose mood settled over him. He remained silent which left me confused as to why he had related such a tale.

"Now I'm a king . . . a king of mute whores, grunting idiots, and worthless slaves." He glanced about the hall and slowly shook his head as if discouraged by a deep thought.

Silence filled the hall as I waited for him to speak further, yet he only sat upon his great throne, staring out into the vast room, lost within himself.

"I have enough gold amassed to bargain my freedom and live better than ten 'true-bloods' on my planet. With my treasure and mercenary skills, I could lead an army and rule wherever pleased me in my world." Moloc flew into a rage, smashed a fist upon an armrest and slid forward in his throne. "But the fools haven't returned, and I doubt if they ever will!"

So, there is a dent in your armor, I thought, relishing his grief. *You're surrounded by hundreds of Scaths, Drolids, and Indian slaves, yet you feel as alone as I did in my prison solitary confinement. You want your own kind about you and realize you are a prisoner of your own making.*

I held my glee in check, knowing life may well hang in a fine balance if I next spoke wrong. *You controlled the fates of countless countries but have no control over your own fate. How ironic!*

I chose to remain silent and patiently wait for him to speak.

The great creature-king of the Amazon sat downcast upon his throne. An hour passed then his mood changed as if he realized he'd shown weakness, and as had been his nature, Moloc ended my time free of the cell by asking if I wished to live as king.

When I refused, he casually taunted me with details of the Drolids' night with my sister and the agony she surely had endured.

And the painful tale was always followed by an order to beat me.

★ ★ ★ ★

In the thirteenth month of my captivity on one late night, my cell door swung open. Scar Face entered and placed a torch in the wall holder, then removed my chains. There had been no cruelties toward me in the last month and I believed it was because I would soon be taken before the creature. But Moloc had other plans. After Scar Face took my chains away, he locked two Scath women in with me.

My physical health was good at the time, yet my mental state suffered greatly. While I struggled to keep my mind strong and focused, it had been continually weakened through Moloc's constant abuse and all I had been forced to witness. On the first night the Scath women were brought to my cell, I fought my bodily urge at their presence.

You must remember I had been a man alone, without the least act of kindness or love from another human, far too long. Their touch upon my skin was so soothing and pleasurable compared to the sufferings I had endured. The madness I was constantly adrift in weighed upon my mind and had unknowingly worn me down. Suddenly, being the recipient of such skills of passion as the Scath women possessed proved overwhelming to my soul.

They began by sitting near me. As the minutes passed, they gradually touched my hand. Within an hour their fingers were softly roaming my body, massaging tense muscles, and lightly gliding over my hair. Such gentle assaults broke my internal defenses and I involuntarily found myself yearning to be held, wanting some fragment of physical love in my lonely animal existence.

As the night passed I became lost in the oblivion of their arms and cared about nothing else. Excuses could be made and blame laid on my sexual hunger or I could say I was lulled into a hypnotic state, a prisoner to vixen tricks. But stating such would all be lies. I'm ashamed to say I had struck the lowest depths of solitude and bordered on a razor's edge of dark insanity. My soul needed their touch and physical acts to fill a great void within me.

No more can be said other than I drank from their well of passions like a man fresh out of the desert.

★ ★ ★ ★

There were more nights such as that in my thirteenth month of imprisonment. Moloc must have been pleased for he left my shackles off. I bathed regularly and better foods were brought. I was taken out of the cell and placed in a finely-furnished room with a soft bed, pillows, and silk sheets. In a stroke of magnificent deception I convinced him to allow me freedom for the sake of good health to walk about the palace. The privilege was granted because of my performances as his breeding stallion, yet he was not so foolish as to let me walk alone. I was always heavily escorted.

As said earlier, I am guilty of having a strong sex drive, and it served me well. Moloc constantly sent fresh Scaths to my quarters each night. I believe he wanted to insure I bred as many as possible in the event I suddenly stopped and refused to further be of service.

There were weeks when I refused anyone entry to my room. My body needed rest and time for the Scaths' fingernail rakes and bite marks on my body to heal. On those occasions Moloc anxiously appeared at my door to ask why I had turned the women away. My reasons made him laugh loudly and he left satisfied with my obedience to him. But I wisely used my time alone to plan an escape. I never intended to live my life out with a lizard-king.

★ ★ ★ ★

My Drolid guard had grown complacent. I smiled courteously when he brought my food or ushered my night's entertainment through the door, never raising alarm in his dumb mind. Sometimes, while engaged in a fervent sexual act, I would glance at the door and see it was not fully shut. Scar Face had grown to be a voyeur, but that pleased me. When I knew he was watching, I intentionally guided the vixens into different positions or ordered them to take pleasures with each other. After the Drolid's visual appetite was appeased, he often forgot the door was open and returned to his post down the hall.

On a full moon night after the Drolid patrols left for a raid and few were on the premises, I gave a performance with the Scaths that was sure to draw Scar Face's attention. As I suspected, at the sound of my overly loud groans and encouraging shouts, the door eased open several inches and remained so.

The thought of escape gave me renewed energy and I bred that night's women with animalistic vigor. I grew increasingly rougher as the hours passed, yet my actions only heightened the Scaths' passions. They were accustomed to far harsher strikes from Moloc, and mine were merely foreplay for them. When I no longer saw Scar Face peeking through the cracked open door and believed he had retired for the night, I set my plan into action.

I rose onto my knees on the bed and turned one of the Scath women so her face would be buried in a pillow with hips in the air. She understood and moved into position before me while I drew the other vixen close for a kiss. The timing had to be precise in order to avoid the slightest alarm.

Waiting until the first Scath's face was snuggled into the pillow, I caught her companion's head and snapped it as her lips neared mine. She fell onto the bed as I reached out, choked the other, and finished my handiwork. Assured of their deaths, I ran to the door and looked out. Scar Face sat on the floor, head nodding as he slept, slivers of drool hanging from his lips.

He awoke as I withdrew his sword, but the want of freedom filled my head and gave me the needed speed. Before he could move I bashed his head against the stone wall to stun the ignorant beast, and with a two-handed hold on the well-used weapon, I swung with all my might and split him open.

I paused to listen to the sounds of the night, enjoying the rapid beat of my heart. The accompanying anticipation of flight gorged my mind. *Freedom—Freedom.* The thought reverberated through my soul.

The palace was quiet, too quiet then came the light clap of sandals approaching. I searched for concealment, yet none was found. Running down the hall, I halted at a corner, chanced a quick glance, then slipped around it and pressed my back against the stone wall. The clap of the sandals grew louder, closer, and I waited for the moment to strike.

A frail, dark-skinned, slave woman walked past then startled at the sight of a nude man against the wall. Her eyes flared and she was about to scream, but I grabbed her and pressed a hand over her gaping mouth.

Time was precious. Drolids might turn a corner at any moment. Sweat trailed from my forehead and stung my eyes. I glanced to both ends of the hallways and returned my attention to the woman. Her trembling had slowed and I knew I must risk her screams. The pressure of my grip upon her mouth lessened then I stepped away.

"Shhhhh!" I touched a finger to my lips.

Her brow knitted. Gradually, her head began to nod.

It seemed an eternity before she understood my feeble sign language. I pointed to myself, made walking motions with my fingers, waved my arms toward each length of hallway and finally, hunched my shoulders in question while shaking my head. At last she reached out, touched my chest, and swung her hand in the manner of a bird taking flight.

"Yes—Yes." I nodded and smiled in relief.

Without hesitation she started back along the path from which she had come, all the while motioning for me to follow. At every corner she paused, glanced around it and continued onward.

At last we came to an adjacent hall and the Indian woman abruptly stopped. She looked down its length then anxiously nodded and pointed.

I leaned toward her, lightly kissed her forehead and whispered, "Thank you." She stood stunned a moment and I assumed she had not received a simple act of kindness in many years. A fragment of a smile formed on her lips as she waved a hand toward the hall.

Dull clumping sounds carried to my ears. She had heard it as well for her eyes flared and she looked in all directions. I grabbed her by the shoulders and gently pushed her away, motioning for her to flee. She didn't hesitate and broke into a fast walk, never looking back.

In the stone halls the least noise echoed and I knew the Drolids might be near or far. I chanced a look around the corner, saw no one and realized my only chance for escape had arrived.

All had gone better than expected. There were no further delays from this point on. My bare feet made little sound as I raced toward an exterior window facing the surrounding jungle. If caught, Moloc would surely have me killed or beaten so mercilessly that I would die. But I did not intend to be caught again. *Never again.*

Grunting chatter grew distinct and the scrapings of weapons against chain-mail became louder. Drolids were drawing closer. I expected guards to round a corner any moment and see me within a few steps of the window.

The night air was as humid and stifling as every other night of the past year, yet it smelled of sweet freedom and I grew intoxicated by its breeze. At the window I breathed deeply and dove through it into the dark night, hoping I wasn't plummeting to my death. Fortune favored me and the drop was no more than eight feet to the ground. I landed atop some type of plant with wide leaves that cushioned my fall and concealed me. Drolid grunts carried from the window above me as I lay still in the black shadows. A soldier's melon shaped head leaned out of the window then quickly swung left and right as he scanned the land. I watched him sniff the air then the head eased back into the hall and I raced across a moonlit field to the thick canopied jungle.

Freedom is a strange emotion. I call it so because of the exhilarating sensation it brings about in us when we first feel it. Our heads reel and our spirits soar as it rushes over us in waves of joy. This is not easily explained to someone who has never experienced captivity. You are momentarily invincible, and if not cautious, can be quickly led into harm's way.

At the jungle's edge I paused to listen to the night and bring my exultation under control. Nostrils flared, I sniffed the air for the stench of Drolids and was suddenly dumbstruck by the enticing scent which filled my nose. I realized it came from me. The Scaths had vigorously slid their sweat glistened bodies over mine in the heat of our lovemaking, and their perfumes had smeared onto me.

If I had kept running through the jungle in my anxiety to escape, I would have not realized the trail I was leaving for my pursuers. In Vietnam, our Recon teams never used colognes and after-shaves for that very reason. They soak into the skin and mingled with sweat, our odors would have forewarned the Viet Cong long before we wanted our presence known.

Pushing on, at the first water crossing I scrubbed with scoops of mud, rinsed myself then repeated my actions. When finished, I looked at my naked body. My light colored skin would shine like a beacon in the jungle, never allowing me to blend with the foliage. But after I had covered myself with mud and leaves, I was well camouflaged and renewed my flight.

With each step I found my senses heightening, and like a predator of the jungle, I grew fully aware of my surroundings. As Zeek had once told me, in Moloc's domain no birds sang nor were animals seen. I used that as a guide to tell me when I had reached the borders of the creature's domain.

By dawn I was miles from Moloc's palace and had found an adequate place to hide among fallen trees. I laid still and took a moment to rest, knowing better than to fully exhaust myself if I wanted to make good my escape. The sun rose and I watched the landscape come clearly into view. It was then that a distant clamorous roar swept the land.

I smiled inwardly at the sound of Moloc's fury and imagined the expression of his green alien face when told I had escaped. My elation was short-lived, though, because I also knew he would unleash his mutant horde to capture me.

Four days later as I crossed a gently flowing river, I heard sounds which had almost been forgotten in Moloc's land. Zeek had spoken the truth about the animals and birds of the rain forest being signs of safety. Now agitated birds flapped their wings as they perched on limbs, monkeys chattered, a parrot squawked, and not far away, a jaguar growled.

Standing on the river's bank, I listened to the music of the jungle. To this day I cannot explain what overcame me. Something broke deep within my soul, and like a child, I wept at the magnificent sounds of freedom ringing in my ears.

Chapter Twenty

At the same instant, fatigue and elation consumed me in such an odd blend I was left drained and numb. I felt hollow within and could only stand on the river's bank and stare at the clouds as they passed overhead. My stupor was broken by the rustling of leaves and sudden shouts of frantic women from the surrounding forest.

I tried to move and discovered exhaustion had taken control of my mind and body. Capture by the Drolids flashed before my eyes and I readied myself to die. I waited, expecting lumped masses of muscle to rush at me, but dark-skinned warriors with tattooed faces, streaked or painted deep red, broke through the jungle with spears, blowguns, and bows held aloft, each staring at me as if I were his worst enemy.

They halted and stood ready, yet never attacked.

Whether my laughter was born from freedom's joy or the sheer madness I had endured for months, I do not know. But I stood in the river bank's thick mud and spread my arms wide, laughing heartily in the realization they were not Drolids.

A gaunt, leathery skinned warrior stepped out from their ranks. He lowered his spear, and as he did, the line of warriors behind him gradually did so too. Across the bridge of his nose and onto his cheeks were the black-stained designs of a tattoo blurred by age. The lines ran down both sides of his throat and flowed in circular patterns over his chest. I took all this to be significant of his rank as the tribal leader. He stood like an ancient bronzed statue and his detached stare made me feel self-conscious. I glanced at my nude body and my elation of freedom became sadness at the sight.

My skin was mottled with mud and the filth of days on end living like a wild beast. There were deep cuts and welts over my chest, arms, and legs where branches had raked me. Leaves and grass were stuck to the mud, and must have made me look demonic to these forest people. I raised a hand to my hair and felt muddy, stiff cords where smooth texture had once been. My hair had long since grown past my shoulders and was a matted mass of twigs and muck. My beard was crusted and I itched from countless ant and other insect bites over my body.

Yes, I was a ghastly sight to the tribesmen, and the months of mental and physical abuse came crashing down upon me with the weight of a great mountain. Tears welled up in my eyes and against my will I began to weep. I was mentally breaking, something I had fought so long against. The cruelties of my years passed before me like storm driven clouds and I could not halt the self-pity flooding my mind. Although I towered over the men before me and my body appeared chiseled from rock, I suddenly felt helpless, weak and small compared to the tribesmen.

My legs crumpled and I sank to my knees, weeping silently from loneliness, heartache, and overwhelming mental anguish. Unless you have personally experienced such a breakdown, I cannot describe the desolation I felt there, kneeling in the muddy bank. My world simply shattered into a thousand pieces.

I looked back across the river to the jungle from which I had come from and wondered if all I had endured was mere madness conjured by my now insane mind. My strength diminished and I could no longer hold myself upright. As I turned to face the warriors again, my eyelids grew heavy. I struggled to keep them open. Fatigue won the battle, though. All I remembered next was falling forward into the mud, slipping into a black pit of sleep.

★ ★ ★ ★

Youthful giggles and laughter woke me. I opened my eyes to find that scores of smiling children, all stair-stepped in heights, had formed a circle about my open-sided hut. They watched me intently and often pressed their hands over their mouths to suppress giggles at my clumsiness. When my eyes focused and I grew more aware of my surroundings, I smiled at the wide-eyed girl child near me. The innocence of her face touched my heart, and I recalled the children carried from Moloc's fields by the Drolids. I never knew their fates, but neither did I want to. They could only have met a cruel end.

The tribal leader appeared; followed by what I assumed were his circle of councilmen. They squatted about me on the hut's floor and smoked strong tobacco as they talked. I understood nothing of their language and we communicated solely by hand gestures as if we were playing some form of a game.

The leader touched his chest and said, "*Tacoma*," several times.

In turn I replied, "Alvarez," and touched mine which evoked approving nods and deep grunts. Pleased with himself, Tacoma began an endless string of words which only left me confused. He pointed toward Moloc's domain and motioned to the river near the village. Whether he was referring to Moloc or merely was curious where I had come from, I do not know, but I remained apprehensive and could not rid myself of the fear that any moment I would be attacked and beaten.

The tribal chief lifted my arms and poked his finger into my biceps. He studied the hard balls of muscle that formed when I bent my arms then compared them to his own. His councilmen laughed and jokingly poked their arms. It was then I happened to glance over myself and realized that during my sleep the Indians had scrubbed the jungle filth from me. I touched my face and felt clean-shaven. I touched my long hair and at its soft feel delightedly plowed rows through it with my fingers. Tacoma nodded understandingly and watched my every move with interest.

Women brought food and began hand-feeding me. I felt starved and grabbed the wooden plate, shoveling the leafy food and bits of meat quickly into my mouth. An elderly woman slapped my fingers and shook her head as she swung a finger in front of my face. Tacoma laughed and spoke to his councilmen. Whatever he said must have been quite funny for everyone about the hut found great humor in it.

Since my escape I had survived on nothing but berries and fruits, and my stomach had shrunk. The Indians' meal set heavy on my stomach and I was forced to pause and let it settle. When I did,

Tacoma held a foul-smelling drink to my lips and gestured for me to swallow.

The odor was putrid. Once I started to drink, I knew better than to stop until the cup was empty. As I gulped it down, Tacoma and his council of warriors intently watched me. Everyone drew quiet and I wondered what was to come next. But I did not have long to wait for an answer.

My world spun and I grew nauseous. I crawled to the edge of the hut and retched until I dry heaved, then rolled onto my back and stared at the swirling thatched roof above me. The drink produced such dramatic effects. I doubt if I can fully recall all that occurred. A rainbow of colors exploded before me as tribal drums beat in my ears. Warriors with faces and bodies painted in elaborate designs and colors all danced with spears in circles about me. I felt myself rising into the air, floating above the mass of people who swayed by a bonfire. A dream-world engulfed me. Voices from the past whispered in my ear, while people I had known whisked before my eyes with lightning speed. Bit by bit I felt my soul emptying its sins, and in time I was awash in the most pleasant sensation of peace. When the river of dreams went dry, I fell into a deep sleep as I have never known to this day.

★ ★ ★ ★

I do not know how long I slept, but I awoke with the hunger of a dozen men. It was mid-afternoon and from my mat I watched the villagers go about their daily affairs without a glance in my direction. I rose on unsteady legs and made my way to the hut's steps. Children pointed and started toward me. Tacoma waved them away in a fatherly manner as he approached with a white man dressed in simple clothes. By the tattered Bible and small bag in the stranger's hands, I took him to be a man of the cloth, although I saw no collar or cross about his neck.

The chief nodded and spoke to me, yet I had no comprehension of his language and only nodded in response.

"Tacoma says he is glad to see the great warrior has returned from his *journey* and is well," the stranger said, removing his sweat-stained straw hat.

The sun made his gray hair shine and by the wrinkles of his hands and face, I guessed him to be at least seventy or more. He smiled and extended his hand. I looked at it and hesitated for a second, feeling awkward about the warmth in his voice and friendship.

"I am Otto Klaus, formerly of Dusseldorf, Germany, now a missionary to the indigenous tribes of the Peruvian-Brazilian border."

Klaus' smile was genuine and his voice carried such sincerity with its accent that I found myself grinning. I introduced myself and forced the apprehensive feelings from my mind.

"What journey is he talking about?"

The missionary chuckled and glanced at Tacoma. "It's the journey into the dreamland where your body may rest and heal its wounds. I've tried to tell my old friend the drink is dangerous, but he insists upon its usage. Horrible tasting, isn't it?"

I grinned and nodded. "You've tried it?"

"Once. The Indians use it to drive away evil spirits which make people sick. I had to drink it to be accepted by this village." Klaus opened his bag and dug through it a moment. "Here, these trousers should fit, unless you prefer to remain native."

I had been without clothes for so long I had forgotten my nudity. As I slipped the trousers on, the cloth felt strange against my skin. The trousers would have fit a heavier man far better, and hung baggy on me, but I happily wore them, a length of rope serving as a makeshift belt.

Tacoma motioned for us to join him in the shade of a tall tree. We sat in silence for a few minutes, enjoying the sight of the children at play, then Tacoma gestured toward Moloc's land and spoke at length with the missionary. There was an exchange of words between them and at last they turned to me for answers.

Again fear rose from deep within me, and it became difficult to speak of the creature-king. As briefly as possible, I explained about escorting Zeek into the jungle and looking for my sister Melinda. When I began to speak of Moloc and the Drolids, I observed a faint mask of disbelief on the missionary's face. Evidently he attributed the village peoples' deaths to the loggers, drug runners and guerrilla forces known to plunder and kill throughout the area. True, it did sound like a fantastic tale, but I had lived it, and did not exaggerate a word. Naturally, since Klaus was a man of the cloth, when I came to the parts about my nights of breeding Moloc's nymph Scaths, I passed over those quickly. Yet as I related the tales of my beatings and witnessing such cruelties to the Indians, I once more felt immense pain rising within me.

"You have had quite an adventure, Mr. Alvarez," said the missionary, his tone consoling yet implying the skepticism which I expected. "The jungle shows no pity to anyone and the trauma of seeing innocent people murdered will cause the mind to play tricks to ease its suffering."

Anger flashed within me. *You fool,* I thought, staring at the man. *You have no idea what horrors lie in that jungle!* But I gradually calmed and restrained the urge to grab his shoulders and shake him violently. The tale of Moloc's palace and the atrocities I had seen did sound like the ramblings of a lunatic. Even I, still to this day, have difficulty accepting what my own eyes had seen and the tortures my body had endured. If I have such doubts of my own sanity, then how was I to expect others who have never seen Moloc to accept my experiences with a reptilian alien. My anger subsided and I realized there was little to be gained by wasting further effort trying to convince this man of GOD—a god Moloc had fabricated for all of mankind to believe. Yes, the devil had done well to disguise himself.

Tacoma spoke to Klaus then patiently listened while the German translated all I had said. I watched the missionary's every expression and felt he was adding his own interpretation of my story.

When my gaze carried to Tacoma, his dark eyes stared intently at me with a piercing look. He seemed to understand my inner distress, and that there was more to the story than Klaus had explained. With an almost imperceptible nod to me he returned his attention to the missionary. They spoke again and Klaus smiled as if in approval at Tacoma's decision.

"As the *cacique*, chief of his tribe, Tacoma has ordered your adoption into the jaguar clan of his warriors. It is an honor few receive, Mr. Alvarez," said the missionary. He leaned slightly toward me and whispered. "Accept it, my friend. He must think highly of you.

Most white men are killed the moment they are discovered near his village."

Straightening my posture, I placed my right hand over my heart and bowed in a show of respect and gratitude to the solemn *cacique*. The chief accepted with a curt nod then rose and walked away.

Chapter Twenty-one

Klaus and I spent the next two days of his visit walking about the village, talking at leisure, him attempting to answer my endless barrage of questions.

"They are Matsés Indians, Mr. Alvarez. Some people also refer to them as the Mayoruna Indians," Klaus paused and slowly scanned the village. He spoke with sadness in his voice. "This is one of their few surviving groups here in the Amazon."

"Surviving from what? Wars with other tribes?"

The missionary grinned and shook his head as if amused by my lack of knowledge. He lifted his hat and wiped sweat from his wrinkled brow. Using it as a pointer, he motioned toward a passing group of warriors then repositioned the hat on his head.

"It seemed as if they were at war with everyone outside of their own village, especially with the Peruvian government. The Matsés had a long tradition of raiding Spanish and Portuguese speaking settlements for tools and women. The kidnapped women were integrated into their tribe and in the mid-1960's the government ordered them to stop the kidnappings. When the Matsés refused, the president of Peru directed his Air Force to bomb their communities with Napalm. Shortly after that, the Peruvian Army invaded and burned whatever remained."

"Their own president dropped Napalm on them?" I stood stunned.

"Yes, and as a former military man, you well know what Napalm does to the human body."

I could only nod in reply. The memories of its use in Vietnam will always remain vivid.

"No man fights harder than one fighting for his family. The Peruvian Army, with all their sophisticated automatic weapons, never believed they would be beaten by Indians with simple bows and arrows, and blowguns. But the Matsés put them in such retreat your American Marines were asked to fly in from Panama to assist in the evacuation. Not long after that the Matsés abandoned their settlements and fled deeper into the rainforest."

As he spoke, I glanced at the villagers, clothed only in loin cloths, walking about us. The warriors carried their bows and arrows, pausing at times to laugh and talk with their women and children. With the exception of jaguar necklaces, red painted faces and tattoos, the men did not particularly display a warrior's physique or military bearing. I learned a healthy respect for these gentle people who had gone into battle against a formally trained army and sent them running.

"Don't be fooled by the women, either," Klaus said, as if reading my mind. "They will often go hunting with their men and they know the jungle better than you know the back of your hand. The women spot the game and take part in the chase. They retrieve the hunters' arrows then kill the wounded animals with machetes or sticks, and carry the game home and prepare the meals."

A grandmotherly woman knelt and fed sticks into a nearby cooking fire. She looked at me for a moment, adjusted her necklace of seeds and frog bones then returned her attention to the preparation of a freshly killed monkey. Her face gave me no indication of what she might have been thinking.

"They are an odd lot. You would think a tribe which kidnaps women would be cruel to them, but the Matsés hold a deep respect for their women's knowledge and wisdom. If a man is caught abusing a woman, the *cacique* sentences him to a special 'ceremony.' It is my understanding that if you survive the ceremony, you will never abuse a woman again," Klaus said, his lips forming a crooked smile.

We continued our walk through the village and I smiled inwardly at the sight of several women surrounding a warrior. They eagerly served him food and poured water for him from a gourd into a small cup. The missionary swung a hand in their direction.

"As long as I have known Kana, his wives have treated him like a king. According to the other men, his prowess evidently extends to his sleeping mat."

"Wives?"

A broken smile appeared on the elderly missionary. "They are polygamists, Mr. Alvarez. I don't know if they are limited to a specific number, but every warrior has several wives." Klaus shook his head lightly in disdain. "Adultery is not uncommon here either. I have preached against it, but jealousy doesn't seem to be a factor among the men. With so many wives, the husbands choose to turn their heads."

I grinned and the missionary looked slightly confused.

"Kana doesn't have to worry about his wives on another man's sleeping mat," I commented.

"No, but the other men have to worry about their wives going to his," Klaus said as he began to laugh from the depths of his chest.

Hearing the missionary make such a joke made me laugh aloud as well, and for the first time in months, possibly years, I found myself enjoying the freedom to do so.

★ ★ ★ ★

A distant rumbling preceded the bombardment, then the explosions swept over the land with such swiftness that all blended into one. The black night became day in blinding, brilliant flashes and a deafening roar sounded in my ears and shook me to the very core of my soul. My stomach kept tightening and twisting into knots until I wanted to scream. My muscles refused to obey my command to move. Stern, Franklin, and Nakai stood over me in silence, staring with hollow caverns where their eyes had once been. Nakai offered a hand as if to help me rise from the ground, but I couldn't move and terror began to flow like fiery lava through my veins. I wanted to reach out, take his hand in mine and hold fast until the horror subsided, but my arms felt as if they were being held back. Nakai spoke but I could not understand him. Within the next instant his face faded and Tacoma's gradually appeared.

I blinked until my eyes focused on the chief. Was he real? Where had my team gone? I tried to look about me but felt so sluggish.

Nakai's hand before me was now the *cacique's*. Sweat stung my eyes and trailed down my face. My body was drenched as if I had been standing beneath a waterfall. I lurched forward but the hands which tightly gripped my arms halted further movement. Tacoma's shaman stood beside him whispering, and several men from his tribal council were about me, staring with eyes devoid of any detectable emotion.

My senses returned and, as they did, Tacoma motioned his warriors to release their hold on me and leave us. As they filed out the hut door and vanished into the night, I watched lightning streak across the sky. A thunderclap immediately followed and a horrific explosion of power shook the land. A torrential storm inundated the village with rain so fierce the night was consumed with a continuous dulled roar. And as I glanced at Tacoma, I gradually understood that I had been having a nightmare. In my thrashings upon the floor, someone must have grown fearful of evil spirits attempting to possess me and sent for him and the shaman.

Tacoma was wise though and must have realized I needed to combat the remaining demons within me because he had allowed my thrashing to continue until I awoke on my own.

Extending his hand once more, he helped me rise from my sleeping mat. I walked on unsteady legs from the hut and stood in the mud, letting the cold raindrops pelt my body and wash away my terror.

In the Amazon, rain storms often pass as swiftly as they arrive or may seem to remain without end. From the cell window in Moloc's palace, I had often watched the captive Indians laboring in the field, one moment with dust rising about them, and the next, bogged down to ankle-depth in mud. Never were they allowed to pause and seek shelter from the ferocity of the storms. Only those who wished their misery to end cast away their tools for the Drolids to see.

I've rarely mentioned the rain storms because they are so common an occurrence. After all, the Amazon is nothing but a rainforest and the rains come and go during certain seasons. But on this night, the rain which fell seemed different. Its cold penetrated my mind and washed every fiber of my soul. I was being cleansed, inch by inch, with each fierce shiver of my body. For some mistaken reason, I took this physical abuse of my body as punishment for the wrongs I had committed in life and believed I was deserving of every suffering I underwent. I know there is no logic in such thinking, but a person whose mind borders on the purest insanity finds all personal thoughts quite logical. If I had been devoutly religious, I would have believed God was purging my sins from me—but my faith has always been weak, and Moloc had crushed what little remaining hope I had for a merciful God to one day love me. The kind of person I had been in life never went to Heaven.

As the lightning dissipated and the rain slowed, I turned and saw Tacoma standing in the mud at the foot of the hut's steps. He had stood in the rain the same as I, but in a hand by his side, he held a bow with one arrow nocked, ready to be drawn and launched. We stared at one another, no words passing between us. His passionless gaze told me he had decided to allow me to live. He nodded and slowly removed the arrow from the bow. I watched as he walked to his hut, a part of me wishing he had chosen otherwise.

Chapter Twenty-two

"Who are you?"

My voice held the dregs of sleep as my eyes focused on the woman lying beside me. I eased upright and rested my weight on my left arm. She had come during the night, and I must admit to being embarrassed at not having heard her.

She rose and sat on the mat, stretching as if to ease stiffness from her body then combed her long hair with fingers to straighten it.

"I am Kache," she said in Spanish. Her gaze held mine with bland emotion as if merely awaiting my next question.

There is a homely appearance to most Matsés tribal women, one which does not necessarily make them unpleasant, but simply plain to the viewer's eye. Their noses are a bit wider than normal and their Indian ancestry gives their overall facial features a passive nature. While all have black hair, although not the rich, raven black of Oriental women I've known, several of the Indian women have light streaks of brown mixed in that I took to be the genetic traces of women kidnapped from other tribes or settlements. But their true beauty lies in the purity of their souls which is somehow reflected in their faces, and it was this which made me understand why the Matsés warriors treated their women with respect and admiration.

Against my will, my gaze traveled over her smooth, athletic body while my mind struggled to understand why she had been sleeping beside me. Her eyes held a tint of brown different than the other women I had seen in the village, and faint brunette streaks painted her hair. She was mature, yet age is difficult to judge in women of the rainforest unless they are quite old. Small, firm breasts rose and fell gently with the rhythm of her breathing and I quickly looked away. The last thing I needed at the moment was to have her husband enter the hut and find me staring at his wife's nipples.

"You . . . You should go now," I said, stammering like some school-boy as I scanned the area for anyone approaching, especially carrying a bow.

"Tacoma has ordered me to live with you, to teach you the ways of our tribe," Kache replied, her Spanish sounding rough as if she had not spoken it in years. "I am to care for you."

And so she did; becoming my constant shadow each day, my interpreter and teacher, often my hunting partner, and in time, I believe the only woman I ever truly loved.

★ ★ ★ ★

Kache was, as I suspected, one of several women kidnapped in their youth from Spanish settlements. In time, though, she had grown to accept the Matsés tribe as her own people. From what I understood from our long talks, life among the Matsés was far better than what she could have expected from her true family. Remaining in the settlement would only have destined her to a life of prostitution in order to survive, or worse, she would become a baby-factory for an abusive, drunken husband just to keep a roof over her head.

Her Matsés husband, brother to Tacoma, had been killed two years before in a short territorial war with another tribe. There were no children from the marriage, but the tribe's shaman said the jungle spirits had chosen it to be so for reasons unknown to the tribe. After his brother's death, Tacoma took her into his home with honor as if she were a sister. Upon my arrival the wise *cacique* believed the jungle's reason had now become known to him and thus, he ordered her to my hut.

The villagers found humor in the sight of her trailing my every step. I was tall; she was short. I was well muscled; she was slender, lithe, and moved with the silence of a jungle cat. In time, as we became accustomed to one another's constant presence, I felt odd when apart from her. When we reunited, my heart warmed at the sight of her gentle smile. These were new emotions to me, emotions which I distrusted and relished within the same breath.

The rainforest may be fraught with danger for a city dweller, but in the eyes of its indigenous people beauty abounds at every turn. Kache walked me through the forest trails, pointing out exotic but poisonous flowers, the colorful yet poisonous tree frogs, edible plants and those which cured ailments of the body. She could mimic the squawks of birds with such clarity they often flew to us as if responding to their mates, and seeing them light upon nearby branches always brought a tender smile to her face. Whereas I always believed myself to be quite knowledgeable about jungle due to my experiences in Vietnam, Kache made me quickly realize I was merely a novice in comparison to her.

My warrior's training in the Corps was not wasted, though. Tacoma personally accepted the role as my teacher of tribal weaponry and hunting, and grew impressed with my swift mastery of their use and uncanny ability to stalk peccary and monkeys. I never conquered the blowgun, but I maintained a good measure of confidence with a bow and arrow.

The Matsés believe there is no separation between the spiritual and physical world. To the tribe, souls or spirits exist within us as well as in all things such as animals, plants, rocks, mountains and rivers. And in some odd manner, which I never fully came to understand, all spirits are connected or may blend with one another for reasons that only the jungle knows.

My training continued and two months swept by before Tacoma, with Kache translating for him, spoke of my coming initiation into the Jaguar clan. My jungle schooling had progressed well, or so he understood from Kache's reports, and now with my weapons training almost at an end, I would soon undergo the clan's rituals to become a warrior. But as I was to learn, the jungle maintains its own timetable of events.

★ ★ ★ ★

The day's hunt had been grueling, covering the roughest terrain I ever encountered in the Amazon. Our hunting party had made a wide sweep of the land, skirting miles around the village, and our efforts were rewarded with success in the afternoon. When we turned homeward our path took us along a narrow, winding game trail. It was to be a shortcut of sorts for we were heavily laden with two fat peccaries and a large boar slung from thick branches cut into carrying poles and borne on the shoulders of warriors. The hour had grown late and we realized the dim light of dusk was quickly blanketing the land. The rainforest is treacherous enough during the day and the thought of walking it in the pitch black only hurried our steps.

Tacoma led our hunting party home. Having shot the boar with several arrows and tracked him through the jungle, I walked on the *cacique's* right side as a place of honor, followed by the game bearers. While Tacoma kept glancing at the sky to judge our remaining light, I began to grow restless. My gaze swept the surrounding jungle, yet nothing out of the ordinary was visible. I felt as if we were being followed, as if someone paralleled our route home. The feeling would not leave me.

At times I glanced to the rear, expecting to see unknown faces approaching, but all I saw were the warriors of our party. I proudly looked at my boar and the pigs hanging from the poles. It was then I realized they had continuously bled a mixed stream of gelled blood and bodily fluids, leaving a thin trail behind us as we walked. The sight of it bothered me, yet my mind didn't register the full extent of its danger.

My senses tingled and, as years ago in combat, I unconsciously drew ready for the unexpected. I was about to face front again when a wide body of tawny yellow painted with black spots, sprang from one side of the trail in a blur and swept a game bearer off his feet. I heard the bearer's screams blend with the jaguar's deafening roar of attack until they were one. The savagery and speed of the animal stunned me.

The pigs crashed into the dirt as the bearers released their holds on the poles and struggled to arm themselves with their bows. As they spun and defensively crouched, over their heads I could see the jaguar attempting to drag its prey away. In its mouth with teeth sunk deep into the skull was the head of Chawa, a warrior I had become friends with while on the day's hunt.

Claws sliced his body with blinding speed, shredding flesh with each stroke, spewing crimson streaks that spread in fine mists through the air. Chawa's eyes bulged outward from the immense pressure of the jaguar's bite on his skull, and only the great cat's muted growl was heard as he shook his head to sink teeth deeper for a firmer grip.

I reacted without thought, turning at the waist to allow me to swing my bow fully about and draw down on the rib cage of the massive jaguar standing over Chawa. The great cat was far larger than I believed existed in the jungle and from its girth I guessed it weighed more than two-hundred-fifty pounds. The jaguar straddled Chawa and pushed forward, trying to carry its fresh kill off by the head into the thick jungle growth.

Time slowed and all sound faded as I drew my bow string. The string touched my cheek, my fingertips flexed, and I watched the arrow sail through the air. When the fierce cat's back hunched I knew then my arrow had found its target. Three more arrows followed from my fellow hunters, striking the jaguar within inches of mine. Time flowed as if the attack were all occurring in slow motion. As Tacoma turned I saw the hilt of his prized knife. It was a trophy he treasured for it had been taken in battle from a drug cartel patrol that had trespassed upon tribal land. I tore the knife free from his makeshift, palm leaf belt and started toward the animal.

Chawa may have only become my friend on this hunt, but I would never have abandoned Nakai, Stern or Franklin to such a lingering death, and Chawa would be no different. We couldn't wait for the jaguar to bleed to death. He carried four arrows and showed no signs of weakening—and no man should die while others stand idly by and watch.

I ran with arms wide, Tacoma's large knife gripped tightly in hand, and dove toward the great cat. When I collided with the animal, the impact was unexpectedly hard, as if striking a wall of pure iron muscle. We barely moved because the beast kept its balance through outstretched legs and teeth still lodged deep in Chawa's skull.

Lying along the length of its spine, I took a death grip upon its throat with my free hand, rode the beast, and drove the knife's blade up to its hilt into the wide, tawny-yellow hide. A maddening fury possessed me. I shoved the knife deep, twisted, turned and slashed, never slowing, trying always with each stab to slice a wide gap to reach the great cat's beating heart. Its teeth broke free from their wedge upon Chawa's skull and the jaguar's full rage was released upon me. The cat's furious screams bombarded my ears as its claws found their mark and viciously raked me.

We toppled off Chawa and I fell onto my back with the jaguar upon me, its weight pinning me down. Adrenaline coursed through my body and gave me the strength to retain my hold on the flailing animal and to keep its belly turned skyward while I stabbed and ripped wildly. Blood showered me and I was unsure whether it was mine or the jaguar's. Pain swept through me, yet I refused to release my hold upon the cat's throat.

My grip slipped from the fierce twisting of our struggle. I felt the cat turning, trying to face me, and its claws slit my flesh as paws found traction to force its body about. I lost my hold on the knife after burying it inside the animal then reached within the cat's gaping chest. My fingers wrapped about whatever organs I touched—and I tore them free.

A final scream of fury came from the great cat then it went limp atop me.

My arms crashed to the ground, weighing heavier than the giant trees of the rainforest rising about me. All strength left me. I could not move my body and felt paralyzed. Rolling my head to the right, I saw the jaguar's beating heart clutched in my hand.

I looked at Tacoma. His lips parted, but I heard no sound. Then he became a blur before my eyes, and faded.

★ ★ ★ ★

My eyelids felt weighted and at first refused to open. As consciousness returned, I blinked and gazed at the thatch roof above me, confused as to where I was. A sense of security returned when Kache hovered over my face for me to see her.

She stirred something in a bowl, dabbed leaves in it then gently wiped my chest with the wet leaves. Each time she touched my skin I felt sharp, stinging pains shoot through my veins. The concoction, whatever jungle medicine it was, stung like a scorpion and then burned. I grimaced yet she never slowed or removed her attention from the leaves except to glance at my face. Her frown told me of her displeasure with the manner in which I had received my wounds.

"Chawa is dead," Kache stated bluntly as if knowing that would be my first question.

Before I could respond, she sat back on the hut floor, looked over the areas where she had doctored me then spoke again.

"When they carried you into the village, I thought you were dead too . . . and—" Her voice broke. She turned her face away but before doing so, I thought I saw tears on the rims of her eyes.

"Where is the boar I killed?" I asked, not knowing what else to say.

Her head whipped back to face me, eyes painted with fire. Lips forming a taut line, she held her tongue and bore holes into me with her stare. But as the fog cleared in my mind, I understood she was more worried than angry with me. Taking up the bowl, she whisked leaves through it again and renewed her dabbing of my wounds.

Garnering strength I laid a hand atop her leg and softly brushed her skin with my fingertips. "I'm sorry to have made you worry." I was surprised by my words, but more so at having touched her.

Since Tacoma first ordered her to my hut, I had never touched her body except upon the hand. Kache slept beside me each night upon her mat, and often I awoke to the feel of her body pressed against my back, but I never took the slightest liberty with her. Something within me held my physical urges in restraint. I would not disrespect her or treat her with the same savage lust as I had unleashed upon the Scaths. She was the gentle flower I feared would be ruined by my touch.

She lifted my hand, gently rubbed it against her cheek and the world grew dark before my eyes.

* * * *

In Kache's skillful hands the medicines of the rainforest worked their magic. I drifted in and out of sleep for days, which allowed my wounds to better heal. When I awoke, Kache decided what meals I would eat in order to best replenish my strength, but she also determined when I should rest once more and made me drink a cup of horrible tasting brew. Within three gulps I would feel the world spin and suddenly the blackest of nights swept over me.

My recovery may have been days or weeks; I'm unsure which because of the sleeping narcotic Kache so frequently administered. At some point she must have determined I would live and the brew's taste changed. I remained awake longer periods and recall once having glanced at the stitched wounds along my arms, chest and legs where the great cat's claws had raked me. It was then I realized her potent jungle drink had been used as an anesthesia, as well as to make me sleep.

Late one night, I awoke with a great hunger and my body feeling rested with few aches. Raising my head from the mat I saw the campfires outside the hut had almost burned out and from the silence knew the village was asleep. I felt a weight on my stomach and saw Kache's head resting upon me. She must have been exhausted. Every time I woke she would be by my side, ready to feed me, give me water, or clean my wounds. Her breathing was labored and she lightly snored. Strands of hair had fallen across her face and with a finger I gently moved them away from her nose. The hairs tickled her face and she wearily swatted the air as if clearing away a fly. I lowered my head back onto the mat and feigned sleep when she stirred. She awoke, groggily looked about the hut then glanced at me. Through lightly closed eyes I watched her lay her head back upon my stomach and felt one of my hands being taken in hers. She pulled it to her breasts as if it gave some form of comfort, then her snoring returned.

★ ★ ★ ★

The sun crossed overhead and was beginning its descent when I walked through the village. Laughing children chased one another in play; women busied themselves with cooking and diligently painting their bodies with designs I hadn't seen before, and the men seemed to inspect and double-check their weapons. Fresh dark paint dotted their faces, necks, and chests in what I thought were similar to a jaguar's coloration. My first thought was that our village had declared war on a neighboring tribe, yet as I looked closer, I sensed these were all some form of official preparations. Even Kache, who accompanied me on my walk, appeared to carry herself with shoulders back and chin raised slightly higher than normal. A glow of pride filled her dark eyes.

At my approach the villagers paused in their work to smile, nod, and say things to me which I didn't understand. But I quickly realized they were treating me with respect, as if I were of some importance.

Tacoma strode from a nearby hut, spoke to Kache, nodded sharply and walked away.

"Tonight you undergo the ritual to enter the clan," Kache said, her eyes growing brighter. "The *cacique* will personally initiate you."

I understood then why she seemed to be carrying herself with a prouder step. She was my woman, and as such, soon to be the woman of a Jaguar Clan warrior.

★ ★ ★ ★

At dusk the campfires ringing the open area of the village were stoked with massive logs to burn like infernos well into the night. Several large, freshly cut leaves were laid over the flames to create pillars of smoke that mingled with the smoke of other fires to create a hazy wall about us. Kache briefly explained that the special leaves when burned helped repel the mosquitoes and other flying insects that were a common nuisance, and again I was amazed at all the rainforest provided.

Families brought food to share with their neighbors and soon a banquet was in progress. The children were the first to be fed, then next the women as I expected because they were treated with such reverence by the Matsés. The tribe's warriors stood grim-faced in a ring about us all, weapons in hand, displaying their protection of the villagers. In time they ate as well, but not before they opened the night's ceremonies with their demonstration of courage.

Sitting on a log, from my place of honor at the right side of the *cacique*, I watched everyone. Although I had seen the women beginning to paint themselves earlier in the day, now they were fully adorned with lengthy shell necklaces, multiple bracelets, and jaguar-like black spots painted across their breasts and backs. Long, slender wisps of wood pierced the sides of their noses and upper lips to fashion a jungle cat's whiskers, and their movements slowed to a feline grace as they strolled about the area.

As Kache moved past me, her head lowered slightly like a jaguar on the hunt and she gazed at me as if I were her prey. There was something erotic in her walk and my stomach drew tight.

Tacoma stood and motioned me to follow him out into the middle of the circle formed by the tribe. Women and children took their seats upon the ground while Jaguar Clan warriors with faces and bodies painted in wide swathes of muted yellow with black spots ringed us once again with solemn gazes and weapons in hand.

While the *cacique* spoke, the warriors chanted a primal song that evoked images in my head of a fierce hunt. Kache's voice softly penetrated the chant as she stood behind me translating Tacoma's narration of my battle with the great jungle cat. I felt her hand resting upon the small of my back as she leaned close to insure I heard each word; her slightest movement of fingertips upon my skin arousing me against my will.

The hide of the jaguar I had killed was swung through the air by the *cacique* for all present to see. Its immense size blocked firelight and cast areas into darkness which caused small children to cry from fright until it was thrown aside. A necklace made from the jaguar's long, thick claws next rose into the night, hanging from Tacoma's left hand, and in his right he clenched the treasured knife I had insanely used to slay the beast. A chill shot through me as I suddenly felt Kache's fingernails rake a path down my back.

"Look at the scars the jaguar has left upon his chest. The jungle has made them brothers. Their spirits are joined. Their blood has flowed together upon the ground and now they are one . . . ."

A warrior laid the jaguar hide over my shoulders as Tacoma placed the claw necklace about my neck. Taking hold of my right wrist, the *cacique* raised it to stomach level and placed the knife in my hand. This honor elicited a louder primal chant from the warriors and the women rose to their feet and joined them in their odd song.

Warriors brought bowls of yellow and black paint in which Tacoma dipped his fingers and trailed them over my chest. When finished he stepped back and proudly presented me to the tribe as the newest member of the Jaguar Clan.

The ceremony went on late into the night and when the end arrived, Tacoma abruptly raised a hand and everyone quietly walked away. I looked for Kache, but had lost track of her earlier in the evening. My walk to our hut seemed long without her yet I was sure she would return the next day. At first I believed her disappearance may have been part of the ceremony and initiated warriors were supposed to sleep alone in some soul-searching journey—but upon entering our hut and seeing her waiting for me, I knew sleep would not come soon.

She stood in silence, shadows wavering across her painted body from the faint light of a campfire. A long shell necklace draped her breasts and it was all she wore.

Taking my knife and removing the jaguar hide from my shoulders; she spread the hide over our sleeping mat for us to lie upon and laid the knife beside it. She walked to me and brushed her fingertips across my throat and claw necklace. Her fingers trailed down my chest and next I felt my loin cloth fall away.

Kache's hands guided me to the mat where I laid on my back and stared at her standing over me. She knelt upon hands and knees and moved atop me like a jaguar stalking its victim. Cupping her fingers in claw-like manner, she lightly raked the scars on my chest.

Her ability to mimic jungle creatures was amazing, but that night as she crept the length of my body, I closed my eyes and listened to the purr then deep, guttural growl of a hungry, great cat.

An excited gasp escaped her lips as she settled herself atop me. Her necklace swayed in gentle rhythm over my face then swung faster as a growl rose in her throat and her body undulated. Fingers dug deep into my chest as her hunger rose and her body tightened. Her thick black hair fell about my face when she leaned forward and sank her teeth into my flesh. Her lips searched, found mine, and closed over my mouth to mute her passionate cry. Such pure desire between lovers can never be explained; only experienced.

She gave herself to me and I took her with the fury of a wild animal until dawn's first light.

Chapter Twenty-three

The months which followed were magical for me, living with my wife among the Matsés. I hardly thought of the past anymore, only the present and the future held any importance. My soul had been cleansed by Kache's love, and my sufferings at Moloc's hands became mere clouded dreams. My position as a warrior within the Jaguar Clan gave me a new life and prominence among the villagers and with Tacoma's approving nod I led hunters into the jungle to gather meat for our cooking fires. Such things may seem trivial to the outside world, but were great honors within the tribe.

The village became my home and the tribe, my family. Through Kache's persistence I learned enough of the language to make life among the Matsés much easier. For the first time in more years than I could remember, I found peace.

On the third morning after watching Kache rush to the edge of the hut and retch until beads of sweat formed across her forehead, I grew more worried.

"Is there one of the women I can call to help you with your sickness?"

Glancing at me as if I were the dumbest man alive, she shook her head, rinsed her mouth with water and then spat on the ground. Once her stomach calmed, she leaned against a hut pole and grinned.

"The hour for a woman to help me will come soon enough," Kache said, laying a hand tenderly upon her belly.

My confusion made her laugh. I shook my head, puzzled even more at what she found so humorous.

"Soon the jaguar will have another brother—a little brother."

Her words stunned me.

She nodded and warmly smiled. "Your son grows stronger each day."

That was how I learned of the new clan I was to enter—*fatherhood*.

★ ★ ★ ★

Kache's belly swelled until I believed she would surely burst. With each passing month her walk gradually became more of a waddle yet she never slowed her pace about the village. I tried to help her with daily chores, worried she might hurt herself, until one day Tacoma summoned me to him as he sat in the shade beneath a towering tree.

"Women have given birth to children longer than the years of this tree . . ." he said, motioning to the wide branches overhead without looking at them. "When it is her time, the village women will know. These are things for women to concern themselves with, not a warrior of the Jaguar Clan."

"As always you are right, *cacique*," I said, not fully believing my words.

He nodded, letting his gaze flow across the village then staring off into the jungle. Something in Tacoma's weary expression told me there was more on his mind than talking to me about Kache, but I knew better than to ask directly. A chief lets his thoughts be known as he wishes them to be known. Until such time I could only sit patiently and wait. But the wait did not last long.

"Weda came to me this morning. He says the spirits of the jungle are disturbed."

"May I ask why?" I wanted to be respectful of Tacoma yet my curiosity forced me to ask. The shaman was not one to speak lightly of the spirits, especially when problems existed with them.

"Tucum came to me too," the chief said, ignoring my question. "He found boot tracks of soldiers traveling across our land."

"Do you believe the tracks are what Weda sensed from the jungle?"

Weda's premonition and Tucum's observations seemed to be a natural match, both coming within so short a time. The shaman's hallucinogenic-induced visions were strong medicine within the tribe and Tucum, who ranked as one of the best hunters in the village, had never been known to exaggerate his reports.

Tacoma stared at me for a long time before speaking. His expression implied an apprehension I had never seen before. A slow nod came in confirmation yet he didn't seem confident with his answer. He turned his face to watch children running between the huts. When they were gone from sight, he looked at me again.

"The tracks could be from the drug people or the guerillas. The loggers do not wear soldier boots. Take six hunters and find the ones who crossed our land. Feed them to the jungle."

I understood my orders well but was surprised at Tacoma remaining behind and not leading his hunters. As if reading my mind, the *cacique* rose from his seat upon a log and exhaled hard.

"I must stay here," and having spoken, Tacoma slowly walked away, the weight of his thoughts bearing down on him.

★ ★ ★ ★

Kache sat in the hut, calmly rubbing her stomach, remaining silent as she watched me inspect my bow and arrows. When I pulled my knife from its sheath, she leaned forward to better see the weapon. It was a German made knife of the finest steel, dull black in color from tip to grip, razor sharp, with a ten inch long overall construction designed for the rigors of a Special Forces mission. Someone had probably paid a high price for the knife, but thankfully, in a violent exchange of ownerships, it had made its way to me courtesy of Tacoma.

"Are you going to sharpen it?" Kache asked, her tone telling me she was only making conversation.

"I did yesterday."

She gave a gentle nod then repositioned herself to be more comfortable. "How many hunters will go with you?" she asked.

"Tacoma said to take six."

"Be sure to take Kana. He is a good warrior and his wives have said they need a night's rest . . . ."

I chuckled, slipped the knife back into its sheath and placed it on my palm leaf belt. "Yes, I've heard he has a busy mat."

We laughed, but Kache's smile faded.

"When you return, will you take more wives for your sleeping mat?"

The question caught me off-guard. I paused, laid my weapons aside and looked into Kache's eyes. "Why would I need more wives for my mat when I have you?"

The words were evidently what she hoped to hear because a warm smile appeared as her dark eyes took on a shine.

Moving to behind her, I sat, wrapped my arms about her shoulders and softly rubbed her bulging stomach. She laid her head back into my chest and we sat in silence, enjoying the moment.

"I will miss you," I said, whispering in her ear.

She squeezed my arms. "We will be waiting for you," she replied, patting her stomach.

This was the moment of truth when I realized how much my life had changed, how Kache had changed me, and all for the better.

★ ★ ★ ★

The dawn sky still held a pink, yellowish glow along the horizon when the chosen hunters arrived at my hut. Kana, Binan, Tucum, Yava, and the ones I called Runt and Frog, both fierce warriors, stood waiting for me; black streaks painted their faces, and their chests were dotted with the black spots of a Jaguar Clan warrior. In their hands were the bows, spears, or blowguns I knew each man could so expertly use.

Tacoma stepped from behind them and approached as I walked out of the hut. His expression was as solemn as when we last spoke.

"Tucum believes he knows where to find them. Let him lead your way. Within three days you should be returning. Do so quickly," the *cacique* said, his eyebrows drawing tightly together to create deep furrows across his forehead.

No further words passed between us. His gaze rose to look over my shoulder then he left. I turned to find Kache standing on the steps of our hut, my bow and knife in her hands. She held them out to me but her gaze followed Tacoma as he walked away. A moment later her attention returned to me, her eyes filled with worry.

I stood confused. A hundred questions consumed me. Why would Tacoma remain in the village when normally he would have led the hunters? He seemed bothered yet would not speak his thoughts. What had Kache sensed from him or was my mind playing games with me? *Return quickly?* Why would he say such a thing? Did Weda have another vision? Had the shaman told him we would die on our mission?

As I took the weapons from her, Kache's hands wrapped about mine, squeezed hard and walked back into the hut. Lowering my gaze to the steps I saw bowls of red and black paint sitting off to the side. I dipped my fingers into them; smeared streaks across my face and dotted my chest with jaguar-like spots.

Once my knife was positioned upon my hip I nodded and Tucum spun toward the jungle, leaving at a light run. I fell in behind him and the others followed. Questions still bothered me but they quickly vanished when the village was lost from sight.

* * * *

Tucum's initial pace burned my lungs as I fought to draw each breath in the thick jungle humidity. We had often run before on hunting trips, but never for such a distance as this day. Gradually he settled into a trot which ate the miles and allowed my body to adjust to the physical demands. Rather than cut through the rainforest as I expected, he took us along wide trails that were almost roads to reduce our traveling time. Sweat stung my eyes and dripped from my face in torrents, yet each time I glanced at the men following me, they appeared as fresh as when we had left my hut. Whether out of embarrassment or simply to conserve my energy, I stopped looking back.

Our run lasted two hours before the least break came. When a rain storm passed over us, Tucum slowed for better footing in the mud, but that was the extent of any rest we received. I had my second-wind and, once settled into the distance-eating run, my body and mind shifted into a void which closed off all physical pain.

Time was lost to me. We ran until sometime mid-morning then halted at a stream. Tucum left us while we knelt and scooped water with our hands. I was drinking when a hand tapped my shoulder.

"Here. Chew this as we run," Runt said, handing me several dark green leaves.

Taking them, I sniffed one then put it in my mouth. As I began to chew, I experienced a tingling sensation in my jaw which then moved into my chest. I suffered no ill effects from the leaf, but I felt a resurgence of energy. Whatever stimulants were in the leaves worked their magic. I felt revived, almost anxious to run again. When I glanced at Runt, he nodded complacently, slipped another leaf into his mouth and began to inspect his blowgun. I looked at the warriors about me and realized they too were chewing leaves.

Runt was as fierce and tireless a warrior as the others, but far shorter. None in the village were very tall, but when I memorized my fellow hunters' names in the Jaguar Clan, his stature made it easier to nickname him 'Runt.'

The warrior I called 'Frog' earned his name from working with the little creatures. His specialty was harvesting the brightly colored green frogs in the rainforest, tying them carefully to short stakes then extracting their highly poisonous secretion for use on arrow tips, darts, or in ceremonies. An arrow or blow gun dart dipped in the poison could kill or incapacitate its victim. The quantity of the poison used was the deciding factor. In ceremonies, which I refused to take part in, small cuts were made on the participant's arm and droplets of poison were dripped into the wound. This created a light form of paralysis and flashes of intense pain which the Matsés believed opened doors in their souls, through which, the jungle spirits and their visions visited them.

Feeling refreshed, I sat looking about the area, waiting for Tucum's return, wondering how many men we would find in the camp. A bush swayed, its branches making no noise, and then Tucum appeared as if he had walked out of the plant.

"They are no more than a half day ahead of us. We should find them tonight," he reported, kneeling in the mud on one knee to drink from the stream. He saw the green leaves held in my hand and nodded approval. "Weave them into the strands of your palm leaf belt . . . You can pull one free to chew as we run."

Once I had done so, Tucum glanced at his brother warriors, wiped his mouth with the back of a hand and rose from the ground. He took a moment to get his bearings then trotted away.

We entered a denser part of the jungle, our run now slower than before, made more difficult by the vines which stretched across the narrow game trails. Although I tried to be as nimble and silent as Tucum, I stumbled at times when my toes snagged a vine, and made noise when my arms thrashed in the air to regain balance. There was much I had yet to learn from the Jaguar Clan.

The canopy grew thicker, blocking the sunlight and leaving me unable to judge the hour. As we moved deeper into the rainforest, dark shadows painted the surrounding jungle and blended to become large swathes of black about us. At one point Tucum motioned to halt. He raised his nose and sniffed the air as a hunting dog would to catch a scent. I watched him make a slow, confirming nod before he looked to see if I smelled it too. At first there was nothing but the fragrance of the forest, the green plants and odd budding flowers, yet after lifting my nose into the air and inhaling deeply several times, I caught a faint, stale odor of tobacco smoke.

We crept forward for what seemed to be hours and stopped when wavering firelight danced off the trees hundreds of yards ahead. Our prey's night vision would be ruined by their roaring campfire while the darkness surrounding us allowed a clear view of them.

Squatting in a circle, we huddled to plan our attack in whispers. We would wait and allow our quarry to settle for the night and become complacent. As the smell of cooking food carried through the air, I knew the soldiers would eat, become lazy, and grow over confident because of their numbers or the weapons they carried. They would probably sleep, leaving the youngest among them to stand guard. I had few doubts about their failings because no well-trained team smoked as they walked or made a bonfire and freely cooked as they were now doing.

One hour passed, then two before we edged closer. Binan, Tucum, and Yava swung wide to the left while Kana, Runt and Frog went right. We chose to catch them in a crossfire ambush with me at one of the open ends to deal with would-be escapees.

My team of Jaguar Clan warriors well deserved the honor of being brothers to the great jungle cat. They moved into position about the soldiers with magnificent stealth and sat patiently waiting to attack. Although they were only a short distance away from me, I neither heard nor saw them. At that moment I realized I was as proud of them as I had been of my Recon team in Vietnam.

Moving a wide leaf aside I studied the trespassers on our land, wanting assurance of their numbers, their position in the camp, and whether they watched the surrounding land as if awaiting the return of a companion. They were either a bold or a stupid lot, I'm not sure which because they laughed and talked so loudly without care for their safety. Their words were confusing—some South American dialect—but body language and tones of voice were all I needed to understand them.

Their military manner of dress made it difficult to decide whether they were soldiers, drug runners, or guerrillas, but the automatic weapons slung from their shoulders were not a sign of danger but themselves dangerous.

I counted eight uniformed bodies about the camp fire, each person paying little attention to the surrounding area. One slender man tossed wood onto the already crackling fire while a heavier set soldier sank his fingers into a bowl he held and scooped food into his mouth. When finished he licked and sucked his fingers clean, and swiped them across his shirt. Another man sat with knees raised and arms wrapped about his legs. His head was lowered, resting on his knees, burying his face from sight. Someone spoke to him but he didn't move, and short laughs came from several of the men.

The soldier I took to be their leader stood, stretched and walked with an exaggerated swagger to the perimeter of their small camp site. His wide back was to me but I could tell he was relieving himself. All I could hope for was that none of my men were within his stream's range. He swung his hips as if writing his name in urine across the bushes, and yelled over his shoulder in a braggart's tone. The one he spoke to rose from a log and took a defiant stance with hands on hips, perfectly silhouetted by the firelight. At that moment I saw the outline of hefty breasts which I certainly had not expected to see this night.

When the leader ran out of urine, he wheeled from the jungle and shook his erect manhood at her. His words came low and cold, followed by a lecherous smile. I needed no translation to understand what he wanted from her, but the woman calmly drew an impressive sized knife from the small of her back, swung it before her and made slicing gestures at waist level to show her intent as well.

The slovenly leader threw his head back as he brazenly laughed and stroked his erection—but the laughter abruptly stopped. His face lowered. He stood with mouth agape and eyes flared, gazing at the world in disbelief. He looked at the ground, and as if in slow motion, fell forward like a cut tree. The soldiers nearest him recoiled as if he were a viperous snake then shouted at the sight of the arrow shaft protruding from the back of his neck. It had been a perfect shot; striking a major nerve center, severing as it sliced through to penetrate the brain, immediately breaking the link between mind and body. Death did not come instantaneously, but swift enough.

A mad flurry erupted in the camp as one soldier pushed another aside to take up defensive positions against their invisible attackers. Two soldiers grabbed large backpacks and bolted toward the jungle. Arrows pierced their throats and cut short their flight. But the woman didn't run. Instead, she dropped to a knee, swung a short automatic weapon up to her shoulder and opened fire in the directions the arrows had come from.

My warriors were well camouflaged because the soldiers fired wildly up into the trees and about the surrounding area, unsure where their attackers were hidden. Long yellowish-red streaks spewed from the muzzles of the automatic weapons as brass casings streamed into the air.

The roar of the weapons grew deafening, bombarding our ears, masking the screams of the frightened and dying soldiers.

A soldier slapped at himself as if swatting a mosquito, only to find a long, feathered dart lodged in his neck. Within seconds he wobbled, lost balance and began to crumple into the dirt. An arrow struck his stomach and buried itself deep within him as he fell.

The remaining soldiers raked the jungle with a continuous barrage of bullets then all drew eerily still and quiet in the jungle. Rather than use fire discipline, they had swiftly expended their ammunition within the first minute and were all forced to reload at the same moment. This proved to be a fatal mistake on their part.

Poison-tipped arrows sliced through the firelight, found their targets, and drove into flesh. A soldier grabbed his face when an arrow pierced an eye, but once the tip penetrated his brain, he immediately dropped where he stood.

The woman's head turned. Her attention seemed focused on something in the jungle. A gut feeling told me she had spotted one of my warriors.

Still kneeling to maintain a low profile, she spun in that direction and brought her weapon to bear on a target. But before she could fire, my arrow struck her side and buried itself until only the feathers of the shaft could be seen. She howled in agony and fell back, squeezing the trigger of her short length machine gun. Muzzle flash swept in a long arc across the night as she went down. Bullets spewed until the magazine emptied and then the weapon fell silent. When she crashed into the dirt, her finger still squeezed the trigger.

There was no rush to inspect the soldiers. My warriors were patient and remained concealed. We waited for the wounded to die or attempt an escape. As a soldier tried to stand, an arrow or feathered dart from a blow gun immediately struck him. When only a few groans were heard in the camp, we walked into the clearing.

"Anyone hurt?" I asked, looking to each warrior for wounds.

They shook their heads in reply as they cautiously moved from soldier to soldier cutting their throats.

I opened the two large backpacks to see what was valuable enough to make soldiers risk their lives. The contents was as I suspected; dozens of large, well-wrapped bricks of drugs. Slicing through the plastic wrapping of one, I held it out at arm's length and let the white contents cascade onto the ground.

We rummaged through the packs and equipment to see what could be salvaged and taken to our village. I found the woman's knife beside her, partially buried in the dirt, and wiped it clean on her shirt. Rolling her over, I removed the empty sheath from the small of her back and eased the big knife into it.

"This will be for Tacoma," I said, holding it up for the warriors to see. Scanning the camp, I pointed to the bodies. "His orders were to feed them to the jungle."

They understood. Yava withdrew his knife, knelt beside a body and began to slice the clothes off and remove the arrows and darts. The warriors followed suit and busied themselves with pulling arrows free and removing clothes until each drug runner lay nude.

Hearing the splatter of urine, I turned and saw Runt relieving himself on the dead leader's face.

"This pig sprayed me," the short warrior said without removing his gaze from the dead man. "Now it is his turn."

My companions grunted approval, grinned, and returned to their work of clearing the campsite.

The woman's body was left for me to undress which I did quickly, slicing through her uniform and boot strings with ease. My arrow had lodged deep in her, driving at an angle through lungs and evidently piercing her heart. I worked the shaft free with short, hard jerks but the arrow head remained in her.

At a distance she had appeared tall but in reality was as short as Runt. She looked young, no more than twenty. Her narrow face was heavily pock-marked and her high cheek bones suggested some Indian ancestry. But in spite of her being a woman, I gave her credit for being a worthy adversary. She had let her leader know his desires would come at a high price, and during our assault, while her companions tried to flee, she remained and fought. Her firm body bore several scars, one of which appeared to be an old bullet wound. These further confirmed my belief about her courage and the rough life she must have lived. I was fairly confident from her melon breasts that she had learned at an early age to defend herself against every man with the urge to mount her; lessons she undoubtedly learned the hard way. But my warriors paid little heed to her. They glanced at her breasts, nodded approval of their weighty size then walked away.

Kana gathered the automatic weapons and remaining ammunition boxes, placed them in a mound with dry firewood beneath, and then spread the uniforms atop it all. A blanket was laid across the ground to act as a makeshift fuse for the mound and to provide us time to be clear before the explosions came. The hard-packed bricks of cocaine were sliced opened and dumped on the ground near the ammunition. The explosion would spread the cocaine across the campsite so it could never be retrieved.

The two oversized backpacks were set in front of me to inspect. Kuni had stuffed them with canned food, knives, and other salvaged equipment from the drug runners. There was no need to review his work, but as the designated leader of the team it was my responsibility to give approval on everyone's actions. I glanced at the packs, grunted and waved a hand as I had often seen Tacoma do. Kuni appeared proud of his work and tied the packs closed.

All was soon ready for our departure. No sign remained of Matsés warriors having been present. Every arrow and dart was accounted for then returned to its rightful owner to be used again.

"When we leave, Binan will set fire to the mound. The soldiers' clothes will burn a long time before the bullets explode. We will be safe in the jungle by then," Tucum explained. He glanced at the drug runners laid out in the camp site. "In two days the bodies will be nothing more than bones and no one but us will know how they died. The ants and our brother jaguars will eat well. In five days many of the bones will have been carried off into the forest."

My gaze traveled across the campsite. There was no evidence to connect the dead with my Matsés warriors. And Tucum was right; the rainforest ants and jaguars would devour the flesh from the bones within two days. I had seen it before when the ants cleaned the meat from a jungle pig's body.

I had lost all concept of time once we entered this area of the jungle with such thick canopy overhead. Glancing skyward, all I could observe were tree limbs and leaves illuminated by the firelight. Taking a wild guess, I estimated the hour to be after midnight. We had run all day without halting to eat and then moved straight into the attack without rest. The fight with the drug runners had lasted no more than twenty minutes from the release of the first arrow until we were packed for departure. I knew our adrenaline rush mixed with the potent green leaves had helped keep us going, yet each warrior never faltered. I thought how efficient and focused they were, and the fact that they had not mutilated the corpses or touched the woman made me respect them more.

The drug runners' bonfire had burned down to half its original size and still there was sufficient light to see by in the camp. But within twenty feet of the campsite all was pitch black. I waited until each warrior appeared ready then motioned to the jungle.

"Lead the way, Tucum. Let's go home." I smiled at the sound of *going home.*

★ ★ ★ ★

We were well away from the camp when the ground lightly shuddered beneath our feet. The distant roar of an explosion, muffled by the dense jungle, carried through the air. Trees trembled enough to sprinkle leaves upon us then silence returned to the forest.

Before leaving the camp we had discovered Claymores and other perimeter defensive explosives laid off to the side in packs. I believed the drug runners had been too lazy to establish a proper perimeter because doing so takes time, patience, and expertise—qualities they lacked. But, for whatever reason they were negligent, I was thankful the explosives had not been used. Hearing the power of their detonation at such a distance made me realize our good fortune.

It was not long after the explosion before Binan caught up with us on the trail and took up position as rear guard. A team once more, we renewed our slow trek through the dark to the village.

As we walked I realized a faint light began to illuminate the jungle. The canopy was thinning and moonlight shone through its gaps. Fatigue was rapidly taking hold of me, yet I kept pace with Tucum. The long day must have been wearing on him as well because soon he stopped, scanned the area, and motioned us to a slight clearing off the trail.

"Sleep now. When the sun rises we will find food then go until we reach the village."

I didn't give him an argument. My body needed rest, and from the swift manner in which everyone began cutting large elephant-eared leaves to make a bed, the others felt the same way. Frog sniffed several of the bushes as if judging the fragrance of their leaves. When satisfied, he cut short branches and brought several to me.

"Lay on these. The smell keeps the ants and their friends away," he said, pointing to the ground. I did as he instructed and added it to my many lessons of jungle life.

Lying against one of the large packs, I tried to relax. Possibly I was too tired to fall asleep immediately or my mind wouldn't stop replaying the events of the day, but something bothered me. Shifting my body into a more comfortable position, I stared out into the distance at the beams of moonlight penetrating the canopy.

Thoughts of Tacoma came and went. Kache's voice rose as a shout in my ear, startling me, making me look about before realizing I must have dozed off and dreamed of her. As the moon traveled across the sky I could see its full, white orb through a break in the canopy. Its brilliant light bathed the jungle wherever it cast its beams, outlining the trees and plants.

A disturbing sensation enveloped me yet I could not understand any reason as to why. My eyes gently closed but a face flashed in my mind which I had long tried to forget; Moloc. Startled, I sat upright again, anxiously glanced about the rainforest, and let my gaze carry skyward. I couldn't take my eyes from the Amazon moon.

★ ★ ★ ★

The remaining hours of night passed tediously slow. When the moon vanished behind the canopy I tried to sleep yet found myself constantly tossing about for better comfort. My heartbeat grew rapid and my palms were slick with sweat.

At the break of dawn I rose with my warriors, glad we would soon depart. Fruits and berries pulled from trees and bushes served as our breakfast, and thick vines were cut and passed among the team for the water they provided. By all rights I should have been hungry, but an anxiety which makes a man pace about without reason dulled my appetite. Even Tucum must have noticed a difference in me for he kept glancing in my direction as we ate our breakfast.

Runt approached with more of the small green leaves in hand, nodded with a grin, and gave me more to replenish my depleted stock.

Tossing the peelings of a banana-like fruit into the undergrowth, Tucum swiped his hands clean, eased off the log he was sitting on, and motioned in the direction of our village. The warriors gathered their weapons and stood waiting while Runt and Kana adjusted the packs upon their backs. Tucum walked to the trail and without looking back, left at a trot. Slipping a leaf into my mouth, I followed him feeling anxious without knowing why.

The first three miles allowed me to settle into a rhythm and clear my head for the long journey home. A runner's 'second-wind' came easier this time and my lungs didn't burn with each breath as before. Sweat drenched me, head to foot, but the physical demands of the run upon my body felt good.

Streams of light from the rising sun cut through the canopy, painting the landscape with varying intensity. Morning droplets of dew upon the sea of leaves reflected the sunlight and made each droplet sparkle as if they were jewels strewn across the jungle. The serenity of the rainforest at that moment should have been soothing to my soul, yet was not.

We ran all day, stopping only to relieve ourselves or to find the vines to cut and quench our thirst. During one such break, Yava, brow furrowed as he spoke, told me the vine water was better to drink than stream water. Properties within the vine mixed themselves with the water and served to strengthen the body. This was unlike the energizing 'running-leaves' which held some form of stimulant and pumped your heart. Again, I had received another valuable lesson.

Our pace increased slightly as we drew closer to the village. Leaves and branches slapped my arms and face as the trail narrowed, yet I felt very few as I grew more excited about seeing Kache again.

Tucum slowed so abruptly that I almost ran into him then he came to a halt and scanned the jungle canopy. The sun had lowered on the horizon and shadows were forming in the forest. His eyes narrowed as he turned and looked high into the trees about us. He glanced at me with a questioning gaze then his nose rose to sniff the air. Lowering his face, he slowly shook his head and stared in the direction of the village. My stomach drew taut when he laid an arrow across his bow and held it at the ready by his side. Runt, Frog, and the other warriors readied their weapons.

"Do you hear it?"

My senses were electrified.

"No . . . nothing," I replied.

"You hear silence. Where have the birds and animals gone?" Tucum asked, voice lowered into a whisper.

Beads of sweat trickled down my face as I raised my nose into the air and inhaled deeply. There was no fresh jungle scent as it should have been. Instead, my nostrils caught a light odor of smoke mingled with a stench which never leaves your mind once smelled—burnt flesh.

Runt and Kana eased their backpacks off and lowered them to the ground. With a nod to us, Tucum left at a trot, bent low as if ready to drop any moment to the ground and take cover. We followed suit, moving as silently yet as swiftly as possible along the narrow trails.

When we neared the village Tucum knelt and stared in the direction of where we should already be seeing the tops of the first huts, but there were none. Only thin wisps of smoke spiraled into the air. We crept forward to the perimeter of the village then stood unable to move, unable to speak, as we stared at the decimation before us.

My stomach twisted into knots. Dread and nausea struck hard as I forced myself to walk forward. The huts were mere charred remains, their thatch roofs now caved in and burnt. Smoke rose in light pillars across the area where hut poles had fallen and become smoldering fires. As far as one could see lay the corpses of men, women and children, massacred in the most savage of ways.

Burnt bodies lay in the destroyed huts in contorted positions. In the large campfires used at night to ward off animals and light the village were tangled masses of bodies so badly mutilated that it was difficult to tell whether they were men or women. Only the children could be defined because of their size.

The ground throughout the village appeared a dark maroon, stained from the streams of blood which had flowed from the butchered masses. At first I tried to step over the bodies and wide areas of blood soaked ground then realized I could not avoid it and forced myself to walk through the muck. I felt my stomach churn and bile rise into my throat. The stench of burnt flesh assaulted my nostrils and I fought the rising nausea.

No, I had seen such things before when the Viet Cong had left a village after punishing the peasants for any of a dozen senseless reasons. But this wasn't the heartless work of the Viet Cong, and I walked among the dead in a disoriented state.

The pain-gorged scream of Kana in the distance shattered my confusion. More shouts of agony filled the air from Tucum, Frog, and others of my team. I looked about the village and saw them at what had once been their huts. The sight of the warriors holding the remains and lifeless bodies of their loved ones tore at my soul and drove home my greatest dread—where was Kache?

At first, with every hut burnt to the ground and mutilated bodies sprawled where ever I looked, my hut was lost among the destruction. When I got my bearings and determined which hut had been mine, I pushed aside smoldering poles and dug through the ashes. A part of me hoped she had survived, yet in the carnage of the village I knew such thinking was only false hope.

I stumbled through the remnants of the village, searching the corpses, my mind numb from the savagery to which these innocent women and children had been subjected. The Matsés warriors lay butchered and sprawled by them, showing me they had put up a valiant fight before being killed.

Having walked through the village I paused and let my gaze carry across the sea of madness. It was then I saw Kache, or what was left of her—and our son. With each step I took toward her I felt the world caving in on me, nausea rising until finally I could not stop myself from vomiting. I collapsed into the dirt at her feet, retching until my chest heaved in pain, my mind lost in a maelstrom of insanity. I am not ashamed to say I was on hands and knees, moaning, weeping, and clawing the ground into fistfuls of dirt. My soul felt as if it were being shredded by hot knives within me while my mind splintered in agony.

No man should ever have to find his loved ones in such horrific condition. Not like that—not with his wife holding fast to their child after it had been gutted from her stomach.

I cried out like a wounded animal and wept until there were no more tears, crawled to her side and fell into the dirt. I remember only laying an arm over her and my lifeless son, and then a black void engulfed me.

Chapter Twenty-four

My name reverberated through the canyons of my mind. The more I heard it called, the more confused I became. My body shook slightly and my eyes opened to see men standing about me, silhouetted by a large campfire.

Forcing myself to move, I lifted my arm from Kache and the baby. I was back in that terrible moment when I found them butchered, and my heart felt as if it too was dead.

When Runt saw that I was awake, he released his hold on my ankle and moved to stand beside the other warriors. I rose onto unsteady legs, stared at their hollow expressions and realized I must look the same to them. They waited in silence for me to speak, to lead them and give order to their present world of chaos.

Glancing at the gruesome spectacle of my wife and son, I shook my head and exhaled deeply.

"There are too many to bury. We will have to place everyone together and burn the bodies," I said, looking to the warriors.

"We found Tacoma. He wants to talk with you. He still lives—for now." Kuni's words were as flat and emotionless as his stare.

Following them to where the *cacique* lay I knelt by his side and took one of his limp hands in mine. Cuts and bruises covered his body yet none were of such degree that they were life threatening. But when he couldn't move I realized his back must be broken. He was paralyzed from the neck down. His eyes bore the anguish of his physical and mental torture, yet he shed no tears.

"Weda's visions told of this attack . . . told him we were in danger. But he had seen the soldiers . . . the spirits were too restless for him to understand his vision," Tacoma said, each word difficult to form.

"Who did this to our village, *cacique*? The ones we found in the jungle were the drug people. Did soldiers or the logging people do these things? Was it another tribe?"

His eyes slowly closed. For a moment, I believed he had died.

"They came when the moon was full . . ." Tacoma's eyes opened wide as if he were seeing the attackers once more. ". . . I have never seen such men—no, they were not men . . . they were—."

My anxiety rose as everything came together in my mind. I had been a fool all this time, lulled by the fact Moloc's Drolids had never ventured this far. Tacoma's odd character before we left should have made me pursue the truth with him—but last night, the full moon, Kache's voice, and my vision of Moloc, all should have alerted me to the attack.

Moloc still hunted for me, furious at my escape, and the village had paid the grave price for his revenge. Now, though, there would no longer be a need for him to hunt for me—I would hunt him.

★ ★ ★ ★

Tacoma, great *cacique* of the Matsés tribe, died that night while I was at his side. To honor him, my warriors found paints to adorn his face and chest with markings that befitted a leader of the Jaguar Clan. We carefully laid his body to rest in the middle of the open village area with a bow and two arrows placed upon his chest so his spirit could roam the jungle and hunt as he wished.

The remainder of the night we carried the dead to lay beside him so they would have his protection when their spirits walked the land. I placed Kache and our son next to him then asked the great *cacique* to watch over them until we were a family once more. Before turning away, I pulled the jaguar claw necklace from my neck and laid it across my son's corpse so the jungle spirits would recognize him as a warrior.

The night's labors were the worst ever forced upon me. We worked in silence, our grief making us unable to speak as we carried our families and friends to join Tacoma. Tucum wept as he gathered the horrid remains of his children, and Kana walked in a dazed state as he carried several of his wives to the funeral pyre. The other warriors wept as well over their loved ones. They were all overwhelmed by the carnage because never had they seen such acts committed by other tribes during their wars. There were still women and children unaccounted for, yet I feared they were now Drolid prisoners, a fate no human should endure.

Throughout the night I saw the warriors pause to stand and stare at the rising mound, numbed by the sight of the mutilations. There were easily eighty dead or more; I'm not sure of an exact number for I had stopped counting long ago.

Then we began the task of cutting firewood for the pyre.

★ ★ ★ ★

By midday we had covered the bodies and reached a point of throwing the firewood up onto the mound. Half-burnt hut poles and anything else that would burn was scavenged and positioned against the pile. We were beyond the point of exhaustion, yet the agony in our hearts refused to let us stop. At last we did, though, but only because our arms had lost all strength.

Yava and Kuni passed out torches to us that they had made. Once the torches were lit, we stationed ourselves about the wooden mountain, and as one, all shoved the torches deep within it. At first the fires were slow to catch but once the flames began to spread and join, its intense heat drove us farther and farther back.

The inferno's wall of reddish-orange flames began to dance eerily and above it all a massive pillar of spiraling gray and black smoke billowed skyward, blotting out the sun as it spread across the horizon. The fire roared as its intensity grew. Within the fire I heard loud crackling, pops, and hisses which I hoped were from the wood. But when logs shifted I caught sight of fluids spewing from bodies, and witnessed the creation of the horrendous sounds.

My nostrils were already filled with the stench of the dead from carrying them to the mound. With each breath, we could smell little else. But when the wind shifted and carried smoke over us, it bore the pungent odors of burnt flesh that sickened even the strongest of men.

I stood mesmerized by the wavering flames, staring at them, realizing all hopes of a new life for me were being incinerated. No matter how hard I searched for happiness, I realized it was never to be for me.

* * * *

The funeral pyre burned late into the night before crumbling into a dune of red coals. Scanning the decimated village I realized there was little left to show of the Matsés once having lived here, and within a year the rainforest would reclaim the land.

The last two days took their toll on us and fatigue finally forced sleep upon every warrior. I awoke to the sunlight of a new day, not knowing when I had gone to sleep during the night. I felt drugged, barely able to move, and my head throbbed with each beat of my heart.

Walking into the rainforest, I sliced bark from a particular tree and began chewing it to relieve my headache as Kache had taught me to do. After plucking fruits and berries from the jungle, I carried them into what had once been the village. Frog, Runt, Tucum, and the other warriors met me in a clearing and we shared a communal breakfast. Still no one spoke, but I knew the time had come to discuss the attack on the village, and decide our next actions.

Glancing at each of the warriors, I realized we were all covered in dried blood, dirt that had become smears of gory mud, and still wore partial amounts of sweat-streaked paints across our bodies. As warriors, we were a miserable lot to behold.

In the last year my hair had grown far past my shoulders and now it was matted with twigs, leaves, and was thick with chunks of mud. My beard, which always has grown fast, had not been shaven from me in days. Kache kept me clean shaven because she disliked the coarse feel and scratches it left upon her cheeks—and she wanted me to be slick-faced as other Matsés warriors were so I would blend with the villagers. Now none of that mattered. All that mattered was preparing my warrior team for what was to come.

"We will bathe, gather our weapons, and prepare ourselves for war. The ones we seek are not like any tribe you have seen before, but they can be killed. I was once a prisoner in their land and escaped. They came here to find me; to return me to their chief to be punished."

No one asked any questions. By the stoic expressions each warrior wore I knew they only wanted to avenge their loved ones' savage deaths. Yet how could I explain to them the Drolids were not simply another tribe? How would these brave warriors hold up mentally when they went into battle against a mutant adversary?

"The ones we seek are evil spirits." My words hung heavy in the air, making their brows furrow as they looked at me. I waited. No one asked a question. "They live far from here and have only been gone a full day's march. If they have taken some of our people prisoner then their travel will be slow."

I knew that was a lie. The Drolids would willingly kill any prisoner that faltered, but I did not want to tell the warriors that a trail of the dead would lead us to them. This was a fact I believed they already understood.

We finished our meal in silence then went to the river and washed the caked gore from our bodies. Finding our weapons, we made necessary repairs, gathered large quantities of the running-leaves, and then searched for the plants needed to make our paints. Kana knelt and scraped dirt from the ground where the darkest blood stains still appeared then mixed it with water and red ochre dyes. I understood his actions. It was only right that we should bear the blood of our families as the foundation of our war paints.

This was our private moment; a time each warrior used to prepare himself to take vengeance at all costs upon our enemy, a time to focus our minds upon what must be done. With bowls of black and red paints before me, I sat with closed eyes and saw Kache walking toward me through the village, smiling as she approached. I dipped my fingers into the black paint and felt her hand upon mine as if she would guide me in my preparations. As my fingertips glided diagonally across my face and chest leaving wide streaks, the sight of her began to fade. I could still feel her touch as I dipped deep into the bowl of red paint and adorned my face. Then the gentle feel of her hand upon mine vanished and my ears were filled with the purring of a great jungle cat. Opening my eyes I looked about me, no longer immersed in the pain of my loss. Such was my transition, my return to a killer's mindset.

Chapter Twenty-five

Tucum led the way, although there was no need for his expert tracking skills. The Drolids had crushed the vegetation so badly that we believed we were walking in a narrow road. From the wide footprints mashed into the ground, Tucum estimated the Drolids numbered at least thirty and had taken no more than twenty prisoners. Reading the ground, Tucum believed their route home appeared to be no different than when they first came.

As I suspected, bodies marked the Drolids' direction of travel. The first corpses found were the old ones whose health or state of shock didn't allow them to keep pace. But next we began to find the children, and knowing the Drolids as I did, I knew they had killed the little ones because their crying irritated the creatures. Unfortunately, while Moloc's prisoner, I had witnessed too many such acts from my cell window.

Using our knives we buried them in shallow graves wherever we discovered them, and then renewed our trek, running to make up for the lost time.

An hour before dusk we drew to a halt. Tucum left to scout ahead while the remainder of us gathered food and cut vines to quench our thirst. Shadows were blending into dark swathes throughout the rainforest when at last he returned.

"The evil ones are in a valley over the next hill." He paused, raised his mouth and held a vine high to drink. The water drained from the thick vine in a steady stream, and when he had his fill, he let it run over his head to refresh him. Casting the vine aside, he knelt in the dirt to draw a map with his knife.

"We are here. They are camped here—and a patrol of the drug people is now moving through the jungle in this direction."

The point of Tucum's knife cut a line in the dirt from the drug people directly through the Drolids encampment.

I stared at the markings in the dirt and realized the possibilities of the situation. The Drolids could sustain an arrow strike to the chest but were vulnerable to the automatic weapons the drug dealers carried. And I wanted those automatic weapons for when I next met Moloc.

"The patrol is probably searching for their missing friends," I said. "Let them attack the evil ones and reduce their numbers. We will strike when they think they've finished their fight."

The warriors nodded, glanced a last time at the dirt map then looked at me.

"Yes, *cacique*."

★ ★ ★ ★

Walking out from under the jungle canopy and into the open valley, I was glad to see the faint light of the moon's last quarter. It allowed us to move faster across the land, yet with our painted bodies, we blended with the shadows whenever we drew still.

We found the best vantage point on the hillside and squatted in the dark beneath wide tree limbs to wait out the hours. Below us in the valley lay the Drolid encampment, its single campfire burning wildly as if stoked to last for days. Unintelligible shouts rose through the night and at a distance we could see the evil ones formed in a ring as if watching a spectacle. My first fear was that a villager had been chosen to be the night's entertainment, but when two Drolids' broke through the ring I saw they were engaged in deadly battle with one another.

The brush lightly moved thirty feet directly in front of me and I drew my bowstring, ready to shoot once my target came into sight. Frog immediately touched my arm and shook his head.

"Binan," he whispered as the slender warrior came into view from the jungle growth.

Binan knelt before me, his eyes wide, telling me he had seen the Drolids up close.

"They are not men like us, *cacique* . . . and they are bigger than you!" He shook his head in bewilderment and spread his arms wide to depict their immense size to the other warriors.

"But they bleed like us, and can die like us," I said before Binan spoke again. "This I know." My calm reassured the warriors, yet I wondered what my brave team would think if they saw Moloc.

"The evil ones keep our people off to one side. The two evil one's that are fighting were arguing over one of our women."

I listened but wasn't surprised by his report. As I was about to ask if he knew where the drug people were, the steady staccato of automatic weapons fire carried through the night. Drolids shouted then I heard two explosions, which I took to be grenades. There was more gunfire; another explosion, then quiet settled over the area for several seconds. A man shouted in some South American language and immediately I heard the indiscriminate sounds of semi-automatic gunfire which told me the patrol was bringing their assault to an end.

Having watched the path of the patrol's tracer rounds burn through the night, and seeing how the drug patrol had set up on the side where our villagers were held, I realized their leader was better qualified than the last one we had killed. This leader had planned his ambush well and positioned his men to reduce the risk. Our assault on them would have to be well-timed.

"We go now . . . make each arrow a kill so they cannot use their rifles on the villagers or us." I divided my team and sent half to the left and half to the right, as we had previously done.

The closer we drew to the camp, the louder became the voices of the drug patrol, reflecting their surprise as they moved into the encampment and got their first close-up look at the Drolids. This was exactly what I had hoped for because their attention would be focused on the mutants and they wouldn't be watching the surrounding area.

Positioned on the side opposite of the villagers to draw gunfire away from them, we edged forward, halted, and spread out as planned. The drug patrol was perfectly outlined by the raging campfire as they prodded the dead Drolids with their boots and jumped back quickly, ready to shoot if the mutants moved. Their curiosity got the best of them and they slung their rifles over their soldiers while they talked and began a closer examination of the creatures.

I counted five men, each well-armed and appearing quite fit for jungle warfare. But we now had the advantage of surprise, courtesy of the Drolids. The soldiers of the drug patrol were so fixated upon the mutants that they had almost forgotten about the silent villagers huddled behind them on the far side of the fire.

A bird sang out to my right, and another answered to my left. The drug patrol never paused from their examination of the Drolids. A woman captive struggled to stand, swayed and grabbed her chest, and cried out in pain. The soldiers spun to look at her, turning their backs to me as they slid their weapons off their shoulders. They were scanning the captives when the first arrow struck a soldier in the skull with deadly accuracy.

I took aim on the man I believed to be their leader and let fly an arrow that struck him in the base of the neck. He danced about in the firelight trying to reach the shaft, but he appeared to have little control of his arms.

Arrows flew, creating light whooshing sounds as they traveled through the night. They struck their targets with solid thuds, but not before a soldier turned and fired wildly into the jungle before collapsing.

We waited in the surrounding growth until the downed soldiers had stopped moving then entered the camp and ensured no adversary remained alive.

★ ★ ★ ★

At first a huddled mass on the ground, the captives raced towards us. There were cries of anguish, and tears flowed from almost every face, including my courageous warriors when they discovered a loved one among the group.

While they rejoiced in their reunions I stripped grenade bandoliers, ammunition belts, and automatic weapons from the dead soldiers. Holding one of the automatic rifles, I turned it in my hands, relishing its feeling after not having held one for so long. I inspected it closely, not knowing its brand or make, yet familiar enough with weapons to release the magazine and reload.

"*Cacique.*" The voice came softly from my warriors.

I glanced behind me to see who had called. Yava and Binan entered the camp carrying Runt's limp body in their arms. My brother of the Jaguar Clan had taken several rounds into the chest when the soldier had fired indiscriminately.

"Take him into the jungle and bury him. I do not want our brave brother buried near the evil ones or the drug people."

Yava and Binan acknowledged with nods and left. Frog trailed them into the jungle with his head lowered. Kana stood watching, his arms wrapped around two of his wives that had been captives. His gaze slowly lowered to the ground. Runt had long been a close friend to all.

A woman Kuni was consoling broke from his arms, grabbed a stick and began to smash one of the Drolids' head. Her face was a twisted mask of fury, and when she finished, she stabbed the mutant through his eye. I could only guess at what the Drolids may have done to her.

Eighteen villagers, mostly women with older children by their sides, had been freed from their captors. Counting the Jaguar Clan warriors, there were twenty-three total. They were all that remained of the Matsés tribe.

Tucum helped me carry the soldiers' ammunition and equipment to the far side of the encampment, away from the Drolids. Once Yava, Binan, and Frog returned from their burial detail, I ordered everyone to quickly strip the Drolids of weapons and take any food they found in camp. When the people slowed, I urged them on and motioned everyone to assemble at my confiscated weapons. The last thing I wanted was to let shock take further control of them. Everyone had been traumatized in some manner, and I realized they must keep moving.

I positioned myself before them so their backs were to the carnage about the campfire. My gaze swept across the group and my heart sank as I looked into their eyes. I knew what must be done and summoned Tucum to stand near me.

"You are the last of the Matsés—you are my family." My words grew difficult to speak. I removed a knife and sheath from my vine belt and held it high for all to see. "This knife was taken in our last battle and was to be given as a gift to our great *cacique*, Tacoma. Now I give it to your new *cacique*—Tucum—who will lead you to safety so you may be a tribe once more."

Having spoken, I turned and presented the knife to Tucum. He recognized it as the knife I had removed from the dead woman soldier.

"I do not understand," he said, his brow furrowed in question. "What of you?"

"Take our people far from here and make a new life for them. Everyone has suffered much and their hearts must heal. Where I go now, none of you may follow. This is my last order as your *cacique*."

We stood in silence. He looked at the villagers then to me.

"Return to us, brother," Tucum said.

He extended his hand and we clasped as warriors do, hands gripping tightly to one another's forearms.

I nodded, unable to speak, and watched them turn to walk away. Only the crackling of the fire broke the night.

Kana was the last warrior to reach the edge of the camp. He paused, looked back at me, raised his bow in salute, and then vanished into the jungle.

I stood listening to the fire with the dead sprawled about me.

Chapter Twenty-six

After Tucum and the villagers left, a dark mood swept over me and I sat in the dirt, staring at the Drolid corpses. My heart wanted revenge and pure hatred pumped through my veins like a raging river. My soul burned with the fury of an inferno and my worthless life flashed before my eyes in glimpses, reminding me of what a pathetic creature I had come to be. But the thought of righting all the wrongs in my life rose like the morning sun appearing through a fog's mist. Moloc and his mutant army could no longer be allowed to harm innocent villages. It was then I began to feel better and regain control over my hate and fury.

I accepted my life would soon end. In some odd manner, I found peace in this realization. Throughout my years the only mark I had left upon the world was pain and suffering to others with little to show for good intentions. Maybe it was time for my judgment day to arrive. If Moloc was right about all he had told me, then there was no heaven or hell to be concerned with—yet if God existed . . .

My conflicted thoughts rambled on until dawn's first light. I assembled what equipment I needed, looked about the camp and stood ready to leave on my final journey.

Anyone from civilization would have laughed at the sight of me; my loin cloth was tattered, a vine leaf belt circled my waist and held the knife Tacoma had given me upon my initiation into the Jaguar Clan. My face and chest were painted with wide black and red swathes for war—and bandoliers of grenades and ammunition crisscrossed my chest. Throwing my bow into the campfire, with an automatic rifle in hand I turned toward the east and set out at a trot along the trail the Drolids had beaten from Moloc's fortress.

★ ★ ★ ★

Upon the afternoon of the fourth day of grueling travel I found myself at Moloc's kingdom. Its bleak presence made me restless and reminded me of my time in his captivity. No birds flew, no animals were ever seen, and even the jungle bore a forbidden, eerie existence with its deep shadows and snarled trees.

Circling the vine covered, massive stone walls of Moloc's castle, I wondered who had constructed it. My curiosity was cut short, though, when a Drolid walked out into view then turned toward the fields. I breathed deep to calm my nerves and reminded myself I wasn't on an archeological expedition.

My reconnaissance allowed me to locate where the captive Indians were housed and to find the area through which I had once escaped. I returned to the jungle and lay camouflaged beneath wide-leafed plants and brush for a day to watch Drolid patrols come and go, escorting the slaves to the fields in the early morning and late evening hours. All had to be well executed if I was to gain entry and wreak havoc upon Moloc's empire. My only hope was that the massive room had not been emptied of the weapons and armaments the Drolids had collected from soldiers they had encountered throughout the years.

Moving to a better position, I sat for hours in the cover of dark jungle shadows and stared at the stone walls, mentally replaying the paths I once walked throughout the fortress. My palms grew slick with sweat. Each beat of my heart pounded against my chest with the fury of a hammer striking an anvil. Edging back into the jungle, I searched for food to replenish my strength then found a towering tree to climb and sleep in for the night. Thick branches with intertwined vines formed a perfect hammock and, camouflaged by leaves, I was sheltered from the searching eyes of any who might pass below.

I slept light, waking at times to the distant noise I took to be Drolids on patrol about the fortress. Through the holes in the canopy I could see patches of the brilliant star-filled sky and, as a child would, I wondered how space could go on and on without end. In time I must have fallen asleep because when I next awoke the sky had begun its transformation to a pale shade of blue. My day of retribution had arrived.

★ ★ ★ ★

Three well-worn trails led from the fortress into the jungle. The Drolids followed these deep into the forest before intersecting with other trails to travel in various directions. I had little time to set proper traps at each but knew even crude devices would prove their worth in delaying my pursuers should I manage to escape.

I buried grenades along both sides of the trails, leaving only their tops peeking above the loosely packed soil. Stretching slender vines across the trodden paths, I tied the ends firmly to the tops of the grenades then eased their pins free. The spoons were held in place by the dirt, yet if one of the heavy-footed Drolids snagged a vine, the grenades from both sides of the trail would be torn from the earth and like bolos, wrap about ankles or legs. The clink of the spoons freed from the grenades would be the last sounds a Drolid would ever hear.

Leaving the camouflage of the jungle I set out, bent low as possible, toward the fortress and crossed the hundred yards of waist high grass. My own weight was bad enough, but the additional bulk of the bandoliers, ammunition, and the automatic weapon slung from my shoulders only added to my discomfort. The muscles in my thighs began to burn, yet I knew there was no other choice but to travel the vast distance in such a crouched and squatting form. As I reached a wall and rose to full height, I stood for a moment to regain control of my legs and use the time to scan the area for Drolids.

The first group of Indian slaves, their faces lowered to avoid making eye-contact with their captors, were led out to the fields as the sun broke over the horizon. Back pressed against the wall's stones, I waited until the last group passed then with knife in hand, scurried through the fortress door they had just left.

My lungs heaved like a bellows and I fought my anxieties to bring my breathing under control. I milked my grip upon the knife and felt the sweat in my palm. My imagination, running wild, made me afraid my heart, pounding hard against my chest, might be heard in the quiet hall.

I followed the hall until reaching a wide set of decaying double-doors. Pulling one side open only enough to ease through, I entered and discovered luck was still with me. This was the oil storage room, the sole supply for every brazier, sconce, and torch in the fortress. At least ten rows of giant wood casks, most taller than me, lay stacked upon their sides.

The air grew thick with a petroleum odor as I moved deeper between the rows and chose casks hidden from view. Prying their plugs free, I let the oil drain onto the floor and watched it flow beneath other casks and begin to form pools. Soon I had a steady stream flowing across the floor and to my delight it ran unseen beneath casks toward the rear of the cavernous room.

The creak of rusty hinges carried through the room, followed by rough grunting sounds I recognized as a Drolid giving orders. I knelt and waited at the end of a row, my knife poised to strike. Beads of sweat formed across my forehead and I could feel them begin to glide down my face. Another noise came which I couldn't identify yet something told me it belonged to a slave.

Looking around the corner I saw an old, frail Indian woman at a cask with a jug in hand. The jug's weight pulled her down as it filled. The Drolid walked further into the room and stood with his back to me while he watched the slave work.

The woman glanced in my direction, saw my painted face as I edged toward the Drolid, but calmly returned to her chore. The long blade of my knife pierced the mutant's neck and drove deep as I forced it in to the hilt with a fierce twist. As the creature crumpled to the stone floor, I withdrew the knife and motioned the woman to remain silent. She did and I breathed easier.

In the dim light of the room I could see life still shining in the woman's dark eyes, but her weary, wrinkled look made her appear far older than her true years. Being Moloc's captive, as well as enduring Drolid cruelties, would age anyone quickly—if they survived the insanity.

Her gaze swept over my face and body with a look of confusion that asked why I was so big, appeared to be a white man, yet was painted like an Amazonian tribesman. There was no time though to stand and answer questions.

"Are your people all in the fields?" I asked in Spanish, hoping to find a common language.

Her head canted as if the memory of a spoken word had long been forgotten. A second passed. Her eyebrows rose as she gradually began to understand. She nodded then paused and held up four fingers and pointed to the ceiling.

"Four—up there . . . ." She struggled to speak the words.

These were four people I realized I may not be able to save if they were in the upper levels of the fortress.

"Can you carry water to the field?"

Her eyes flared and she nodded anxiously.

"Take water to your people in the field. Tell them to wait until they hear trouble in here then run south into the jungle. Do you understand? Go south into the jungle, *not west!*"

At first she gave no reply. I had to make sure she understood not to travel 'west' because that route led to the booby-trapped trails. Ready to repeat myself, she suddenly acknowledged.

"Yes . . . to the south."

"Good. After you tell your people, find a Drolid in the field and tell him you saw a sick one in this room."

Her face grew ashen and she drew back from me.

"Is the creature in the big room?" I asked.

No movement came from her.

"Woman, is the creature upstairs in the big room?"

She replied with a slow nod.

"Go now . . . take the water and do as I said so you and your people can be free."

I pushed her toward the door and watched her leave. Setting her half-filled jug of oil by the dead Drolid, I turned him onto his stomach and settled his weight upon a grenade. Careful to keep the spoon pressed against the grenade, I eased the pin free and tossed it away. I placed another grenade beneath his thick neck and removed its pin as well.

Each precious second that passed was one less I had to rush upstairs and find Moloc before the Drolids entered and discovered this body. If all went as I hoped, the explosion here would be the tactical surprise I needed. But the big *'if'* in my plan was *'if'* the Drolids entered the room and turned the body over to start the chained reactions I hoped for.

Unsnapping the magazine pouches along my bandolier so as not to slow my reloading, I pulled the automatic rifle from my shoulder and thumb clicked the safety off. I had three grenades left and I was unsure where or how I would use them, but time was wasting and I had to leave.

Chapter Twenty-seven

I left the supply room, found a stairwell leading to the upper levels of the fortress, and started climbing it two steps at a time. At a small window half way up the narrow passage I paused to look out across the fields at the slaves. The woman gave a water jug to a skinny man leaning on a shovel. He looked about and nodded as she turned in the direction of a Drolid.

How long before the Drolids discovered their dead companion? Where was the main force of Drolid soldiers?

I suddenly became aware of someone drawing near. A Scath rushed down the steps, in her right hand was a knife, its blade gleaming as she raised it to strike me. Her mouth was opened wide as if to scream, but as I learned during my captivity, Scaths are mute, and she could not utter a word.

My reaction came without thought as I butt-stroked her with my rifle. She took the full blow square in the face, spun off her feet and tumbled past me down the stairs. I turned to leave but took one last look out into the field. The Indian woman was speaking to a Drolid overseer. He knocked her to the ground with a wide arm-swing then started a waddling run toward the fortress. Drolids along the sides of the field abandoned their guard posts and hurried after him. My time was about to run out. I needed to find Moloc.

Taking two and three steps with every jump, I raced up the stairs, ready to unleash my automatic on anyone barring my way. At the top of the stairwell I turned right and followed the bend of a wide hallway. Everything appeared familiar. Moloc's cavernous room was ahead, but a partially opened door captured my attention. I slid to a halt and glanced inside. It was the munitions room where the Drolids had mounds of weapons, explosives and equipment they confiscated from the drug patrols, guerillas, and government soldiers they had fought in the jungle.

There was no time to rig a trap or select more weapons. I had to keep moving. But a thought crossed my mind. Somewhere directly below this room and Moloc's main hall was the huge, oil flooded supply room about to explode. At first my stomach tightened into a hard knot at the thought of its imminent danger—but the madness of my plan took hold of me. I wanted it to explode. I came to kill Moloc, and die with him if necessary. My tensions eased and I laughed aloud.

Rhythmic pounding of heavy-weighted feet rose in the hall, growing louder by the second. I took a quick look out the door and saw a wall of Drolid soldiers running in my direction. Pulling the pin on a grenade, I leaned out and let it fly. The spoon clinked when it popped free; the grenade was live, and I dove back into the room for cover.

The explosion was deafening as it reverberated throughout the hall.

I threw a second grenade and let it clear a path for me to Moloc's hall. A resounding boom shook the walls and cast a hazy cloud of dust across the air. Soon all that could be heard were the odd groans of dying Drolids.

The stones of the hall floor were slick with blood and entrails but I raced through it all, careful not to slip, anxious to reach Moloc and let him know it was me that was bringing about his death.

At the entrance to Moloc's massive throne room, I pulled the pin on my last grenade, held it at the ready in my left hand and with my right, pressed the stock of the rifle against my side. I drew in a deep breath; my mind ready to explode from the adrenaline flooding my body. Hopefully, the oil supply room would blow soon—and if luck remained with me, detonate the munitions storage room. I felt no fear. No, I relished the thought of death being so near. This was payback time for Kache, and every hour of suffering in my life.

I shoved the massive doors open with my shoulder and made a grand entrance; a war cry pouring from my mouth, welcoming the release of my pent-up pressure—and all the while enjoying the rage of gunfire I was unleashing upon anyone in the room.

Chaos ruled the morning as I hurled my grenade toward the reptilian-like creature king upon his throne. His bodyguards bent and released two screaming leopards then they burst toward me, racing behind the attacking animals.

The grenade exploded in the middle of the cavernous room, its shrapnel flying in all directions as the concussion swept the area. One of the leopards was bashed aside by the blast while the other rolled to a heap, severely wounded yet trying to crawl in my direction. The bodyguards both lay still on the floor, but my joy was short-lived. Behind them in the distance a dozen more Nubian-like warriors sprang into view, running toward me.

Scaths raced from the dais and were bashed out of the way by Drolids taking up defensive positions before their ruler. When the warriors reached the mid-way point of the massive room, I heard an echoing roar of anger and saw Moloc standing on the dais, head thrown back with mouth agape, his arms spread wide and shaking with hands drawn into knotted fists. He had flung his great crimson cloak through the air and the sight of his wrath held a chilling appearance.

Releasing the empty magazine from the rifle, I shoved a full one into it as I dropped to one knee, aimed and calmly squeezed the trigger, leveling the front line of warriors racing toward me. Some of their followers managed to leap over the bodies but many tripped and fell into piles. This arrested their charge. I continually fired at the mass of them, emptying magazines and reloading as swiftly as possible. Although the body count mounted, there seemed no end to them.

My rifle jammed and I slung it at a charging Drolid. Drawing my knife I waited for a warrior no more than ten feet away to finally reach me—then Moloc's furious voice thundered through the room and every assault on me drew to an immediate halt. He raced off the dais and climbed atop the mound of bodies that had separated us. His arms swung wide, displaying the massive bulges of granite hard muscles on his body. The demonic look of his face paralyzed me momentarily. He was the worst evil I could ever imagine encountering, but the moment passed and I waited. His gaze never left me as he slowly descended the mound to stand upon the level floor.

"Do not worry. They will not interfere," the creature king proudly said, waving a hand at the Drolids and warriors surrounding me. His tone of voice lowered. "I will give you pain as you have never known."

"I made a promise I would kill you—and I never break a promise."

"I've always admired your spirit, John, but too much can be detrimental to your health." His mouth formed a sneer. "You don't mind if I call you 'John', do you? After all, we are almost family."

The creature walked toward me then paused, straightened his posture and lowered his chin as he kept his gaze locked on me. "Oh, wait—you don't have a family anymore, do you?"

Rage flowed through me at his taunts. He was reading my thoughts but I was determined to kill him.

"You'll never be a 'true-blood' on your planet," I shouted. "All that gold you have to bargain with, your hopes of returning home a hero—and you're stuck here, a forgotten, low-life prisoner from your world!"

Moloc laughed at my bravado and began to circle me, crouching slightly, arms spreading, ready to wrap about me. I circled too, knife held ready. His size was deceiving. At first I assumed he would be slow moving, but he cleared the distance between us with the speed of a jungle cat. I lunged forward and we collided with the force of two fighting bulls. Running into him felt as if I had crashed into a stone wall. It stunned me. His thick arms wrapped about me and squeezed until I thought I would surely burst, but he stopped abruptly and cast me aside as if I were a leaf.

Sliding across the floor, I gasped for air and shook my head to regain my senses. I looked up and saw him staring at his chest in disbelief. His face rose and a piecemeal smile appeared on his lips as his left hand pulled my knife out of his chest. The blade had driven deep, yet evidently not deep enough. He let the knife fall to the floor.

I stood and squared myself for his next attack. He was wounded. He bled. He could be beaten. My confidence grew, but was short-lived.

In two steps he was upon me, raked my chest with his claw-like nails, and drove a fist into my stomach with such strength that the blow took me off my feet and back into the Drolids behind me.

Moloc had spoken true. The pain shooting through my body was like none I had ever endured in my lifetime. My eyes watered and my mouth was open, gasping to fill my empty lungs. Landing amid the Drolids' legs, I looked up to see Moloc straighten to full height and waver slightly on his feet. Anguish painted his face. His wound was worse than he wanted me to know.

I clamored to my feet, still gasping for air, but as I did, I tore a battle axe from the hands of a nearby Drolid and spun toward Moloc. The creature had begun to walk toward me once more when I flung the axe at him with all the strength I could muster. His eyes widened and I knew he had not expected such a tactic from me.

Time slowed as I watched the battle axe spin end over end through the air, traveling directly at his chest. The axe was about to penetrate his alien flesh when suddenly a maelstrom of explosions made me lose sight of him.

A wall of orange-red fire, streaked with black, erupted from the floor where the mound of warriors lay behind Moloc. It spewed toward the ceiling with a deafening roar that bombarded my ears as bodies and stone were carried upward by the explosion. The floor rippled with the ferocity of an earthquake and everyone was thrown off their feet and fell into one another.

Within the same second the throne room's floor erupted to my right. A thundering boom pounded my ears and the explosive force sent me tumbling in another direction. I was struck by bodies and rocks that flew through the air like artillery shrapnel.

The entire fortress shook violently and its walls began to cave in. Boulders flew past me, cutting a brutal swathe through the Drolids. More debris became treacherous shrapnel, and then blinding sunlight burst into sight as the fortress roof caved in.

I was thrown back and forth, struck by so much that I could not know what exactly hit me—and suddenly there was no more floor to stand upon. A sense of weightlessness overcame me as I seemed to hang in the air. Then I began my descent into hell.

The explosions were devastating. Massive stones shot in all directions, brutally slaying those in their way as they rocketed through the mass of warriors and Drolids. Swirling clouds of blackish, gray smoke and dust swept through the fortress with hurricane force. Sunlight flashed then vanished with strobe-like effect. But all was lost to me as I felt myself falling through the air to the lower floors, my body constantly being pelted. In that bleak moment I felt the oddest sensation of arms wrapping about me.

Something struck my head and all went black.

Chapter Twenty-eight

A great weight was upon me. I tried to open my eyes, felt pain shoot throughout my body, and wondered if this was what death felt like. My head hurt worse though, and I lay unable to move from the contorted position I was in. Inch by inch I pushed and pulled until one arm was free and then the other.

Pausing at times to rest, I realized Drolids and rocks covered me. I was partially buried by them, but the mutants' bodies had protected me from the debris. But what of the arms I had felt as I fell? Had they been some hallucination? My head throbbed and I stopped trying to recall anymore.

I worked my way free of the rubble and sat looking about the remnants of the fortress. The surviving walls were broken and jagged, and the roof was gone. Arms and legs stuck out of the debris like objects scattered at random and left me confused until my mind replayed all that had occurred.

A faint fog of dust floated over the destruction as I struggled to stand. The world spun before my eyes and I was about to fall back into the rubble, but I managed to keep my feet.

Fires still burned wildly in spots and black smoke rose into the sky in slender pillars. As my mind gradually cleared and my vision focused, I looked at the markings on the walls and realized how far I had fallen. The sun was lowering on the horizon when I scanned the surrounding fields. No slaves were in sight and I hoped they had made good their escape.

Stumbling over the debris that had once been Moloc's vast fortress, I searched for any signs of his body, wanting confirmation of his death. I noticed an oddly colored arm and hand protruding from beneath a mound of rocks. Only the creature would have such a flesh tint—but it was then the sounds of a distant patrol carried to me and raised alarm in my soul. What a fool I had been, never considering how the explosions would make every patrol immediately return—and possibly cut off my path of escape.

Overcome with an insane need, I rushed to the arm and began pulling at rocks to see what lay beneath. The patrol drew closer and the muffled rattling of their equipment became more distinct.

I threw a heavy rock aside and fell exhausted to my hands and knees on the rubble. At that moment I looked down and realized I was staring at his evil face. His eyes opened and his gaze fell upon me. A feeble attempt was made to speak, but I never hesitated.

Raising a large, jagged stone over my head with both hands, I looked directly into his eyes. "I always keep my promise." My words came low and cold then I drove the rock downward with all the strength I could muster. The first blow split his head open between his eyes, yet I repeatedly smashed his face until it was pulp.

Moloc was no longer evil. He was dead.

My moment of victory was fleeting though. The clamor of the patrol grew louder and anxiety mounted within me. I had to leave, yet my body refused to move. For a moment I thought of giving up; letting them kill me. It was over. Moloc was dead. I felt dead. But a voice, something I cannot describe, called out to me and urged me on.

I had never quit anything in my life, and refused to do so now. No strength remained in me, yet I crawled and stumbled across the rocks and debris until clear of it all. When I slid into the dirt and felt my face pressed hard against blades of grass, a spark of hope grew within me. I forced myself to rise then made my way westward into the jungle.

Fortunately, I still retained enough presence of mind to remember the vines across the trails and bypassed them. As I struggled to put distance between myself and the patrol, I heard the dull thumps of exploding grenades. My traps had bought me precious time.

Nothing of my flight remains with me except flashes of scenes, mere glimpses in my mind. I remember moments of being on hands and knees, clawing my way along dirt paths, injured and weak, yet refusing to stop for fear of being taken prisoner if the Drolids still followed. In my insanity I found the 'running-leaves' and gorged myself upon them for strength. For that, I spent a night hiding in the forest, sick and retching until the agony subsided in my stomach.

Hallucinations came and went in my delirium but one dream still haunts me. I was lying on the ground and soft hands gently cradled my head as water was poured into my mouth. I never saw a face, yet before my world went black again, I felt arms wrap about me.

I lost track of the days and nights that passed. The last memories I have are of running, stumbling and falling into a river—and a boy pulling me from the water . . .

Chapter Twenty-nine

Layers of faint blue, faded yellow and orange-red hues painted the horizon as night began its transition into day. The full moon, with its perfect white orb, had long since vanished from sight as the two men sat below and talked through the night. Now the fires used to ward off predators had burned down to glowing coals and awaited the arrival of the village women to stoke them and begin the daily cooking.

John Alvarez sat on the steps of the hut, leaning back against one of the structure's many poles, letting his head rest on it. His chest rose and fell in calm rhythm as he stared at a distant tree in the forest still partially concealed by shadows. In time he let his gaze carry to the old man sitting on a lower hut step, forearms resting on knees, face lowered in deep thought.

"The boy was my grandson. Ignacio found you that day." Papito paused. "*Madre de Dios*, the things you have said are . . ." His words were barely above a whisper and filled with sorrow. He never raised his head as his voice tapered off to silence.

Returning his gaze to the tree, Alvarez sighed. "Impossible to believe? Yes, I know. I didn't expect you to believe me."

The village elder slowly turned in his seat and sadly looked at Alvarez. "No, the things you have said are difficult for me to think about—to know why my son suffered as he did."

Alvarez acknowledged with a nod but remained quiet and stared ahead.

"And now, John? Must you keep your promise and find the *cabrones* Clements and that other man?"

"Henderson."

"Yes, the ones you promised to kill."

Daylight gently began to bathe the village and dissolve the jungle shadows. Alvarez gradually sat upright, staring all the while at the distant tree. He squinted hard, trying to focus on shadows about it. Standing up, he slowly walked down the hut steps and stood staring at the jungle.

"John? John?" Papito rose and stood beside him, unable to get his attention. He glanced in the direction the big man stared but observed nothing.

Alvarez turned, briefly looked at him and then spun back to face the jungle. "I'm going home." His voice held a tone as gentle as the rising of the sun.

"What?" Papito's brows rose. "Stay with us! *Por favor*, please. Do not return home to kill those men—forget your promise."

Renewed life shined in Alvarez's eyes as he wheeled toward the old man. "Do you believe in the jungle spirits?"

"Yes, from a boy I have always believed." Papito nervously made the sign of the cross. "And I believe in GOD too."

A smile formed on Alvarez's lips as he nodded.

"Goodbye, my friend, and thank you." Without a further word Alvarez started walking toward the tree he had been watching.

Papito slowly shook his head, lips forming a thin line as he stared at the big man's back. "But you are going the wrong way. Your home is that way!" he shouted. He quickly raised a hand and pointed northward.

The warrior of the Jaguar Clan never broke his stride.

"No," Alvarez whispered, "My home is *this* way." His gaze remained locked on the *cacique,* woman and warriors who stood in the shadows and awaited his arrival. The woman's smile warmed his soul.

The village elder watched until the lone man walked into the jungle and was gone from sight.

"Goodbye, John Alvarez," he called out softly.

AFTERWORD

The writing of *Amazon Moon* was truly an interesting, personal journey for me as an author. I set out upon the path of wanting to write a good, action-adventure story with a bit of sci-fi set in the deep, mysterious Amazonia region—and ended with a discovery of problems that I did not know so fully existed. The goal of every author is to be a good storyteller, yet as writers, we hold a responsibility to educate our readers as well about certain facts as we move them from chapter to chapter until the end. Such responsibility was better understood by me once my protagonist entered the rain forest.

A psychologist might have a field day analyzing John Alvarez; the boy who longed for love, became lost within himself when his family was killed, yet as a man, eventually found home within the Spartan environment of the Marine Corps to anchor his soul to. He learned warfare well, possibly too well. That could be debated, and then came the insanity thrust upon him by finding Moloc and having to doubt the truths of all he had learned. But as I wrote this novel, John took a slightly different path in his life than I originally intended. The variation began when he met the indigenous people of the Amazon and discovered their plights.

Simply saying, "The Amazon," invokes images of thick jungle, wild animals, hidden tribes, and the immediate setting of danger at every turn. It's one of the last bastions of immense territory in the world yet to be fully explored. Yet, with all its hazards and menace, we owe so much to this region.

The bio-diversity of the Amazonia rain forest is vital to our eco-system and pharmaceuticals. Climate change is heavily dependent upon it and we need the forest to keep it in balance. Over two-thirds of all mass produced drugs are derived from medicinal plants. In the Amazon, 650 species of plants with pharmaceutical value have been discovered. Gold, oil, and other resources are within this region as well. The value of the rain forest is immense, and it is home to many indigenous Indian tribes.

The history overall of the Amazon is fascinating and truly worthy of reading. But it is saddening as well, often to the point of being comparable to what our Native American Indians endured as the government and gold seekers chose to steal their rich lands.

There may be predatory creatures in the Amazon—black caiman, jaguar, cougar, piranha, bushmaster snakes and anacondas—but none so vile and vicious as the "civilized" men and governments who decided they wanted to drive the tribes out in order to fill their pockets from the sale of the region's rich resources.

Every country the Amazonia region touches is guilty in one form or another of injustices against the indigenous tribes. That in itself should be an embarrassment to mankind, yet little has been done to protect these native people or the Amazon. What has been done is nothing more than a façade to display to the world.

Imagine if your family lived in a rain forest village under primitive conditions. In addition to the daily struggles to provide food for your family, you must be concerned with brutal Maoist guerilla factions such as the Shining Path traveling through your land; drug cartels and their trafficking, their soldiers killing anyone they find in order to protect their drugs; land grabbers and 'loggers' raping and savagely killing your loved ones then burning your village to the ground because they want the trees for lumber—or the gold seekers who murder villagers in order to stake a claim and destroy the land as they mine for gold. But worse, is when governments such as the Peruvian government use their military to bomb your village and then send in militia to drive you out.

The indigenous tribes of Amazonia once numbered in the thousands, now due to civilized society's gifts of rape, torture, murder, infectious diseases, venereal diseases, and violent land grabbing, some tribes are near extinction and others only number in the hundreds.

Does this all sound similar to our own embarrassing United States history in the dealings with Native American Indians? Unfortunately, it is almost verbatim.

In one disgusting account, I read that loggers used a different approach to rid themselves of a tribe. They donated clothes to the tribe. It sounds quite peaceful and generous until it was discovered that the clothes had all been worn by people sick with small pox and other infectious diseases—then was intentionally given to the Indians. The outcome was as expected by the loggers. The majority of the tribe died.

It would take another full novel to fully tell of the injustices performed and being performed today on the Amazonia tribes. My hope here is to inform readers there is far more story to be known than what I have now written.

I encourage you to seek out the information and read it for yourself. Use the Internet and search for "indigenous tribes of the Amazon" then begin reading about the atrocities committed against them. Perform a search on "rainforest loggers" and "Amazon gold miners" and see for yourself the volumes of real-life horror stories that will appear.

Thank you for reading *Amazon Moon,* as well as my other novels, and hope you will continue learning about the Amazon.

One day mankind may learn to not repeat the mistakes we have made throughout history.

Sincerely,

Glenn

ABOUT THE AUTHOR

Glenn Starkey is a former USMC Sergeant, Vietnam veteran, Texas law enforcement officer, and retired from a global oil corporation as a Security Manager. He's been a Security Consultant, public speaker on various subject matters, and was the interim Security Director for a major Texas Gulf Coast port to oversee security and federal projects. His background, travels and experiences provide the foundation for realism in his novels.

    Returning to writing fulltime, he lives south of Houston, Texas with his family and a 98 pound Labradoodle. During the school year, Glenn volunteers to assist children with their reading skills. You can contact Glenn through his website, http://GlennStarkey.net.

CPSIA information can be obtained at www.ICGtesting.com
Printed in the USA
LVOW05s1517130913

352212LV00003B/5/P